*Amy Cross is the author of more than 200 horror, paranormal, fantasy and thriller novels.*

OTHER TITLES
BY AMY CROSS INCLUDE

*American Coven*
*Annie's Room*
*The Ash House*
*Asylum*
*At the Edge of the Forest*
*B&B*
*The Bride of Ashbyrn House*
*The Cemetery Ghost*
*The Curse of the Langfords*
*The Devil, the Witch and the Whore*
*Devil's Briar*
*The Disappearance of Lonnie James*
*The Dog*
*Eli's Town*
*The Farm*
*The Ghost of Molly Holt*
*The Ghosts of Lakeforth Hotel*
*The Girl Who Never Came Back*
*Haunted*
*The Haunting of Blackwych Grange*
*The Haunting of Edward House*
*The Haunting of Nelson Street*
*The House on Fisher Street*
*The House Where She Died*
*How to Make a Ghost*
*I Married a Serial Killer*
*Lights Out*
*Mary*
*The Night Girl*
*The Purchase*
*Stephen*
*The Shades*
*The Soul Auction*
*Trill*
*Ward Z*

# THE TED ARMITAGE TRILOGY

AMY CROSS

This edition
first published by Blackwych Books Ltd
United Kingdom, 2021

Copyright © 2021 Blackwych Books

*Out There* originally published in February 2021
*Twist Valley* originally published in March 2021
*The Great Beyond* originally published in April 2021

All rights reserved. This book is a work of fiction.
Names, characters, places, incidents and businesses are
the product of the author's imagination or are
used fictitiously. Any resemblance to actual persons,
living or dead, or to actual events or locations,
is entirely coincidental.

Also available in e-book format.

www.blackwychbooks.com

# CONTENTS

## Book One
## OUT THERE

**PROLOGUE**
*page 15*

**CHAPTER ONE**
*page 17*

**CHAPTER TWO**
*page 19*

**CHAPTER THREE**
*page 25*

**CHAPTER FOUR**
*page 31*

**CHAPTER FIVE**
*page 37*

**CHAPTER SIX**
*page 43*

**CHAPTER SEVEN**
*page 49*

**CHAPTER EIGHT**
*page 57*

**CHAPTER NINE**
*page 63*

CHAPTER TEN
*page 69*

CHAPTER ELEVEN
*page 75*

CHAPTER TWELVE
*page 81*

CHAPTER THIRTEEN
*page 87*

CHAPTER FOURTEEN
*page 93*

CHAPTER FIFTEEN
*page 99*

CHAPTER SIXTEEN
*page 105*

CHAPTER SEVENTEEN
*page 111*

CHAPTER EIGHTEEN
*page 117*

CHAPTER NINETEEN
*page 123*

CHAPTER TWENTY
*page 129*

CHAPTER TWENTY-ONE
*page 135*

CHAPTER TWENTY-TWO
*page 141*

CHAPTER TWENTY-THREE
*page 147*

CHAPTER TWENTY-FOUR
*page 153*

CHAPTER TWENTY-FIVE
*page 159*

CHAPTER TWENTY-SIX
*page 165*

CHAPTER TWENTY-SEVEN
*page 171*

CHAPTER TWENTY-EIGHT
*page 177*

CHAPTER TWENTY-NINE
*page 183*

CHAPTER THIRTY
*page 189*

EPILOGUE 1
*page 195*

EPILOGUE 2
*page 199*

**Book Two**
**TWIST VALLEY**

PROLOGUE
*page 203*

CHAPTER ONE
*page 205*

CHAPTER TWO
*page 213*

CHAPTER THREE
*page 219*

CHAPTER FOUR
*page 225*

CHAPTER FIVE
*page 231*

CHAPTER SIX
*page 237*

CHAPTER SEVEN
*page 243*

CHAPTER EIGHT
*page 249*

CHAPTER NINE
*page 255*

CHAPTER TEN
*page 261*

CHAPTER ELEVEN
*page 267*

CHAPTER TWELVE
*page 273*

CHAPTER THIRTEEN
*page 279*

CHAPTER FOURTEEN
*page 285*

CHAPTER FIFTEEN
*page 291*

CHAPTER SIXTEEN
*page 297*

CHAPTER SEVENTEEN
*page 303*

CHAPTER EIGHTEEN
*page 309*

CHAPTER NINETEEN
*page 315*

CHAPTER TWENTY
*page 321*

CHAPTER TWENTY-ONE
*page 327*

CHAPTER TWENTY-TWO
*page 333*

CHAPTER TWENTY-THREE
*page 339*

CHAPTER TWENTY-FOUR
*page 345*

CHAPTER TWENTY-FIVE
*page 351*

CHAPTER TWENTY-SIX
*page 357*

CHAPTER TWENTY-SEVEN
*page 363*

CHAPTER TWENTY-EIGHT
*page 369*

CHAPTER TWENTY-NINE
*page 375*

CHAPTER THIRTY
*page 381*

EPILOGUE
*page 387*

## Book Three
## THE GREAT BEYOND

PROLOGUE
*page 391*

CHAPTER ONE
*page 393*

CHAPTER TWO
*page 399*

CHAPTER THREE
*page 405*

CHAPTER FOUR
*page 411*

CHAPTER FIVE
*page 417*

CHAPTER SIX
*page 423*

CHAPTER SEVEN
*page 429*

CHAPTER EIGHT
*page 435*

CHAPTER NINE
*page 441*

CHAPTER TEN
*page 447*

CHAPTER ELEVEN
*page 453*

CHAPTER TWELVE
*page 459*

CHAPTER THIRTEEN
*page 465*

CHAPTER FOURTEEN
*page 471*

CHAPTER FIFTEEN
*page 477*

CHAPTER SIXTEEN
*page 483*

CHAPTER SEVENTEEN
*page 489*

CHAPTER EIGHTEEN
*page 495*

CHAPTER NINETEEN
*page 501*

CHAPTER TWENTY
*page 507*

CHAPTER TWENTY-ONE
*page 513*

CHAPTER TWENTY-TWO
*page 519*

CHAPTER TWENTY-THREE
*page 525*

CHAPTER TWENTY-FOUR
*page 531*

CHAPTER TWENTY-FIVE
*page 537*

CHAPTER TWENTY-SIX
*page 543*

CHAPTER TWENTY-SEVEN
*page 549*

CHAPTER TWENTY-EIGHT
*page 555*

CHAPTER TWENTY-NINE
*page 561*

CHAPTER THIRTY
*page 567*

CHAPTER THIRTY-ONE
*page 573*

CHAPTER THIRTY-TWO
*page 579*

EPILOGUE
*page 585*

Book One

# OUT THERE

# PROLOGUE

As more huge clumps of soil and stone crashed down against her, Charlotte scrambled through the darkness on all fours and finally took cover by crawling through the police car's broken window and stopping for a moment next to its upturned back seat.

More dirt was falling into the pit, slamming into the car with a series of constant heavy thuds. Trying not to panic, Charlotte looked around and saw the two dead bodies wedged into the car, and then she saw several bags that had been thrown in for good measure. Pulling one of the bags open, she found that John had gathered together anything that might show that there'd been visitors to the house over the previous few days. The contents of her pockets, which he'd removed when he'd first taken her prisoner, were in the bag, along with a few of Ted's items too.

The car shook as more dirt crashed down, and when she looked out Charlotte realized that the pit was filling up fast. She could see a huge cloud of dust filling the air, partially blocking the light from above, but a moment later more soil tumbled into the pit, partially obscuring the night sky. In that moment, she realized that soon there'd be no way out.

Crawling over Mack's body, she reached for the car's radio and tried desperately to call for help.

"Hello?" she said, pressing every button but succeeding only in eliciting a clicking sound from the unit. "Is anyone there? Can anyone hear me? Please, you have to hurry! He's going to kill me!"

# CHAPTER ONE

*Three days earlier...*

"Do you know what freaks me out the most?" Richard asked. "Child actors. Like, children should *not* be good at acting. At all. Whenever I see a child in a film or a show who's really good at acting, I just wonder what the hell is going on there. Like, how did that happen?"

Realizing that she'd allowed her thoughts to drift again, Charlotte stared at him across the table and tried to work out exactly how the conversation had strayed onto the topic of child actors. She briefly considered trying to bluff her way through an answer, before realizing that she was better off just being honest.

"I'm really sorry," she told him, as a waiter headed over to the next table with some plates, "but I..."

Her voice trailed off for a moment.

"My head's really not in a good place tonight," she admitted finally.

"I noticed."

"I'm so sorry," she continued, feeling awful for making such an admission. "I was looking forward to this date all week, and then, to tell you the truth, my mum called me yesterday and she lives hundreds of miles away and she lives alone and she had a fall and because of work I can't go to her until tomorrow and so here I am sitting here trying to be a good date but my mind..."

She hesitated, and then she sighed.

"I completely understand," Richard told her.

"I'm so, *so* sorry."

"No, it's fine," he replied, as he twirled some more pasta onto his fork. "Your mum needs you, and you want to be with her. I'd think something was wrong if you *were* able to concentrate on my rambling semi-humorous thoughts about the movie industry."

"Everything you said was fascinating," she said. "The parts I heard, anyway."

"It's all available on my blog," he explained. "You can pretty much download my podcasts and hear 90% of the stuff I told you tonight. The other 10% was really just awkward little pauses sprinkled with a few attempts to check whether you were actually listening."

"I'm really sorry."

"I didn't mean to sound passive-aggressive there," he added. "Damn it, I'm over-analzying things again, aren't I? I always do that. It's like, I just keep talking even though I know I should stop, probably because I feel like silences are just too awkward and I have this need to fill them. That's actually pretty useful when I'm recording my podcast, it's a good skill to have, but..."

He froze for a moment.

"I'm doing it again, aren't I?" he said with a groan.

"No, honestly," she replied, even though she'd caught herself thinking about her mother again, "it's really interesting."

"Hey, my ego's not that fragile," he continued. "No harm done and I am in no way offended. I could actually see your eyes glazing over a little, so actually I'm relieved."

"You are?"

"Not that your mum's sick!" He sighed. "I mean, I'm relieved that I know *why* you weren't getting swept up by my witty conversation. At least now I have some context. As first dates go, this is far from the worst I've had."

"I should have canceled," she told him.

She waited, but she could see from the look in his eyes that he agreed.

"I nearly *did* cancel," she continued, "but then Hayley called and told me I'd be fine, and I listened to her. Since she's the one who set us up in the first place, I figured she knew what she was talking about."

"In the ten years I've known Hayley, her longest relationship has been about a month," he replied.

"Yep, me too." Leaning back in her chair, she sighed again. "You seem like a really nice guy, Richard, and I'm sorry for wasting your time like this."

"You haven't wasted my time. And, hey, when you get back from your mum's, we can always try again. Right?"

\*\*\*

"I'm just so sorry," Charlotte said – for what must have been the hundredth time – as she and Richard stepped out of the restaurant half an hour later and began to walk across the dark car park. "I feel like I dragged you out tonight under false pretenses."

"Not at all," he replied. "So even my hilarious London hotel spa anecdote didn't cut through, huh?"

"London hotel spa anecdote?"

"Wow. And that's my best story."

"Again, I'm sorry," she said, stopping and turning to him, then putting her hands on her face. "I just kept thinking about my mother all alone in that house and even though I tried really hard to focus on dinner, I couldn't do it."

"If you apologize even one more time," he told her, "I'll be forced to storm off in a huff and ignore you if you try to call me."

He paused for a moment.

"Assuming... I mean, do you think there's a chance you *might* try to call me again?"

Lowering her hands, she stared at him, momentarily lost for words.

"Yes!" she blurted out finally, worried that she'd taken too long to answer. Although she'd felt no real spark with Richard, he seemed like a nice guy and she figured she should at least give it another go. "Of course. Sorry, I didn't mean to act like I was having to think about that, I was just..."

"Thinking about your mum again?"

"I've been a mess this evening. Please feel free to tear me to shreds when Hayley inevitably calls you up for a debrief."

"I'll do no such thing," he told her. "I'll simply bid you goodnight, and hope that you do indeed call me again some time once you get back. And I'll tell Hayley that I found you charming and witty. At least in the brief moments during which you were aware of my existence."

He hesitated, before surprising her by stepping closer and planting a brief kiss on her cheek.

"I *will* call you," she told him, feeling more than a little uncomfortable. "I promise."

"And now I'm going this way," he added, before turning and walking away.

After a few paces, he glanced back at her, and Charlotte managed a faint smile and a little wave. Richard smiled in response, but he kept walking and soon he was over by his car in the farthest corner.

Figuring that she shouldn't simply stand and watch him drive away, Charlotte turned and headed to her own car, while fishing her keys from her pocket. She still felt dreadful for having been such an awful dinner companion, and she told herself that it would only be polite to call Richard once she got home from visiting her mother up north. She didn't really hold out any hope that the date might lead anywhere, but she reminded herself that she wasn't exactly drowning in offers.

Reaching her car, she unlocked it and then looked back just as Richard drove past. He waved, and she waved back, and then she climbed into the car and pulled the door shut.

"You're an idiot," she said out loud, once she was safely away from anyone who might overhear her. She looked in the mirror. "You know that, right? Hayley set you up with a perfectly nice guy and you couldn't even keep your mind on him for a couple of hours. He probably thinks you're the rudest woman in the world, and he probably won't even answer if you try to call him in a week or two."

She took a deep breath, and then she started the car. Just as she was about to reverse out of the parking spot, however, her phone buzzed. Checking the screen, she was surprised to find a message from Richard:

*Had fun tonight. Good luck with your mum.*
*Hope to see you again some time.*

The message was sweet, she had to admit that, so she quickly typed a response:

*Thank you for understanding. Will call. Night!*

She waited a moment, just to make sure that there wouldn't be any further replies, and then she set the phone down as she once more set about reversing out of the spot.

"Stupid," she muttered under her breath as she drove toward the exit of the car park. "Stupid stupid stupid..."

Still feeling frustrated, she steered the car out onto the main street and began the short journey home. After a moment, she glanced in the mirror and saw the lights of the restaurant disappearing into the distance, and she felt a flicker of relief that at least the evening was over. Now all she had to do was pack for the trip to see her mother and get an early night so that she'd be able to hit the road early the following morning.

Glancing in the mirror again, she saw that the restaurant's lights were now completely out of view.

## CHAPTER TWO

"No, I think disaster is pretty much the opportune word to use," she said later, as she stood in her bedroom and looked at her half-packed suitcase. "I'm sorry, Hayley, he genuinely seemed like a nice guy, but I shouldn't have been there."

"Richard is by far my hottest single friend," Hayley replied over the tinny speakers of the phone, which was resting on the bed next to the suitcase. "Okay, he can be a little geeky, but that's not necessarily a bad thing. You just have to overlook the fact that he collects toy soldiers. Sorry, I meant... action figures. And did I mention that he does triathlons?"

"Only about a million times."

"That means he has good stamina. You know the other time good stamina comes in handy, don't you?"

"Yes," Charlotte said, rolling her eyes.

"What am I going to do with you, huh?" Hayley continued. "I made it my mission to hook you up with a nice man, but I honestly never thought that it'd be this difficult."

"Have you considered the possibility that I'm a hopeless case?" Charlotte asked as she headed to the wardrobe and began to take out a couple of sweaters. "Think about it, I'm thirty years old and I've never had a really stable relationship. What if I'm destined to always be alone? It might be better to just accept that fact and try to live without this crushing sense of hope."

Once she'd picked a few sweaters, she turned to go back over to the suitcase, but then she hesitated as she glanced out the window and saw a figure outside. Down on the street, a little way from the pool of light cast by a streetlamp, a man was standing and apparently staring straight back up at her. Charlotte waited for him to walk away, but although his features were hidden in the shadows, she could tell that he was still watching her.

"You're not destined to be alone," Hayley told her. "No-one is. There's someone out there for you, and I still think Richard could be that someone. When do you get back from your mother's place?"

Still waiting for the man to walk away, Charlotte didn't immediately answer.

"Huh?" she said finally, turning and heading to the suitcase, where she took a moment to pack the sweaters. "Sorry, I got distracted there. I don't know how long I'll have to be with her, it all depends on how she's doing after her fall."

"She said she's okay, didn't she?"

"She'd say that if her leg had fallen off."

"When you get back, you need to arrange another date with Richard, pronto. And in the meantime, it wouldn't hurt you to keep the texting going a little."

"I don't really know what we'd talk about."

"Try to make it sexy."

Again, Charlotte rolled her eyes.

"I heard that," Hayley added.

"Heard what?"

"You rolled your eyes. Admit it. The point, my dear Charlotte, is that it wouldn't hurt you to try a little sexting with this guy."

"I'm not texting him any nudes. I don't do that sort of thing."

"Of course not, that'd be way too desperate. You need to tease him."

"I really didn't sense that kind of thing between us," she replied as she headed back to the wardrobe. Looking out the window again, she told herself that the man would be gone, but instead she felt a shudder run up her spine as she saw that he was still out there.

Still staring up at her in the window.

"Then you need to *make* it happen," Hayley said. "Be the spark."

"What?"

For a moment, Charlotte could only watch the figure. She tried to convince herself that she was wrong, that the guy was looking the other way; the more she waited, however, the more she realized that her initial instinct had been right. For whatever reason, the guy was still staring at her window, and she figured that he'd been out there for at least a few minutes now.

Was it Richard?

The build wasn't that dissimilar.

"So are you going to text him tonight?" Hayley asked.

"How well do you know him?" she replied.

"What's that got to do with anything?"

"Why's he single? He hasn't got any kind of reputation, has he? You know, for being... weird."

She kept her gaze fixed on the man, almost daring him to turn away first.

"What are you rambling on about now?" Hayley said. "I've presented you with a perfectly nice guy and you're finding new and increasingly ingenious ways to screw the whole thing up."

Charlotte looked over at the phone, and for a moment she realized that Hayley might be right. Then, turning back to the window, she saw to her relief that the strange man had disappeared. Leaning closer to the glass, she looked both ways along the dark street, but there was no sign of the man at all and she couldn't help but breathe a sigh of relief.

"So are you going to send him a message?" Hayley asked. "How about a photo? Nothing too on-the-nose, just something to remind him what he's missing. Charlotte? Are you going to send Richard a photo?"

\*\*\*

"No, Mum," Charlotte said as she sat began to scrape the stir fry onto her plate, "I'm coming tomorrow and that's the end of the story."

"Why do you have to make everything such a big deal?" her mother asked. "It was only a small fall, and I'm fine. I'm not some pathetic, ancient old thing, you know."

"No-one said that you are," Charlotte replied, "but it can't have been a small fall if you had to see Doctor Henry."

"Oh, why won't people stop fussing?"

"I should be there tomorrow evening. I'm setting off really early, and I'll have to stop for a bite along the way, but I reckon I'll be at your door around six."

"The main road to the village is closed."

"Since when?"

"I don't know since when, it's just closed. Something to do with floods."

"Then I'll take the scenic route, Mum, but you're not going to stop me. As long as I can see that you're fine, I'll be out of your hair by the weekend, okay? Please, just accept that as your only child I'm somewhat concerned for your well-being." She waited for an answer, and then she heard her intercom buzz. "Hang on," she continued, carrying the phone through to the hallway and checking the screen on the wall, "there's someone -"

Stopping, she saw that the video showed only the step outside, with no sign of anyone out there. She waited, but after a few seconds she realized that most likely some passing kid had simply hit the button for a joke. That kind of thing happened, especially when people were spilling out from the local bars.

"I went hiking last week," her mother told her.

"What's that got to do with anything?"

She made her way back into the kitchen.

"It shows that I'm not as fragile as you think I am."

"Well," Charlotte said with a sigh, "I'm still -"

Before she could finish, the buzzer rang again. Turning, she looked through to the hallway, and this time she couldn't help but feel a hint of concern in the pit of her stomach. Even from a distance, she could see that there was nobody on the intercom's screen, so she decided to keep watching in case she spotted someone ringing for a third time. She told herself that there could be no link to the shadowy man she'd seen earlier, out on the pavement, but she still couldn't get rid of a lingering sense of suspicion in the back of her mind.

"I'm coming tomorrow, and that's that," she said finally, forcing herself to stay focused on her mother. "I don't care if all the roads in the entire county are closed, I'll find a way to reach you. I'm going to make sure that you're alright, whether you like it or not."

"Fine," her mother muttered, "if you want to waste your time and money, then that's your choice. Now, if you'll excuse me, I have to go down to the basement and fetch some boxes."

"I really don't think you should be going into the -"

She heard a click, and then she looked at the phone.

"Did you just hang up on me?" she asked, although she already knew the answer. "Damn you, Mum, sometimes -"

Suddenly the buzzer rang out for a third time. Looking over at the intercom again, she once more saw no sign of anyone, but this time she was determined to find out for sure. Heading to the stairs, she hurried down until she reached the front door and then she stood on tiptoes so that she could peer out through the frosted glass. Although she couldn't see too clearly, she was at least able to make sure that nobody was lurking nearby. She almost opened the front door, but then – thinking better of that approach – she turned and headed back up to the kitchen.

The buzzer didn't ring again that night.

## CHAPTER THREE

The following lunchtime, sitting at a table at a motorway service station, Charlotte bit into a burger and looked out across the dining area. Having been driving for six hours already, she knew that she needed to take a break, although she also didn't want to waste too much time. After all, she still wasn't sure which roads were closed near her mother's village.

After setting the burger down, she picked up her phone and brought up her last text message exchange with Richard. She read the messages again, checking for any sign that he might be a crazed stalker, and then she told herself that she was probably being a little paranoid. The guy outside her flat had most likely been some random person waiting for a friend. He hadn't even been the right build for Richard.

She thought for a moment, and then she typed out a message:

*Hey, sorry again about last night. I've been on the road since six. Should be back in town in about a week. Try dinner again?*

She tapped to send the message, and within a couple of seconds she saw a notification that it had been read. She waited, and then – realizing that she was perhaps being a little too obsessive – she looked out once again across the dining area and watched the crowds of people flooding all around the large open space.

She took another mouthful of the burger, and then she glanced down at her phone again.

Still no reply.

Although she told herself that there were millions of reasons why he might not have got back to her yet, she couldn't ignore a niggling sense of concern. She figured that if she'd blown it and Richard was no longer interested, she wanted to at least know, so – against her better judgment – she typed another message:

*No worries if not. I totally get it. Maybe see you around some time.*

She debated whether or not to add some emojis at the end, but she decided against that idea before tapping to send the message. Again, it took only a few seconds for him to read what she'd written, but there was no sign of him replying.

"Okay, then," she muttered, as she realized that trying again would simply reek of desperation. Closing the app on her phone, she focused on finishing her burger, and she told herself that it was already soon going to be time to hit the road again.

\*\*\*

A couple of hours later, having taken a rural route through the forest in order to avoid some closed roads ahead, Charlotte gently steered the car around a lazy bend. Since she was unfamiliar with the local area, she glanced a couple of times at the view, although all she could really see was the forest spreading off for miles and miles in every direction.

Grabbing her phone from the passenger seat, she did what she'd sworn not to do: she checked yet again for a reply from Richard, only to find that there was still nothing. Although she'd told herself that she wasn't too bothered, she realized now that she was pretty disappointed, although she couldn't really blame him for giving her the cold shoulder. As she set her phone back down and focused once again on the road ahead, she tried to imagine how she'd have reacted if the situation had been reversed, and she realized that she might well have decided not to bother with another date.

After all, unless he'd felt a real connection, why would -

Suddenly she heard a loud pop, and the car instantly began to steer wildly to the left. Slamming her foot on the brake pedal, Charlotte steered to the right, but she succeeded only in putting the car into a half spin that ended with an unceremonious bump against the barrier on the outside of the next curve.

Cutting the engine, she sat completely still for a moment as she tried to work out what had happened. Her heart was racing, but after a few seconds she unbuckled her seat-belt and climbed out of the car, and then she walked around to the front and saw that the left tire had somehow been shredded.

"What the..."

Crouching down, she took a closer look at the damage. Something seemed to have sliced straight through the carcass of the tire, and after a moment she realized that she could see something sharp and metallic poking out of the hole. Reaching inside, she struggled to pull the foreign object out, and finally she found herself holding what appeared to be a thick metal spike with several barbs on its sides.

She looked back along the road, and then she looked forward, but there was no sign of anything similar. Turning to the tire again, she could already tell that there was damage to the actual wheel, and she knew that her limited tire-changing expertise likely wouldn't be enough to get the car back up and running.

"What the hell happened here?" she whispered, before realizing that the 'what' was less important than the 'how'; namely, how she was going to get help.

Still holding the mysterious object, she headed back to the other side of the car and climbed inside. She set the object down on the seat and grabbed her phone, and she immediately felt a thud of despair in her chest as she saw that she had no signal.

"You've got to be kidding me," she said, clambering back out of the car and waving the phone around, hoping to at least pick up one bar.

When that failed to work, she tried dialing 999 anyway, to no avail.

"Not today," she muttered, waving the phone around again, "come on, I don't have time for this crap. This is the twenty-first century, everywhere's supposed to have network coverage by now!"

She walked several meters from the car and tried again, and then she tried doing the same thing in the opposite direction, but nothing seemed to work. Looking out at the forest, she realized that most likely the trees were blocking the signal, although that realization didn't help much. She briefly considered setting off on foot to find somewhere she could call from, although she knew that she'd been driving through the forest for quite a while and she was worried about abandoning her car.

So many different options ran through her head, but finally she decided that her best bet might simply be to stay put and wait for someone else to pass along the road. Sure, she was out in the middle of nowhere, but she figured that she couldn't be the only person to head out that way on a warm spring day.

"A road is a road," she said, hoping to give herself a little more confidence. "If people didn't drive this way, they wouldn't have built it in the first place. Therefore, it's simply logical to assume that there'll be more cars along before too long, and then I can get to the next town."

She paused, running the idea through her head a few times.

"That makes total sense," she added finally. "All I have to do is wait."

Sitting back in the car, she tried her phone again and again, hoping that eventually she'd get lucky. Although she felt frustrated, she knew that everything would be alright so she leaned back and focused on staying calm. She was perfectly aware that the next car would come along in its own sweet time, and that getting angry wasn't going to solve anything, so instead she closed her eyes and tried to meditate. She'd never really meditated before, but she figured that it couldn't be that difficult, so she tried to enter some kind of peaceful state of mind.

And then, just a few minutes later, she heard the unmistakable sound of a car approaching.

Opening her eyes, she looked in the mirror and saw that a small truck was heading her way. Filled with a sense of profound relief, she climbed out of the car and waved at the truck, just as it pulled over nearby and the engine stopped. She waited for a moment, until one of the doors opened and a late middle-aged man stepped out.

"Well, hello there," the man said, removing his hat and sunglasses as he made his way over to her, "what seems to be the problem?"

"My wheel's wrecked, I think," she told him. "I've got no signal, I was sitting here and waiting, hoping that someone would come by who might give me a life to the next town."

"I can do better than that," he replied with a smile. "My name's Ted Armitage and I happen to know my way around a car. I've even got a load of tools with me. If you like, I can take a look at the damage and hopefully get you back on the road in no time."

"That'd be amazing," she said, before letting out a sigh of relief. "Thank you so much. You're a lifesaver!"

## CHAPTER FOUR

"You know," Ted said, about half an hour later, as he continued to examine the underside of Charlotte's car, "you've been lucky. Sure, there's some damage, but nothing that'll keep you off the road."

"That's a relief," she replied. "Do you have any idea how long it'll take to fix?"

"Well, that's the tricky part." He scooched a little further under the vehicle, until only his legs were visible. "No, hang on, scratch that. I think patching you up won't be too hard at all, although you're gonna need to get to a garage at your earliest convenience. This thing won't exactly pass an M.O.T., if you catch my drift."

"I just need to get to my mother's house."

"And where's that?"

"A village called Arlingham."

"Never heard of it."

"It's about two hundred miles from here."

"That'd explain that, then. Nice place, is it?"

"It's small," she told him. "It's the kind of place where everyone knows everyone. Not that that's a bad thing, it's certainly what my mother wants. It's also a bit of a pain to get to."

He scrambled out from under the car and got to his feet, and now there were smudges of grease on one side of his face.

"Listen," he continued, "I can get your car roadworthy and I'm sure she'll take you a couple of hundred miles, but then you really need to get her checked over properly. You have to promise me that you'll do that. Do we have a deal?"

"Absolutely. Anything." She paused. "How... much will it cost?"

He stared at her, and then he let out a raucous laugh as he turned and shuffled over to his truck.

"You're funny," he told her. "I'm not charging you. You're a damsel in distress by the side of the road, what kind of man would want money for helping out? I'm just glad I came along, that's all."

"Thank you so much," she replied, stepping over to the driver's side door and grabbing her phone. She checked once more for signal, but still she found none. After settling her phone back on the seat, she made her way around the car again and saw that Ted was taking a bag of tools from his truck.

"There's about an hour's work under there," he told her.

"Is there anything I can do to help?"

"You got any way to make coffee?"

"Sorry."

"Don't sweat it," he replied, stepping past her and then stopping for a moment. "Actually, could you grab the little red kit bag from my truck? You should see it easy enough."

"Totally."

Keen to help however she could, Charlotte hurried over to the truck and leaned into the back. She immediately saw an assortment of different bags, although only one was red. She took a moment to pull it out from under some metal bars, and then she looked at all the other stuff piled into the back of the truck. There was a ladder, along with several ropes and pieces of equipment, and even what looked to be a bright yellow drone. She paused for a moment, and then she began to take the red bag back over to Ted. Spotting him round by the damaged wheel, she carried the bag to him and then set it down.

"I don't know what I'd have done if you hadn't shown up," she told him.

"I must've been sent by an angel."

Smiling, she headed around to the other side of the car. She'd been obsessively checking for signal every few minutes, but this time – as she reached down to the driver's seat – she saw that her phone had disappeared. She leaned down and reached under the seat, in case it had fallen, but once again she found nothing. Hesitating for a moment, she tried to work out where it might have gone, and then she peered round at Ted as he shuffled back under the car and got to work.

She opened her mouth to ask him whether he'd seen her phone, but at the last second she held her tongue. There was no way he could be responsible for its disappearance, so she told herself that she just had to keep looking.

"You're lucky with the weather," he observed after a moment.

"Yeah," she replied, still puzzled, as she checked all around the seat again.

"Out here," he continued, "I'm sure you can get all sorts of different storms and things like that. Have you ever heard of micro-climates? I wonder whether they get micro-climates in this part of the world. Anyway, I bet it can get real muddy out here, real quick. I wouldn't like to be stuck on this road in a downpour, that's for sure."

"Me neither."

She checked down the side of the seat, but there was still no sign of her phone, and she was already running out of places to search.

"There's something quite impressive about a woman setting out all alone to drive pretty much across the country," he said. "I know in this day and age I probably *shouldn't* be impressed by that, but still, anyone taking such a long drive is a hero in my books. So many people do things the easy way and hop on a train, or even fly, but driving's the best way to really see the country you live in. I drive everywhere, I don't mess around with any other forms of transport."

"Sure."

Still trying to find her phone, she dropped to her knees and reached under the driver's seat, hoping against hope that somehow the damn thing had slipped down there. Although she wasn't panicking, at least not yet, she still couldn't help but feel that her phone seemed to have simply vanished without a trace. The only possible explanation was that, in an absent-minded moment, she'd put it someplace completely different.

Getting to her feet, she began to check all her pockets again.

"Even at my age," Ted continued, "there are parts of this fine country that I've never visited. Can you believe that? I'm coming up on fifty-five years of age soon and I'm starting to realize that I haven't traveled enough. My late wife wasn't much of an explorer, you see, and work always kind of held me down, but lately I've been getting this bug for getting out there and seeing what the world has to offer. Hell, you probably think I'm just some rambling old man, but I guess what I'm saying is that you reach a certain stage in your life and you realize that there's only a finite amount of time left for you to do all those things you've been dreaming of for years. Does that make any sense at all to you?"

"It does," she muttered, still racking her brains to try to figure out where she could have put her phone.

"I'm probably talking too much. I do that. People always tell me that I go on and on, even when nobody's listening."

"Sorry," she said, making her way around to the other side of the car and looking down at his legs as they continued to poke out from the side, "I know this might seem like a weird question, but have you seen a phone anywhere?"

"A phone?"

"Yeah, I seem to have..."

Her voice trailed off.

"I'm sorry," Ted said, "but I don't think I can help you."

"No, it's fine," she muttered, heading back to the front of the car, still determined to find her phone. She knew that it had to be around somewhere, and for a moment she tried to think logically about all her actions over the previous hour or so.

The phone had to be somewhere.

A moment later, hearing Ted getting to his feet, she turned to see him smiling at her from the other side of the car.

"Found it?" he asked.

"Not yet."

"Huh."

She waited for him to get back to work, but for a few seconds he seemed content merely to stare at her.

"You know," he continued, "there's just one thing I've really got to ask you."

"What's that?"

"Well..."

He paused.

"No, forget it," he added, shaking his head, "it's none of my business, not really."

"It's fine," she replied. "What's wrong?"

"Well, it's just been eating at me, that's all."

"What has?"

She waited, and again he merely stared for a moment.

"Well," he said finally, clearly choosing his words with care, "I just can't help wondering... Why *didn't* you cancel your date with Richard at the restaurant last night?"

She opened her mouth to reply, before realizing in an instant that there was no way he should know anything about her date.

"That was his name, wasn't it?" he continued. "Richard? Yeah, it was, I'm sure. Anyway, I just can't help thinking... If you knew you were in no fit state to be out, why didn't you do the right thing – the polite thing – and cancel before you showed up and wasted his evening?"

## CHAPTER FIVE

"I'm sorry," Charlotte said cautiously, her mind still racing as she tried to figure out whether there was some reasonable explanation, "but did you just..."

She stared at him, and he stared back.

"Oh, I just happened to be there," he said finally, with a half-smile. "I know what you're thinking. What's a guy like me doing at a fancy restaurant like that? The truth is, sometimes I like to treat myself. I was alone, I was actually at the table right behind you, and you know what it's like, you can't really help overhearing conversations from nearby."

Still staring at him, Charlotte felt as if she was missing part of the explanation. She told herself that she had to be misunderstanding, that there was no way that this guy could actually have been at the restaurant.

"And it's been bugging me ever since," he added. "The normal thing to do in that situation, the right thing to do, would have been to call him beforehand and politely inform him that you'd be unable to attend the date. He seemed like a reasonable guy, I can't imagine he would have kicked up a fuss. You could have at least given him the opportunity to prove to you that he wasn't an asshole. Instead, you showed up anyway and just demonstrated a complete lack of respect for his time."

Charlotte opened her mouth to reply, but at that moment she thought back to the sight of the man who'd been watching her flat the night before. At the time, she'd told herself that there was no reason to worry, although a part of her had considered the possibility that Richard might be some kind of crazy stalker type. Now, however, as she looked at Ted, she realized that *he* was a better match for the general physique of the mysterious figure. She told herself that she was simply overreacting, but at the same time she was starting to feel increasingly uncomfortable.

"You know what?" she said after a moment, trying to act as if nothing was wrong, "I don't want to put you out, so I think what I might do is I might just walk to the next town. It can't be far."

"I think it's pretty far."

"Well, still, I think -"

"It really is pretty far," he added, interrupting her. "Honestly, this stretch of road is more or less the worst place to break down. You're basically equidistant between the two nearest towns, and they're both a real good distance off. Plus, I honestly don't know if there's a garage at either of them, so you could end up having a long wait, plus any work would be expensive. Please don't take this the wrong way, but I don't get the impression that you're exactly swimming in money."

"I think I'll be fine," she said through gritted teeth.

"Why be fine, when you can be *more* than fine?" he asked with a chuckle. "I'm more than capable of looking after you. Didn't you see all that equipment I've got with me in my truck? I've been doing this type of work all my life, it's my bread and butter. It doesn't matter where you go, you won't find anyone who's better than Ted Armitage when it comes to fixing this sort of damage."

"It's okay, really."

"You don't want my help?"

"I just feel like it'd be better if I went and found someone who can fix the car up properly," she explained. "You said it yourself, it might not be entirely up to scratch, so I should probably just go and try to find a garage."

"Huh."

He stared at her.

"And how far," he said after a moment, "do you think you'll have to go to find a garage out there? You're pretty far from anywhere."

"Sure, but..."

Her voice trailed off.

She waited.

"Okay, then," he said with a shrug, "suit yourself. I was just trying to be helpful, that's all, but I'm not a pushy guy. I'll get my things and be out of your hair."

With that, he crouched down out of sight, and Charlotte heard him starting to gather his tools.

"Thank you," she said quietly, and then she headed back to the driver's seat and started looking for her phone again. Part of her worried that she'd been too quick to turn down Ted's offer of help, but she still couldn't figure out exactly how he'd ended up chancing upon her after apparently overhearing her date with Richard the previous night. The story just didn't add up.

All she knew was that she wanted him to leave, and that then she could come up with another plan.

She searched for her phone for a moment, and then – realizing that she could no longer hear Ted – she got to her feet. The man's truck was still parked nearby, with the rear still open, but there was no sign of Ted himself and she couldn't hear him collecting his tools. She waited a moment longer, and then she stepped around the car and looked down to see his red bag resting on the ground.

She looked over her shoulder, then back toward the truck.

"Are you okay?" she asked.

The only response, save for the gentle rustle of nearby trees, was silence.

"Ted?"

When he still failed to answer, she stepped over to the bag and crouched down. She half expected to find that he was fully under the car, carrying out some final piece of work, but instead she saw no sign of him. Looking around, she tried to work out where he could have gone, but the man seemed to have somehow disappeared into thin air.

Standing again, she stood completely still and listened out for any hint of footsteps.

"Ted?" she called out. "Hey, is anything wrong?"

After a few seconds, she walked around to the other side of the car, but he still seemed to have vanished. She looked toward the truck, and then she wandered over and looked into the front. Yet again, Ted was nowhere to be seen, and a moment later she looked back toward her own car as she tried to figure out exactly where the guy might be hiding.

No.

Not hiding, she told herself.

Just...

She looked out into the forest, convinced that he'd probably just gone to take a pee, but there was still no sign of him. Although she told herself that there was no reason to be alarmed, she was starting to think that something about Ted Armitage really didn't seem quite right, and after a few more seconds she began to make her way back to her car. She really wanted to find her phone, not only because she wanted to go and find some signal but because she was also starting to wonder whether there was any chance that Ted might have grabbed it from the front seat. She told herself that some mid-fifties guy was hardly likely to be a psychopathic serial killer, but as she reached her car and looked in at the seat again she realized that she was running out of explanations for her missing phone.

Stepping around the car again, she saw that Ted's red bag was still on the ground.

"Hey, Ted," she said cautiously, convinced that he had to be close enough to hear her, "I think I'm just going to go and head on down the road and try to find a garage or something. There has to be one somewhere, and they'll probably be better equipped to do whatever needs doing."

She looked around, hoping that he might respond.

"So, I just wanted to thank you for helping out," she continued. "I hope I didn't delay you too much. Thanks again and I really appreciate the offer, and I hope you have a nice journey, wherever you're going."

Realizing that there was little prospect of him answering, she grabbed her keys and locked her car, and then she stepped back and looked at the entire scene. She saw the car and the truck, and the red bag on the ground, but somehow Ted had absolutely vanished. She even crouched down, just to check one more time that he wasn't under one of the vehicles, but it was as if some hidden force had reached down and plucked the guy straight out of existence.

"Okay, then," she muttered under her breath, before turning and starting to walk away. "Sorry, I -"

Suddenly someone grabbed her from behind and plunged a needle into the side of her neck. She gasped and tried to pull away, but already her body was starting to feel very heavy. The last thing she felt, as she passed out, was the sensation of somebody gently lowering her down onto the tarmac.

## CHAPTER SIX

Stirring slightly as the truck ran over a bump in the road, Charlotte opened her eyes and found that she was on her side in the rear of the vehicle, surrounded by Ted's various bags and ladders and ropes. The yellow drone was right next to her face, but she could barely keep her eyes open. Already, she felt herself slipping back into unconsciousness.

She tried to cry out, but she could only muster a faint murmur as he eyes slipped shut and she drifted into darkness.

## CHAPTER SEVEN

The next thing she knew, the sound of the truck's engine was gone and suddenly she felt very still. She managed to open her eyes, only to find that her vision was somewhat blurred, but she blinked a few times until finally she was able to see a bare bulb on the ceiling high above, lighting the room.

"What the -"

She immediately began to sit up, only to find that she was flat on her back with her arms and ankles tied to the four corners of a wooden bed. Shocked, she instinctively tried to pull free, only to realize that the ropes were tied far too tight. She looked around and saw that she was in a fairly small, bare room. A window on the far side offered a view of darkness outside, and other than the bed there was only one piece of furniture, a large wardrobe that stood against the opposite wall. The walls themselves were covered in peeling paper that retained just enough of a faded greenish pattern to suggest that once – long ago – someone had taken care to try to make the place look nice.

A long, *long* time ago.

Pulling once again on the ropes, she began to bang the bed's wooden posts against the wall, but she didn't let the noise stop her. She was trying desperately to keep from panicking, and she told herself that there had to be some way out of the ropes, but her wrists in particular were already starting to chafe as she tried to twist them free.

"Come on," she muttered, "you can do this."

She tried to find a weak spot in the structure of the bed itself, but a moment later she heard heavy, thudding footsteps making their way up from the ground floor, and she turned to look over at the open door. She waited, and her heart was racing as she finally saw Ted stepping into view.

"Ah, there you are," he said, and now he'd changed into what appeared to be some kind of hunting gear, complete with a pale green baseball cap. Leaning against the jamb, he grinned as he looked through at her. "You woke up a little faster than I expected, but not a great deal. It's all good. You must be a little heavier than you look."

"What do you want from me?" she snapped.

"Well, first I'd like you to chill out a little," he said, before taking a bite from a sandwich he'd been carrying in his right hand. He chewed for a moment. "There's no need to be rude just because you've found yourself taking something of an unexpected diversion," he continued, speaking with his mouth full. "The truth is, I knew you'd never reach a town if you just went wandering off. You'd most likely have died of exposure, so I very kindly decided to bring you back to my place."

He took another bite from the sandwich.

"Let me go!" she said firmly.

"I don't exactly know if you're the grateful type," he muttered.

"Let me go!"

"You're not really making a good case for yourself. In fact, you're coming across pretty poorly. It's not generally considered polite to start making such a racket in a stranger's home."

"Someone'll come looking for me," she told him. "They'll realize that I'm missing by now. They'll find my car. They'll start searching."

"I'm sure they will," he replied, "but I imagine they'll be a little off target. We're about a couple of hundred miles from where I left your car, so -"

"You followed me!"

"That's a big accusation to make."

"Why?" she continued. "What did I ever do to you?"

"Absolutely nothing. Apart from turning down my offer of help, that is." He took another bite. "I didn't like your tone last night, when I overheard you in that restaurant," he explained. "You caught my attention and I decided to check you out. That happens to me a lot, I notice people being rude or unpleasant and I get this itch to figure out what's going on with them. The nature of my job means that I travel a lot, so it was no big deal for me to trail you for a while. As you might have guessed by now, I'm not actually a mechanic."

"What... what are you?" she asked.

"I'm a mortgage broker," he replied. "I help people... it's complicated, but I help people get the best deal for their new home, or for their existing home if they're thinking of trying to refinance. Tell me, that flat of yours, do you own it or rent it? Because if you own it, I think I could help you out by comparing some of the different -"

"Let me go!" she snapped angrily.

"Just think about it for a minute," he continued. "You'd be amazed at the difference a good broker can make when it comes to -"

"Help!" she screamed, looking toward the window. "Somebody help me!"

"We're fifteen miles from the next house," he told her. "More, maybe. Who exactly do you think is going to come running to your assistance?"

"Help me!" she yelled, desperately hoping that he was lying. "I'm up here! He's holding me hostage!"

"Am I?" he replied, furrowing his brow. "I think you might have your terminology wrong there. You're not a hostage. If anything, I'm keeping you here for your own benefit, until you calm down a little and start to realize what's good for you. Frankly, back on that road, you struck me as someone who was on the verge of some kind of psychotic episode. Was I really supposed to just leave you there?"

"What did you do with my phone?" she snapped.

"I have no idea what you're talking about."

"Where's my phone?" she shouted.

She waited, but now he was simply chewing again.

"I won't tell anyone," she continued. "Obviously there's been a mistake. Did you think I was rude to you earlier? I'm sorry, I can come off like that sometimes, but I promise I won't get you into any trouble. I just want to go to my mother's house, she's elderly and she's frail and she had a fall, and if you'll just let me go then I swear no-one'll ever hear about any of this."

Again she waited, but Ted simply took another bite from his sandwich.

"Please," she added, and now there were tears in her eyes. "It doesn't have to be like this. Can we talk about the situation like two adults? I'm more than capable of apologizing and owning up to any mistakes I might have made. You're a reasonable man, aren't you? Let's not let a little misunderstanding get out of hand."

Ted stared at her, while slowly chewing, and then he popped the last piece of the sandwich into his mouth.

"Please," Charlotte sobbed, "I'm sorry..."

He took a moment to finish chewing, and finally he swallowed.

"You know what I think you need?" he asked after a few more seconds. "I think you need some time to cool off and gather your thoughts."

"No," she replied, "I just need to -"

"I'm going to let you think things over," he continued, stepping back and reaching out to pull the door shut. "I need to go and talk to someone anyway, so I'll come back through in the morning and see how you're doing."

"No!" she shouted, pulling again on the ropes. "You can't leave me in here!"

"It's only for one night," he told her. "Now, do you want the light on or off?"

"Please let me out," she sobbed, still trying to get out of the ropes. "I'll do anything you want, but just untie me and let me go."

"Light off, then."

With that, he switched the light off and then pulled the door shut.

"I'll do anything!" she screamed, pulling so hard on the ropes that the bed's wooden frame once again began to bang against the wall. "Come back! Just tell me what you want!"

Hearing footsteps heading back downstairs, she realized that she was being ignored.

"Someone's going to come looking for me!" she yelled. "There's still time to put this right! All you have to do is let me go and no-one has to know that I was ever here! Do you hear me? Let's end this madness before it gets out of hand! I'm sorry! Do you hear me? I mean it, I'm sorry!"

She heard a door bumping shut somewhere downstairs, and she let out an angry sigh as she realized that Ted – if that was even his real name – hadn't listened to a word that she'd just shouted. Although she still didn't want to believe that he was some kind of psycho, she began to look around the dark room as she tried to think of another way to get free. She told herself that there had to be a way, that there was always a way, and that she simply needed to be smart enough to figure it out before morning.

"Someone *is* going to come looking for me," she whispered, as more tears streamed down her face. "They're going to find me, and then everything's going to be okay."

## CHAPTER EIGHT

Several hours later, bathed in moonlight that shone through the window, Charlotte struggled to push against one of the bed's wooden posts, hoping to break it free so that she could loop the rope away. She'd been working on the same post for a while now, and she hadn't felt it give so much as a millimeter, but she told herself that she had no other option.

Finally, feeling a burning pain in her shoulder, she slumped back down for a moment.

The house had been silent ever since Ted had gone downstairs. She had no idea of the time, although she assumed that it must be at least midnight. Was he asleep in a chair down there, or had he gone out? She had no clue, but she told herself that she had to get free before morning, because she felt certain that he was planning something.

Glancing around the room, she looked for any sign of hidden cameras. There was nothing so far, although she couldn't really make out the darker corners and she was worried that Ted might have some kind of high-tech system set up, perhaps even with night vision. She looked at one corner, then at the next, but she was more and more certain that there were no cameras, although that didn't make her feel too much better. She'd seen enough horror movies to know that men didn't tend to kidnap women and take them to rural locations simply for their own good.

Once her shoulder had stopped hurting so much, she leaned up and set to work once more trying to break the wooden post. She felt its great, solid immovability withstanding her pressure, but she told herself that she had no other options. She adjusted her position slightly and tried pushing at a slightly different angle. Although she felt certain that Ted would have tested the bed, she had no better ideas and she couldn't just wait passively for him to return. She changed her angle again, then again, determined to find a way to -

Suddenly her shoulder pushed hard against one of the slats, breaking it in the middle. Startled, Charlotte looked at the damaged slat for a moment before using her shoulder to push it again, this time knocking the upper section out and leaving a large, damaged piece of wood poking out. She thought for a moment, before leaning closer and trying to use her teeth to grab the wood and break it free. At first she struggled, but after a few more attempts she was able to break the piece of wood away, leaving it damaged at both ends with large, sharp shards exposed.

Her heart was pounding as she managed to reach down and take the shard from her mouth, and then she began to run one of the broken ends against the rope. She knew that the odds were against her, but she couldn't help hoping that somehow she might be able to break through and escape.

\*\*\*

The bedroom door creaked open, and a moment later Charlotte peered out at the dark landing. She was still fairly sure that Ted was downstairs, although she didn't want to take any chances. The landing was almost pitch black, although a patch of moonlight allowed her to see that all the other doors were shut. A set of stairs offered a chance to get downstairs, although – as she stepped over and looked down toward the hallway – she had no idea what might be waiting for her.

She listened, but the house remained silent.

A million questions raced through her mind. Where was Ted? Did he keep any weapons in the house? Was he asleep? Was he waiting for her? Hadn't it been a little too easy to get away from the bed, or was she simply being paranoid? Was she being tested? Had she just been lucky? Was Ted about to step out from any direction and smack her in the head with an ax? Did she genuinely have a chance of getting away, or was she a dead woman walking?

Was he playing some kind of sick game?

Trying to remain positive, she made her way to the top of the stairs and once again looked down. She was starting to think that her best option was simply to get outside and run, and to keep running until eventually she found civilization. Sure, she wasn't exactly the athletic type, but then neither was Ted and she felt fairly confident that she could outrun him. Besides, what other options did she have?

Still, she hesitated, worried that she was walking into a trap. All she could see at the bottom of the stairs was a small part of the hallway, which meant that there were plenty of places where Ted could be hiding. She knew that at any moment he could suddenly lunge at her swinging a baseball bat, or wielding any other weapon. She couldn't simply stand at the top of the stairs and wait, however, so finally she forced herself to start making her way down, while simultaneously preparing to run back up if necessary.

By the time she reached the hallway, she was starting to feel a little more confident. All the lights were off and the house remained silent, and she found herself wondering whether – inexplicably – Ted might have gone out. She knew she was probably getting her hopes up way too much, that there was no way he'd have simply wandered off and left her alone in the house, but as she made her way over to a nearby doorway and peered through, she saw a darkened front room and realized that there was still no sign of the guy.

And then, looking over her shoulder, she realized she could see a hint of light coming from somewhere outside.

She hesitated, and then she crept over to the window and looked out; sure enough, there was a light on in a large barn on the far side of a wide, open yard. Ted had to be in there, she realized, although she had no idea what he might be up to. A moment later, however, she spotted a shadow briefly appearing in one window on the side of the barn, and she realized that she had to get away while he was distracted.

Finding that the front door to the house was unlocked, she pulled it open and stepped outside, and then she turned to run toward the road.

Suddenly a cry rang out, piercing the night air, and she spun around and looked back toward the barn.

She knew instantly that the cry had belonged to a woman, and after a moment she realized she could also hear a shuffling sound coming from the barn. She stood frozen in place for a moment, and then she turned once again to run.

"No!" a woman's voice screamed, causing her to stop again. "Please, don't do this!"

Charlotte's heart was racing now as she looked over at the barn. All she wanted was to run and get as far away from the house as possible. At the same time, she could tell that the woman was in agony, and she realized that she couldn't simply abandon someone who was clearly in need of help.

She looked around for some kind of weapon, and then she began to make her way slowly toward the barn.

"Why are you doing this to me?" the woman cried, followed by the sound of clanking chains. "Just let me go. Please, I'm begging you, I have a husband and a child, you have to let me go..."

As she approached the door to the barn, Charlotte realized that she could hear more chains moving inside. She stopped for a moment as she looked toward the open door, and then she spotted a window in the barn's side. After glancing around one more time to make sure that nobody else was around, she crept over to the window and ducked down, and then she very carefully craned her neck and began to peer through to the barn's interior.

At first, bright lights made it impossible for her to see anything. She squinted, and then she turned to look along the barn, and finally she froze as soon as she saw the Ted was standing at the barn's far end. For a moment she was unable to make out anything beyond him, but as he stepped aside she was able to see a naked woman hanging from a set of chains.

Horrified, Charlotte pulled away for a moment, just as the woman cried out again.

"What do you think that's gonna achieve, huh?" Ted asked, sounding distinctly irritated. "I already told you, I've got your replacement lined up. We both knew this day was going to come. And you have to admit, you've caused me a fair old bit of trouble lately."

Hearing the sound of something heavy being dragged across the barn's concrete floor, Charlotte looked around and tried to work out what she could use as a weapon. She knew that she had to get into the barn and save the woman, and after a moment she spotted an ax resting against the side of the building. She stepped over and took the ax, and then she tried to figure out exactly how she was going to get the jump on Ted. She briefly considered running instead, and trying to get help, but deep down she knew that she wouldn't be able to get back in time.

"No!" the woman screamed suddenly, before letting out a series of guttural cries.

Charlotte stepped back over to the window and looked through, and to her horror she saw that Ted was cutting the woman's belly open. She told herself to get in there and help, but in that moment she watched as the woman's intestines slopped out from the wound, and she realized that she was already too late. Although the woman was still just about alive, her body was shuddering and blood was pouring from her split belly, and a moment later Ted plunged the knife into her chest.

"Don't feel bad," he said firmly. "You were good. She's just better, that's all. I think she and I are going to have a lot of fun."

As Ted stepped around the woman, Charlotte pulled back to make sure that she couldn't be seen. Part of her still wanted to go into the barn and make Ted pay, but she quickly told herself that she'd likely be no match for him. After a few seconds, she turned and stumbled along the side of the barn, figuring that she needed to pick a direction and run. And then, reaching the barn's far end, she looked around the corner and saw yet another horrific sight in the moonlight.

Clamping a hand over her mouth, she just about managed to keep from screaming as she stared at a long, vertical metal pole. The heads of a dozen or more women were arranged on the pole, with the lowest heads almost skeletal while the heads toward the top were fairly fresh. So many dead eyes stared out from the awful scene, and open mouths hung open in silenced screams, as Charlotte took a few steps back and tried to tell herself that the heads couldn't possibly be real.

Finally, still holding the ax, she turned and raced toward the forest.

## CHAPTER NINE

Scrambling down a steep hill in the dark, struggling to keep hold of the ax while remaining upright, Charlotte felt as if at any moment she was going to slip in the wet leaves and tumble down the rest of the way. Somehow she made it to the bottom of the hill, and then she turned and looked back up, terrified that at any moment she was going to see Ted Armitage coming after her.

She waited, but all she saw were the trees.

Although she wasn't sure how much time had passed since she'd left the barn, she felt that she'd been running for at least half an hour. Breathless and terrified, she took a couple of steps back before bumping against a tree, and then she stopped to listen to the forest. All she heard was the sound of trees rustling in a late-night breeze, but somehow the dying woman's scream still seemed to be echoing in her mind.

For a moment, back at the farm, she'd seemed to have been in the middle of something truly horrific. Escaping from the bed had been difficult, yet at the same time she couldn't help but wonder how it had been possible at all; if Ted had tied several woman to that thing before, why had only *she* been able to get free? Had she been lucky, or had she somehow been meant to escape? That last idea seemed unlikely, but her head was starting to fill with paranoid thoughts as she looked around and waited in case there was some sign that Ted was close.

Had she escaped?

Was it really that simple?

A few seconds later, she turned and stumbled away through the dark forest, keeping her arms out to make sure that she didn't slam into any trees. She wasn't sure which way she was going, so all she could do was try to keep going in a straight line and hope that eventually she could find her way back to civilization.

*** 

An owl hooted in the distance, as Charlotte stopped a short while later and leaned against a tree. As she struggled to get her breath back, she looked all around, but the forest seemed like an endless nightmare that offered no obvious way out. She'd been deliberately heading downhill for a while, hoping to reach a river, but she wasn't even sure that this strategy was likely to work

Looking up, she saw the vast starry sky above, and she realized that there was obviously no source of light pollution anywhere nearby. That, in turn, meant that she must be far from a town, but she told herself that she had to keep going so she pressed on, picking her way as quickly as possible down the slope while keeping her hands out to make sure that she -

Suddenly she pressed against some kind of fence. Unable to stop herself in time, she dropped the ax and fell forward, and she felt sharp pains in her hands and against her face. For a moment, hanging in the darkness, she had no idea what was happening, but a moment later she felt a small, sharp metal spike against her right hand and she realized that she'd stepped straight into some barbed wire. She instinctively tried to pull back, only to find that there were in fact several lengths of wire running through the air, and each had snagged against her.

Every time she tried to get free, she felt more barbs cutting into her face and hands, and some were even breaking through her jeans. She stopped for a moment and tried to figure out a plan, and then she began to pull back, only to feel more wire against the nape of her neck. Not understanding how some of the wire could now be *behind* her, she turned and tried to climb back up the hill, only to feel yet more wire catching against her shirt. The more she struggled, the more she seemed to be stuck, like a fly in a spiderweb.

"Come on," she muttered, determined to get free, even though she knew she should stay still and try to come up with a proper plan.

Reaching out, she tried to find the ax, but she quickly realized that it was lost in the darkness. She tried to lift her arms away from the wire, but then she let out a pained gasp as she felt something slicing through her left arm. Taking a moment to regroup, she attempted to solve the problem logically, and after a few more seconds she turned and tried to lift her left leg back so that – one limb at a time – she might be able to unhook herself from the barbs.

As that plan seemed to be working so far, she steadied herself and tried to extract her right leg. For a few brief seconds she began to think that her plan was going to succeed, only for her left foot to slip suddenly in the mud. Letting out a pained gasp, she tumbled forward until the wire caught her, and she felt barbs digging into her belly and arms and face. She froze, too scared to move in case she caused more damage, and as she hung in the darkness she realized she could feel one particular barb digging into her right cheek.

Despite the pain, she already knew that she had to try again to get free. Unable to see anything at all, she took a deep breath and stared straight ahead as she tried to muster the courage to move, and then she began to lean forward.

She immediately flinched as she felt something scratch against her right eye.

Pulling back, panicked, she blinked furiously. The damaged eye felt extremely uncomfortable, but she was fairly sure that she hadn't actually punctured her eyeball. Still, she was terrified to move in case she caught herself again, although she knew that she couldn't simply hang in the wire until morning. Figuring that the wire most likely marked the boundary of Ted's property, she realized that he must have noticed by now that she was missing. She imagined him hurrying through the forest, desperately trying to track her down, and she knew that sooner rather than later he'd start checking the perimeter fence.

"You have to do this," she whispered to herself, trying to find the strength to simply push through the wire. "It'll hurt, but..."

She told herself that by now she was so tangled, getting through to the other side likely wouldn't be much more difficult than backing out. Besides, even if she did make it back, she'd still need to find some way through.

"You *can* do this," she told herself, trying to cling to that belief even as she began to imagine the pain that she was about to endure.

Her best bet, she decided, was to try to free herself as much as possible, and then to throw herself through in the hope that the pain would at least be brief. Sure, she knew that some of the barbs would catch deep, but she'd be fine so long as she avoided any cuts to her eyes, and she tried to focus on the fact that the barbs – while sharp – were still fairly small. The biggest danger would be to remain trapped, to end up dangling in the darkness until Ted eventually caught up.

"You're going to do this," she whispered, as she tried to summon every last ounce of strength that she possessed. "Cuts are just superficial. You're going to get away from this maniac."

With that, she began to carefully lift the wire so that she could reach through. To her surprise, she found that moving slowly was actually much better than attempting to rush, even though she felt the urge to throw herself forward into the darkness. She felt a few occasional snags trying to hold her back, but she resolutely pushed through those until – miraculously – she reached down and felt her hands press against the cold, hard dirt on the other side of the fence. Part of her, at least, was through, even if she could still feel the wires against her chest and legs.

"Just do it," she said, once again trying to give herself a little extra courage. "You're so close now. All you need is one final push."

She tried to work out exactly how many barbs were still digging into her, and where they were located, but deep down she knew she was only delaying the inevitable. She was going to have to push through, and she was going to have to keep going even when she felt some of the barbs slicing through her flesh. The pain was going to be intense, but at least it would be brief and it would end, and then she'd be free to keep running.

"One," she whispered as she tried to prepare herself once more, "two..."

She waited.

*Please don't hurt too much.*

"Three."

Throwing herself forward, she immediately felt barbs cutting into her belly and waist, but this time she was determined to keep going. Even as her clothes tore, and as she felt blood bursting from wounds all over her lower body, she scrambled through into the darkness, screaming as she clawed at the ground and tried to drag herself free.

## CHAPTER TEN

Morning sunlight streamed through the treetops as Charlotte limped down a muddy hill that seemed to have no end. Almost numb now to the pain all over her body, she didn't much mind letting her thoughts drift away. Better that, she figured, than being fully aware of her plight.

And then, as she passed a small clearing, she realized she could hear a very faint buzzing sound somewhere in the distance.

She turned and looked back up the hill. Already tense with fear, she told herself that Ted couldn't have caught up to her already, that he couldn't even know which way she'd walked away from his house, but the buzzing sound was moving closer and now it was starting to seem more like a low, consistent hum that was coming from somewhere fairly high up. For a moment Charlotte began to hope that a helicopter was on the way to rescue her, but then she took a step back as she realized that the sound seemed to be something different, something smaller.

Suddenly, spotting movement at the hop of the hill, she scrambled down to the ground and crawled behind a tree, and then she listened as the humming sound moved even closer.

She carefully shifted a little further around the tree, and then – forcing herself to be brave – she leaned back the other way and tried to see what was coming.

A yellow drone was whirring as it made its way down the hill, and Charlotte flinched as she realized that she'd seen the exact same drone before, in the back of Ted Armitage's truck.

Pulling out of the way, she listened to the drone and tried to figure out which way it was going. Once she was sure that it was passing the tree and heading further down the hill, she craned her neck to take another look. Sure enough, the drone seemed not to have noticed her, although after a few more seconds it stopped and simply hovered in the air as if waiting to see which way it should go next.

*He's hunting me.*

Charlotte immediately understood what the drone meant. Preferring to cover a greater distance than he could manage alone on foot, Ted was using the drone to try to spot her somewhere on his land. As the drone continued to hover, she tried to work out whether bad luck had led it so close to her, or whether she'd left some kind of sign to indicate the direction she'd taken. Thinking back to the barbed wire in the night, she realized that most likely some pieces of fabric – not to mention blood, and maybe even flesh – had been left on the fence.

The drone turned toward her, and Charlotte pulled back behind the tree. Hearing the humming moving closer, she began to worry that she'd been spotted, but then she saw the drone slowly moving past and she was fairly sure that it had only one, forward-facing camera.

As the drone stopped nearby, Charlotte spotted a long, broken branch on the ground, and she realized that she could use that to bring the damn yellow bastard crashing out of the sky. At the same time, she'd be giving away her location in the process, so after a few more seconds she scrambled behind the tree again and waited, hoping that this time the drone would head off in another direction.

"Please," she mouthed silently, uncertain as to whether the drone could detect sound, "go away."

For a moment, she imagined Ted watching the drone's footage on a phone or some other device, searching for any sign of her location. She felt a shudder pass through her chest at the thought of his face, and she imagined him dragging her into his barn and chaining her up like the girl she'd seen before. Had he already taken that girl's head, she wondered, and added it to his sick collection?

The humming sound continued for a couple more minutes, as if Ted was unsure about his next move, but finally the drone began to head off down the hill again.

Leaning out from behind the tree, Charlotte watched as the drone disappeared into the distance. She glanced around to make sure that Ted was nowhere in the vicinity, and then she got to her feet and began to make her way in a different direction, walking along the side of the hill in the hope that she could get as far away from the drone as possible.

\*\*\*

Several hours later, exhausted and barely able to put one foot in front of the other, she stopped as she realized that she'd finally found what she'd been searching for. Ahead, at the bottom of yet another steep slope, she could see a wide, rapid river coursing through the forest.

Picking up the pace, she began to clamber down the hill, desperate to reach the river so that she could try to follow it out of the forest. Not that she was certain that course of action would succeed, of course; she simply hoped that following a river would turn out to be the best approach, although she knew that she might still have many miles to go.

Once she reached the riverbank, she stopped and dropped to her knees. After glancing around to make sure that there was still no sign of either Ted or the drone, she reached down and cupped some water in her hand. As she drank, she realized that she had no way of telling whether the water was clean, but that didn't stop her and she drank for several more minutes before sitting back and realizing that she couldn't afford to rest.

Not yet.

Hauling herself up, she began to follow the river, heading in the same direction as the fast-running water. Her feet were sore and she felt as if she might collapse at any moment, but she thought of her mother and she told herself that she had no option but to keep going.

*That bastard Ted isn't going to win.*

Already, the first elements of a plan were starting to form. Once she found a town, she was going to get someone to call the police, and then she was going to lead them straight to Ted's farm. She had no idea how a guy like Ted could possibly have killed so many women without getting caught, but she figured that wasn't her mystery to solve; instead, she was going to make sure that he was taken away, and that he spent the rest of his life rotting in jail. She thought of all his victims, and of all the families who'd probably given up hope that they might ever find out what had happened to their loved ones, and she told herself that justice would eventually be served. She didn't care who Ted Armitage really was, or why he was a killer; she just wanted him locked up.

She stumbled a couple of times and almost tripped, but for the most part she was able to keep a consistent pace as she followed the river's meandering course. All she saw on either side was the forest, with trees covering the land all the way up to the tops of distant hills. Having lost track of exactly where Ted had taken her, Charlotte really couldn't even begin to guess what part of the country she was in now. She'd been somewhere near Oxford when she'd met Ted, but she knew that now she could be pretty much anywhere. Still, she told herself that she'd find a town eventually, and that she'd be able to get some help soon enough.

Looking down at her hands, she saw that they were badly torn. She could still move her fingers and clench her fists, but her palms and wrists in particular had suffered significant damage from the barbed wire. She'd refrained from checking her injuries in too much detail, figuring that there was no point, but she couldn't help wondering just how much skin and flesh she'd left behind on those metal barbs. Her clothes were torn, she knew that much, but at least the weather wasn't too bad. She told herself that she could keep walking for as long as it took to reach the first town.

Plus, while she knew almost nothing about drones, she figured that they must have a limited range, and that with each step she was hopefully getting further and further away from Ted.

Suddenly she stopped, as she realized she could hear a rushing sound ahead. Her first thought was to take cover and wait to see whether a boat was approaching, but instead she listened as the sound continued. Finally, cautiously, she began to walk again, and after just a couple more minutes she rounded a curve in the river and saw the cause of the rushing sound in the distance.

Unless she wanted to go back the way she'd just come, her only way forward was straight down a waterfall.

## CHAPTER ELEVEN

Stopping at the edge of the wet rocks, she looked over the edge and saw that the bottom of the waterfall was about three hundred feet down, maybe a little more. The sound of the crashing water was intense, and she could feel spray against her face, but she was already trying to work out whether she'd be able to climb down.

Although the rocks were wet and no doubt slippery, she was just about able to spot what seemed to be a route. If she followed a zig-zagging path, she'd be able to avoid the steeper parts, and she told herself that even if she only got partway she could drop the rest of the distance and hope for the best. Besides, even an ignominious death at the foot of a waterfall sounded better than getting dragged back to Ted's barn, and she certainly didn't have the stomach for heading back the way she'd just come and trying to find another path.

"You can do this," she whispered, not for the first time, in an attempt to gee herself up. She could feel a nagging sense of doubt at the back of her mind, but she quickly told herself that if she'd managed to get out of the barbed wire, she could do just about anything.

Realizing that there was no time like the present, she began to pick her way down the steep collection of rocks that led to the first ridge. The rocks were even more slippery than she'd expected, so she had to move carefully, and after a moment she turned around and got down onto her hands and knees. With each move, she wondered whether she was out of her mind, but finally she was able to get to the ridge, at which point she looked down and saw another set of rocks that looked – to her untrained eye, at least – fairly simple to navigate.

After adjusting her position again, she edged down past the largest rock, and then she passed the point of no return as she climbed down to a second, smaller ridge that brought her a little closer to the waterfall itself. Water was constantly spraying against her now, soaking her clothes, and she knew that she couldn't climb back up even if she tried. The only way was down, but when she looked over the edge she momentarily felt a little giddy. Forcing herself to stay focused, she spent a moment working out the next part of her route, and then she began once more to descend.

Almost immediately, her right foot slipped. She clung desperately to the rocks and managed to steady herself again, but her heart was racing and she was starting to worry that the rocks were too wet to be used for support. At the same time, she knew that she had no choice, and that she at least had to get far enough down that jumping the rest of the way wouldn't be suicidal.

She took a deep breath before trying again, and this time she managed to not slip. She edged her way further and further down, and although she didn't immediately come upon another ridge, she managed to move slowly but steadily. The route was taking her a little further away from the waterfall itself now, and after a couple more minutes she finally found a spot where she could take another break.

For a moment, she could only listen to the sound of the crashing water far below, and to her own desperate attempts to get her breath back.

Suddenly she heard a humming sound, and a moment later the yellow drone rushed down in front of her and stopped with its main camera pointed directly at her face.

"Go to hell!" she screamed, clinging to the rocks.

The drone simply stayed in place, with its four little engines whirring loudly.

"Go away!" Charlotte yelled, before grabbing a small rock from nearby and throwing it at the drone, hitting it on the front but failing to knock it out of the sky. "Go on, get out of here!"

Reaching out, she tried to grab the damn thing. Although it was close, it quickly pulled back out of her reach, and she had to take hold of the rocks again in order to keep from falling.

"What do you want?" she shouted, once more imagining Ted watching her through the camera. "Why can't you just leave me alone?"

Wobbling a little in the continued spray from the waterfall, the drone merely continued to keep its camera trained on her face.

Grabbing another rock, Charlotte tried again to knock the drone down, then again. These second two rocks missed completely, but she was more and more certain that one well-aimed missile would knock out one of the engines and perhaps caused the entire machine to plummet down to the rocks below.

She took hold of another rock, but this time she hesitated as she tried to time her attack perfectly. Staring into the drone's main camera, she took a deep breath and imagined Ted grinning from ear to ear at the prospect of having found her again. She had no idea of the drone's range, so she couldn't be sure whether or not Ted was nearby, but she felt certain that he was already on his way to recapture her and drag him back to his barn.

She adjusted her grip on the rock.

The drone continued to hover just a short distance from her face.

"You think this is funny?" she sneered. "You're sick, do you realize that? There's something wrong with you, I saw what you were doing to that girl in the barn, and I'm going to make sure you pay for all your crimes."

She waited, in case the drone was equipped with some sort of speaker.

"You're going down," she continued through gritted teeth. "You realize that, don't you? You're not going to keep your crimes hidden anymore, not after I tell everyone about you."

The drone continued to hum and whir in front of her.

"And as for your stupid little toy," she added, "well, I'll tell you exactly what I think about that."

She hesitated, and then she threw the rock straight at the drone's camera. At the last second, the drone swung back and the rock missed, falling helplessly and hitting the ground far below.

"I hate you!" Charlotte screamed, before reaching out once again and trying to grab the drone, which easily flew out of her reach before settling in a new position just a little further away. "You think you've got me?" she continued. "You think I'm powerless, and that you can just hunt me down? Do you really think I'd ever let you get your hands on me again?"

She turned to start climbing again, and she took a moment to adjust her grip before resuming her slow descent. Although she was trying to take things slowly, anger was surging through her body and pushing her to rush. Her feet almost slipped a couple of times, and then – just as she was starting to let her frustration boil over – she heard the humming sound starting to fade away.

Looking up, she saw that the drone was rising up the waterfall, and after a moment it disappeared entirely over the top.

*It'll be back.*

After taking a deep breath, she set off yet again, following a torturous route that took her closer to the waterfall several times. Surprised that she was making such good progress, she nevertheless made sure to take care. She knew that one wrong move could send her crashing down, and that depending on where she fell she could either hit the rocks far below or the water. The rocks would be fatal, and she had no idea how deep the water would be and whether she'd survive, so she focused on clinging to the rock-face as tightly as possible as she made slow but steady progress down toward the bottom.

Finally, she reached another ridge about twenty feet above the raging water, and she realized that she was stuck. No matter which way she looked, there was simply no way to go any further, and she realized after a moment that she was going to have to jump. She looked down at the water and imagined large, dark rocks beneath the surface, but she told herself that she might be much luckier.

Adjusting her position, she prepared to jump, although she took a moment to imagine what might happen if she slammed straight into hidden rocks and died instantly.

"I love you, Mum," she said, as tears filled her eyes. "Always remember that, okay? And when they find my body..."

Her voice trailed off.

*Enough with this morbid shit.*

Without giving herself a chance to change her mind, Charlotte threw herself off the rock. Screaming, she plunged through the immense spray, and then her scream was abruptly cut off as she hit the water and vanished into the darkness below.

## CHAPTER TWELVE

Gasping for air, Charlotte hauled herself out of the water and rolled onto her back. Drenched and terrified, she felt her heart pounding in her chest as she looked up at the waterfall and saw the steep rocky path that she'd taken, and then she sat up.

*I made it.*

"I made it," she stammered, and then she took a moment to check that she had no broken bones. She'd felt nothing under the water after crashing into the depths, and she'd managed to swim to the shore quickly enough, but she still checked carefully before finally stumbling to her feet and looking around.

The river snaked away, once more running through a thick forest, although at least here the ground was a little flatter. Charlotte looked up, to make sure that there was no sign of the drone, and then she set off along the riverbank. She was limping slightly, due to a nasty blister on her right foot, and her clothes were soaked, but she told herself that she had to be getting close to civilization.

A town, or at least a road or a hut, could well be waiting for her around the river's next bend.

\*\*\*

Several hours later, as the afternoon sky began to darken, Charlotte stopped and leaned against yet another tree. Her legs were aching and she felt as if she was about to drop to the ground, but she told herself that she had to keep going. Still, the thought of enduring a second night in the forest made her feel sick to her stomach.

"Where are you?" she whispered, still convinced that soon she had to stumble upon at least a scrap of civilization. "Please..."

Looking up at the sky, she realized that she couldn't even see any sign of planes passing overhead. Wherever she'd ended up, it was as if she was completely separated from the rest of the human race, and she felt a flicker of doubt in her chest as she began to wonder whether she was ever going to get home. At first she'd assumed that her options were either to die at Ted Armitage's hands or to get to safety, but now she was starting to realize that there was a third possibility: what if she simply dropped dead in the forest, never to be found, and her bones ended up getting picked clean by wild animals?

"No," she said, before starting to walk again, albeit swaying slightly. "You're going to make it. You're going to -"

Stopping suddenly, she realized she could hear a familiar whirring sound. She spun around, and to her horror she immediately spotted the yellow drone heading straight for her, following the course of the river.

"You've got to be kidding me," she stammered, momentarily too shocked and exhausted to know how to react.

Turning, she forced herself to start clambering up the hill that led into the forest. She had to drop to her hands and knees, but she quickly reached the treeline. When she turned and looked over her shoulder, she saw that the drone had already changed direction and was coming after her, and she realized that there could be no doubt that she'd once again been spotted.

Looking around for something she could use to attack the drone, she quickly spotted a long branch. Scrambling across the ground, she grabbed the branch and got to her feet, just as the relentless drone buzzed closer.

Crying out, Charlotte swung the branch as hard as she could manage, and to her amazement she managed to hit the drone on the side, sending it crashing into a nearby tree.

She pulled the branch back and swung again, but this time the drone was already flying away, albeit with what appeared to be some slight damage to its casing. Rushing after the machine, Charlotte tried to hit it again, swinging the branch wildly but missing this time.

"You want a piece of me?" she screamed, swinging the branch again, this time just managing to clip the side of the drone, causing it to veer wildly to the right. "Come on, you coward, why don't you show yourself?"

She swung the branch again and again. The drone banked sharply to the right again, as if trying to get away, so Charlotte stumbled after it and tried once more to smash it against one of the trees. For a moment, thinking of Ted Armitage watching smugly through a phone, she wanted nothing more than to bring the drone down and then smash it to pieces with her bare hands.

"You're scared, is that it?" she continued, waving the branch toward the drone. "Why don't you come on down here and let me teach you a lesson, huh?"

The drone rose a little higher into the sky and continued on its way, beating a slow but effective retreat as Charlotte – trembling with rage – finally dropped to her knees and threw the branch aside.

"That's right," she said breathlessly, watching as the drone disappeared into the distance, "come near me again and I'll finish you off. I'll turn you into a pile of scrap!"

She listened as the drone's hum faded away, and then she slumped back against a nearby tree and slid down to the ground. For a moment, she felt as if she might never get up again, but deep down she knew that she couldn't let Ted win. She took a few seconds to gather some dregs of energy, and then she winced as she pulled herself up. Grabbing the branch, she used it as a crutch this time as she turned and began to make her way once more through the forest, still following the course of the river but choosing this time to stay a little way back, so that she might be less easily seen.

\*\*\*

"Damn it!" she muttered, stumbling and almost falling for what must have been the second or third time in a minute.

Stopping for a moment, she leaned on the branch and tried to regather her composure. Afternoon was becoming evening now, and she'd given up hope of finding help by sundown. Still soaked from her time in the water, she was starting to wonder just how she was going to get through the night without freezing, and she could already tell that the temperature was plummeting. At the back of her mind, she was starting to worry that she might freeze after all.

She listened for a moment to the sound of the wind whistling through the forest, and then she set off again, forcing herself to climb up a shallow hill. All she knew was that -

Suddenly her right leg gave way and she fell, landing hard on her knee. She let out a gasp of pain, and she leaned heavily on the branch for a moment as she tried to get her strength back. She felt as if she was becoming weaker with every step, and her original plan to simply walk through the night now seemed hopelessly unrealistic. Starving and barely able to think straight, she stared straight ahead for a moment before starting once again to get to her feet.

*If I drop dead, I drop dead, but I'm going to keep walking until I can't take another step.*

Feeling a burning pain in her right ankle, she took a moment to prepare to walk again. A moment later, glancing to her right, she realized to her shock that she could see a faint warm glow coming from somewhere over the next ridge. She hesitated, listening in case there was any hint that the drone was returning, but the forest remained fairly quiet so finally she began to make her way to the ridge. She dropped down low as she got closer, choosing to crawl the last few meters, and eventually she peered over the top of the ridge and to her astonishment she saw the source of the glow.

Down at the bottom of the next hill, a house lay nestled in a large clearing. A few lights were on inside the house, but otherwise there was no sign of life.

Scrambling around the side of the ridge, she scurried down to the edge of a narrow dirt track that led toward the house. She was still worried that Ted Armitage and his drone might reappear at any moment, but as she looked at the house she realized that there were no cars parked anywhere nearby. A large shed stood a little way from the house, so she figured any vehicles might be parked in there.

Looking at the house again, she watched the bright windows and waited for some hint of life. And then, shivering and exhausted, she got to her feet and began to make her way along the dirt road, finally entering the yard and stumbling toward the house.

"Please," she whispered, barely managing to keep walking, "somebody, help me..."

## CHAPTER THIRTEEN

Slamming into the front door, she let out a gasp of pain as she reached up and knocked hard with her left fist. She waited, hoping against hope to hear somebody rushing to the door's other side, but instead the only answer was silence.

"Come on," she said, slurring her words slightly as she stumbled to the nearest window and looked into the house. "Where are you?"

She saw a large, sparsely-decorated room, but one that appeared to be pretty comfortable. A fire was burning in the hearth, although it appeared to have not been tended for several hours, and the far wall was covered in book-lined shelves. Charlotte waited for a few seconds, in case somebody stepped into view, and then she limped back to the front door and knocked again.

"Hello?" she called out. "Is anybody here?"

Still receiving no reply, she made her way to another window. This time she was able to see into the kitchen, and again the house seemed to be in a decent state. There was still no sign of anyone, but the place obviously wasn't abandoned so she headed back to the front door and grabbed the handle. Expecting to find it locked, she was surprised when the door clicked open, and she found herself staring into a gloomy hallway.

She waited, but there was still no sign of life.

"Hello?" she said, still hoping against hope that somebody would help her. "Please, if you can hear me, I need you to call the police."

Silence.

She stepped forward, until her toes were almost over the threshold, but she held back from actually entering without an invitation.

"A man's after me," she explained. "I know this is going to sound crazy, but I really, genuinely need help right now. I don't know where he is, but he can't be far away, and he's got this drone that keeps coming after me and I don't know how much longer I've got before..."

Her voice trailed off.

After glancing over her shoulder to make sure that there was no sign of anyone, she looked back into the hallway. The last thing she wanted to do was enter somebody else's house before she'd even spoken to them, but at the same time she couldn't shake the fear that Ted Armitage – or his drone – might show up again at any moment.

Finally, almost shaking with fear, she stepped into the house. Although she knew she was trespassing, she figured that in the circumstances she was within her rights to try to find a phone as quickly as possible. She made her way to the foot of the stairs and looked through a doorway, and she saw the fire still burning in the hearth.

"Hello?" she shouted again, raising her voice a little more this time. "I don't know if anyone's here, but my name is Charlotte Walker and I really need some help. A man's after me and..."

Her voice trailed off as she realized that she might have made a terrible mistake by leading Ted Armitage to the house. She took a deep breath, and then she limped through to the kitchen, desperately trying to find a phone. Spotting nothing, she went into the living room, but there was still no phone to be seen anywhere. As she felt her frustration starting to boil over, she tried to figure out what to do next, and she quickly told herself that the homeowner would surely be back soon.

She just had to wait.

She walked back into the kitchen and made her way straight to the fridge. Unable to stop herself, she pulled the door open and looked inside as the hunger began to burn in her gut. The fridge was surprisingly empty, but some scraps of meat had been left on a plate so she took a few pieces and shoveled them into her mouth.

Finally, telling herself that she shouldn't take any more before the owner of the house returned, she shut the fridge and made her way back out into the hallway, and then she looked up the stairs.

She listened.

Silence.

"Hello?" she shouted. "Is anyone here?"

She waited.

"Please," she continued, feeling a fresh rush of fear as she realized that she might not be safe yet. Tears were welling in her eyes, and after a moment she lowered herself onto the bottom step and leaned against the wall. "I'm sorry I ate some of your food," she sobbed, "I was just so hungry, I couldn't stop myself. I've been walking for over a day now and I just want to get out of here. My mother's waiting for me, and there's this madman chasing me through the forest, and he's already killed a lot of women. Someone has to stop him."

Starting to feel a little delirious, she closed her eyes as the silence of the house seemed to envelop her. She knew that she couldn't afford to nod off, but at the same time she was struggling to stay conscious, and finally she forced herself to stand again.

"I won't sleep," she murmured. "I *can't* sleep. I still have to get out of here."

Stumbling up the stairs, she tried once more to find a phone. She knew that one had to be hidden away somewhere, but as she checked each of the bedrooms she began to feel more and more frustrated. After all, she figured, what kind of person wouldn't have at least one phone in their house?

"Damn you!" she snapped finally, stopping and leaning against a wall on the landing, and taking a deep breath. "What's wrong with -"

And then she saw it.

On the wall opposite, just above a small table, a mirror showed her reflection. Before she had a chance to look away, she was by shocked her pale, bloodied face and her torn clothes, and she finally realized just how badly she'd been hurt by the barbed wire. Taking a few steps forward, barely able to believe what she was seeing but utterly incapable of not staring, she approached the mirror with a growing sense of dread in her chest.

Reaching up, she touched the side of her face, but then she flinched. Several thick cuts had been left in her cheek and forehead, and she'd picked up two black eyes from somewhere. She knew she'd been through a lot, but until that moment she hadn't quite appreciated just how much of a beating she'd endured, not just from her initial encounter with Ted Armitage but also from her attempt to get to safety through the forest.

She leaned closer to the mirror, hoping to prove to herself that the damage wasn't really too bad, but if anything she was starting to see that it was worse. Somehow she'd managed to put her injuries out of her mind while she was pushing on through the forest, but now she could see the damage in all its glory.

Finally, shocked, she pulled away and looked down the stairs, and at that moment she felt extremely nauseous. For a moment she worried that she was actually going to throw up, but she managed to calm herself enough to start making her way back down to the ground floor. She felt a little woozy, as if she might faint at any moment, and as she reached the front room she dropped to her knees and found that she could no longer contain her sense of panic.

"Help me!" she screamed, putting her hands on the side of her head. "Where are you? I need someone to help me! There's a maniac out there in the forest and he's trying to kill me and I just need you to call the police! Why can't you call them?"

Rolling onto her side, she was unable to keep from sobbing wildly. At that moment she knew that if Ted Armitage suddenly appeared, she'd no longer have the necessary strength to even begin fighting him off. She tried to sit up, only to find that even that required too much effort. All she knew for certain was that she needed the house's owner to return so that he or she could help her get to the police. Without that, she was still just a sitting duck.

Finally she managed to sit up and lean against the wall, and a thousand terrifying possibilities were already rushing through her thoughts.

What if the owner of the house was dead?

What if the owner was gone for a while?

What if the house had been abandoned?

She tried to deflect those possibilities with logic, telling herself – for example – that the house couldn't be abandoned if the fire was still burning downstairs. Still, nothing quite made sense and she was starting to worry that Ted had perhaps killed the owner. While at first he'd seemed like some bumbling middle-aged guy, Ted now seemed far more dangerous, and Charlotte couldn't help but wonder just how far he was willing to go in order to track her down. She knew that she certainly couldn't expect him to give up. He was out there somewhere, hunting her, and sooner or later he was bound to find the house.

"Please help me," she whimpered, struggling to stay conscious. "Please, I'm begging you, someone..."

Her voice trailed off, and after a moment her eyes slipped shut as she passed out.

## CHAPTER FOURTEEN

Jolting awake a couple of hours later, Charlotte instantly knew that she'd heard something. She stumbled to her feet and looked around, waiting to see whether the house's owner might have come back, but the place was already silent again.

What had she heard?

She tried to remember, but she'd been drifting in and out of sleep and all she knew was that she'd suddenly been roused from sleep by...

By what?

"Hello?" she said cautiously, even as the hope began to drain from her heart. "Is anybody -"

Before she could finish, she heard a bump coming from somewhere far off, perhaps from outside. She instantly bristled, and then she told herself that she had to at least go and investigate. She'd seen nothing she could use for a weapon, but finally she began to make her way through to the hall, even as some of the boards creaked beneath her feet. With each step, she was fully prepared to turn and run back upstairs, and to perhaps barricade herself in one of the bedrooms, and as she reached the doorway she was starting to wonder exactly what could have caused the noise.

Suddenly she heard it again, and she instantly turned to look at the front door. Someone seemed to have knocked, although she couldn't understand why the owner of the house would knock on his own door.

Stepping closer, she peered through the hole in the door and looked outside, but there was no sign of anyone. She began to wonder whether someone – a friend, perhaps, or a neighbor or even a delivery guy – had dropped something off. She looked around, although she couldn't really see much of the yard outside the house, so finally she grabbed the handle and pulled the door open.

To her surprise, she saw absolutely nothing.

She waited, just in case someone appeared, and then she began to shut the door.

In a flash, the yellow drone dropped into view, its engines suddenly whirring loudly. Horrified, Charlotte stumbled back and bumped against a table by the foot of the stairs, but already the drone had begun to fly into the house.

"No way," she said through gritted teeth. "This is impossible."

The drone stopped above the doormat, flying at around head height. Its engines, whirring furiously, seemed so much louder in the confines of the house.

"How did you find me?" Charlotte screamed, and now she was starting to feel as if she was never going to get away. "What's wrong with you? How did you know that I'd be here?"

Stepping back, she watched as the drone continued to hover just inside the doorway. She looked around, hoping to spot something she could use, and she quickly grabbed a vase.

"Okay," she said, turning back to the drone as it began to move forward, with its camera resolutely trained on her face, "you've messed with me for the last time. You're about to -"

Suddenly a gunshot rang out and one side of the drone exploded. Crying out, Charlotte fell back as pieces of shattered plastic and metal rained down on her, and the rest of the crippled drone slammed to the floor as its engines surged and then died.

The vase also fell, breaking against the floor.

Horrified, Charlotte stared at the ruined machine and tried to understand what had happened. The drone's engines were still whirring furiously, sending the casing skittering across the floor and bumping into the walls. A moment later, she heard the sound of somebody stepping toward the house.

"Come out with your hands up!" a man's voice yelled. "I won't tell you again! This is my property and I don't like coming home to find people playing games on my property!"

"It's not a game," Charlotte stammered, too scared to move. "Please, I -"

"Don't make me tell you again," the man said firmly. "Hands up and get out of there right now!"

Charlotte hesitated for a few seconds, before realizing that she really had no other choice. She got to her feet and cautiously edged toward the door. She picked her way past the shuddering drone before stopping on the mat as soon as she saw a figure standing out in the yard with a rifle aimed at her head.

"I said put your hands up!" he yelled.

Instantly doing as she was told, Charlotte opened her mouth to start explaining what had happened, but somehow she was unable to get any words out.

"Are you alone?" the man barked.

"Yes," she replied, her voice trembling with fear.

"Are you sure about that?"

"Yes!"

"What was that thing doing here?"

She paused, before realizing that he meant the drone.

"It's not mine."

"Then who does it belong to?"

"His name's Ted Armitage," she replied, "at least... I think that's his name. He was chasing me through the forest."

"Why was a man by the name of Ted Armitage chasing you through the forest?"

"He -"

"No, forget that," the man said, interrupting her. "More importantly, what the hell are you doing bringing your little game to my doorstep?"

"I told you, it's not a game," she replied, with her hands still raised. "Please, I can explain everything. He was using the drone to track me, and it was just by pure chance that I found your house. If you have a phone I can use, I need to call the police and get them to come out here because Ted Armitage..."

Her voice trailed off. She wasn't sure how to explain further without sounding like a complete lunatic.

"I think he's a serial killer," she continued finally, "or something like that. He's killed some other women."

"What women?"

"I don't know!" she snapped, before reminding herself to stay calm. "I really don't know," she continued, "but that's something for the police to look into. I just want to get out of here, and I'm sorry I was in your home but the door was unlocked and I was desperate. I mean, I *am* desperate. Please, you have to help me."

"I don't *have* to do anything."

"Please believe me, he's out there and even though his drone's been destroyed he knows where I am now, and he's going to come after me."

She waited, but the man kept his rifle aimed at her.

"I just need to use your phone," she added, with fresh tears in her eyes, "and I need you to drive me to the nearest police station."

Again, she waited.

"Please?"

Slowly, the man lowered his gun, and Charlotte saw that he was about her age, perhaps a year or two older. Ruggedly handsome and with an intense stare, he seemed to be not entirely convinced by her claim, although she figured that at least he was no longer aiming a loaded weapon at her face.

"Do you *have* a phone?" she asked.

"I do not," he replied.

"Okay," she said, swallowing hard, "then you have to... I mean, please, would you mind driving me to the nearest police station? Or if there isn't one, at least to the nearest town, so that I can call for help."

"Your story doesn't quite add up," the man pointed out.

"Believe me," she said, as she began to lower her hands, "I know how it sounds, but this guy is out there and he's going to come for me, and we're not safe until we've managed to get the police down here. Please, I'm begging you, you're my only hope."

The man hesitated, before stepping over to her and then looking through at the remains of the drone on the floor. Its engines were still running, but the drone was unable to take off.

"You broke my vase," the man pointed out.

"What?" She looked past the drone and saw the pieces of the vase near the foot of the stairs. "Oh, yeah, I... I'm sorry."

The man stepped past her and crouched next to the drone. Picking it up, he fiddled with the side and then flicked a switch, causing it to finally fall still.

"This hunk of junk really isn't yours?" he asked.

"It belongs to him. It's what he was using to track me."

"And he tracked you here?"

"I escaped. I was trying to find a town."

"There's no town round here for miles."

"Then -"

"There's not even another house for a good twenty," he added, carrying the remains of the drone to the door and tossing its carcass outside, and then taking his rifle through to the kitchen. "You're soaking wet. You'd never have survived a night out there."

"I'm just -"

"All I want is to be left alone. Is that too much to ask?"

"No," she stammered, not daring to move from the hallway. "I want to be left alone too. By him, I mean. But the thing is, I don't think he's going to stop. He's going to keep coming after me, because he knows that I know what he does out there at his place, and he won't want anyone to find out."

"Is that right?"

"Do you really not have a phone? Not even a mobile?"

She waited.

"What do you prefer?" the man asked. "Tea or coffee?"

"I just want to get -"

"What do you prefer?" he asked again, more forcefully this time. "Tea or coffee? And shut that door and get in here. You're letting all the heat out of the house."

## CHAPTER FIFTEEN

Gingerly stepping into the kitchen doorway, Charlotte watched as the man poured some water into a kettle. She could tell that he knew he was being watched, but for a moment she genuinely had no idea what she should say to him.

"I'm not lying," she managed finally.

"I never said that you were."

"He's insane," she continued. "I saw him kill a woman."

He turned to her with a furrowed brow.

"He had heads, too," she explained, and her voice was once again trembling. "He had them on a spike."

"Heads on a spike?"

"It was like something from a film," she told him. "It was awful."

She paused, fully aware that the story sounded insane, but at the same time she had to tell him the truth.

"It was like he's collecting them," she continued, "and they were just there, all piled up in a column. Some of them were old, but some of them were really new and I think he was planning to add that other girl. I know this must seem like something from out of a crazy movie, but I saw it with my own eyes."

The kettle was starting to boil on the hob.

"And this guy is now tracking you down, is that right?" the man asked.

She nodded.

"Why *you*?"

"I don't know," she told him. "It's a long story and I don't even understand it all. I just know that he has to be stopped, and that I need to call the police and bring them here."

"That's not going to happen."

"I'm sorry?"

"The police are not coming to this house," he muttered, as he grabbed two tea bags and set them in a couple of mugs. "Not now, not tomorrow, not ever, do you understand? I have a habit of keeping myself to myself, and I have no intention of going against that habit." He paused. "No police. Not ever."

"But -"

"No exceptions," he added, glancing at her again.

"This is an emergency!"

"No emergencies."

The kettle was already starting to boil.

"I don't think I've explained this very well," she continued, desperately trying to work out how to make him understand. "This man is a maniac. He's killed multiple people and now he's coming after me. I literally watched him gut a woman in his barn, and then I saw a kind of spike in his yard with a load of heads on it, and I think he's been doing this for a long time and nobody's managed to stop him. He's completely out of his mind, and it's only by some kind of miracle that I managed to escape, and I don't have my phone and even if I did I don't know if I'd get any signal and this guy's still out there and he's coming for me and I need you to help me. Even if he doesn't recapture me, he's obviously a psychopath! He's going to kill again!"

The man stared at her for a moment.

"That's really none of my business," he said finally, before turning back to the kettle.

She waited, convinced that she must have misheard.

"None of your business?" she asked cautiously. "I'm sorry, I don't think I..."

Her voice trailed off.

"There's a killer out there," she continued finally, unable to hide the sense of exasperation in her voice. "He's already killed a whole lot of people, and now he's after me, and I'm asking for your help! You can't turn someone away when they're being hunted down!"

"Can't I?"

"Not unless you're a monster!"

Again, she waited for him to get the message, but he simply busied himself with preparing the tea.

"I keep myself to myself out here," he said finally, "and I really don't have any time or interest in getting involved with the affairs of other people. I prefer to just let the world sail on by while I get on with my own thing."

"Even murderers?"

"I've told you how I see things," he replied, glancing at her briefly before returning his attention to the cups as the kettle began to whistle. "I'm sorry I can't help you, but I really can't be doing with any of this. I have my way of doing things and I stick to that way."

Staring at him, she realized he was serious.

"You're welcome to stick around for a while," he added, a little uneasily. "It's getting late, I guess you can even stay for the night if you want."

"Do you really not have a phone?"

"I really do not have a phone."

"What about an internet connection?"

"Get real."

She looked around the room, and she realized after a moment that she'd spotted no modern devices at all, not even a television. Although she found it difficult to believe that someone could live that way, she told herself that not everyone wanted or needed to be plugged into the modern world all the time.

Sighing, she tried to think of an alternative.

"Will you at least drive me to the nearest town?" she asked. "You don't even have to come in anywhere with me, if you just drive me there and drop me off I can..."

Her voice trailed off as she realized that he seemed far more interesting in making tea than in actually helping her. She watched as he took the kettle and began to pour water into the two cups, and she tried to work out how she was going to get through to him. He seemed intelligent, yet at the same time he either couldn't or wouldn't understand that her life was in danger.

"Milk and sugar?" he asked, turning to her. "I think I even have some biscuits somewhere."

\*\*\*

"You can't just pretend that none of this is happening," Charlotte said a few minutes later, as they sat at the kitchen table. Outside, darkness had begun to fall. "You can't just sit there and act like I didn't tell you any of that stuff."

"Do you know how long it's been since I had another person in this house?" he asked.

"I don't even -"

"Six years," he added, interrupting her. "No-one visits me. I just get on with things. I work, I farm the land, I fix my equipment when it breaks, and I tend to things around the house. In the evenings, I read. I don't really drink, at least not much, and when I do it's only in moderation. I walk a lot. Occasionally I have to make a run somewhere to get a few supplies that I can't source from the forest or my own land, but other than that I don't have any contact with the outside world."

"You just live here all alone?"

He nodded, and then he looked down at his tea.

"I don't want any complications," he explained. "I don't want any visitors. I just want to be left alone to get on with things."

"And I just want to get home," she told him. "I also want this madman to pay for what he's done. None of that has to involve you, not if you don't want it to. If you can just see your way to driving me to some place where I can get help, I'll be out of your hair forever."

Convinced that she must have finally made him understand, she waited, but once again he still seemed utterly impervious to her reasoning.

"My name's Charlotte," she added finally. "Charlotte Walker."

He stared at her.

"What's *your* name?" she asked.

"John," he replied, as if even this simple admission was a huge challenge.

"John," she continued, "I'm begging you to help me, John."

She waited, and this time she decided that the best option would be to simply let him think for a moment rather than bombarding him with more pleas. She felt certain that he was a reasonable man and that sooner or later he was going to come around to her way of thinking. He clearly wasn't a bad person; rather, he seemed like someone who'd been on his own for a very long time, and who was taking a little time to get used to dealing with the world again. No matter how desperately she wanted to beg him to understand, she was starting to think that she should let him come to the right conclusion in his own time. Hopefully that wouldn't take too long.

Suddenly she realized that lights were approaching the house, and she turned just as a car bumped its way across the gravel and came to a halt near the front door.

"It's him," she said, feeling a thud of dread in her chest as she saw that the car was in fact a very familiar-looking truck. "John, it's him! He's come for me!"

## CHAPTER SIXTEEN

"Don't open the door!" Charlotte hissed, hurrying after John before stopping as she saw that he was already sliding the bolt back across. "No!"

She quickly pulled out of sight into the front room, just as she heard the front door creaking open.

"Hello there!" Ted said, and the sound of his voice instantly made Charlotte's skin crawl. "I'm really sorry to disturb you so late in the evening, but I've got a bit of a problem and I was hoping you might be able to help me out."

"I doubt I can," John replied.

Charlotte looked over at the fireplace and spotted several metal pokers. She couldn't believe that Ted might manage to charm his way into the house, but at the same time she wasn't willing to take the risk.

"The thing is," Ted continued, "I'm out here looking for my daughter. She's something of a troubled kid, I won't go into her entire life story, but let's just say that she's recently absconded from a psychiatric hospital about a hundred miles from here and I'm trying to track her down before the police have to get involved. You can understand that, can't you?"

Gritting her teeth, Charlotte had to force herself to stay quiet.

"I don't know what you're talking about," John said firmly.

"I guess what I'm asking is whether you've seen her," Ted replied. "She's about this tall, with mousy hair and kind of a slim build. She'd probably be on foot by this point, wearing a white and blue plaid shit and jeans. Now, it pains me to say this, but I imagine she might also be in something of a heightened state of anxiety, she might be babbling on about things that she's imagined in her mind."

Charlotte waited, but for a moment neither man said anything.

"So have you seen anyone matching that description?" Ted asked.

"I'm in the middle of something," John told him, "so I'd really rather just get back to it, if that's okay."

"Sure," Ted replied, "absolutely. I understand. There's just one other thing. I know this might sound even stranger, but I was using my new drone to try to track poor Charlotte through the forest, and I actually did spot her. And I'm pretty sure that I tracked her right to this house. In fact, I can see the drone, or what's left of it, right over there just outside your door. Looks like it's in a bad way, like maybe it's been in the wars a little. That's fine, I can always get another drone, but what I can't always get is another daughter. So you see, if you can help me talk to her before I have to get the cops involved, that'd be really appreciated."

"Go to hell," Charlotte mouthed silently.

She waited.

"You'd better come in," John said suddenly.

Horrified, Charlotte raced across the room and grabbed one of the metal pokers, and then she turned just in time to see Ted stepping into the doorway.

"Well, there's my little angel," he said with a big grin, immediately making his way over to her. "Daddy's here now and -"

"Stay away from me!" she screamed, swinging the poker at him, almost catching his face as he stepped back.

"Careful there," he replied, still smiling as he turned to John. "See? I told you she might be a little anxious. To be honest, even though I had no option but to have her committed a while back, she still blames me. It's so hard dealing with this sort of illness in a family."

"That man is a murderer!" Charlotte shouted, waiting for John to see the truth. "Don't you get it? He's lying! I'm not his daughter! He wants to kill me!"

"I just want to take her back to the hospital so she can get some treatment," Ted told John, before turning to Charlotte again and holding his hands up. "I want to take you back there myself," he continued, "rather than having you get dragged in. Do you remember how horrible that was for all of us last time, sweetie? Do you remember the men in white coats who had to sedate you while you were kicking and screaming?"

"That didn't happen!" she snarled. "I know what you are! I saw you kill that woman in your barn! You gutted her!"

"Please don't say things like that."

"I saw those heads on that spike!"

Ted opened his mouth to reply, and then he sighed.

"You're not going to make this easy, are you?" he muttered. "You've broken your mother's heart, Charlotte, do you realize that? And mine, too. We both ask ourselves over and over whether we could have done something more for you, whether we could have -"

"Liar!" she screamed, lunging at him and swinging the poker.

Ted ducked out of the way, just as the poker rushed past his face and slammed against the table.

"I'm so sorry about this," Ted said, turning to John. "She's really not herself right now!"

"Hold him!" Charlotte yelled at John. "Even if you don't believe me, then at least keep him here so I can get away!"

"I don't want anything to do with any of this," John replied. "You both -"

"Why won't you believe me?" she sobbed, with tears in her eyes. "This man is a serial killer!"

"I'm a worried father, is what I am," Ted said with another sigh. "I'm just another in a long line of men who really don't understand what they did wrong. But I'm willing to learn, Charlotte, and to grow as a person. I'm ready to listen, but first you need to come back to the hospital with me."

"You kidnapped me from the side of the road!" she snapped, before reaching up and touching the side of her neck. "He injected me with something," she continued, turning her neck so that John would be able to see. "Is there a red mark there? There has to be!"

"That's from the hospital, sweetheart," Ted said, laughing nervously as he turned to John. "Do you see how she twists everything around? The worst part is, she seems to really believe all this crap she comes out with. It's like everything's all muddled up in her head and she's completely lost touch with reality. Would you mind helping me to restrain her?"

John looked at him, and then he turned to Charlotte.

"How can you not tell that he's lying?" she shouted, still holding the poker. "I'd never even met this man until yesterday!"

"You'll be your old self again soon, Charlotte," Ted said, as he reached into his jacket's inside pocket. "It's just going to take a little time, but time is something we have in abundance. I'm going to take you away from here and give you the help you need. Let's just get going and leave this nice man alone, huh?"

With that, he began to hold up a gun.

"No!" Charlotte shouted, lunging at him and knocking him back, just as the gun fired and blasted a hole in the far wall.

Landing hard on the floor, Charlotte grabbed Ted's right arm and slammed it against the edge of the nearest chair, knocking the gun from his hand. She tried to grab the poker, but Ted quickly elbowed her in the face, knocking her back with such force that she felt she might be about to lose consciousness.

"I'm sorry about that," Ted said breathlessly, getting to his feet and turning to John. "This little misunderstanding can be quite quickly cleared -"

Before he could finish, John swung a punch at him, hitting him square in the jaw and sending him crashing back down to the ground with a thud. Letting out a gasp of pain, Ted spat blood and tried to get back up, only for John to grab him by the collar and then punch him again, this time knocking him out cold. After letting out a faint groan, Ted crumpled down against the floor.

Breathless and horrified, Charlotte stared at Ted for a moment, as John stormed out of the room.

"Thank you," she stammered finally, as she began to get to her feet. Touching the side of her face, she felt a sharp pain. "I told you he wasn't my father. We have to tie him up and get him to the police, and then they can go to his place and uncover all the evidence of what he's been doing."

She turned as John marched back into the room and hurried toward her.

"Please," she continued, "now you have to -"

At the last second, she saw that he was carrying some kind of rag. She opened her mouth to ask what he was doing, but he quickly grabbed her head and pushed the rag against her nose and mouth. Startled, she tried to fight back, but she was already breathing noxious fumes and she felt herself weakening. No matter how hard she struggled, the fumes were filling her lungs, and finally she passed out and slumped down onto the floor, landing next to Ted.

## CHAPTER SEVENTEEN

"Hey," a voice said, breaking the silence and darkness, rousing her from a deep stupor. "Hey, wake up. Hey, can you hear me?"

Opening her eyes, Charlotte realized that her head felt very heavy. She blinked a few times, trying to clear her vision, and then she realized that she could hear somebody shuffling about nearby. She took a moment to gather her strength, and then she turned and looked to her right, and to her horror she saw Ted Armitage staring at her.

"Hey," he continued, "we need to -"

Panicking, Charlotte turned to run, only to find that her hands were tied tight behind her back, and that thick ropes were holding her against a heavy wooden pillar. She looked around and saw that she was in some kind of basement, with the only light coming from a small window at the top of the far wall. Turning the other way, she tried to get free from the ropes, but she could already tell that they were far too tight.

"Can you stop doing that for a moment?" Ted asked with a sigh.

"What do you want from me?" she snarled, looking back over at him. "How did you get me here?"

"We're kind of in the same boat," he replied, turning so that she could see he too was tied to a post. "Congratulations, Charlotte. Your new buddy up there seems like a real nice guy. Real swell. I honestly have no trouble whatsoever understanding what you see in him."

"What are you..."

Her voice trailed off as she tried to make sense of what was happening. The last thing she remembered was John pressing the rag against her face, and she realized after a moment that he must have knocked her out. Morning light was streaming through the small window, so she figured she'd been unconsciousness for several hours. When she looked over at Ted again, she remembered that he too had been knocked out, albeit with a fist rather than some kind of chemical on a cloth.

"The irony of the situation is not lost on me," Ted told her. "Listen, I fully understand that I'm probably not your favorite person right now."

Staring at him, she began to wonder whether he might in fact be a hallucination.

"There's two of us and one of him," he continued, "and we have to make that count for something."

Ignoring him, she started tugging on the ropes.

"That won't work," he told her. "I woke up a couple of hours before you, and believe me I've tried everything. If your ropes are tied even half as well as mine, there's no way you're going to get out of them. I have to admit, this guy really puts me to shame. Then again, you're the first one who ever got away from me, so I guess I'm not *that* bad at what I do. Anyway, I doubt you want to hear all that right now, so instead let's focus on how we're going to get out of here."

Still ignoring him, she began to twist around, convinced that there had to be some way to slip her wrists out of the ropes.

"So are you going to just pretend that I'm not here?" he asked. "I've gotta tell you, that's not a very -"

"Help me!" she screamed, hoping that John would be able to hear her upstairs in the main part of the house. "You've made a mistake! You have to let me out of here!"

She waited, but there was no sign that he was even up there.

"He's not going to listen to you," Ted told her. "I didn't get much of an impression of him, but I don't think he's really the kind you can negotiate with. In fact, he doesn't really seem like much of a talker at all."

"Shut up!" she snapped.

"We have to work together."

"John!" she shouted, pulling against the ropes even though she was succeeding only in hurting her own wrists. "You've made a mistake! You have to untie me!"

"He really doesn't," Ted pointed out.

She turned and glared at him.

"As someone who's been on the other side of this type of arrangement," he continued, "let me assure you that no amount of begging or pleading is going to work. It'll accomplish precisely diddly-squat, and really you're just wasting time and energy. Plus, you're letting him know that you're awake, which might not necessarily be a good thing. Don't show your whole hand at once, young lady. You need to get into his mind and try to work out how he thinks."

"Don't talk to me!" she said angrily. "Don't even look at me!"

"We need each other."

"I don't need you!" she yelled.

"I'm sorry," he said, with a faint smile, "but you do. And I need you, otherwise we're both going to end up dead in some ditch somewhere."

"He's not going to kill us."

"And what makes you think that? Do you think he's just tied us up while he makes dinner, and then he's going to invite us to the dining room?"

"We haven't done anything!" she told him. "I mean, *I* haven't done anything. I mean... he's not a killer. He's not like you."

"Why not? Because he's more handsome? Because he's hotter? I've got news for you, young lady, the early signs coming from this guy aren't particularly good. Now, I'll freely admit that I haven't got him entirely figured out, but I might be seeing him a little more clearly than you are." He paused for a moment, with a faint smile lingering on his lips. "What's the matter? Have you got the hots for him?"

"Go to hell!" she spat.

"I get it, you're angry. People from your generation really need to learn how to control their emotions better. This whole ranting and raving thing isn't a good look and it's entirely counterproductive. Despite the severity of our situation, we both need to keep cool heads. Can you do that, Charlotte?"

Staring at him, she realized that he was serious.

"He's *going* to kill us," he said firmly. "That's the harsh reality of the situation. He's put us down here while he thinks things through, while he tries to come up with a plan. My guess is that maybe he hasn't done anything like this before, but here's the rub, he's not going to change his mind. You can promise him all you like that you won't tell anyone, but he's not a moron. He's not going to believe that for a second."

"Don't talk to me," she said through gritted teeth.

He rolled his eyes.

"We're not in this together!" she yelled.

"The ropes would seem to suggest otherwise. We have to work as a team, if we're going to have any hope of getting out of here."

"You want me to trust you?"

"I don't think you have any choice," he replied. "Listen, I get that it's hard, but I promise you that for as long as we're on this man's property, I won't lay a hand on you. Think of it as a marriage of convenience. We're just two people who wouldn't ordinarily get along, who had a bumpy start and -"

"You tried to kill me!"

"I don't think I did," he pointed out. "Certainly not yet, at least. Although to be fair, I'm splitting hairs, I totally would have ended up killing you eventually. Right now, however, we're two people who happen to be in the same dire straits, so it would be useful if we teamed up. Does that not sound like a good idea?"

"Why the hell would I believe you?"

"Honor among thieves," he suggested.

"I'm not a thief!" she shouted. "And neither are you, you're a murderer!"

"I've done my share of thieving over the years," he replied, before sighing again. "Listen, you're getting bogged down in the semantics, when what really matters is that we get out of this place. I doubt we have much time, he's going to want to get rid of us as soon as he's worked out exactly how to do it."

"Why would he kill *me*?" she asked. "I haven't done anything!"

"And yet here you are," he pointed out. "Do you really want to wait and see whether this guy has a change of heart? That seems like a risky move when you have a much better alternative."

"What's that?" she asked cautiously.

"Well, you see," he continued, "I have one thing that you don't have right now. I have a plan. I know exactly how to get out of here, but it's not something I can do alone. Which is where you come in."

"Why the hell would I help you?" she asked.

"Because you'd be helping yourself at the same time," he said firmly. "Can't you get that through your thick head? We're in this together. Now, are you finally ready to be smart?"

## CHAPTER EIGHTEEN

"It's in my shoe."

"What is?" she asked.

"You've seen me in action," he continued with a sigh. "You know the kind of thing I get up to. Don't you think I've prepared for different eventualities? Well, not this one specifically, but... the point is, I have something in my shoe that we can use to get out of here, but I can't get to it. I thought about slipping my shoe off and trying to kick it round to my hands, but I don't have good joints, I'd most likely miss. But you..."

He paused, watching her carefully.

"I can get the knife out of my shoe and slide it over to you," he explained, "and then you can use it to cut through those ropes."

"What -"

Hesitating, she tried to work out whether there was any way he was trying to double-cross her. On the face of it, his offer seemed surprisingly positive, but she still wasn't sure that she was able to trust him.

"I'll show you," he muttered, and then he used one foot to pry the shoe off the other. Tilting the loose shoe, he managed to give it a shake, and a moment later a small knife fell out onto the basement's concrete floor. "See?" he continued. "Its serrated edge should make short work of the ropes. That's another reason why I don't think this fellow has done anything like this before. Most people would have checked for hidden weapons."

Charlotte stared at the knife, before telling herself that she had nothing to lose. Sure, Ted was untrustworthy, but she really couldn't see how he was hoping to screw her over by giving her a knife.

"Send it over here," she said cautiously.

She waited, but Ted hesitated.

"You see," he replied after a moment, "now *I'm* the one who's in a spot of bother, because I need to know that you won't just free yourself and leave me down here."

"Didn't you just say that we have to trust one another?"

"Sure, but the moment you have that knife, you might think you don't need to work with me." He paused again. "I need you to understand something. You won't be able to get out of here without my help, and you won't be able to reason with that guy, so you *have* to untie me once you're free. No funny business."

She considered his suggestion for a moment, and then – realizing that he had no way of enforcing the agreement – she nodded.

"Deal?" he asked.

"Deal," she said, reluctantly.

Ted hesitated for a moment longer, and then he twisted his foot around and prepared to push the knife across the floor.

"I have to get this just right," he muttered, "or we're back to square one. Are you ready?"

"Just do it!"

"Make sure you don't accidentally -"

"I said do it!"

He sighed, and then – after preparing for a few more seconds – he kicked the knife and sent it sliding across the floor until it came to rest right next to her right foot.

"Perfect shot," Ted said with a grin.

Charlotte immediately kicked off a shoe and began to shuffle the knife around to her hands. At first she struggled a little, but after a few seconds she got the hang of the situation and she managed to take the knife and she started frantically cutting the rope.

"Can you reach it?" Ted asked.

"I've got it."

"How's it working?"

"Fine."

"Is it cutting through the rope?"

"Just let me get on with it."

"Are you -"

"Can you shut up for a second?" she snapped, still furiously cutting through the rope while taking care to not slash her wrists open. "It's working just fine, but it's going to take a minute or two."

"If you cut against the grain -"

"Will you just shut up?" she snapped. "I'm going as fast as I can, but it doesn't help if you're constantly peppering me with questions!"

For the next couple of minutes, she worked carefully. Finally, just as she was starting to wonder why everything was taking so long, the rope snapped and she managed to pull one hand free. She quickly got to work on the other, and after a few more minutes she pulled both hands away from the post and scrambled to her feet.

"Fantastic!" Ted said with a huge grin. "I knew you could do it! From the very first moment I saw you, I could tell that you were a very capable woman. Now hurry, get over here and help me!"

She opened her mouth to reply, but then – staring at him – she thought back to the woman she'd seen dying in the barn, and to the heads on the spike. The mere sight of Ted Armitage was enough to make her stomach churn, and in that moment she realized that there was no way she was willing to be responsible for him getting back out into the world.

"I'm sorry," she told him, "but... I can't."

"What do you mean?"

"I mean, you're a monster."

Sighing, he rolled his eyes.

"You're a murderer," she continued, as tears filled her eyes and she thought back to the dying woman in the barn, "and a killer, and a torturer, and you're sick! If things had gone according to plan, I'd have been hanging in that barn by now, wouldn't I?"

"You need to -"

"Wouldn't I?" she shouted.

"Keep your voice down!" he hissed, before hesitating. "Fine, yes, you would have been. You'd still be alive for the moment, but obviously I had certain... designs on you. I tend to keep my... friends... alive for a while, sometimes for months on end. Listen, I really don't want to go into the details. That's all in the past, and I'm pretty sure that a few minutes ago you agreed that we'd work together. You're not the kind of woman who goes back on her word, are you?"

"I'm not the kind of woman who lets a serial killer go free, either."

"I helped you!"

"It's a little late for that."

"So you're just going to leave me at that bastard's mercy?" he asked. "Seriously? Anyway, do you really think you can just waltz out of here? Call me paranoid if you must, Charlotte, but I'm pretty sure that it won't be that easy. Sure, you made it out of my place, but I think we both know you had a lot of luck there. Are you so deluded that you think you can do something like that again? You could really use someone to watch your back!"

"I'll take my chances."

"No!" he snapped, pulling hard on the ropes. "I won't let you do this to me!"

"I guess now you know how it feels to be tied up and helpless," she replied, before turning and heading to the door. "Don't worry, I promise I'll send plenty of cops here to pick you up once I get to safety. Then you can explain exactly what's been going on at your farm."

Reaching out, she grabbed the handle, only to find that the door was locked. She tried a couple more times, and then she stepped back as she realized that she had no idea how to get out of the basement. Her mind was racing and she felt certain that there must be a way, although she was fairly certain that the window was too small to crawl through; she briefly wondered whether she could ambush John when he inevitably arrived with food or water, but that prospect seemed far too risky.

A moment later, hearing a low, rumbling laugh coming from somewhere over her shoulder, she slowly turned to look back at Ted.

"Don't sweat it," he said with a chuckle, "I was only messing with you. I fully expected you to take the high horse and announce you were going to ditch me." His laugh ended abruptly. "The thing is," he continued, "I was also fairly sure that you'd have no idea how to pick that lock, whereas I happen to be a dab hand at such things."

"Tell me how to do it!"

"Not a chance," he replied. "Fine, you're out of the ropes, but that's not going to be much use if you're still stuck down here when that asshole comes to get us. I'm 99% certain that I can get that door open, but I can't do it from here and I sure as hell won't tell you any secrets." He shuffled around until she could see his bound wrists. "Now, how about you reconsider your decision to not help me? 'Cause the way I see it, you really don't have any other options."

## CHAPTER NINETEEN

"You go first."

"No," Ted replied, as they stood outside the open door and looked up the stairs, "*you* go first."

"I'm not turning my back on you," she whispered.

"Is it going to be like this every step of the way?" he asked with a sigh. "That's going to get real tiring, real fast. I've given you my word that you're safe while we're on this guy's property, so what more do you want? Fine, you're safe after we get out of here, too. I won't try to hurt you. You can run away unhindered."

"Do you expect me to believe that?"

"Whatever. *I'll* go first, then."

Stepping past her, he began to make his way up the stairs, although he stopped once he was about halfway.

"What is it?" Charlotte asked.

"Nothing," he replied, turning to her. "That's just it, I don't hear him at all. Either he's gone off somewhere, hunting maybe, or he's hiding and waiting for us to make a mistake." He hesitated for a moment. "Excuse me for being paranoid, but something about this situation just doesn't quite sit right with me. I'm worried that he's got some kind of trick up his sleeve."

"There's only one way to find out."

Ted hesitated, before turning and heading to the top of the stairs, and then he turned left and disappeared from view.

"Ted?" Charlotte hissed, before realizing that she had to go after him.

Taking her time, she walked carefully up the stairs, and when she reached the top she saw that Ted was going from window to window, looking out at the yard beyond the house.

"What are you doing?" she asked.

"My truck's gone," he said, turning to her.

"I'm sorry?"

"I know where I parked it," he continued, "and it's gone. Why would he go to all the trouble of moving my truck?"

"I have no idea," she replied, "but is that really what matters right now? If he's not here, then we just need to run."

He opened his mouth to say something, but at that moment they both heard a banging sound coming from somewhere outside. They turned and looked toward the living room, and then Ted stepped over and peered out toward the other end of the yard.

"I see him," he said after a moment.

Charlotte hurried over and looked out, and she saw that John was chopping wood in the distance.

"That seems like an odd thing to be doing right now," she pointed out.

"Maybe it helps him think," Ted suggested. "Whatever's going on, it's pretty obvious that he's been a busy bee while we were down there."

"So what do we do?" she asked. "Can't we just find the back door and go out that way?"

"Just let me think for a moment," he muttered, turning and pacing across the room, heading to another window and then looking out. Once again, he could see John over at the edge of the barn. "He's either a complete idiot, or he's very relaxed about the whole situation, or something else is going on."

"He thinks we're tired up in the basement," she replied. "He probably figures that he has all the time in the world."

"You know he's not your friend, right?"

She turned to him.

"You have to remember that," he continued. "He's not on your side, and he's never going to be won over, no matter how much of an impassioned speech you try to give him."

"Who said anything about a speech?"

"Please, I know what women are like. You probably think you can help the poor bastard and change his life, make him see the light." He paused. "I wouldn't even be surprised if you've got a bit of a crush on him."

"You're sick," she replied.

"I'm just being realistic. I get that he has a certain appeal, aside from the whole locking you in the basement thing. I can see it in your eyes, you think he's a nice bit of rough."

"Go to hell!" she snapped.

"Keep your voice down."

"You don't know what you're talking about," she hissed. "I'm not -"

Before she could finish, they both heard the sound of a car approaching. Looking out the window, Charlotte saw a police car rumbling across the gravel, and she immediately turned to rush over to the door, only for Ted to pull her back and clamp a hand over her mouth.

"Not a chance!" he snapped.

She tried to struggle free, but he was holding her too firmly.

"Think about it!" he continued, keeping his voice low as the police car ground to a halt right outside. "If you cause a fuss, you might provoke your dreamboat guy and make him do something rash!"

Still trying to get free, Charlotte momentarily managed to pull away, only for Ted to grab her and push her against the wall as he once more clamped her mouth shut.

"Fine, that was a bullshit excuse," he said firmly. "The truth is, if you go running out there and start squawking at those cops, I'll be dragged off and it'll all be over for me. I'm sorry, Charlotte, but I don't believe for one second that you'd keep your mouth shut about what you know, so don't even try to make me that promise." He paused, before craning his neck to look outside. "We've got this. We're getting out of here. We're just waiting for the cops to move on first."

He watched as the two officers made their way over to talk to John.

"It can't be a coincidence that they're here," Ted continued. "They must have found your car by now, and I'm sure someone will have noticed that you're missing. Most likely, they're going door to door, checking to see whether anyone knows anything about you. They'll just ask him a few questions and move on, and then we'll be on our way." He adjusted his grip, making sure to hold her even tighter. "Just be patient, and everything'll be fine."

Charlotte was still struggling, but no matter how hard she tried, she couldn't get free.

"They're still talking," Ted muttered, sounding increasingly irritated. "Your buddy doesn't look very comfortable, but I guess he's worried that they might ask to take a look around. The last thing he needs is for two officers of the law to stick their noses into his basement. After all, he still thinks we're down there."

Trying to call out, Charlotte knew that she'd be saved if only she could attract the two officers' attention.

"Still talking," Ted went on. "This is taking a while, huh? You'd think they'd have other places to check. Wait, now they're leaving. I suppose he told them that he hasn't seen any sign of you, and they believe him. They should be gone within a minute or two."

Charlotte could hear the police car's engine starting again, and she was starting to come up with a plan. She figured that if she bit the palm of Ted's hand, she might be able to get away.

"Off they go," he said with a faint smile. "Okay, we should -"

Suddenly Charlotte bit him hard. Letting out a gasp of pain, Ted fell back, and Charlotte raced to the window, only to see that the police car was already disappearing into the distance. She briefly considered running outside and shouting for help, but she knew that she was too late, and after a moment she stepped back out of sight so that there was no chance of being seen by John.

"Smart girl," Ted muttered, as he examined the slight cut on his hand. "Vicious, but smart. I can see I'm going to have to keep a close eye on you."

"They would have saved us!" she snapped, turning to him.

"They would have saved *you*," he pointed out.

"It's not my fault you're a serial killer."

"Sticks and stones," he replied with a faint smile. "Listen, sooner or later that bastard's going to be done chopping wood, and we need to be out of here by then. First, we need to find weapons, and I'm sure this loser must have a few guns hidden around the place. We've got to find them."

"And then what?" she asked.

"Simple," he continued. "We each take a gun, and we head away from this place in different directions. That way, no-one can double-cross anyone. I don't care what you do once you're free, and you don't have to care what I do. And trust me, even if you break your word and tell everyone what I've been doing, no-one'll be able to track me down. I'm more than capable of keeping myself out of sight."

"You'll still be out there, though," she replied. "You'll still be killing people."

"That really won't be any of your business," he said, before nudging her arm. "Come on, let's find a couple of guns before he comes back inside. The sooner we do that, the sooner we can be out of here. I don't know about you, but I *really* want to get this day over with."

## CHAPTER TWENTY

"I still can't find anything," Charlotte said a short while later, as she stood on a chair and checked the top of another cabinet. "Have you considered the possibility that you might be wrong? What if he doesn't have any guns tucked away in the house?"

"There are guns here, alright," Ted replied, watching through the window as John continued his work with the firewood. "I can smell them."

"Or maybe -"

"He has guns!" he snapped, before taking a moment to compose himself. "Trust me, I know guys like this, I know how they think. A man who lives in a place like this and tries to block the world out is going to have a whole load of guns knocking around, waiting for the day when the world comes knocking on his door. It's just a matter of working out where he keeps the damn things."

"Then maybe *you* should do the looking," she said with a sigh, "because I'm not finding anything. Are you really sure that guns are the answer?"

"What's he doing out there?" Ted muttered, keeping his gaze fixed on John. "He's been chopping wood for a hell of a long time now. It's almost as if he's forgotten all about us. Either that, or..."

His voice trailed off.

"Or what?" Charlotte asked as she climbed down from the chair.

He turned to her.

"Or he's delaying," he suggested. "He knows exactly what he has to do next, and he's putting that moment off for as long as possible. I told you this guy wasn't a seasoned professional when it comes to holding people as prisoners, and I was right. He's leaving it as long as he can before he..."

Again, his voice trailed off.

"Before he *what*?"

"Do I need to draw you a picture?" he asked. "The guy's blatantly going to kill us. For all we know, he's planning to burn our bodies. At least that might go some way toward explaining all that wood. But he hasn't done it before, or at least he hasn't done it very often, so he's still not comfortable with the whole thing." He watched John for a moment longer. "Goddamn amateur."

"He wouldn't murder us."

"And how do you know?"

"He just wouldn't!"

"Face it," he said with a smile, "you don't know this guy. Sure, he might not be quite like me, but he's no angel either. Your dreamboat has his way of life and he sees us a threat, and there's only one thing to do when you're facing a threat. You neutralize it."

"He's not my dreamboat!"

"Whatever."

"I..."

She wanted to tell him that he was wrong, but deep down she realized that there was a certain logic to his assumptions about John's intention. A moment later, as Ted headed across the room and set about searching for guns, she told herself that all she had to do was put up with him for a little longer, and that then she could go to the police and tell them everything. For her efforts to be worthwhile, however, she needed more information.

After glancing out the window and seeing that John was still chopping wood, she turned back to Ted.

"So is that your real name?" she asked.

"Is what my real name?"

"Ted Armitage."

He glanced at her.

"Why wouldn't it be?"

"And why do you do what you do?" she continued. She looked outside again, and she saw that John was still working. "I mean, no-one kidnaps and murders people unless they've got a good reason."

"Are you sure about that?"

"Did someone hurt you?"

"Save the psychological investigation," he replied, as he checked under one of the sofas. "You don't know anything about me, and you don't *need* to know anything. As far as you're concerned, I'm just someone you had a little run-in with, and soon I'll be out of your hair. I'm not some puzzle, waiting to be solved."

"But what about -"

"I know what you're doing," he added, as he went out to check the hallway. "You want some more information you can pass on to the cops when you eventually go and tell them everything. Relax, don't deny it, I already know that's what you're planning to do. The truth is, I'm not too worried. Sure, it would have been fun to get to know you a little better, but I honestly don't think you pose much of a threat."

She looked out at John to make sure he was still working, and then she turned back to Ted.

"Once we say our goodbyes," he continued, "that'll be the end of it. It'll be as if I just vanish into the forest. I've been doing this for long enough to know how not to get caught. I'd sure appreciate it if you don't tell anyone about me, but to be honest I doubt you'll be able to contain yourself. Honestly, it's no biggie either way."

"So kidnapping me was just completely random?"

"I'm not getting into a deep conversation about this," he replied, before stepping back into the doorway and looking at her, "unless..."

"Unless what?"

"Well..." He took a step toward her. "I do sometimes open up to people, about my background and so on, but only in very special circumstances. I happen to have had quite a lousy few days before I met you." Making his way even closer, he looked down into her eyes. "While you were busy escaping from my place, I was finishing off your predecessor. I'd had her chained up for a while, and I'd told her a fair bit about what makes me tick. Call me crazy, but that's the only way I can really talk about myself honestly."

He paused, before reaching out and putting a hand on the side of her face.

"If you truly want to get to know me," he added, "you can always come back home with me and we'll pick up where we left off."

"Go to hell!" she replied, pulling back and glancing out the window. "I'm not -"

Stopping suddenly, she saw that John was no longer cutting wood. She hurried over and looked out across the yard, but there was no sign of him anywhere, and after a moment she turned back to Ted.

"This way," he said, gesturing for her to follow him through to the dining room. "Hurry, we might not have much time."

For a moment, she remained frozen.

"I won't tell you again!" he snapped, grabbing her arm and forcing her to follow. "Damn it, sometimes I think you *want* to get murdered!"

Once they were in the next room, they headed to the back door, and then they both looked out for a moment as they waited to see whether there was any sign of John. Realizing that the coast seemed to be clear, Ted carefully opened the door and stepped outside, and then he turned to Charlotte again.

"I guess this is it," he told her.

"What do you mean?"

"You run that way," he continued nodding past her, and then he nodded over his shoulder, "and I'll run this way, and I guess we'll never meet again. Good luck out there."

"Wait," she replied, "I -"

Before she could finish, Ted turned and ran, hurrying away from the house and scrambling toward the forest. Charlotte hesitated for a moment, somewhat shocked by the fact that it had all ended so suddenly, and then she turned and ran the other way, rushing past the end of the house and over toward another stretch of the forest. After a few seconds, she ground to a halt and tried to figure out which way to go next; she had several options, and she was worried that if she took the wrong route, she might be easy to track. She told herself that she just needed to -

"Freeze!" John yelled, and suddenly a patch of ground exploded right in front of her.

Startled, Charlotte turned and stepped back, quickly stumbling and falling to the ground. She was horrified to see that John was already stepping toward her with his rifle raised.

"What the hell are you doing out of the basement?" he snapped angrily. "Where's the other one?"

"I -"

"What are you doing out here?" he yelled, stopping right in front of her and aiming the rifle directly at her face. "How did you get free?"

"Please," she stammered, holding her hands up as she began to get to her feet, "I just -"

"Stay on the ground!" he shouted.

Dropping back down, she stared at the barrel of the gun. For a moment, too terrified to know what to do next, she could only wait for him to pull the trigger.

"I knew you were going to be trouble," he continued, moving the gun forward until it was almost butting against her forehead. "I'm sorry, but this has to end. Now."

## CHAPTER TWENTY-ONE

"Hey, asshole!" a voice shouted suddenly. "Over here!"

As John turned and looked over his shoulder, Charlotte was shocked to see that Ted was standing at the other end of the house, waving his arms frantically.

"I'm gonna get those cops back here," Ted yelled, "and then we can all have a nice long chat as we explain ourselves! How does that idea grab you?"

Raising the gun, John fired again. Ted ducked out of the way just in time, as the bullet blew a chunk off the corner of the house. Already starting to reload, John muttered something under his breath as he hurried after Ted, leaving Charlotte trembling with fear on the ground.

Once again, she had no idea what to do, and she could only watch as John disappeared round to the other side of the house. Finally realizing that she needed to get to safety, she stumbled to her feet and took a step back, and then she turned and began to hurry through into the forest. Just as she reached the treeline, however, she heard Ted cry out, and she turned to look back over at the house.

Seeing no sign of anyone, she hesitated for a moment before turning again. In that second, another shot rang out, hitting the tree next to her and sending her crashing to the ground. As splinters rained down on her, she began to get up, only to hear footsteps racing closer, and she turned just in time to see that John had found her. She cried out, but he grabbed her and swung her round before shoving her back out into the clearing.

"That really hurt!" Ted yelled in the distance, as John glared down at Charlotte. "Man, you really know how to piss a guy off, don't you?"

\*\*\*

"Why did you come back for me?" Charlotte asked an hour later, as she and Ted walked through the forest at gunpoint, with John just a few paces behind.

"I'm asking myself the same thing," Ted muttered. His cheek was bleeding following the impact with the rifle's butt. "I suppose I just thought that since we were still on that bastard's property, our agreement still stood. I suppose that deep down, I still have some sense of honor. Is that so hard to believe?"

She opened her mouth to ask if that was the real reason, but then she hesitated. In her mind's eye, she couldn't help but think back to the sight of the gun aimed at her face, and she wondered whether – without Ted's intervention – she'd already be dead. She tried to tell herself that John would never have done something like that, but she worried that she was being naive.

"Where are you taking us?" she asked, looking back at John.

"Just keep walking."

"But where -"

"Keep walking!" he barked.

Looking forward again, she tried to work out exactly what was happening. John had simply told them both to start walking, without explaining why, and now they were quite some way from the house.

"You know what he's doing, don't you?" Ted asked after a moment. "Please, Charlotte, tell me you're not *that* dumb."

"I -"

"Your dreamboat lover-boy is going to kill us," he continued. "My bet is that he'd already dug a pair of graves. Or, more likely, he's just dug one and we're going to have to share. How do you feel about that, huh? You and me, down there in the darkness forever, or at least until someone -"

"You talk too much," John said darkly.

"It's a sign of nerves," Ted replied, before glancing over at Charlotte again. "You know you're an idiot, right? You could be far away by now, and so could I. All you had to do was run and keep running."

"I told you, you didn't have to come back for me!"

"I know that now!"

"Will you both please stop talking?" John asked.

"You're about to execute us," Ted said, "and you won't even let us talk in our final moments? Come on, man, you don't want to be a complete meanie, do you?" He kept his gaze on Charlotte for a moment. "We've still got a lot to talk about, don't we?" he continued. "I feel like you and I have been through a lot, even if we've only known one another for a couple of days. And let's be honest, you face some degree of culpability for the fact that I'm in this position right now."

"*I'm* to blame?" she replied, shocked by the accusation. "You're the one who kidnapped me!"

"Fair point," he said, rolling his eyes. "Then again, you're the one who got this bundle of joy involved. He still owes me for a new drone, by the way. If we get out of this, I want a like-for-like replacement and -"

He stopped as he saw that they were approaching some kind of clearing.

"Well," he continued, "looks like we're arriving at our destination. And I think I see something rather familiar parked just ahead."

A few seconds later, they stepped out onto a cliff-edge overlooking a huge lake, and they stopped next to Ted's truck.

"I wondered where this baby was," Ted muttered, his voice filled with concern as he turned to John. "Seems odd for you to have gone to all the trouble of driving this thing here and then bringing us to join it. Why didn't you just bring us in the damn thing in the first place?" He paused, before looking at the truck again. "You seem to be taking everything slow. I get the distinct impression that you really don't want to do whatever it is that you're about to do."

"You've left me with no choice," John said darkly.

"We won't tell anyone," Charlotte told him. "Please, listen, if -"

"Ignore her," Ted said, cutting her off, "she's still trying all those pathetic attempts to reason with you. Next she'll probably start fluttering her eyelashes and undoing the top button of her shirt." He stared at John for a moment. "The truth is, my friend, you and I are cut from the same cloth. I recognize a fellow outsider, and I'm sure you've worked out by now that I'm not this woman's father. It seems to me that a series of overlapping situations might have collided with one another, and the result is something of a mess. I can only hope that cool heads are going to prevail."

"Get in the car," John said. "Both of you."

"I can't help noticing that there's liquid on the ground," Ted continued. "Is that brake fluid?"

"Get in the car."

"Are you letting us go?" Charlotte asked cautiously.

"He's not letting us go," Ted said, still watching John. "He just wants to get us out of his hair, and he figures the best way to do that is to toss us over the edge of a cliff. Literally. Make it look like an accident."

"You can't be serious," Charlotte said, shaking her head. "John, I know that you don't like being disturbed, and I know we've come crashing into your world, but we can figure out some way to make sure that everything's okay."

"Get in the car," John said yet again, with the rifle aimed at Ted. "Don't make me tell you again."

"You have us at quite a disadvantage," Ted pointed out, slowly holding his hands up. "The thing is, in every situation, there's always a way to -"

"Get in the car!" John snapped, stepping toward him and pushing him toward the truck. "Why are you so -"

Suddenly Ted lunged at him, grabbing the rifle and pulling it from his hands. John immediately swung Ted against the side of the car and tried to take the rifle back, but for a moment both men struggled before John finally managed to punch Ted several times, sending him crumpling to the ground. Without wasting another second, he grabbed Ted by the collar and bundled him into the front of the truck, before shifting him around so that he was in the driver's seat.

"Hey, man," Ted groaned, slurring his words as blood ran from his mouth, "I'm only -"

Punching him in the side of the face, John knocked him out cold before reaching past him and starting the truck's engine. After setting the vehicle into gear, he scrambled back just as the truck began to roll forward toward the edge of the cliff.

"No!" Charlotte shouted, rushing forward, only for John to shove her back and send her stumbling to the ground. "You can't do this!"

Without answering, John watched as the truck reached the edge and tipped over. A moment later the truck disappeared from view, although it could be heard crashing down the side of the cliff until it slammed into the water far below.

"We have to get him out of there!" Charlotte stammered, hurrying to the cliff's edge and looking down, only to see that the truck was already sinking. For a moment she spotted Ted's unconscious body in one of the front seats, before the entire vehicle disappeared beneath the water's surface.

Realizing that there was no way to get down in time to help, she slowly turned to John and saw that he was once again aiming the gun at her.

"There's been a change of plan," he explained, clearly a little flustered. "Come on, we're heading back to the house."

## CHAPTER TWENTY-TWO

As she made her way toward the front door, Charlotte saw that the remains of Ted Armitage's yellow drone lay on the ground nearby, partially covered by a section of tarpaulin. For a moment, she couldn't help but think of the sight of his body disappearing into the lake.

"Stop," John said.

Obeying, she stopped dead in her tracks, before slowly turning to look back at him. As she watched his features, she searched for some hint of compassion, for some look that suggested he was rethinking his approach, but at the same time one big question filled her mind and she knew that she had to ask.

"I was supposed to be in that truck with him, wasn't I?" she said cautiously.

She waited.

He simply stared at her.

"It's okay," she continued, "I already figured it out. Then Ted made you angry, and you weren't thinking straight, and you didn't think before you killed him. But if he hadn't tried to fight you..."

Her voice trailed off.

"I'd be down there in that truck with him, wouldn't I?" she added. "You were going to put us both in there and roll the truck over the edge, and you hoped that eventually we'd be found and it'd look like an accident."

She waited.

He nodded.

"Thank you for... *not* doing that," she said.

"Go inside," he replied, "but don't try anything. I need to think."

"The guy you killed was a serial killer," she told him, as tears ran down her cheeks. "There's a way to make all of this okay. If you let me go, I swear I won't -"

"I told you to go inside," he said, interrupting her. "I'd have thought the events of the past couple of hours might have made you realize that you shouldn't disobey me. Get into the house and go to the kitchen, and sit down. And please... stop talking." He paused, waiting for her to do as she'd been told. "Please," he added. "I won't tell you again."

\*\*\*

Sitting on a chair in the corner of the kitchen, Charlotte waited as John finished handcuffing her to the radiator. She hadn't said a word since entering the house, and she was once again hoping that leaving him to think would work better than begging him for help. He seemed like the kind of guy who hated being told what to do.

Finally, once the handcuffs were firmly in place, John got to his feet and took a few steps back.

"Thank you," she said, before she could stop herself.

"I'm sorry?"

"For not putting me back down in the basement."

"I learned my lesson," he replied, turning and heading to the fridge. "I figure this time it's better to keep you where I can see you."

She watched as he opened the fridge door and took out a can of beer. Although she desperately wanted a drink, she told herself to keep her mouth shut and she simply watched as he drank. Once he was done, he set the can aside and turned to her again. She could tell that he was lost in thought; she desperately wanted to know what he was thinking, but she figured that she needed to let him take the lead.

"So you were telling the truth," he said. "About him being some kind of killer, I mean."

"I saw the bodies at his farm," she explained. "At least, I saw the heads. They were on a kind of spike, it was like they were trophies. I think he must have been killing people for years."

"And where exactly is this farm of his?"

"I'm not sure. I've kind of lost my bearings."

"There aren't many places within walking distance of here," he admitted. "I had no idea that someone like that was in the area, although I haven't really checked into my neighbors very much. It's not exactly surprising that people might be up to no good round these parts. It's not hard to disappear into the forest, and the local police spend more time extorting people than dealing with problems."

"I saw a police car here earlier," she told him. "Were they looking for me?"

"They found your car," he replied, "and they're trying to figure out where you went. They think you might have broken down and wandered off to find help, and that you got lost. I told them that I had no idea. I'm sorry, but I really didn't want to get involved in whatever's going on. The local police and I have a... *complicated* relationship."

"I can understand that," she said, hoping to get on his good side. "Out here you just want to be left alone, right?"

"My business is nobody else's business, and vice versa." He sniffed. "The police are bored, so they look for trouble. If they can't find any, they try to make some. One of the first things I learned round these parts is that you should never put yourself out there. Never make those bastards start thinking that you'll be a good distraction for an hour or two. Matters can escalate very rapidly. That's why I keep them at arm's length."

"That's how it should be."

"Damn straight," he muttered, taking another beer and drinking from the bottle. "That's the problem with the modern world, everyone's all up in what everyone else is doing. The human mind wasn't built for that kind of life. It's in our nature to keep things to ourselves, but modern life is twisting and subverting all of that. Eventually I got sick of it all and I made my way out here to..."

He paused.

"Never mind," he added. "I shouldn't be drinking. I don't do it very often."

"No, I'm interested," she replied. "What do you do out here all by yourself?"

"I get by. There are plenty of ways to live off the land, if you really know what you're doing. I'm not talking about those people who dig a pit and store five thousand tins of beans in the dirt, waiting for the end of the world. I'm talking about understanding how to cultivate the soil around here. How to hunt. How to fish. How to know what you're doing. How to be completely self-sufficient. Honestly, I'm never bored."

"I can see that."

"I really don't know what I'm going to do about you," he said, with a hint of frustration in his voice. "You've put me in a very difficult situation."

"I know, and I'm really sorry."

"I should have realized that something like this was going to happen," he continued. "I tried to block the world out, and I was doing pretty good for a while, but I should have known that eventually it'd break through. There's just nowhere to escape to, is there? Not permanently."

"If there's anything I can do to reverse the damage," she said cautiously, "I'll do it. The last thing I want is to cause you any more trouble."

"So I should just let you go and trust that no-one ever finds out about what happened here?"

"I didn't say that."

"No, but you're thinking it," he said. "The problem is, life doesn't work like that. Do you really think you could keep your mouth shut about that guy I just killed?"

"Yes."

He shook his head.

"I can!" she blurted out, as she began to hope that she was making progress. "Okay, I admit that it's not exactly my first instinct, but I *can* make myself stay quiet."

"And what about all his victims?"

"There has to be some way to make sure that justice is done."

"See?" He turned to leave the room. "You're already breaking your word."

"No!" she called after him. "I won't think about them! If you let me walk away from here, I won't look back! You can trust me, I swear!"

She watched as he left the room, and she was starting to worry that the chance to escape was slipping away.

"I won't break my word!" she shouted. "I can walk away from here and forget about all of it, I promise! I can just pretend that it never happened!"

She waited, and a moment later she heard him shutting a door somewhere far off in the house. Although she felt certain that she'd begun to get through to him, she knew that the moment had slipped away and that she was going to have to find some other way to persuade him to let her go. Deep down, she felt certain that John was a good man, and that he'd only killed Ted because he felt that he had no other choice. He'd had plenty of opportunities to kill her, and he'd taken none of them, and she had to hope that this was a good sign.

"I just want to go home," she whispered, as fresh tears filled her eyes. "That's all. I want to go home and forget that any of this ever happened."

## CHAPTER TWENTY-THREE

After several hours, sitting by the kitchen window and staring out at the yard as the sun began to set, Charlotte was still trying to come up with some way to persuade John to let her go. She knew that it wouldn't be easy, but she remained certain that there was something she could do – something she could say, or perhaps offer – that would allow her to win her freedom.

She just had to figure out *what*.

Lost in her thoughts, she didn't notice the car at first. When she did, she turned and looked out the window, and she was surprised to see a police car bumping along the dirt road and stopping outside. A moment later, hearing a door creaking open elsewhere in the house, she looked over her shoulder just as John stormed into the room and dropped behind her.

"I -"

"Quiet!" he hissed, placing a hand over her mouth just as they both heard the police car's engine being switched off. "It's the same two losers who were here earlier. I didn't think they'd be back so soon. They must have finished their shift and decided to poke around. Damn these morons and their empty lives. Don't they have anything better to do?"

Taking hold of the chair, he dragged it away from the window so that they wouldn't be seen, and then they both listened to the sound of footsteps making their way toward the front door. A moment later, a loud knock rang out through the house.

"I'm going to have to go and talk to them," John said, before hesitating for a moment. "If you call out, if you make any kind of noise at all, things are going to get very ugly, very fast. Do you understand?"

She nodded.

"I'm still trying to figure out how to let you go," he continued, "but none of that'll happen if you cause trouble. I'm only going to give you one chance to do the right thing."

He paused, and then he moved his hand away from her mouth.

"I won't shout out," she whispered, her voice trembling with fear, "I promise."

She waited for him to reply. For a moment, she simply watched his face, searching for any clue as to what he was thinking. She knew she was probably imagining things, but she was starting to think that she and John understood one another on some level, and that they'd made a connection.

"It's going to be okay," she told him. "I promise."

Although he still seemed uncertain, he got to his feet and made his way through to the hallway. Left alone, Charlotte listened to the sound of him unlocking the front door. Part of her desperately wanted to call out, and she wasn't sure how John planned to punish her if she did; after all, two officers would most likely be able to overpower him fairly easily. At the same time, she'd seen him in action and she knew she couldn't take the risk of upsetting him. Choosing to believe that he was sincere when he said that he wanted to release her, she decided to stay quiet.

"Good evening, John," she heard an unfamiliar voice say, "we just thought we'd swing by and see whether you'd had any thoughts about that matter we discussed earlier."

"I still haven't seen anyone, if that's what you mean," John replied.

"I've got to tell you," the man continued, "we're getting pretty worried. We thought the Walker woman must have simply wandered off to get help, but we've been searching the area near her car and there's absolutely no sign of her. We're starting to think that certain other possibilities are more likely."

Hearing more footsteps, Charlotte realized that the second officer was making his way toward the window. She hesitated for a moment, and then she dropped off the chair and climbed under the table, hoping to keep well out of sight.

Looking up, she could already see a shadow at the window.

*Am I being an idiot?*

For a moment, she wondered whether she should change her mind and call for help. She knew that would set in motion a certain chain of events, and she was worried that John might have a gun he could access quickly. Too terrified to do or say anything, she waited and watched as the shadow moved away.

"We're wondering whether she followed the river," the officer at the door said. "If she was smart but she got lost, that's one of the more obvious options. And if you think about it, if she headed downhill from that area, the river doesn't run too far from your place, does it?"

"I already told you, I haven't seen anyone."

"And you wouldn't have any reason to lie, would you?"

Looking through into the next room, Charlotte realized that there were several other windows that might allow her to be seen. Sure enough, a moment later she spotted movement in the distance, and she instinctively ducked away just as the second officer appeared at the window in the laundry room. Although she was fairly sure that she hadn't been seen, she was still worried that at any moment all hell might break loose. She barely even dared to take a breath.

"I've told you everything I know," John said firmly.

"Are you sure? We can always come in and take a look around."

"Not without a warrant."

"Is there some reason why you're opposed to us coming inside, John?"

"I don't like to be disturbed."

"But you could be helpful. You could help put our minds at rest."

"I'm really not too interested in any of that."

"And how are you doing out here, anyway?" the officer continued. "We often think about you, living all by yourself in the middle of nowhere. You're a man of mystery, John Harrison, and that kind of catches our attention from time to time."

"I can't help that."

"No, I suppose you can't. You go out hunting a lot, don't you?"

"I'm fully entitled to go and -"

"Oh, I know," the officer continued with a somewhat unconvincing chuckle, "I'm not casting aspersions. I just wondered whether you saw any sign of someone having been out there. This woman is a city type, so she's probably not very good at surviving alone in the forest. You know what these idiots are like. They fall apart at the first sign of a little dirt."

"I've seen nothing."

"Her name's Charlotte Walker."

"You told me that before."

"Did I?" He chuckled again. "Forgive me, John, but I get easily confused. You see, I'm just a dumb rural policeman who isn't very observant and who doesn't join the dots together very well. It's very easy to pull the wool over my eyes."

"Is there anything else I can do for you?" John asked. "I'm busy."

"Got a lot on your plate, huh?"

Charlotte waited, but John said nothing. After a moment, hearing a rustling sound, she looked up and realized that the other officer was back at the window, seemingly trying once again to peer into the kitchen. She took a moment to pull her feet a little further out of the way, just in case there was any chance that they'd been visible.

"I guess we'll leave you alone, then," the officer at the door said. "Oh, but hey, there's one other thing I was going to mention. Danny Kendricks down at the petrol station claims he heard someone discharging a firearm in the area. You know how that sound can travel, right? And the thing is, you're the only person round here who has any weapons registered, so I was wondering if you'd been... I don't know, shooting at anything..."

"As you noted earlier," John replied stiffly, "I often go out hunting."

"So you were hunting today?"

"I was."

"And who were you hunting? Sorry, slip of the tongue. I meant, *what* were you hunting?"

"Deer."

"Is that right? Any luck?"

"Not today."

"Well, that's a shame. We'll be off now, but remember to let us know if you spot any sign of that poor woman out there in the wilderness. To be honest, if we don't find her soon, we're probably going to be looking at a fatality. Anyway, you keep on being you, John. Never change."

As footsteps headed away from the house, Charlotte heard the front door bumping shut, followed by the sound of the bolt being drawn across. She instantly began to wonder whether she'd made the wrong choice, whether if she'd just cried out she might be free by now. For a moment, she wondered if she'd been completely crazy to keep her mouth shut. A few seconds later. she watched as John stepped into the room.

"Someone was at the window," she explained as she crawled out from under the table.

"I know," he replied. "I was hoping you'd do the smart thing."

"I told you," she said, "you can trust me. I meant it."

"Those two idiots swing by and bother me on a regular basis," he told her as he stepped over to the window and watched them driving away. "Any time they're bored, they come and poke about. It's like they think I'm some kind of freak, just because I like to keep myself to myself."

"At least they're gone now," she pointed out.

"For now." He looked down at her. "They'll be back tomorrow, though, even if it's just to entertain themselves. They're pretty predictable. They'll be getting drunk soon in some bar, coming up with their next plan to bother me. That means that sooner rather than later I have to get you out of here."

"I just proved to you that you can rely on me," she replied, still staring up at him from the floor. "Doesn't that count for something? Now you know that I won't scream at the first policeman I see, do you understand that you can trust me to keep quiet?"

She waited, but he simply stared at her for a moment.

"Get back on the chair," he said finally. "You'll be more comfortable."

## CHAPTER TWENTY-FOUR

Several hours later, once darkness had fallen, Charlotte – with one wrist still chained to the radiator – sat at the table and dipped her spoon back into her soup. She hesitated, and then she looked across the table and watched John for a moment.

A candle burned between them.

"You know," she said, "the sad thing is, this isn't even the most awkward dinner I've had with a guy."

John glanced at her.

"I went on a date a few nights ago," she continued, "that went so badly, it might as well have been a scene from some dumb comedy. It wasn't the guy's fault, it was mine, I was totally spaced out and I barely listened to a word that he said to me. Even though I knew it was going badly, I was powerless to stop myself. I was worried about my mother. I still am. And that bad date is really what caused me to end up in this mess in the first place."

She waited, but he simply stared at her with a somewhat puzzled expression.

"Not that I'm suggesting *this* is a date," she added suddenly, correcting herself. "Sorry, I get chatty when I'm nervous and I just go on and on. I guess all I meant was that..."

Her voice trailed off.

She'd been trying to get another conversation going, even though John hadn't been very receptive. She desperately wanted to know what he was thinking, and what he was planning, and her attempt to simply leave him alone seemed to have only worked to a certain extent. Deep down, part of her was worried that she was falling victim to some kind of Stockholm Syndrome, that she'd been insane not to call out to the police, but she quickly reminded herself that she was trying to be smarter than that.

Looking down at her soup again, she tried to think of some other way to understand John Harrison.

"You're the first person who's been in this house in a long time," he said suddenly. "Other than myself, obviously."

"How long have you lived here?"

"Ten years."

"Wow. You must have been young when you bought it."

"We thought it was a good project."

"We?"

She waited, but he seemed reluctant to continue, as if perhaps he regretted his little slip.

"It's a long story," he muttered, taking a moment to stir his soup. "She said she wanted the outdoors life, away from everyone, but it turned out that she got very bored. She was a city girl at heart and she didn't last a year. We didn't keep in touch after the divorce."

"I'm sorry."

"It's just what happens sometimes," he continued. "The more I embraced this lifestyle, the more she hated it. Anyway, it's so long ago now, it doesn't even matter."

"It might if -"

"I said it doesn't matter."

"Sorry."

Worried that she'd pushed too far, she took a moment to try to figure out another approach. As she glanced out the window and saw nothing but darkness outside, she felt that John definitely seemed to be opening up a little, even if she still didn't understand him fully. All she knew for certain was that she still needed to nudge him a little more, to prove her trustworthiness, in order to get away without any further trouble. She was so close.

"The soup's really good," she told him. "You're pretty good in the kitchen."

"I get by."

"All my soup comes in tubs and packets," she explained with a faint smile. "I definitely wouldn't say that I'm much of a cook. I mean, I can follow instructions and whip something up, but I'm never going to -"

"I'm done," he said, suddenly getting to his feet and carrying his bowl over to the counter.

"Sorry," she replied, "was I talking too much?"

"No." He headed to the door, and then he stopped with his back to her. "I left the front door open for her."

She waited, not quite understanding.

He turned.

"You must have thought it was odd," he continued, "that the front door was unlocked when you arrived here."

"I wondered," she admitted.

"She used to mock me for locking it every time we went out," he explained. "She used to tell me that I was getting paranoid. I told her that we could never be too careful, but it became a big thing for her." He paused. "Now I leave it open sometimes when I go out, just so that if she ever drops by for an unannounced visit, she'll see that I've changed. Not a lot, but... that I listened, in the end."

"Maybe she will," Charlotte suggested.

"No, it's stupid," he muttered. "I won't be doing it again. I always said that eventually some lunatic might enter the house while we were gone, and it turned out that I was right after all."

"Who's the lunatic?" she asked. "Me or Ted Armitage?"

"Finish your soup," he replied, before turning and heading through to the hallway. "I'll bring some bedding down for you soon."

*\*\**

"What's going to happen to me in the morning?"

As soon as those words had left her lips, Charlotte worried that she'd made a mistake. She'd managed to avoid asking that question all evening, but now – as John set a duvet and two pillows on the kitchen floor – the words had slipped out of her mouth.

She waited, watching him to see how he'd react, but after a moment he simply got back to work arranging the duvet.

"I'm sorry I can't move you upstairs," he said, "but that would just be impractical. You'll be fine down here. It's warm, and I'll make you comfortable."

"Anything's better than the basement, right?"

She hoped that he'd laugh, but instead he didn't even look at her.

"I'm not a bad person," he said finally.

"I know that."

"What I did to that Ted guy -"

"You won't hear me complaining," she said, interrupting him. "You didn't see what he was doing to people on that farm. I watched him literally cut open a woman's guts while she was hanging from chains. I don't know if you even follow the news, but wait until it all gets out and it's in the papers. I'm going to make sure that everyone knows what he did, just as soon as I get out of here."

Again, she worried that she might have said the wrong thing.

"I mean, *if* I get out of here," she added. "Or I won't tell anyone. Sorry, I forgot, it was just instinct. I'll pretend I never met him. I'll tell everyone that I just got lost in the forest. After all, I'm from the city. All trees look the same to me."

"People like that Armitage guy shouldn't exist," John muttered, getting to his feet. "They're the worst of the worst and I'm glad that he's gone, even if..."

He paused.

"I've never killed anyone before," he added.

"If he hadn't acted the way he acted," she replied, "would you really have put us both in that truck and sent us both over the edge?"

"I just wanted to be left alone."

"But would you have gone that far?"

She waited for an answer.

"In the morning, I'll have a plan," he told her. "I don't know what it'll be, but at least it'll be something we can work to. There's no need for anyone else to get hurt, just so long as we're both clear about what we have to do. There's a way out of this, and it doesn't even have to be complicated. It just has to be something we can both agree on."

"Absolutely," she replied, feeling a flicker of hope as she realized that he *was* planning to release her after all. "You just tell me what you want me to do, and I'll do it. No questions asked."

He paused, as if he was about to say something, and then he took a step back.

"Try to get some sleep," he said, before turning to leave.

"Can you do one thing for me?" she asked.

"What?"

She looked at her handcuffed wrist, which was still attached to the radiator.

"I'm not quite sure how I'm going to be able to sleep with this held up," she told him. "It just doesn't quite seem like it'll work." She glanced back at him. "If I promise that I won't try to pull any stunt or try to run, is there any chance at all that you can remove the handcuff?"

He stared at her for a few seconds, and then he headed to the door.

"I'm sorry," he muttered. "I'll be back down early in the morning. We can talk then."

Sighing, Charlotte turned and looked once again at the handcuffs. She gave them a brief, perfunctory tug that she knew wouldn't really help, and then she shifted around and leaned back against the wall. Although John had begun to hint that everything would be okay, she still worried that at any moment she might do or say the wrong thing, and that she might set back all the progress she'd made. Figuring that there was little she could do about that while she was still being held captive, however, she told herself that she simply had to focus on getting through the night.

And then, in the morning, she'd have to prove one more time that she really could be trusted.

## CHAPTER TWENTY-FIVE

Opening her eyes suddenly, Charlotte stared ahead across the dark kitchen and realized that she had – at last – fallen asleep. For a few minutes, anyway. Leaning against the wall, preferring that to any attempt to rest on the duvet – she'd managed to doze off, but after a few seconds she began to realize that she'd been woken by a noise.

She turned and looked toward the open doorway, but the house was quiet now. She assumed that John was upstairs, perhaps asleep, but after a few seconds she looked up at the window.

The noise had seemed to come from outside.

Shifting onto her knees, she peered out and saw the moonlit yard. There was no sign of anyone, but with each passing second she was remembering more and more about the sound that had caused her to stir in the first place. Something had made a kind of rustling, hissing noise somewhere in the dark night air, and she was already certain that this 'something' had to have been alive. She told herself that it was perhaps one of the deer she knew John liked to hunt, or some other passing wildlife, but at the same time she couldn't help wondering whether she'd heard a person.

Ted Armitage.

With a sickening sense of dread, she thought back to the sight of the truck disappearing over the edge of the cliff, and she realized that she hadn't seen a body. Neither had John. The truck's impact with the water had surely been powerful, and the vehicle had quickly sunk, but she began to wonder whether there was some way Ted might have escaped. And if he had, was he the kind of man who'd return for vengeance? She wasn't sure whether that idea fit with what she knew of his personality, but she also didn't know him well enough to count the idea out. As she watched the yard, she began to worry that Ted might have returned.

For a moment, in her mind's eye, she imagined a whole range of possibilities. Had Ted woken up just in time and thrown himself from the truck before it hit the water? Sure, he'd most likely have been injured, but he could easily have survived. Or had he been in the truck when it had crashed into the lake, only to then force his way out? Again, the prospect seemed somewhat unlikely, but she couldn't help picturing him – soaked and bloodied – staggering away from the crash site, keeping out of view for a few minutes and then setting off relentlessly for revenge.

Suddenly, hearing a clicking sound, she spun around and looked toward the front room.

The sound persisted for a few more seconds before stopping abruptly, but Charlotte was more and more certain that somebody was outside the house, and that they seemed to be trying to get inside. She considered calling out for John, but at the last moment she reminded herself that she'd be putting herself in danger if she gave away her position. She waited, listening as the clicking sound returned, and then she flinched as she heard a slow, ominous creaking noise coming from one of the other rooms, like...

Like a door opening.

Again, she almost called out. This time, telling herself that perhaps John was sneaking around and was trying not to disturb her, she wondered whether she should simply let him know that she was awake. She watched the doorway that led into the front room and she waited for some sign that John was nearby, but then she heard a bump coming from a different direction and she turned to look across the hallway and over toward the dining room. Whoever was in the house, they seemed to be making their way cautiously through the rooms.

She opened her mouth once more to shout John's name, but she held back.

A moment later, a flashlight's beam caught the dining room wall, and she realized to her horror that someone had definitely broken in from outside. She pulled back, terrified in case Ted appeared, but then she heard whispered voices and after a few seconds two figures stepped into view.

The flashlight's beam swung around until it was aimed directly at her, and she had to shield her eyes from the brightness as she heard footsteps hurrying into the kitchen.

"Ma'am," a voice said, as a man dropped to his knees next to her, "are you okay?"

Turning to him, she realized that he was one of the police officers from earlier.

"I knew that sick son of a bitch was hiding something," the officer continued. "I felt it right in my gut."

"I told you I saw movement earlier," the other officer said, looking around for any sign of John. "I was peering through that other window and I thought I saw just the very tip of a shoe. I wasn't wrong. I'm never wrong."

"My name is Mack Carter," the first officer told Charlotte, "and this is my colleague Kevin Watkins, and we're going to get you out of here. You *are* Charlotte Walker, aren't you?"

She hesitated, and then she nodded.

"Well, Charlotte Walker," Mack continued, reaching past her and trying to pull the handcuff free from the radiator, "you don't have to worry now, because we -"

Before he could finish, a radio began to buzz with static. Looking up, Charlotte watched as Kevin quickly switched if off.

"I thought I told you not to bring that thing!" Mack hissed at him.

"I'm sorry," Kevin replied, "it was supposed to be off."

"We need to get you free," Mack muttered, turning his attention back to the handcuff for a moment before turning to Charlotte again. "Ms. Walker, do you know where John Harrison is in this house right now?"

"I..."

For a few seconds, she wasn't sure whether she should answer.

"He's upstairs," Kevin said. "He has to be. The bastard's probably sleeping soundly in bed and dreaming about all the sick things he's doing to do to her in the morning."

"Ms. Walker," Mack said, "it looks like we can't free you immediately, but we're going to get you out of here just as soon as we can. In the meantime, my colleague and I need to go and incapacitate Mr. Harrison. Do you understand?"

"There's a man named Ted Armitage you need to know about," she told him. "He -"

"Is he here right now?" Mack asked. "This Ted Armitage guy, I mean."

"No, but -"

"Then we need to deal with one thing at a time," he continued. "We've had our eye on John Harrison for quite some time. We knew he'd slip up eventually, I'm sure keeping you here is just the tip of the iceberg."

"What did he do to you?" Kevin asked. "Did he touch you? Did he force you to -"

"There'll be time for that later," Mack said, turning and glaring at him, before getting to his feet. "Ms. Walker," he continued, "do you happen to know what kind of weaponry Mr. Harrison has up there?"

"I don't," she replied, "but listen, I think -"

"This is one sick individual," Mack said firmly, interrupting her. "They laughed at us back at the station when we said we were going to bring him in, but they won't be laughing when we show up with him tonight. I've got a feeling that we're gonna find a lot of secrets buried in this house once we tear it apart, starting with the mystery of what really happened to his missing wife."

"His wife is missing?" Charlotte asked.

"Didn't she leave him and move to Wales?" Kevin asked, furrowing his brow.

"That's far from confirmed," Mack replied, before taking a deep breath and then looking up at the ceiling. "There's a hell of a lot that's not confirmed about this guy, but that's about to end. One way or another, we're dragging his sorry ass out of here tonight." He turned back to Charlotte. "We'll be back in a few minutes, Ms. Walker. Don't you go anywhere."

With that, he and Kevin began to make their way through to the hallway.

"Wait!" Charlotte hissed. "What are you doing?"

Placing a finger against his mouth, Mack turned and signaled for her to stay quiet.

"You can't just go up there!" she continued. "Do you have a warrant? Are you even on duty right now?"

"What's wrong?" Mack replied, stepping back over to her. "You haven't started to like the freak, have you?"

"He promised to let me go in the morning," she told him. "Please, you don't have to be violent. I don't think he's a bad person."

"We'll be the judge of that."

"What if she warns him?" Kevin asked. "I've heard of that happening. Sometimes they fall in love with their captors and they try to help them."

"That's a fair point," Mack muttered, stepping closer until he was towering over her. "Say, when we were here earlier, you didn't call out to us. Why not?"

"I..."

As her voice trailed off, she realized that she wasn't quite sure how to explain that decision.

"We can't risk her making this complicated," Kevin said. "If she warns him, he could get a jump on us."

"Can we trust you?" Mack asked, kneeling in front of Charlotte. "Are you completely on our side?"

"I just want to go home," she told him. "Please, my mother had a fall and I just want to go to her and make sure that she's okay."

"We're going to get you to her," Mack replied, placing a hand on her shoulder, "but first we need to make sure that we get you out of this hellhole. And my colleague here is right to worry that you might have fallen under this man's spell."

"I haven't fallen under anyone's spell," she protested, as Kevin stepped around to her other side. "Listen, I think you've got the wrong impression of John, he only -"

Suddenly Kevin placed a gag over her mouth and tied it tight. Before she could react, he also slipped a rope around her free wrist and secured her more fully against the radiator. Struggling to get free, Charlotte twisted in several different directions but she was unable to fight back as Kevin secured the gag properly.

"That's better," Mack said, nodding sagely. "This is for your own good, Ma'am. Try not to worry." He gave her shoulder a firm squeeze. "We're here to rescue you."

## CHAPTER TWENTY-SIX

Several minutes later, with Mack and Kevin having left the room to go upstairs, Charlotte desperately tried to get free. She was already starting to pull her wrist out from the rope, and she knew that she'd then be able to remove the gag. After a few more seconds she managed to twist her hand away and she reached up and pulled the gag aside.

Suddenly hearing loud, heavy footsteps stomping down the stairs, she looked over at the open doorway just in time to see that Mack and Kevin had returned.

"He's not there," Mack said, clearly shocked. "Where is he?"

"Are you sure?" she asked, looking at the ceiling. "He has to be."

"We checked every room," Mack continued, looking around the room as if he expected John to leap out from the shadows. "I'm starting to think that the good Mr. Harrison might have already flown the coop."

"What if he guessed we were coming and he ran?" Kevin asked. "That chickenshit coward's probably all talk and no action. When we catch up to him, I've got a mind to teach him a valuable lesson."

"I don't think he's the running type," Mack muttered, as he made his way over to Charlotte, "but I *do* think he's the type to sneak away and find his guns."

"We should call back-up," Kevin suggested.

"I see you got the gag off," Mack said, peering down at Charlotte and furrowing his brow. "And you got out of that rope, too. Did you manage that all by yourself, or did you have a little help?"

"Where is he?" Kevin asked, clearly starting to become agitated as he too stepped over to her. "If you're trying to help him get a jump on us, you should know that you can be charged with aiding a criminal. And trust me, I would personally make sure that you got the book thrown at you."

"I don't know where he is," she replied through gritted teeth, "but I think you're in danger of escalating this into a really bad situation."

"Your friend Mr. Harrison has already done that," Mack replied, before reaching into his jacket and holding up a gun. "Don't worry, though, he's not the only one who's ready to defend himself. You know, I happen to think that our American cousins have the right idea when it comes to law enforcement. Fortunately, I'm more than capable of defending myself."

"You can't be serious," Charlotte said, trying not to panic. "Please, just undo this handcuff, I want to get out of here."

"We need to find the key first," Mack said. "Just stay put, and keep your mouth shut, and -"

Before he could finish, they all heard a loud thud coming from one of the other rooms. Turning, Mack aimed his gun at the doorway, while Kevin backed away into one of the corners.

"John Harrison," Mack called out, "I need you to put down your weapons and come through with your hands up, otherwise I'm going to come in there and I'm armed. I will *not* hesitate to use deadly force."

He waited.

"Do you hear me?" he continued. "You're only getting one warning, Mr. Harrison, and after that I'll feel compelled to do whatever's necessary. I really hope you're not going to turn this already difficult situation into one that could get a thousand times worse."

He turned and gestured for Kevin to go through to the other room, so that they could try to trap John in a kind of pincer movement. Kevin hesitated, before doing exactly as he was ordered.

Charlotte watched with a growing sense of horror, but she had no idea what she could do to keep the situation from spiraling even further out of control.

Suddenly Kevin's radio burst to life again.

"Cut that thing off!" Mack hissed.

"I'm sorry," Kevin stammered, flicking a switch on the side of the radio. "I swear I did it already!"

"Okay, Mr. Harrison," Mack continued, with his gun still raised as he stepped out into the hallway, "we're coming for you. Don't say you weren't warned."

As the two men disappeared through to different sides of the house, Charlotte began once again to pull desperately on the handcuff that was still keeping her attached to the radiator. She quickly realized that she was going to have to try another approach, so she turned and tried to reach the nearby drawers, in the hope that she might find something she could use to pick the lock. She was just about able to grab the top drawer, and she quickly pulled it out and let the contents spill out noisily onto the floor.

Immediately starting to sort through the various utensils and other items, she tried to think back to how Ted had picked the basement lock, although at the time she hadn't paid much attention.

Finding an attachment for some kind of device, she tried to slide the sharp end into the lock on the handcuff, but to no avail; she looked through the utensils for a moment longer, before pulling out another drawer, then another, convinced that soon she had to find something that would work.

Suddenly a shot rang out from elsewhere in the house, followed swiftly by a second, and Charlotte looked toward the doorway and froze. She couldn't be sure, but she felt that the shot had seemed to come not from a rifle but from a smaller gun, perhaps the one that Mack had been wielding.

"Did you get him?" she heard Kevin shouting.

"Mr. Harrison, you need to surrender!" Mack yelled. "This isn't the time for heroics, this is the time for calm heads to prevail!"

Looking back down at the contents of the drawers, Charlotte once again tried to find something she could use to get free. All she wanted was to get away from the house and run, and to never look back. The more she searched, however, the more she began to realize that she had no hope of breaking out of the handcuff, although after a moment she found a screwdriver and she turned to look back at the radiator. For a few seconds, she tried to figure out whether there was any way she might be able to remove the entire radiator from the wall and loosen the pipes, and she quickly realized that this idea – while somewhat unlikely – might be her best chance.

Her *only* chance.

She set about trying to remove some of the screws holding the radiator in place, although after a moment she stopped as she heard another gunshot.

"Get him!" Kevin shouted excitedly.

Two more shots rang out, followed by the sound of running footsteps somewhere in the house. All hell seemed to be breaking out in the other rooms.

"Come on," Charlotte muttered under her breath, working furiously on the screws, before suddenly she was interrupted by the sound of another shot.

Looking over at the doorway, she realized that this shot had seemed to come from a much larger gun, perhaps the kind of rifle that she'd seen John with earlier. A moment later she heard another shot, this time accompanied by an agonized scream.

Hearing more footsteps, she looked over at the other door, just in time to see Kevin stumbling into shot. Clutching his bloodied belly, he slammed into the wall and tried to hold himself up, and then he looked over at Charlotte as blood ran from his mouth.

"He killed Mack!" he gasped, barely able to get the words out. Blood was dribbling from his wound and splattering against the floor. "That psycho killed Mack!"

"Where is he?" Charlotte stammered.

"He's on the floor in the other room!" Kevin sobbed. "His head's been blown off!"

"Not him!" Charlotte snapped angrily. "Where's John?"

Kevin tried to take a step forward, only for his legs to buckle. He just about managed to grab the table, and as he swung around he didn't even notice his radio fall onto the floor.

"Where's John?" Charlotte shouted.

"We need backup," Kevin spluttered as he tried to make it to the hallway. "Help... please..."

"John, where are you?" Charlotte called out.

Kevin crawled out of view, and a moment later the front door could be heard opening. Horrified, Charlotte looked out the window, and she was just about able to see Kevin in the moonlight as he staggered toward the forest. Before he could manage another step, however, a third shot was fired and Kevin's chest exploded as he fell forward and landed in the mud.

Pulling away from the window, Charlotte realized that the house was now quiet again. She waited for some sign that John was on his way, but she heard nothing at all until – a few seconds later – the radio crackled to life on the floor.

Charlotte looked over her shoulder and realized that somehow the radio was still on.

"Officer Burnside," a static-filled voice could just about be heard saying, "come in, do you read me? Kevin, are you and Mack out there somewhere?"

Frozen for a moment, Charlotte tried to work out what she should do next, but then she reached over and grabbed the radio.

"Kevin, Mack, are you there?" the voice continued as Charlotte held the radio up toward her ear. "If you guys are playing with this thing in the pub again, you're gonna be sorry. Didn't you hear what Reggie said about taking equipment out after hours? You guys are in so much trouble."

Charlotte hesitated, before tapping at several buttons on the radio.

Suddenly she sensed movement nearby, and she turned just as John stormed into the room and grabbed the radio from her hands. He quickly threw it to the floor and stamped on it with his right foot, crushing the device, and then he aimed the rifle and fired, blowing the radio to smithereens as Charlotte let out a startled cry and pulled back against the radiator.

"I wasn't going to call anyone, I swear!" she gasped, looking up at him. "Please, you have to believe me..."

"I actually thought I could trust you," he snarled, aiming the rifle at her face. "I should have known right from the start, you were just like all the others."

## CHAPTER TWENTY-SEVEN

Barely daring to move, Charlotte remained kneeling on the kitchen floor as she listened to the horrific sound of heavy machinery out in the yard. At least a couple of hours had passed since John had stormed out of the room, and all she knew was that he was out there doing something that required large machines and lots of bright lights.

Sitting up again, she looked out the window, but she still couldn't quite figure out what was happening. Whatever John was up to, he was round the far side of the house, and the entire building was trembling as the ground continued to shake. For a moment, Charlotte felt as if John was ripping the whole world apart, and she half expected him to suddenly ride straight through the middle of the house and flatten everything. He'd seemed to be in such a rage, she wasn't sure that anything could be written off as too extreme.

Finally, with the machinery still running outside, she heard John making his way back into the house.

"Hey," she said as he hurried into the kitchen and grabbed the remains of the radio from the floor, "you have to believe me, I wasn't going to call for help!"

Ignoring her, not even looking in her direction, he made his way back outside.

"I wasn't!" she called after him. "I swear!"

She listened to his footsteps heading away.

"Did you kill your wife?" she shouted.

The footsteps stopped.

"They told me she's missing," she continued. Her voice was shaking with fear and she knew she shouldn't provoke her captor, but at the same time she had to know the truth. "They seemed to think that you had something to do with it."

She waited.

"So did you?"

Again she waited, and now her mouth felt so dry. Her heart was pounding in her chest, and she was worried that she might have pushed John completely over the edge.

After a few more seconds, his footsteps resumed, heading out of the house.

"Come back!" she yelled. "John, please! I just want to know what's really happening here!"

Peering out the window once more, Charlotte was shocked to see that John had grabbed Kevin's bloodied corpse and was dragging him round to the side of the house, over toward the source of the deafening noise. She'd seen him doing the same to Mack's body earlier, but she still had no idea exactly what he was planning. A moment later she saw him hurrying back out across the yard, and he quickly disappeared along the driveway.

"Come on," she whispered, once again trying to find some way out of the handcuffs, "you need to get away from here."

She tried to think of some way to break free, but after a moment she realized that she was all out of ideas.

Suddenly noticing another bright light outside, she turned to see that a car was approaching the house. Hoping against hope that perhaps someone knew what Mack and Kevin had been up to, and that more officers were arriving to save the day, she was shocked after a few seconds to see that in fact John had fetched a police car, which he was now driving across the yard. She briefly saw his determined face in the light, and then the car disappeared around to the side of the house.

"I'm sorry!" she screamed, hoping that he might somehow be able to hear her as tears streamed down her face. "I wasn't helping them, I swear! I just picked the radio up, that's all!"

She waited, but all she heard – above the relentless sound of the machinery – was a loud crashing sound.

"I wasn't helping them," she whimpered, sinking back down onto her knees as she felt all the hope draining from her heart. "I promise. I just want to get out of here. I just want to see my mum and go home."

A moment later she heard footsteps in the house once more, and she turned to see that John was storming through from the back room. She flinched, and then she watched as he stopped in the doorway.

"What are..."

Her voice trailed off for a moment.

"What are you doing out there?" she asked, her voice trembling with fear.

"Something I should have done right at the start," he said bluntly, staring at her with an intense expression.

"What are you going to do with *me*?" she stammered.

"All I wanted was to be left alone," he replied. "I didn't ask for anyone to come here. Not you, not that other guy, not those idiots from the police station. I didn't ask for anyone to interfere in my life!"

"I was only -"

"I just wanted to be left alone!" he shouted, as his rage momentarily erupted, and then he managed to calm himself just a little. "That's not too much to ask for," he continued. "Everyone should be left alone if that's their choice."

"I totally agree," she told him. "Please, you have to believe me..."

She waited, but for a moment he simply stared at her.

"Those two idiots were here on their own time," he continued finally. "That's good, it means that there won't be as much of a paper trail connecting them to this place. It means people won't necessarily come here to search for them, at least not at first."

"What.... what are you doing to do?" she asked.

Again she waited, as the house continued to tremble. After a moment she looked out the window and saw the bright, blinding lights in the yard, and then she heard footsteps approaching. She turned back to John, just as he reached down and began to unfasten the handcuff. As soon as she was free, she began to rub her wrist, which was worn sore from all her earlier efforts to get away.

Stepping back, John grabbed the rifle from the hallway and aimed it at her.

"Get up," he said firmly. "Go outside. Now."

"Why?"

"Just do it," he replied, and Charlotte noticed that he seemed reluctant to look her in the eye. "Move."

Slowly getting to her feet, Charlotte tried to figure out exactly what John was planning. Her mind was racing as she considered all the possibilities, but she quickly told herself to remember that he wasn't – at heart – a bad man. He was confused, and troubled, and he clearly had certain issues, but she still felt certain that deep down he was a decent and honorable guy who'd never do anything truly awful. Ted Armitage, and the two cops, had provoked him. She was innocent.

"Don't try anything," he continued, stepping aside and gesturing for her to go out the door. "Don't make me do something I don't want to do."

Raising her hands, she made her way to the hallway and then to the open front door. As soon as she stepped outside, the sound of the nearby engine seemed so much louder in the night air; so loud, in fact, that she instinctively stopped until she felt the rifle pressing against her back.

"Keep walking."

Doing as she was told, Charlotte headed around to the side of the house, and then she had to use a hand to shield her eyes from the lights. Struggling to see properly, she was just about able to make out some kind of huge digger nearby; this was the source of the immense sound, and of the huge vibrations that had been shaking the house, and as its engine continued to run she took a few more steps across the mud and saw to her shock that John had used the machine to dig a huge pit.

"Don't stop," John said, keeping pace right behind her.

Stepping forward, she saw that the pit was easily twenty feet wide and twice as long, and maybe ten feet deep. She had no idea how he could even have dug such a thing in just a few hours, but after a moment she saw several other machines parked nearby. Looking over her shoulder, she realized that John must have been storing a huge amount of equipment in the barn. She spotted the remains of the old yellow drone poking out from under a tarpaulin, and then she turned to see that John was still aiming the rifle at her.

Looking back down into the pit, she saw that a battered police car was resting at the bottom, with Mack and Kevin's bodies having been placed inside.

"What are you going to do?" she whispered, before turning to John again. "Are you going to bury them?"

"I'm going to bury all of it," he replied through gritted teeth. "All this stuff came into *my* world. Your things, their things, that psychopath's things. They weren't invited. They didn't ask. They came and tried to hurt me, and I've had enough!"

"You can't just bury them and hope no-one finds out," she told him. "They're police officers! That's a police car! Someone's going to -"

"Someone's going to come and ask if I've seen them, sure," he replied, "but they won't ever realize that they're here. Believe me, I know how to cover any sign that the ground has been disturbed."

"You can't -"

"That's where the past belongs," he added. "Underground. Buried. Forgotten."

"You can't just pretend that none of this happened!" she shouted, trying not to panic as the huge digger continued to rumble next to her. "That's not how it works, John! You can't pretend that the world doesn't exist!"

"That's where you're wrong," he replied, before pausing for a moment. "Get in the pit, Charlotte."

"What?"

"Get in the pit!"

"You can't be serious," she stammered. "John..."

"I never wanted anyone to come here," he said firmly, his voice trembling with rage. "I never wanted a single person to ever disturb me. All of this has to go away, and I'm sorry but..."

His voice trailed off for a moment, and then he stepped closer to Charlotte with the gun still aimed at her face.

"I'm truly sorry," he added, "but you have to get in there with the rest of them."

"I won't ever tell anyone that I was here," she replied, with tears in her eyes. "You have to believe me, John, I wasn't trying to call anyone on that radio. I'll just leave and never mention any of it."

She looked down at the car, and at the two bodies.

"I'll pretend like it never happened," she continued, turning back to him. "I promise."

She waited, and slowly he lowered the gun.

"Just like you believed me when I told you that my wife left me?" he asked.

"It'll all be fine," she added, hoping that he'd finally seen sense. "It'll be like I was never here."

"I know," he replied, "and I'm sorry."

Suddenly he swung the butt of the rifle, slamming it hard against the side of her head and sending her toppling back. She tried to steady herself, but she could only cry out as she tumbled down the sloping, muddy side of the pit and finally landed in a heap at the bottom. Letting out a gasp of pain as she felt a twisting sensation in her ankle, she saw that she was right next to the police car, and for a moment she could only stare in horror at the sight of the two dead officers wedged inside.

A moment later, hearing an even louder rumbling sound, she looked up just in time to see that John was in the digger. Before she had time to react, she saw that he was pushing a huge pile of dirt and soil into the pit. As massive chunks rained down on top of her, all she could do was raise her hands for protection and scream.

## CHAPTER TWENTY-EIGHT

As more huge clumps of soil and stone crashed down against her, Charlotte scrambled through the darkness on all fours and finally took cover by crawling through the police car's broken window and stopping for a moment next to its upturned back seat.

More dirt was falling into the pit, slamming into the car with a series of constant heavy thuds. Trying not to panic, Charlotte looked around and saw the two dead bodies wedged into the car, and then she saw several bags that had been thrown in for good measure. Pulling one of the bags open, she found that John had gathered together anything that might show that there'd been visitors to the house over the previous few days. The contents of her pockets, which he'd removed when he'd first taken her prisoner, were in the bag, along with a few of Ted's items too.

The car shook as more dirt crashed down, and when she looked out Charlotte realized that the pit was filling up fast. She could see a huge cloud of dust filling the air, partially blocking the light from above, but a moment later more soil tumbled into the pit, partially obscuring the night sky. In that moment, she realized that soon there'd be no way out.

Crawling over Mack's body, she reached for the car's radio and tried desperately to call for help.

"Hello?" she said, pressing every button but succeeding only in eliciting a clicking sound from the unit. "Is anyone there? Can anyone hear me? Please, you have to hurry! He's going to kill me!"

She waited, but there was no sign that the radio was working at all.

"Hello," she continued, trying more buttons, even though she was sure she'd pressed all of them at least once already, "I don't know if anyone can hear me, but I'm at..."

Her voice trailed off as she realized that she didn't even know how to describe her location. Even if she managed to get through to someone, she might be able to do little more than let them know her name, and that she was about to die.

"Please," she stammered, "if anyone's out there, my name's Charlotte Walker and a man named John Harrison is..."

Again, she couldn't quite finish the sentence.

"Can anyone hear me?" she asked again, but all she heard in response was static.

Glancing over her shoulder, she saw Kevin's body. The dead man's eyes were staring almost directly at her, almost as if he was accusing her of being responsible for his death. After all, she realized, none of the madness would be happening if she hadn't been kidnapped on the road a few days earlier, if she hadn't attracted the attention of a psychopath. If she hadn't gone on that stupid date with Richard.

"Sorry," she said finally, before reaching past Mack's bloodied corpse and searching for any other radio or phone that she might be able to use. "If you guys have anything here, now would be the time to come back to life for few seconds and let me know."

Dropping the radio, she turned and tried to find anything else in the car that she might be able to use to call for help.

Looking back into the bag, she spotted her wallet. She knew that wouldn't help, but a moment later she saw Ted's phone. Grabbing it with shaking hands, she tried to switch it on, and she was surprised to find that it still had a little battery. As dirt continued to rain down all around the car, she tried to use the phone to call the police, but after just a few seconds the battery died.

"No!" she shouted, realizing that her last hope was lost. "Please, come back!"

She tried again to switch the phone on, but she already knew that she was too late.

She threw the phone aside and slumped back, and for a few seconds she simply waited to die. She looked over at the bodies of Mack and Kevin and she realized that she was about to join them, and she began to consider the possibility that John's plan was going to work, that she and everything else in the pit would simply be buried and lost forever, that no-one would ever find out where she was or what had happened to her. Even her mother would never know the truth.

She'd just be gone.

She'd vanish, leaving nothing behind, not even a body.

"I'm sorry, Mum," she sobbed, as the car shuddered under the weight of more and more soil falling into the pit, "I was coming to help you, I swear. I didn't just flake out on you."

For a moment, she imagined her mother desperately trying to find her; she thought of police appeals, and searches, and sniffer dogs going through the forest. She thought of her internet search history being checked, and her messages, to see whether she might have run off with someone. She thought of her friends and family being interviewed, of her whole life getting torn apart for clues. And she thought of her mother, lost and alone in the middle of all the madness, never finding out what had happened to her daughter.

And then, glancing at the bag again, she spotted something that looked like another mobile phone. She almost didn't bother checking, but after a moment she grabbed the object and found that it was the control unit for Ted's drone. She flicked a switch on the side, bringing it to life, and she was stunned to see a picture appear on the little video screen, showing a grainy view of the digger from behind.

Somehow, partially destroyed and mostly hidden under tarpaulin, the drone was still at least somewhat active. And its camera was working.

She quickly tried to figure out the controls. She knew that at least a couple of the drone's engines were damaged, but she found that she was at least able to make the damn thing move. The tarpaulin was holding it down, but after fiddling for a moment longer she managed to get the drone to start rising back up into the air. She tried to send it forward, only for it to bump back against the side of the house, and then – finally getting the hang of the controls – she sent the drone on a wobbly path toward the side of the digger.

Staring at the screen, she saw John through the drone's camera, and she realized that she had one chance to distract him. After adjusting her grip on the controls, she sent the drone slamming forward until it hit the window on the digger's side, and she saw John turn and stare in shock as she then turned the drone and began to move it around to the other end of the machine.

After a moment, dirt stopped falling into the pit, and Charlotte managed to turn the drone around so that she could see John climbing down from the digger's cab. She'd managed to grab his attention, and she watched as he hurried toward the drone and reached out to grab it; she swung the drone around, out of his reach, and then she drove it straight into his face. He pushed it away, and she sent the drone back over toward the house and then she watched as John – clearly angry – rushed closer.

*Now.*

Dropping the control unit, she scrambled out of the upturned police car. She had to push chunks of dirt aside, but she quickly made it to the pit's far end and she immediately began to scramble up the sloping, muddy side. She almost fell a couple of times, but after a few more attempts she managed to reach the top. Rolling over onto her side, she stayed low as she looked back toward the other side of the pit, and after just a few seconds she saw John step into view.

He looked down at the partially-covered car, and then he tossed the drone down into the pit before stepping back over to the digger.

As dust continued to swirl in the air, Charlotte had to put a hand over her mouth to keep from coughing. She watched as John resumed his work with the digger, and soon more soil tumbled down into the pit. Within just a few more seconds, the police car was completely covered, and Charlotte thought of the two bodies down there in the darkness. She couldn't see John in the digger's cab now, but she knew he was there, and she began to worry that he might spot her.

Turning, she crawled away from the pit and quickly reached the treeline, where she once again stopped and looked back. Bright lights burned through the huge cloud of dust that was still rising from the pit, and even at a distance of twenty or thirty feet she could feel the ground trembling. The digger's engine rumbled loudly and the mechanical arm seemed almost to scream as it pushed more and more dirt into the pit.

Finally, terrified that she might be spotted, Charlotte turned and stumbled to her feet, and then she set off through the forest, hurrying away from the light, heading into the darkness.

## CHAPTER TWENTY-NINE

Morning light streamed through the forest as Charlotte stumbled between the trees. Barely even conscious, she was somehow managing to put one foot in front of the other, at least for now; she knew that the end was near, however, and that sooner rather than later she was going to collapse and never get up again.

*At least I'll be found. At least he didn't get me.*

As she made her way down a steep slope, her right foot slipped slightly. She steadied herself against a tree, and then she tried to walk again, only to fall and land hard on her knees. She rolled onto her side and waited for a moment to get some strength back, and then she tried to stand, only to find that she was far too weak. Taking a deep breath, she looked out through the forest and realized that she'd found the spot where she was going to die.

"Goodbye, Mum," she whispered, barely able to get the words out at all. "I love you."

She began to close her eyes.

Suddenly, a few seconds later, she heard the distinctive sound of a car driving along a road. She blinked, convinced that the sound had to be all in her mind, but after a moment she sat up and listened as the car disappeared into the distance.

Hauling herself up, she hurried between the trees, and suddenly she realized she could see a road ahead.

"Hey!" she yelled, filled with one final burst of energy as she scrambled between the trees. She could see a car far ahead, heading around a corner, and she started waving frantically. "Stop! Wait! I need help!"

Emerging from the forest, she stopped as she found that she was on a rocky ledge overlooking the road. After taking a couple of steps forward, she looked over the edge and saw that the road was about twenty, maybe even thirty feet down, but when she glanced over her shoulder she realized that she could pick her way down slowly by following a narrow path. And where there was a road, there had to be – eventually – more people.

Turning, she began to make her way toward the path, only to stop suddenly as John stepped out of the forest and blocked her way.

"What -"

For a moment, she couldn't believe that he was real.

"Did you think I wouldn't realize?" he asked. "That drone didn't start flying itself last night. I admit, it took me a few minutes to figure out exactly what had happened. At first I thought maybe the stupid thing had malfunctioned, but finally I understood. After that, it was just a matter of tracking you through the forest. Don't take this the wrong way, Charlotte, but you weren't exactly careful. You might as well have been wearing a big neon suit and firing off flares every five minutes."

"No," she replied.

"No?"

"No," she said again, through gritted teeth. "You're not really here. You can't be. You're a hallucination."

"That'd certainly be a lot easier, wouldn't it?"

"You can't be here!" she screamed, with tears in her eyes. "All I want is to go home! I'm so close!"

"You know that's not going to happen," he told her. "I admit that I've massively screwed up this situation, and for that I'm sorry, but my position remains unchanged. I didn't ask to be dragged into your mess, and I'm not going to let my life get turned upside down by someone else's problems. This ends. Now."

She shook her head.

"You're not really in a good position to argue," he pointed out. "I'm not blind to the fact that you've been through a hell of a lot over the past few days. I'm impressed that you made it this far, but all journeys have to end eventually." He paused. "It would have been better," he added finally, "if our paths had simply never crossed."

She stared at him for a moment, before turning and starting to make her way toward the other end of the ridge. She could already see another path down to the road, and she figured that hopefully John was going to leave her alone, that he was just a hallucination thrown into her path by her addled mind.

"Charlotte."

Suddenly he grabbed her shoulder from behind and pulled her back. Spinning around, she reached up to push him away, but he gripped her wrists and forced her to stay put.

"You shouldn't have come out here," he said firmly.

"It wasn't exactly my choice."

"I'm going to make this very quick," he continued. "I don't want you to suffer."

"Then let me go."

"We're way beyond that point."

"You're insane," she told him.

He shook his head.

"No, really, you are," she continued. "You think you're somehow noble, that you're doing the right thing, but you're no better than that Ted guy. In fact, you might even be worse."

"You know that's not true."

"Then prove it!" she snapped. "Let me go!"

"It'll be over in just a couple of seconds."

"What are you going to do," she asked, "throw me off this thing?"

She waited for an answer, and then she realized that she might be right. She looked down at the road below, and then she turned to him again.

"I don't want to die," she whimpered.

"Some things just have to happen. I'm not a murderer, Charlotte. I'm just a man who wants to live his life without the rest of the world interfering. You, and all those other people, should have just left me alone."

"Please, I'm begging you, I'll do anything but I really don't want to die! Not like this, not now, not here!"

"Don't make this any harder than it has to be."

"Screw you," she replied, before pulling away and trying to run back into the forest. "I'm not -"

Before she'd managed even a couple of paces, he grabbed her from behind and pulled her back. She started struggling wildly to get free, slamming her elbow into his chest, but he'd already managed to put an arm around her and a moment later he carried her right over to the edge of the ridge. No matter how hard she tried to break away, she could feel that John's grip on her was getting tighter, and she knew that at any moment he was about to send her hurtling over the side. Looking down, she saw the road far below, and in that instant she understood that she'd never be able to escape John's clutches.

Suddenly he put his hands on the side of her head, and she realized that he wasn't planning to throw her over the edge at all. Not alive, anyway. He was going to break her neck first.

"It's going to be easy," he whispered. "So easy. You won't feel a thing. I'm so sorry."

"Don't be," she replied, managing to muster a faint smile. "You might actually have a damn good point."

She saw the confusion in his eyes, and she chose that moment to grab his arms tight and throw herself back. He tried to pull away, but he was too late to resist the momentum. Together they tumbled over the edge and fell down toward the road.

For a moment, time seemed to stand still, and that was all the opportunity Charlotte needed. She gripped John's shoulders tight and twisted him around in midair, and in the process she managed to position herself on top of him. Looking down, she saw his horrified face as the ground raced up to meet them, and then she braced herself as she realized that the moment of impact had arrived.

Charlotte landed on top of John as they hit the tarmac, and she immediately felt his ribs – his entire chest, even – break beneath her weight. Blood burst from his mouth, splattering her face, and she felt her own arms crack as she rolled off and fell to the side, landing flat on her back and staring up at the sky. After a moment she turned to her left and she watched as John twitched slightly. He coughed up more blood, but his eyes had already glazed over and a few seconds later he let out one final gasp before falling still.

Feeling intense pain every time she took a breath, Charlotte turned and looked the other way, just as she heard a car approaching. Sure enough, a vehicle pulled up nearby and a horrified man stepped out of his car, clearly shocked by the sight that had greeted him just as he'd driven around the corner. For a moment the man seemed frozen by the awful sight, but then he hurried over and looked down at her.

"Are you okay?" he asked, before turning to John. "Is he..."

He hesitated, and then he pulled a phone from his pocket.

"I'm going to get help," he stammered. "Just hold tight and I'll get someone here who knows what to do."

Charlotte turned back to look at John.

"Sorry," she gasped, as she began to taste blood in the back of her throat. "I really wouldn't have told anyone about what happened at your farm. You should have..."

Suddenly she started coughing, spraying blood from her mouth as the man from the car frantically called for an ambulance.

"I didn't want you to come after me," she continued finally, staring at John's dead face. "You didn't need to. You should have just left me alone."

## CHAPTER THIRTY

"Nonsense," Charlotte's mother Heather said one week later, as she got to her feet in the hospital room, "I'm going to go down there to look after you for a while. You can't live all alone in that pokey little London flat, not after everything you've been through."

"Mum, really, I'm fine," she replied, but her mother had already shuffled around the bed and was busy rearranging the pillows. "You don't have to fuss."

"It'll only be for a short while," Heather continued. "Just until you're back on your feet."

"I'm already walking," Charlotte pointed out, even though she knew that there was no way she'd ever be able to change her mother's mind. "I'm not an invalid. It's just going to take time for my broken bones to heal, that's all."

She paused as she thought back to the moment she'd landed on John. Even one week later, she could still feel his bones shattering, and sometimes she woke up screaming in the night, convinced that his blood was once again all over her face. She'd been offered drugs that the doctors claimed might banish the nightmares, but she was determined to wait for the worst of the terror to go away naturally. That, she figured, was probably going to be a better solution in the long run.

She waited while Heather finished arranging the pillows.

"How long is that going to take you?" she asked finally.

"I'm almost done."

"Honestly, the pillows are fine."

"I'll be the judge of that," her mother said, before stopping. "There. Done. I don't want you straining your back while you're in here."

"You can stay for one month," Charlotte said, somewhat reluctantly. She didn't want to sound too ungrateful. "Tops."

"I'll stay for as long as I'm needed, and that's that."

"Two months and that's my final offer."

"Three."

"Maybe."

"We'll see."

For a moment, an awkward silence fell between them. Charlotte still hadn't gone into a huge amount of detail with her mother; she certainly hadn't told her about the heads on a spike, or about almost getting buried alive in a giant pit, or about quite how she'd survived the final fall. She felt that there were some parts of the story that only the police needed to know.

"I thought I wouldn't ever see you again, Charlotte," Heather said finally, her voice cracking a little as tears filled her eyes. "I tried to keep hoping and praying, but there was a part of me that thought you were gone and that I'd never even find out what had happened to you. It was almost as if that great big forest had just swallowed you up and wasn't ever going to spit you back out."

"I know," Charlotte replied, "I thought the same thing."

Heather hesitated, before reaching over and giving her daughter a big hug.

"I love you, Mum," Charlotte said, struggling to hold back tears. A moment later she saw Chief Inspector Walton stepped into the doorway, and she realized that she was going to have to endure yet another exhausting conversation with the police. "Hey, Mum, I know this is a big ask," she continued, "but would you mind popping down to the shop for a few minutes?"

\*\*\*

"We've finished our work at John Harrison's farm," Walton said a few minutes later, as he stood at Charlotte's bedside. "Everything was exactly as you described it, including the bodies that had been buried inside the car."

"I wasn't lying," she replied.

"I never thought that you were," he told her. "I have to admit, though, that some parts of your story were difficult to believe. I wondered whether you were remembering it all the right way, but most of it's checking out so far. We've been digging into Mr. Harrison's history, and he certainly seems to have been living off the grid for as long as possible. The guy was something of a loner."

"That's the understatement of the year."

"We even spoke to his ex-wife. She confirmed that he'd begun to spiral out of control shortly after they moved out there."

"You found his wife?"

"Samantha Harrison, yes," he replied. "She lives in Wales now. She's remarried. To be honest, she didn't seem particularly keen to talk about her first husband."

"He was telling the truth, then," she muttered, as she thought back to the claims that Mack and Kevin had made about John's wife. They'd strongly suggested that he'd murdered her, although she'd never quite believed that such an awful thing could be true.

And she'd believed them, at least for a moment; at least enough to confront John. She couldn't help but wonder whether it had been that moment that, in his eyes, had sealed her fate.

"The only part of your story that we can't verify," Walton continued, as he flipped back through his notebook, "is this business about a man named Ted Armitage."

"Have you been to his farm?"

"We've scoured the maps, all the records, we've even had people going door-to-door, but we simply can't locate the place that you described. Are you sure that you weren't..."

His voice trailed off for a moment.

"You were under a great deal of stress," he added finally, choosing his words with care. "Do you think it's possible that you might have imagined part of what happened?"

"I was there!" she said firmly. "I saw him kill a woman! I saw heads on spikes!"

"And you can't be more specific about the location of this farm?"

"I told you everything I know!"

"We've even looked at satellite photos," he explained. "It's a very large area to cover, so obviously I can't completely discount the possibility that we've missed something, but we keep coming up blank. I'm going to make sure that the investigation remains active for the time being, but it's really not looking like we're going to find anything."

As those last words left his lips, his phone briefly buzzed. He checked the screen, and then he took a step back.

"I'm sorry, Ms. Walker," he continued, "but I'm afraid I'm going to have to head off. I'll be back in a day or two. I understand you might be leaving hospital soon. That's great news. I'll be in touch."

With that, he turned and headed to the door.

"What about his truck?" Charlotte asked.

Stopping, he glanced back at her.

"Did you find Ted Armitage's truck?" she continued.

He hesitated.

"We did find a vehicle in the location that you indicated," he said cautiously. "The plates were fake. After we did some digging, we determined that the vehicle had been listed as stolen several years back. Of course, since it was submerged, there's very little forensic evidence for us to go on."

"That's *his* truck!"

"We might -"

"What about his body?" she asked. "Did you find it?"

"The truck was empty."

"Then you have to search the lake," she continued. "If you find him, you can identify him properly, and then you might be able to locate his farm. There are so many bodies there, they have to be found, their relatives have to be informed."

"I appreciate that," he told her, "but we've already sent divers down and there's really no sign of a body in the water. We're still working to figure out what happened, but -"

"I told you what happened!" she said angrily.

"Trust to get some rest," he replied, clearly unconvinced. "We'll figure everything out in due course. It's just a matter of putting the pieces together and finding out what fits."

As Walton walked away, Charlotte leaned back in the bed and let out a frustrated sigh. She knew that her story – especially the part about Ted Armitage and his gruesome collection of heads – was somewhat shocking, but she felt extremely annoyed that she wasn't being taken more seriously. She'd shown them that she was right about John Harrison, in which case she didn't understand why they seemed to think that the Ted Armitage part of her claims was suddenly so difficult to accept. Somehow, that man had apparently slipped entirely out of view. Even his corpse stubbornly refused to show up.

"There you are," Heather said, shuffling back into the room, carrying some cans of soda and a few packets of sweets. "I saw that nice policeman on my way back up. He told me he's going to have to talk to you again."

"That's standard procedure," Charlotte replied, suddenly feeling very tired. "They still have so much to pick through, I think it's going to take them a long time to understand everything that happened out there. I'm not sure they quite believe it all yet."

"You're going to need time too," Heather pointed out. "After everything you've been through, sweetheart, the last thing you should do is push yourself."

"I'll be fine," Charlotte said. "What doesn't kill you only makes you stronger, right? And I survived." She paused for a moment as she stared straight ahead and thought back to the vast forest. "I survived all the things that were waiting to try to kill me out there."

# EPILOGUE 1

*One year later...*

"To tell you the truth," Josh said, with a slightly nervous smile, "this is my first date in a long time. I've almost forgotten how they work."

"Me too," Charlotte replied, before glancing around yet again, watching the people at nearby tables and checking that none of them were eavesdropping.

"Is everything okay?"

Turning back to Josh, she realized that she was coming across as being pretty skittish. She tried to calm down, but at the same time she felt she was on the verge of having flashbacks to the last time she'd gone on a date. She was starting to think that perhaps she hadn't been ready to try again. Not yet.

"I'm really sorry," she said finally, "and I know this is going to sound awful, but I think... I think coming here tonight was a mistake."

"Right."

"For me, I mean," she continued with a sigh. "I've just been through a lot of stuff, and I thought I was cool with it, and I let Hayley convince me that I was ready, and you seem like a really nice guy but..."

As her voice trailed off, she looked at Josh and realized that she wasn't being entirely honest. In truth, while she was certainly still feeling the after-effects of her experience a year earlier, she had to admit that she wasn't really getting much of a spark from this Josh guy. Hayley had described him as 'solid' and 'reliable' and 'a rock', and she was starting to realize that these had all just been synonyms for 'dull' and 'bland'. She hated herself for feeling that way, but she couldn't deny the truth any longer.

"I don't think I can do this," she added finally. "Dinner. Drinks. The whole date thing. I'm sorry, do you hate me?"

***

"Well, it was a fun half-date," Josh said as they wandered along the street, heading back to the station. "I mean, what was it... a third of a date? Something like that? A quarter?"

Charlotte felt bad, but she didn't really know how to respond. She knew, however, that she'd done the right thing by ending the date early. She'd detected absolutely no spark whatsoever with Josh, and she was surprised that Hayley had even tried to set them up in the first place. She knew that the guy was probably perfectly nice and entirely inoffensive, but 'nice' and 'inoffensive' really weren't doing anything for her. Even Richard – who was now in a relationship with someone – had seemed more promising.

"So this is me," she said suddenly, stopping at a street corner as she realized that she wanted to get away, even if that meant taking a slightly longer route. "Thanks again for tonight. I hope it wasn't too awful. And I'm sorry again, I wasn't really much fun and I should have canceled before you went to all the trouble of getting a train all the way across town."

"Don't worry," he replied. "To be honest, I don't really get out much, anyway. I know you're probably wondering why Hayley tried to set you up with me, but I actually think it was *me* she was trying to help this time."

"She thinks I'm a charity case," Charlotte told him.

"No! Actually, it's the opposite. *I'm* the charity case in this situation."

"What makes you think that?"

*196*

"She's been on at me lately to see people more," he explained. "A while back I moved a little way out of town, and Hayley thinks it's bad for me to go weeks on end without seeing another soul. She doesn't seem to understand that I like it out there." He shrugged. "Maybe it's a bad thing, but I like people leaving me alone so that I can get on with my shit undisturbed. I don't want to be bothered all the time."

Charlotte opened her mouth to ask him more about his new lifestyle, but then she hesitated as she realized that for the first time that night – in fact, for the first time in what felt like forever – she was interested. The change wasn't just in her head, either; she could feel her body waking up, as if she was reacting to Josh on some kind of deep, primal level. She knew that it was strange to like someone who suddenly reminded her of John Harrison, but she figured that she couldn't help the way she felt. Besides, the lure was magnetic. She could barely keep herself from jumping all over him.

"Have a nice life," he said, before turning and starting to walk away.

"Wait!"

He stopped and glanced back at her.

Although she told herself that she was being irrational, Charlotte couldn't deny that some kind of switch seemed to have been flicked in her soul. Whereas a moment earlier Josh had seemed boring, now everything had been turned on its head and she felt as if she couldn't get enough of him. Not wanting to seem too desperate, however, she took a moment to figure out what to say next.

"Do you want to get a drink somewhere?" she asked.

"With you?" he replied, clearly shocked and a little confused. "I mean... I thought..."

"I know a little place just round the corner," she told him. "They do great cocktails, and I just figure maybe we should get to know one another better. Come on, let's give it one more try."

She waited, and for a few seconds she was worried that she'd already scared him away.

"Sure," he said finally. "Lead the way."

"Down here," she told him, and they began to walk along a smaller side street.

"I have to be honest," Josh said, "I actually thought this date had gone pretty badly. I didn't want to admit that, but I was totally bluffing when I said that it didn't matter. I just thought that I'd bored you stiff."

"Don't be silly," she replied, tucking a stray strand of hair behind her ear and she allowed herself a faint smile. She wanted to jump all over him, but she knew that she had to at least play things cool for a little while longer. "So tell me more about your life out in the middle of nowhere."

"It's stupid, really," he replied. "I just wanted a chance of pace. I wanted to try something new, and more than anything I really wanted to slow down. And do you know the best thing about being out there in the countryside? People leave me alone. Like, they actually -"

Suddenly, before she could stop herself, Charlotte turned and threw herself at him, kissing him before he even knew what was happening. The kiss, which she couldn't control at all, lasted for a few seconds before she pulled back a little. She could see the shock in his eyes, but she was pretty sure that she was even *more* shocked.

"Do you want to skip the bar?" she asked breathlessly. "Do you want to come back to my place?"

## EPILOGUE 2

"Oh come on!" Harriet Ward said with a sigh as she looked down into the bonnet of her car and saw some kind of steam rising from the left-hand side of the engine. "Why does this kind of thing always happen to *me*?"

For a moment she felt utterly, hopelessly lost. She'd always planned to take some kind of course so that she'd know basic car maintenance tips, but she'd never quite found the time, and now she had no idea what to do. Turning, she looked both ways along the barren forest road, and she realized that she was several miles from civilization. She'd passed a town a while back, and she could only hope that there was a garage, so she made her way to the car door and reached in to grab her phone.

"Typical," she said, sighing again as she saw that she had no signal. She waved her phone in the air, but still she had no luck.

Realizing that her only option was to take a walk into town, she began to lock the car, but then she heard the sound of a vehicle approaching. Turning, she was overjoyed to see a red pick-up truck rolling to a halt not too far away, and she began to make her way over as a man stepped out of the truck.

"You having trouble here?" he asked.

"It's something to do with the engine, I think," she told him. "I stopped at a service station a while back, just for a bite to eat, and after I left I noticed a little juddery noise. I should have turned back immediately, but I told myself that it was nothing serious and that I'd be able to make it home, and now look at me. Stranded in the middle of nowhere!"

"Not anymore, you're not," the man replied with a grin. "Today might be your lucky day after all. I happen to work with engines for a living, I'd be happy to take a look and see if I can fix this for you."

"That would be amazing," she told him, almost crying with gratitude. "I won't bore you with the details, but I've had a hell of a day, and I just want to get home and climb into a nice hot bath."

"Hopefully we can get you underway in no time," the man said with a friendly smile, as he made his way to the back of the truck and grabbed some tools. "You know, I don't normally come this way. Not a lot of people do. On another day, you might have been waiting several hours for help."

"I think that would have just about finished me off," she admitted.

"I've never met an engine yet that I couldn't coax back to life," he replied. "I'm sure I can at least bodge it together long enough for you to get home, and then you'll probably have to get it looked at by someone at your local garage."

"You have my eternal gratitude," she told him, as he walked past her and stopped to look at the engine.

"I see the problem," he said after just a few seconds, pointing at one particular spot. "You've got a cut line here. Strange, I don't see how something like that could have happened, but like I told you, I should be able to patch it up. I reckon it'll only take me half an hour or so."

"Thank you," she replied, heading around to the door and reaching in for her phone, only to find that it was nowhere to be seen.

Remembering that she'd left the phone balanced next to the engine, she made her way around to the front of the car, only to once again draw a blank.

"I'm sorry," she said cautiously, "but have you seen a gray phone anywhere around here? I'm sure I left it out."

"Sorry, I haven't seen anything."

"I must be losing my marbles," she replied as she walked around to the other side of the car to continue her search. "I suppose I shouldn't be too surprised. After today, it's a wonder I can even think straight."

She began to search methodically for her phone, although she was becoming more and more certain that she remembered placing it on the front of the car. Still, she knew that it wasn't there now, and the kind gentleman had already told her that he hadn't moved it, so she figured that she must simply have made a mistake.

"Still no luck?" the man asked after a couple of minutes.

"It seems to have disappeared into thin air."

"Do you mind if I ask you something?"

She turned and saw that he was staring at her.

"Is anything the matter?" she asked.

He hesitated, and then he shook his head.

"No, forget it," he told her, "it's not important. I should mind my own business."

"It's quite alright," she replied, although she couldn't possibly imagine what he wanted to know. "What's on your mind?"

She waited, and she couldn't help but notice that his stare now seemed somewhat intense.

"It's just a silly little thing, really," he continued, "but I can't help wondering... Why *didn't* you talk to your sister at the funeral today? It just seems like your own father's funeral would be the perfect time and place to try to heal a little family rift. I suppose I'm just wondering why you zoomed in and out of the funeral without really talking to anyone. Considering the nature of the occasion, that just seemed a little... rude."

She opened her mouth to reply, but the words caught in the back of her throat.

"I just thought to myself," the man added, "Ted, what's going on with this woman? Why did she act like that when she could so easily have done the right thing instead?"

As Harriet tried to work out how to answer, and indeed how the man knew anything about her father's funeral at all, she suddenly became aware of just how far she was from civilization. She couldn't help thinking about the vast forest that stretched out from either side of the road, and about the fact that there was probably not a single other soul anywhere out there for miles.

Book Two

# TWIST VALLEY

## PROLOGUE

"Please save me!" Rebecca screamed suddenly, dropping to her knees and grabbing the front of Ted's shirt. "I'm begging you, you were right all along! I see that now!"

"Of course I was right," he replied, "but -"

"I'll do anything you want," she continued, clutching his shirt as tears rolled down her cheeks. "I didn't see it until now, but it finally all makes sense. Everything you told me was true, I just needed time before I could see it. Please, Ted, help me be a better person. I'm entirely in your hands, I won't resist, not again. I need you to save me."

Staring down at her, he realized that she was sincere. He could see the desperation in her eyes, and he knew that she wasn't lying. She'd finally come around to his way of thinking, and she was willing to open herself completely to his teaching. He just had to decide whether he was still willing to come to her aid, or whether she'd pushed him away one time too many.

"Please," she sobbed, as she leaned forward and pressed her forehead against his belly. "Help me."

# CHAPTER ONE

*Several days earlier...*

"Honey, I might be back late tonight, okay?"

Stopping next to her husband in the kitchen, Rebecca Ballard leaned close and gave him a peck on the cheek.

"Maddy needs me to go through some files at the office," she continued, "and there are so many of them, it'd be a nightmare to drag them all home only to have to drag them back in a day or two. She's never been good at paperwork, and she's let it all really spiral out of control. You understand, don't you?"

"That entire office would collapse without you," Phil replied with a grin. "I understand entirely."

"It's not like that, I just -"

"Becky, I'm glad that they appreciate you there," he added, interrupting her. "I mean, they could appreciate you by paying you more, but I guess that's out of the question." He poured some milk into his cereal bowl. "Just try to be back by bedtime. You know she never settles if you're still out."

"I wouldn't miss bedtime for the world," Rebecca said, heading over to the high chair and leaning down to kiss the top of her daughter's head. "Hey, Chloe, Mummy's going to work now but you'll be in Daddy's very capable hands. It's kind of the reverse of a normal day, but don't get used to it. Full service'll be resumed tomorrow."

She looked down at Chloe's smiling face, and for a moment she felt a flicker of doubt. She'd agreed to spend the day at the office, but she was starting to wonder whether there might be another way to get the paperwork done. At the same time, she told herself that she was being a little unrealistic, and that she shouldn't feel quite so upset at the prospect of being away from her child for just one day. After all, the real world was still out there.

"I'll be back tonight," she told Chloe, before planting a kiss on the side of her face. "I promise. Way before bedtime."

Chloe let out an excited gurgle.

\*\*\*

"So how are things at home?"

"Hmm?"

Looking up from her lunch, Rebecca felt a little as if she'd been caught off guard by the question. She'd been thinking about some of the files from work and her mind had definitely begun to wander.

"Are you aching desperately to go back later," her colleague Michaela asked with a grin, "or are you just grateful for the chance to get away, even if it's only for one day?"

"No, I'm fine," Rebecca stammered, as a woman with a child passed their table in the cafe. "Sorry, my head's just a little bit in the clouds right now. I spent all morning looking through your mis-filed reports, remember?"

"We've been missing you in the office."

"I'll be back soon," Rebecca said, trying not to sound too defensive. "I miss meeting with clients. I miss the one-on-one focus of helping people. Things have just been crazy for a while."

"And you know I think you're a lifesaver," Michaela replied. "I guess I just feel a little guilty for dragging you away." She paused for a moment. "I also can't help but remember the conversation we had six months ago, when -"

"Things are a lot better now," Rebecca said cautiously, interrupting her.

"I'm looking at your eyes, and I'm not sure that I believe you."

"Things are fine."

"So you and Phil are getting on okay again? All that lingering post-childbirth malaise has lifted and you can't keep your hands off each other?"

"It's complicated," Rebecca told her, while glancing around at the other tables to make sure that nobody was eavesdropping on their conversation. "We have a healthy relationship. We talk about these things. I mean, I'm a therapist, I should know how this sort of thing works."

"It's harder when it's your own life you're trying to fix."

"I can manage."

"When's the last time he touched you?" Michaela asked. "In the bedroom, I mean."

"We have a one-year-old girl. Not even that, she's not one for a few more weeks."

"That doesn't mean your lives have to grind to a halt. You're a woman, Becky. You have needs. I'd have thought that Phil must have needs as well. Sorry, I'm probably way overstepping the mark, but when we talked about this before, I could tell that you were really having a hard time. I guess my question is... have you fixed things, or have you merely adjusted to a new normal?"

Rebecca opened her mouth to reply, but for a moment she wasn't quite sure what to say.

"Because new normals don't always work out how you think they will," Michaela added.

"It's fine."

As soon as those words left her lips, Rebecca knew how feeble they sounded.

"We're besties," Michaela continued, leaning across the table. "We've been besties since before we learned to walk. You can tell me anything, Becky. You know that, right?"

"There's nothing to tell."

"So it's all good?"

"It's all good," Rebecca replied, although she could tell that she still didn't sound very convincing.

"And have you talked to Phil about all of this?"

"About all of what?"

Letting out a loud and somewhat melodramatic sigh, Michaela leaned back in her chair.

"There's nothing to talk about," Rebecca protested. "We're just going through a slightly tough time and we'll bounce back soon enough."

"You could at least give him the chance, though. If you're unhappy with something, it's only fair of you to talk to him openly and honestly. Doing that now could save you a whole lot of heartache and trouble down the line. Come on, this is exactly the kind of advice we both give to clients all the time."

Rebecca hesitated, knowing full well that Michaela had a point, but also knowing that the last thing she wanted to do was rock the boat at home. Actually, that wasn't quite true: the very last thing she wanted was to be talking to anyone about her marriage.

"I'm dealing with it, okay?" she said finally, hoping to end that part of the conversation and move on to something more palatable. "Phil and I have been married for five years. Honestly, we're rock solid."

\*\*\*

"I'm heading off now!" Rebecca called out several hours later, as she grabbed her bag and coat and headed to the door. "I got everything I need, so I'll be able to do the rest from home over the weekend."

"Don't work too hard!"

Smiling, Rebecca opened the door and stepped out into the car park. Bright, late afternoon light caught the sides of cars nearby, and she took a moment to slip her sunglasses on before making her way toward the far end. As she walked, however, she happened to see that a figure was standing over by the car park's entrance, right next to the board that listed all the businesses operating out of the industrial estate. She told herself that there was no reason to worry, but as she reached her car and started looking for her keys she couldn't help glancing toward the figure again, just to make sure that it was gone.

He was still there, silhouetted against the road beyond, and for a moment Rebecca really couldn't shake the feeling that she was being watched.

Once she'd found her keys, she unlocked the car and climbed inside, and then she set her things on the passenger seat before grabbing her phone and bringing up Phil's number.

"Hey," she said as soon as he answered, "I'm leaving now, so I shouldn't be too late home. How's Chloe doing?"

"She's fine," he replied, although his voice was a little difficult to decipher as static broke into the call. "I don't want to make you feel bad, but she misses you."

"I miss her too," she told him, before pausing for a few seconds. "I miss you too."

"And I miss you," he said. "Everyone misses everyone. Except me and Chloe, obviously, because we've spent all day together."

"We should go out to dinner soon," she replied.

"What's the occasion?"

"No occasion, I just think it'd be good for us to do something romantic. Something just for us. Your mum can look after Chloe for a few hours, can't she?"

"Are you kidding? I'm sure she'd be delighted."

"We could even stay over somewhere," she added. "Like, in a hotel."

"Are you serious? Last month you told me off for spending too much money on sandwiches at work, and now you want us to fork out for a hotel room?"

"I think it's important for us to do something romantic," she explained. "We used to, remember? It might help us to reconnect. And Chloe loves your mum, you know that. She probably won't even notice that we're away."

"You might very well be right," he said. "Okay, I'll look online and try to come up with some ideas. I'll try to have at least three options by the time you get home."

"Let me do that," she replied. "I want to surprise you. It'll be fun."

"How can I turn that offer down? Drive safe, Becky, and we'll both see you real soon."

Once the call was over, Rebecca fastened her seat belt and switched the engine on, before backing the car slowly out of its spot. As she did so, she glanced toward the entrance again, and to her relief she saw that there was now no sign of the silhouetted figure. Whatever he'd been up to, he was obviously done now, and she felt a little foolish for having allowed herself to get so paranoid in the first place. Making a mental note to try to ignore scare stories in the media, she drove the car toward the car park's exit and then out onto the main road.

And she told herself that when she got home, she was going to book a night away for her and Phil. Something to hopefully put the spark back into their marriage and bring them closer together.

## CHAPTER TWO

"So what we're really talking about with these quotas," the man on the radio said a couple of hours later, as Rebecca drove along an isolated road passing straight through a forest, "is not only the question of where the borders exist, but also where they're actually applied and policed."

Reaching out, she tapped to change the channel. With perhaps two hours still to go, she was starting to feel the first twinges of tiredness, but she didn't want to waste any time by stopping for a nap. Besides, as she glanced at the clock she saw that it was already a little after 6pm, and ahead the sky was darkening. Once she'd found a music channel playing hits from the 80's, she took a deep breath and tried to put any exhaustion to the back of her mind, and she focused instead on the winding, twisty road ahead.

Spotting a rusty old sign, she managed to read the words as she drove past:

*Welcome to Twist Valley*

"What the hell's Twist Valley?" she muttered, and she was pretty sure that she'd never heard of the place before, or seen it on any maps.

As she continued to drive, however, she started to realize that she was really out in the middle of nowhere. Having preferred to avoid the motorways, due to reports of several jams along the route she'd taken on the way down earlier, she'd opted for a scenic route that so far seemed to be taking her miles and miles from civilization. She hadn't anticipated that she'd be quite so alone, but she didn't really mind the fact that she was getting away from the world. After a moment, however, her radio began to stutter and cut out.

"Come on," she muttered, hoping that it'd keep going, "I need my shitty music. How else am I supposed to -"

Before she could finish, the radio fell silent.

"Great," she said with a sigh, although she told herself that the dead zone was most likely pretty short. Any second now, the music was likely to -

Suddenly the car shuddered and a loud pop rang out, and the entire vehicle bucked and swerved to the right. Rebecca immediately slammed her foot against the brake pedal, and the tires squealed as the car pitched around and bumped toward the edge of the road. After a few seconds, the rear nudged a metal barrier and the car came to a halt, and Rebecca found herself sitting with her hands gripping the wheel and her entire body tense with shock.

She waited, but whatever had happened, it was over now.

"What the..."

Unfastening her seat belt, she climbed out of the car and stepped around to take a look, and she let out a sigh as soon as she saw that her front left tire had blown. Crouching down, she took a closer look at the carcass, and after a moment she spotted something metallic poking out. She reached down and fidgeted with the object; once she'd finally pulled it clear, she held it up and saw that it was some kind of thick metal spike with barbs on its sides. She'd never seen anything like it before, and as she turned it around in her hands she realized that it must simply have been resting in the middle of the road.

Either that, or it had somehow have been attached to the tire or the car for a while and had only now caused a failure. She certainly hadn't seen anything ahead while she was driving, although she had to concede that the object was pretty small. Whatever it was and wherever it had come from, it had done a real number on her tire.

"Well," she said, as she looked over her shoulder and saw that the sky ahead was a little darker than it had seemed even just a couple of minutes ago, "looks like I've got some work to do."

***

About an hour later, as the last of the evening's light continued to fade, Rebecca heard the sound of another vehicle approaching. Looking over her shoulder, she spotted a small truck making its way around the bend.

The truck drove slowly past and seemed for a moment to be continuing on its way, but a few seconds later it stopped and then reversed, making its way past Rebecca and then stopping a little way back.

As the door on the truck's side opened, a middle-aged man climbed out wearing a hat and sunglasses.

"Well, hello there," the man said, removing the hat and sunglasses as he took a couple of steps toward her, "what seems to be the problem?"

"Oh, I hit something," she replied, before getting to her feet. "I was just driving along, minding my own business, and then this piece of metal wrecked my tire and almost sent me spinning straight off the road."

"That's bad luck," the man muttered, stepping around her and looking down at the wheel. "If you like, I can -"

"It's fine," she told him. "It could have been worse, I could have ended up upside-down or something like that. As you can see, it wasn't a big job. I had a spare and everything I needed, so it's all fixed now. I'm about to set off on my way."

"I'm sorry?" he replied.

She made her way around to the other side of the car and opened the door on the driver's side. A little part of her, deep down, felt quite proud for having managed to fix the problem all by herself. She'd have hated to have simply sat at the side of the road, waiting for someone to come along and save her bacon.

"Thanks for stopping," she added, "but honestly, it's all under control."

"You fixed it?" he replied, clearly shocked.

"I did indeed."

"Are you... sure?"

"I'm sure." Amused by his sense of disbelief, she stopped for a moment. "My dad was a mechanic, and he taught me pretty much everything I could ever need to know. I was lucky that the wheel itself wasn't damaged, so it was really just a case of switching the tires." She held up the metal object that she'd hit. "I have no idea what this is, though. It shredded the tire real good."

"I'm a mechanic," he replied. "I'd be happy to take a look at the wheel for you."

"There's really no need. I've done that and it's fine."

"But -"

"Thanks again," she added as she climbed into the car and swung the door shut. She lowered the other window and leaned over so that she could look up at the guy. "I'm not going to lie to you, it was hard work and my arms are aching, and it took me longer than it should have, but I'm good to go. I'll get it looked over tomorrow, once I'm home, but I'm really not too worried."

"But..."

His voice trailed off for a moment.

"I mean," he continued, "I *am* a mechanic. It wouldn't hurt to have a second pair of eyes check it over, right?"

"There's really no need."

"Sure, but..."

Again, he seemed utterly lost for words.

"It wouldn't be any bother," he added. "In fact, it'd be my pleasure. Let me just go to my truck and grab a few tools, and -"

"Actually, I need to get going," she told him, sitting up straight again and reaching out to start the engine. "Today has been really crazy and I just want to get home and put my feet up. Thanks for the offer, though, it's really appreciated. Have a nice evening, wherever you're going."

"Back at the cafe," he replied, "why did you say that your husband -"

Before he could get another word out, the engine shuddered to life. Rebecca, who'd been too focused on getting started again, realized that she hadn't really paid attention to what the man had just said, so she leaned over to the window again.

"Sorry," she said a little sheepishly, "I didn't catch that."

"I just said that -"

"I really have to get going," she added. "My husband and daughter are waiting for me. Thanks for offering to help, though. You're a real good Samaritan."

The man replied, but Rebecca had already begun to wind the window back up. She knew she was perhaps being a little rude, but at the same time she was now seriously behind schedule and she wanted to drive on a little further so that she could find some phone signal and let Phil know about the delay. She carefully drove around the man, before performing a three-point turn and then setting off again. She waved at the guy as she rumbled past him, but already her sights were set on the road ahead.

Glancing in her mirror, she saw the man disappearing into the distance. He seemed to be watching her, almost as if he couldn't quite believe what had just happened.

## CHAPTER THREE

Twenty minutes later, with the sun having well and truly set, Rebecca continued to check her phone and radio for signal as she drove along the deserted road.

"Seriously," she muttered, frustrated that she still had no way of contacting the outside world. "You've got to be kidding me. I'm having the worst luck today."

She tapped at her phone again as it lay on the passenger seat, and then – returning her gaze to the road ahead – she realized that she could see a light in her rear view mirror. Sure enough, a vehicle was running about a hundred meters behind, although she could already tell that it was slowly catching up. She briefly wondered whether it might be the guy who'd offered to help her earlier, and after a moment she figured that it had to be him. After all, she'd seen no turn-offs since she'd resumed her journey.

"Come on," she said under her breath, trying the radio yet again. "This is the twenty-first century. How can there still be parts of Britain that don't have signal?"

Still having no luck, she looked ahead and turned the wheel as she threaded the car through a gentle turn. The truck behind her was now maybe only fifty meters back, and she figured that soon enough it was going to overtake. That didn't seem like a big deal, since the road was deserted anyway, so she paid no real attention as she focused on her own route. She had the windows open on either side, letting cool air into the car on what was otherwise quite a warm evening, and she was also hoping that the air would also keep her from getting too tired. Better, she figured, to be a little too cold rather than too warm.

The truck was now even closer, perhaps twenty-five meters behind, although its closing pace seemed to have slowed just a little. There was no reason for it to hang back and not overtake, but Rebecca told herself that the guy was probably just being ultra cautious.

Better that than reckless.

Still, the truck had settled into a position not too far back, and she was starting to wonder whether she should perhaps move out of the way and slow down so that it could pass. That seemed a little rude, so she told herself that the guy would overtake soon enough. Until then, she resolved to stay calm, so she took a moment to check both her phone and radio again, before looking once more at the rear view mirror.

This time, to her surprise, she saw another light, although this didn't seem to be coming from another vehicle. Instead, the new light was somehow smaller than the truck's headlights and appeared to be moving independently, almost as if something had emerged from the truck and was now slowly but surely catching up to Rebecca's car. She tried to stay calm and focus on the road ahead, but she couldn't help glancing over her shoulder as the new light passed the rear of her vehicle and began to advance toward the window on the passenger's side. It was almost as if a little U.F.O. had randomly arrived on the scene.

Finally a drone hovered into view, somehow keeping pace with the car itself.

"What the..."

For a moment, too shocked to really know how to react, Rebecca could only keep driving while glancing at the drone and wondering why it was now maintaining station just outside the car. She couldn't really make out too many details of the device, although she could just about hear the sound of its engines struggling to keep up, and then a few seconds later the drone abruptly lifted up and out of sight.

"Okay," Rebecca said out loud, before looking in her rear view mirror and wondering whether the guy in the truck was actually driving both his own vehicle and the drone at the same time. "This isn't creepy at all."

She looked ahead, but a moment later she heard the hum of the drone's engines getting closer and she turned to her right. Sure enough, the drone had passed over the car and was now right outside the other window, just a few inches from where she was sitting.

"Hey, get out of here!" she shouted, just in case the drone's operator was able to hear her. "You're distracting me! This is dangerous!"

She waited, but the drone somehow maintained pace for a few more seconds before once again rising up and disappearing from view.

"This isn't funny!" she yelled out. "What's wrong with some people?"

Watching the road ahead, she told herself that the guy was obviously just trying to have some weird little joke, and that soon he'd no doubt give up and leave her alone. He'd seemed normal enough when they'd talked earlier, but she knew that sometimes freaks and lunatics were able to pass undetected in normal society, at least for a few minutes at a time. Still, she couldn't help glancing up at the roof, wondering whether the drone was still up there.

All she could hope was that some time soon she'd come across a gas station or somewhere she could pull over and wait while the asshole drove on.

Suddenly the drone dropped back into view over by the passenger-side window.

"I told you to leave me alone!" Rebecca shouted. "You're going to cause an accident if you keep this up!"

Realizing that she needed to just stay calm and ignore the damn thing, and telling herself that she had to simply keep driving, she looked ahead and resolved to stay cool, calm and collected. She certainly had no intention of rewarding some random idiot by reacting to his stupidity, and she focused on the fact that he was simply trying to get a rise out of her.

"Screw you, asshole," she said under her breath, forcing herself to not look at the drone again. "You need to get a life. Is this really the only way you can get people to pay any attention to you? By -"

Before she could get another word out, the drone swung straight through the window and into the car, its engines buzzing loudly as it slammed against the side of Rebecca's face.

"What the hell?" she yelled, struggling to keep hold of the steering wheel with one hand while using the other to push the drone away, sending it bumping back against the frame.

Almost immediately, the four little engines surged again, and the drone turned around until its forward-facing camera was aimed directly at Rebecca's face.

"You're out of your mind!" she shouted, trying to push the drone out through the window, before turning to park at the side of the road. "You're a complete -"

In an instant, the truck rammed her from behind, causing her to let out a startled cry as she briefly lost control. She managed to grab the wheel with both hands and keep the car from racing straight off the side of the road, but when she tried once more to pull to the side and slow down she was immediately rammed again, and she realized that the guy in the truck was determined to make sure that she couldn't stop.

Turning, she grabbed the drone and shoved it over her shoulder, sending it crashing down onto the back seat.

She adjusted her grip on the wheel, but in that moment the drone rose up again and surged forward, although this time it bumped against the back of the driver's seat and had to fall away.

"What's wrong with you?" Rebecca yelled, once again trying to pull over, only for the truck to bump the back of the car and force her to continue. "You're going to make me crash!"

She turned the wheel, sending the car swinging over to the other side of the road, but the truck shadowed her every move. Before she had a chance to try to come up with another idea, the drone let out a loud buzzing sound and rammed the back of her seat, and this time it managed to push through the gap and fly into the side of her face.

Reaching up, she tried to swat the machine away, but it swung around and dropped low, hitting her lap and then filling the space between her body and the steering wheel.

"Stop!" she screamed, but the drone had already hooked the wheel, making it almost impossible to turn.

Rebecca grappled to retain control of the car, but at the last second she saw a bend in the road ahead. She tried to slow and steer, but the drone bumped into her head and almost hit her eyes. Turning away for a moment, she was powerless as she felt the car speed straight off the side of the road and start bumping across the mud.

As soon as she finally managed to turn the wheel, she realized that she was too late. The car began to swing around, only to hit a large mound of dirt and flip over into its side. Rebecca could only scream as the car rolled down a steep slope and then slammed roof-first into a tree. Glass shattered and metal crunched, and Rebecca's head slammed against the side of the window, knocking her out instantly as the lights failed and the drone's engines surged louder than ever before.

## CHAPTER FOUR

The next thing she heard, the sound that stirred her from unconsciousness, was a metallic cracking sound accompanied by a series of annoyed grunts.

Slowly opening her eyes, Rebecca found for a moment that she was hanging upside down in darkness. She blinked a few times, aware of a dim pain in one side of her head, and it took a few seconds for her to remember the crash. Even then, she could only look around and try to figure out exactly what was happening, and she was vaguely aware of some kind of flashing light somewhere to her left. She turned, only to be almost blinded as a flashlight shone straight into her eyes.

Letting out a faint cry, she closed her eyes and turned away.

"Police?" she stammered, still somewhat bewildered. "I'm in here! I'm trapped! Please, you have to help me!"

"That's good, you're awake," a voice said, as more footsteps crunched around to the other side of the car, carrying the flashlight.

Opening her eyes again, Rebecca heard the sound of someone breathing nearby, and she turned just as a gloved hand reached through and started pushing broken chunks of glass out of the window's frame. A moment later she screamed as a foot smashed through, knocking the last of the glass away.

"Help me," Rebecca stammered, looking around for her phone but seeing it nowhere. "Please..."

She reached down and unfastened her seat belt, and in an instant she slumped out of the seat and let out a startled gasp as she slammed against the dashboard. For a few seconds, unable to work out which way was up, she panicked as she tried to twist herself around, and in the process she inadvertently reached out and grabbed the opposite window frame. A piece of broken glass sliced straight into three of her fingers.

"You're not going to get far panicking like that," the man said, as he crouched next to the other window and once again aimed his flashlight at her. "You need to calm down and try to think rationally."

"Who are you?" she shouted.

"Didn't I introduce myself before?" He reached a hand out to her. "The name's Ted. Ted Armitage."

"Help me!" she sobbed. "You have to call an ambulance!"

"I'm not sure that's the immediate priority," he replied. "You seem well enough. The thing is, there's this question that's been bugging me and I just can't get it out of my head."

Trying again to twist around, Rebecca let out another cry as she felt a sharp pain in her right ankle. Looking down, she saw that it was bent to one side and that there was blood caked around the bottom of her skirt.

"Why did you say that you don't need to talk to your husband about your marital difficulties?"

Startled, she turned to him. Shielding her eyes from the flashlight's beam, she squinted as she tried to make out his face.

"Back in that cafe earlier, when you were having lunch with your friend," he continued. "It's apparent that you and – Phil, is that his name? - are having problems, and the obvious solution would be to talk to him about what's going wrong. That way, you can both try to come to some kind of understanding."

"What..."

"Instead, you seem determined to fix it all yourself, and I can't help thinking that you're being a little selfish."

"What are you talking about?"

"You and your husband," he said matter-of-factly, adjusting the flashlight a little as if he was trying to get a better look at her. "Did you get more of a bump on the noggin than I thought? Are you having memory problem in there?"

"Who are you?" she asked again.

"I just happened to be at the next table at lunchtime," he explained, "and I didn't mean to eavesdrop, really I didn't, but you were just going on and on about your personal problems and... Well, you have to admit that you were in a very public place. And I have sympathy for you, really I do. As a married man myself, I know how difficult it can be to negotiate the pitfalls of a relationship, but I truly believe that the key to everything is honesty. If you're honest with each other, you can deal with just about anything that gets thrown at you, but if..."

He paused for a moment, as if he was genuinely lost in thought.

"You're *not* being honest with your husband, are you?" he continued finally. "Don't you think he has a right to know what you're thinking?"

"I..."

Staring at him, she began to realize that he must have followed her all the way from the office. Could he have been the man in the car park?

"And it cuts both ways," he added. "If you open up to him, he'll probably open up to you in return. Don't you think it's just fairer to him if you prove that you're open to some constructive dialogue?"

Rebecca swallowed hard as she thought back to her conversation with Michaela at the cafe. That had been five or six hours earlier, which meant that the guy must have been keeping track of her for at least that long. She looked around as she began to realize that she was out in the middle of nowhere, in a wrecked and upturned car, with a man who was rapidly turning out to be some kind of stalker.

"I can help you," he said suddenly.

She turned to him.

"It's kind of what I do," he continued, and now he sounded somewhat amused by the situation. "You seem pretty smart, Rebecca. Or do you prefer Becky? I saw people using both names on your social media. Anyway, I think you just need a little nudge in the right direction. What do they call it these days? A reality check."

"I need you call an ambulance," she told him, hoping against hope that she could get through to him and make him see reason, "and the police, and then you can leave. I won't tell anyone about this... accident. Because that's what it was, right? You didn't mean for your drone to come into my car, I know that. This was all just a big misunderstanding."

She waited.

"Right?" she added.

Again, she waited.

"Huh," Ted replied, getting to his feet and taking a step back. "Does that..."

For a moment, she began to believe that she might be in luck, and that the maniac might be feeling at least a flicker of remorse. She looked around again, hoping that she might be able to find her phone and that she'd finally have some signal, and then she leaned over and started sorting through the wreckage. Her hands were trembling and her eyes were filled with tears, and after a moment she looked back over at the window and saw that the man was no longer outside the car.

Freezing, she listened to the sound of his footsteps crunching away across the forest floor.

And then they stopped.

All she heard for a moment was silence, and she knew that he had to still be somewhere nearby. Trying not to panic, she looked over at the other windows, worried that he might reappear at any second. She realized after a few seconds that he must have switched his flashlight off, and she was fully aware that if he was planning to drive away, by now she should have heard the sound of his car starting up.

A few seconds later, however, she heard a faint hissing sound coming from somewhere deep in the car's wreckage.

"Hey, I think something's wrong," she said, suddenly worried that the vehicle might be about to explode. "You have to get me out of here!"

She began to struggle, but the roof of the car was mangled and she could barely manage to twist around as she tried to inch toward one of the broken windows. Convinced that at any moment she'd be engulfed by flames, she reached out and grabbed the frame and tried to drag herself free, but after just a fraction of a second she let out a pained cry.

In an instant, the drone burst to life and slammed against her, pushing her back from the window. Reaching up, she tried to push the damn thing away, until finally she slumped back against the opposite window as the drone swung around and shone a bright, almost blinding light straight into her face. The four little engines, meanwhile, were whirring loudly in the cramped space of the wrecked car.

"Help!" Rebecca screamed. "Somebody, please -"

She flinched as she felt something sharp sliding into the right side of her neck. Trying to turn, she realized that someone was leaning into the car and injecting her. Already, even as she used all her remaining strength to pull away, she could feel her thoughts getting heavier. Finally, despite her best efforts, she slumped down and let her eyes slip shut, and there was nothing she could do to keep herself from falling away once more into unconsciousness.

## CHAPTER FIVE

"Now," the voice on the radio said, as Rebecca began to stir in the back of the truck, "what I want to know is, if you're out there and you didn't listen to the show last night, *why* didn't you listen? You know the number to call..."

The presenter continued to talk as Rebecca tried to sit up. As the truck bumped along a dark road, she quickly found that she was tightly tied with some kind of thick cord, and a large ball was strapped into her mouth. She tried to turn around, but there was precious little room, although after a moment she spotted the drone just a few inches from her face. Deactivated and silent, the drone shuddered a little as the truck hit another rough patch of tarmac.

"We've got Stephen on line one," the radio presenter continued. "Stephen's from Coventry, I believe. Stephen, what's your take on all of this? Is it a genuine moment that's going to bring about change, or is it just a load of nonsense that's being spun by both sides to sell more papers? Or, even worse, to get more clicks."

Stephen from Coventry began to explain his view as Rebecca finally managed to twist around and sit up slightly. She still found that she couldn't pull her hands free from behind her back; the most she could manage, at least for now, was to lean against the side and try to figure out exactly what was happening. She was in the back of a moving vehicle, she knew that much, and she remembered the drone attacking her in the wreckage of her car. Pulling again on the restraints, she could already tell that there was no way she'd be able to simply break free, but after a moment she realized she could hear somebody humming nearby.

Slowly, and very carefully, she craned her neck and tried to look over the seat, and sure enough she saw the back of a man's head as he drove the truck along what seemed to be some kind of dirt road. She recognized him instantly as the same man who'd stopped and offered to help her earlier.

"This country's going to the dogs," a voice on the radio complained. "Why are people obsessing over a bunch of celebrities when we've got actually problems we need to deal with?"

"Damn straight," the man in the driver's seat muttered.

"That's exactly what I was saying earlier," the presenter said. "We're expending all this energy on things that don't matter, and at the same time we're ignoring the genuine structural issues that are holding us back. And of course all the politicians in Westminster are perfectly happy for us to carry on like that, because it keeps us squabbling with each other instead of asking for real change."

Rebecca watched the back of the man's head for a few more seconds. She could still hear him humming merrily to himself, and she knew that she had to strike while she still had the element of surprise. At the same time, with her hands firmly tied behind her back, she could think of no idea other than trying to make the guy crash his truck. And what exactly was she supposed to do after that? At best, she might be able to climb out of the wreckage, but even that seemed like a long shot; more likely, she'd still be trapped.

Suddenly the truck slowed and turned to the right, before coming to a sudden stop.

Immediately pulling back down, Rebecca rolled onto her side and resumed the position in which she'd woken up. She heard the engine being switched off, and then the sound of the door opening and footsteps trudging around to the truck's rear door. Just as she closed her eyes, she heard the door swing open and she realized that the man must be staring down at her. She could even hear him breathing. For a moment she considered leaping up and trying to attack him, but she knew that this approach was unlikely to work. Instead, she stayed down until a few seconds later the door was slammed shut and she heard footsteps walking away.

She waited, and then she slowly sat up and looked out through the rear window, only to see that the man was walking toward some kind of house that stood near some trees just ten or twenty meters away. A couple of seconds after that, in the darkness, she was just about able to see that the man was opening the front door, and then a solitary light flickered on in what she assumed must be the hallway.

And then he was gone.

For the next few minutes, too terrified to move – still clinging to the one advantage that she hoped might help – Rebecca simply sat in the darkness and watched the house. She felt as if a plan was about to form in her mind, one that would guarantee she could escape, but she couldn't quite make the details coalesce. Michaela had always mocked her for over-thinking things and being too slow to act, and she knew she might be making the same mistake at that very moment, but she still couldn't bring herself to simply break out of the truck and run, because she knew deep down that the guy would almost certainly catch her again. She needed a better plan.

A *smarter* plan.

Finally, however, she realized that anything was better than simply sitting and waiting for the guy to come back.

She started trying to open the rear door of the truck, only to find that it was firmly locked. After glancing at the house again, she hauled herself up and somehow managed to throw herself over into one of the seats. Her ankle was burning with pain, but she ignored the sensation as she wriggled around and threw herself over another seat, at which point she managed to thump down with her legs in the air. She turned, bringing her legs down, and then she backed toward the door on the driver's side and fumbled for a moment before managing to get the door open. To her relief, it had been left unlocked, so she looked at the house once more before throwing herself down to the ground.

The fall was a little further than she'd expected, and she landed sharply on her shoulder. Letting out a pained grunt, she tumbled onto her side, and then she looked at the house yet again and froze, watching for any sign that the man was on his way back.

Not even daring to breathe, she watched all the downstairs windows. Wherever he'd gone, the man was nowhere to be seen, but she knew he'd be back sooner rather than later.

Looking around, she saw a large barn nearby, and she figured that this would at least give her some cover while she tried to come up with a better plan. She began to stand; the pain in her ankle was throbbing hard now, but she managed to push through and get to her feet. Leaning back against the truck, she took a few deep breaths as she prepared for the inevitable agony of trying to shuffle toward the barn. She felt extremely weak, but then she forced herself to think of Phil and Chloe and she realized that she wasn't going to let anyone stop her seeing them again.

As soon as she tried to walk again, the pain became unbearable, but somehow she forced herself to keep going. She began to hurry, and after just a few more seconds she slammed against the wall of the barn. The wooden panels shuddered slightly, and she stayed completely still for a moment as she waited for any sign that she might have drawn attention to herself. Slowly, she turned and looked over once again at the house, and to her relief she saw that there was still no sign of anyone at any of the downstairs windows.

She waited, before starting to turn away so that she could figure out her way forward. At the last second, however, she spotted a figure out of the corner of her eye. She looked at the house again and she felt a thud of fear in her chest as soon as she saw that someone was standing at one of the house's upstairs windows, shrouded in darkness and seemingly staring down at her. She told herself that she was wrong, that the figure was simply a figment of her imagination, yet somehow it actually seemed to be getting clearer.

She could almost feel the man's gaze burning into her.

Filled with panic, she pulled away, hurrying around the side of the barn in a desperate attempt to get as far from the area as possible. Now that she knew her escape had been noticed, she guessed that she didn't have long, and already she could see a line of trees ahead. The thought of trying to run away through the forest filled her with dread, but she told herself that she was simply going to have to hope for a little luck. Limping along the length of the barn, she finally reached the far end and began to make her way toward the trees, before glancing over her shoulder to make sure that the man hadn't caught up to her yet.

And then she froze as soon as she saw the heads.

Tripping and falling, she let out a startled gasp as she stared up at a tall metal pole. The heads of several women had been placed on the pole, one on top of the other; the heads at the bottom were rotten and discolored, some of them little more than skulls, while the ones at the top were much more fresh. Even in the low moonlight, Rebecca could see the dead faces staring out in terror. One or two of them even seemed to be looking directly *at* her.

"No," she stammered, trying to convince herself that what she was seeing couldn't possibly be real, "this isn't..."

Her voice trailed off.

"Please," she added, momentarily unable to tear her gaze away from the gruesome sight, "this can't be happening."

Suddenly hearing a slamming sound, followed by footsteps, she looked back toward the truck. She spotted a figure pulling the truck's rear door open, and then she saw the man's face as he turned and looked straight at her.

Panicking, Rebecca scrambled to her feet and – despite the pain in her ankle – she raced toward the treeline. She almost got there, too, but at the last second she was tackled from behind and sent slamming to the ground as a heavy figure landed right on top of her.

"There you are," the man hissed, a little out of breath, as Rebecca screamed. "I can tell I'm going to have to keep a real good eye on you."

## CHAPTER SIX

"Let me go!" she yelled, pulling once again on the restraints that were keeping her tied to the bed. "You can't do this! You have to let me go!"

"Or what?" he asked, taking a step back.

"People'll come looking for me," she stammered, still hoping that she might somehow be able to make him change his mind. "I have a husband and a daughter."

"I know you do."

"They're going to be worried about me by now," she continued. "They're not just going to sit around and wonder when I'm coming home. Soon they'll call the police, and they'll send out a search party, and they'll find my car."

"I'd be shocked if they didn't," he muttered. "Even the cops should be able to spot a wrecked vehicle right by the side of the road. In fact, I'd be surprised if they haven't already got to that stage of the investigation."

"Then they'll come for me," she said through gritted teeth. "This is your only chance to end this madness before it begins. If you let me go, I won't tell anyone about you. I'll pretend that I got lost, or that I don't remember anything, or that someone tried to kidnap me but I managed to escape. Please, I'll do anything you want, but I'm begging you to let me go."

She waited, but he simply stared at her for a moment.

"Did you not see the heads?" he asked finally.

She opened her mouth to reply, but then she hesitated.

"You must have done," he continued, using a thumb to indicate the window. "Right out there. Big pile of heads on a spike. You can't have missed it."

"What did you do to them?" she asked, and now her voice was trembling with fear.

"Good, you *did* see them," he said with a sigh. "Now come on, think about it, do you really think those heads belong to a guy who's open to negotiation? Just think about it logically for a moment. What part of *any* of this makes you think that I can be reasoned with?"

"What do you want with me?" she sobbed, as tears filled her eyes.

"Oh, I want a lot of things," he replied, leaning against the wall. "I suppose I want the same thing I wanted from all the others, although as you might've guessed by now none of them were able to oblige. It's really been one disappointment after another for me recently and there are times when I find myself wondering whether all my work is for nothing. Honestly, some people are just -"

"What do you want?" she screamed.

"I want you to stop yelling, for one thing."

"You -"

"It's very uncouth," he added. "I get that you're upset right now, but yelling really never got anyone anywhere, did it? How would you feel if I yelled?"

"Please -"

"How do you like it?" he screamed suddenly.

She flinched and tried to pull back.

"See?" he added with a grin. "It's a complete waste of time and energy."

"You're insane," she said, and now she was starting to shake with fear.

"I've considered the possibility," he admitted. "I mean, I'd be crazy not to. They say the only people who don't wonder about that sort of thing are the ones who really *are* crazy, don't they? It's one of those arguments that kind of ends up eating its own tail if you follow it for too long. But the truth is, I'm completely sane and I simply see the world in a very clear and vivid way. I see things how they are."

"Why were you following me today?"

"I wasn't following you."

"Then why am I here?"

"Alright, you got me, I started following you after I happened to overhear you at lunch," he said with another sigh. "That's how it always works with me. I catch little snippets of conversations, and my curiosity gets piqued." He tapped the side of his head, right above the temple. "I'm almost amazed by the way some people can take really easy choices and screw them up. Instead of just doing the right thing, they complicate and over-complicate everything until it's like they no longer know the difference between right and wrong. Do you in any way get where I'm coming from with all of this?"

"I just want to go home," she whimpered.

"And *I* want you to go home," he said, stepping closer to the bed, "really I do, but only when you've come to terms with your failures. What's the point of you going home if you're just going to make all the same mistakes all over again?"

"I'll do or say anything you want," she told him. "Just name it and I'll do it right now. I won't argue, I'll just do it and then you can let me go."

"If only it could be that easy," he muttered, shaking his head. "If only."

With that, he turned and headed out of the room. As he left, he reached over and switched the light off, plunging the room into darkness.

"Wait!" Rebecca shouted, pulling once more on the restraints. "You can't just leave me here!"

"It's okay, I'll be back," he called back through to her. "Don't worry, I wouldn't just leave you there to starve. I'm not that much of a monster. But don't struggle too much, okay? You'll only be wasting your time. Believe me, I know how to make sure people can't get off that bed. No-one's ever managed to get away."

"Wait!" she shouted, but she could already hear him heading down the stairs, leaving her all alone on the bed. "Come back! You have to let me out of here!"

"Simmer down!" he shouted, before adding something else that she wasn't quite about to make out.

No matter how hard she pulled on the restraints, she was unable to break free, and she could already feel a chafing pain around both her wrists. Realizing that the restraints themselves were never going to break, she tilted her head and looked at the railings of the bed itself, and she began to wonder whether she might instead be able to snap the wood and slip herself out another way.

"Come on," she muttered under her breath, picking one railing at random and pulling with all her strength, "you have to -"

Suddenly an orange glow filled the room, and she turned to look over at the window. A light had been switched on somewhere in the yard, and when she lifted her head she was just about able to see that it was coming from the barn. She had no idea why the man would have gone out there, although after a moment she began to worry that he was preparing some kind of torture equipment. For a few seconds her mind filled with all sorts of gruesome possibilities, and then she returned her attention to the bed's wooden posts. Although she told herself that she needed to work methodically, she couldn't shake a rising sense of panic as she found that the posts were staying firmly in place.

"I'm coming home," she said, thinking of Chloe and wondering how worried Phil would be by that point. "I swear to you, I'm getting out of here and I'm coming -"

Before she could finish, an agonized scream rang out in the distance.

Shocked, Rebecca turned and looked once more at the window. As she did so, she heard another scream, and this time the awful sound continued for a few more seconds before starting to peter out. A shudder ran through Rebecca's bones as she finally understood that the man already had another victim out there in the barn, and she stayed completely still as she listened out for any further hint of what was happening. A few seconds later she realized that she could just about hear a loud sobbing sound, accompanied by what seemed to be the man shouting something.

She flinched as she heard another abrupt scream.

For the next few minutes, the cries never really stopped, and Rebecca could tell that the woman out there must be in absolute agony. She couldn't help but think of all the awful things that might be happening in the barn; she'd seen enough horror films over the years to already have mental images of saws and chains and hot pokers, and she realized that she'd most likely end up out there soon if she wasn't able to find a way to get away. Even as the cries continued, she told herself that she couldn't let them stop her, so finally she turned and started once again pulling on the bed's wooden posts.

"Please," she whispered as tears rolled down her cheeks, and as she heard yet another scream coming from outside, "let me get out of here. I have to see Chloe again."

## CHAPTER SEVEN

One hour later, still pulling on the railing but with increasing desperation, Rebecca felt a single bead of blood run down from her torn wrists.

Stopping for a moment, she looked up in the darkness and saw a line of blood dribbling down to the cuff of her shirt. She'd struggled so hard, she'd already begun to wear through the skin on both wrists, and a few seconds later she spotted a second bead. She gave the railing a brief, angry tug; at first she thought she felt it move slightly, but she quickly realized that she might simply be imagining things. She tried again, and this time she felt nothing. After trying for so long to break free, she'd achieved absolutely nothing, and she was starting to wonder whether she needed to come up with a better plan.

In the distance, another anguished cry rang out.

She looked toward the window and saw the same orange glow as before. The man was still out there in the barn, no doubt doing awful things to whoever he was holding prisoner, and Rebecca knew that at some point she'd be next. Her first instinct was to get back to work on the railing, but for a moment she stayed completely still and tried to figure out whether there might be some other option she could try. Looking around the room, she wondered whether she might see something useful, but there was only an old wardrobe that was too far away to reach. Looking back up at her bloodied wrists, she realized with a flicker of hopelessness that her original plan might in fact be her only chance to escape.

Again, she thought of Chloe. She knew that Phil would be worried by now, and that Chloe would be picking up on that mood. She imagined Phil starting to phone round, checking with all her friends to see whether she might have dropped by to see someone on her way home. He'd probably be trying not to panic, at least so far, but with each passing second he'd be getting more and more concerned. How many times would he have tried to call her? She felt tears in her eyes once more as she worried that he might think she'd simply left him, that she didn't love him anymore and she'd run away. After all, things had been tough between them for a while. What if he thought that she'd given up?

And then, just as she was about to resume pulling on the railing, she heard the faint but unmistakable sound of a floorboard creaking out on the landing.

She looked over at the open door and froze. A moment later she heard the woman screaming in the barn again, but she was certain that she'd heard somebody on the landing and she began to realize that the man might already have returned to the house. There were no lights on, but in her mind's eye she was already imagining him sneaking about out there, just out of sight, maybe enjoying the sound of her struggles.

"I know you're there," she said, her voice trembling with fear. "I heard you."

She waited, but now there was only silence.

"What are you planning to do to me?" she continued. "I heard that woman in the barn, and I'm pretty sure that sooner or later I'll be out there too. What exactly do you..."

Her voice trailed off for a moment.

"What do you do to people here?" she asked finally.

Again, she waited.

Again, she heard nothing.

"So what's the deal with the heads?" she asked him. "You didn't exactly explain it earlier. Is it some kind of ritual?"

He didn't reply, but she told herself that she might be making progress. After all, if she could understand a little more about him, wasn't it possible that she could figure out how to get him to let her go? She spent her working life trying to help people, trying to understand what was going on in their heads, and she'd never met a client yet who she couldn't understand. Sometimes that even involved being a little manipulative, and she had to admit that she was good at that part of her job.

"Your name's Ted, right?" she said, picking her words with great care. "Ted Armitage? I think that's what you told me. Why don't you tell me a little bit about yourself, Ted? I actually... I don't know whether you realized this or whether it's a coincidence, but I actually work as as therapist, so I might have some insight into..."

Once again, her voice trailed off. She wanted, at least for now, to try being very honest with him. Besides, if he'd really been trawling through her social media, he probably knew about her job already.

"There are things you can do," she told him, "so that -"

Before she could finish, she heard the woman cry out again in the distance. She flinched, but she told herself that she had to keep talking to Ted.

"There are things that might make you feel better," she continued. "Things that don't involve kidnapping people and doing awful things to them. You don't actually want to do these things, do you? I think that maybe deep down you're a -"

Suddenly she heard his voice, shouting something in the distance, and she felt a shudder pass through her chest as she realized that he wasn't on the landing at all. He was outside, all the way over at the barn, which meant...

She listened.

After just a couple of seconds, she heard another creaking floorboard, this time closer to the door.

"Who's there?" she called out, figuring that she might have a chance to escape. "Please, whoever you are, you have to get me out of here!"

She pulled on the restraints, and although she only managed to bang the bed against the wall this time, she hoped that the person out on the landing might begin to understand that she needed help.

"Hey," she continued, "you have to hurry, he could come back at any..."

Her voice trailed off, and she began to realize that the person on the landing must already know exactly what was happening. She told herself that some random stranger might have wandered into the house, but deep down she knew that the more likely option was that Ted Armitage didn't live alone. Was he married? Did he have an accomplice? Was he part of a whole family of murderous lunatics? She knew that the person out there might well have been left to keep an eye on her, which meant that escaping was going to be even more difficult.

But not impossible.

She thought of Phil and Chloe, and she told herself that she was going to find a way. She *always* found a way.

"Show yourself," she said firmly. "Come on, whoever you are, you can at least have the decency to show your face."

She watched the open doorway, hoping that the person would step into view so that at least she'd have an idea what she was dealing with. A man? A woman? An adult or a child? She needed to know what approach to take.

"Are you scared?" she continued. "Is that it, huh? Are you too much of a coward to let me see you?"

She immediately realized that she might have been too harsh.

"Or are you scared of *him*?" she asked. "Is that it? Because if it is, I can help you."

Her mind was racing as she tried to understand exactly what was happening. A second later she heard the faintest bumping sound, as if somebody had nudged a wall, and she could tell that the person was just inches from the door. At the same time, she could still hear the woman crying in the barn, followed by the sound of Ted yelling at her.

"Please," she said finally, "I'm a mother, I have a little girl out there and I need to get back to her. I don't want anything to do with whatever's going on here. I just want to go home. I need you to untie me and let me go."

She waited, and a moment later she heard another creaking sound, this time so close that she instinctively looked down at the floor. She expected to at least see a foot appear at the bottom of the doorway; instead she saw nothing, until a moment later she heard the creak again and she noticed that the board shifted slightly.

"I know you're there!" she shouted, unable to contain herself for even a moment longer. "What the hell's wrong with you? Why won't you just let me go?"

She pulled harder and harder on the restraints, and for a moment she was filled with a rush of panic. Although she could feel a burning pain in her wrists, she was unable to stop herself as she twisted violently and attempted to smash her way free using sheer force. Sobbing wildly, she could only think about Chloe as she fought to smash the entire bed apart. When her arms seized and she felt a sharp pain in her chest, however, she was forced to slump back down and take a series of deep, desperate breaths. Tears were running from her eyes, and more beads of blood were dribbling down her arms.

Out on the landing, another floorboard creaked, this time further away. Whoever had been approaching the door, they were now retreating.

"Help me!" Rebecca sobbed. "Why are you letting him do this to me? Please, you have to get me out of here!"

This time, the only answer from the landing answer was silence. Outside, the woman was still screaming and Ted Armitage was still shouting angrily. Inside, the figure on the landing seemed to have completely disappeared.

## CHAPTER EIGHT

"Good morning there," Ted said brightly as he stepped into the room, stopping in front of the window as morning light streamed through from outside. "Did you manage to get any sleep?"

"What were you doing out there?" she asked, exhausted from spending the entire night trying to break free.

"You heard, huh?" He chuckled. "Well, I suppose sound *does* travel round these parts. The truth is, your predecessor's out in the barn because she needed to be punished. She was once right where you are now, but she..."

His voice trailed off.

"Well, let's just say that she turned out to be something of a disappointment," he added, with what seemed like genuine sadness. "She had plenty of opportunities to do the right thing, and to learn, but she just couldn't grasp the chances that I laid out for her. It's a shame, really, because I thought she was smart, and I thought she was going to pay attention and improve herself. Now she's..."

Again, he hesitated.

"Is she dead?" Rebecca asked.

He furrowed his brow.

"She stopped screaming a few hours ago," she pointed out. "I thought..."

"She's not dead," he said after a moment. "I took a little nap for a couple of hours, and I imagine she needed to sleep too. She's still out there, I haven't quite finished with the..."

She waited for him to complete that sentence, but after a few seconds he stepped around to the bottom of the bed and began rooting through the pockets of his jacket.

"You're going to kill her, though, aren't you?" Rebecca asked.

"That's not really your -"

"What's her name?"

At this, he paused again.

"Tell me her name," she continued.

"Now why would you want to know a thing like that?" he asked. "I didn't realize it until just now, but you seem to have a very inquisitive streak."

"Can you even bring yourself to say it?"

"Of course I can bring myself to say it."

"Then tell me her name."

He stared at her, as if he was genuinely puzzled by the question.

"Emily," he said finally.

"What's her surname?"

"Now that's really none of your concern."

"What's her surname?" she asked again. "Come on, tell me, I'm curious."

"I'm not getting drawn into all of this," he muttered, before pulling a large knife from his pocket.

"Why not?" Rebecca asked, trying to stay focused even as the blade glinted in the light. "You already have one woman here. Why kidnap me as well?"

"You wouldn't understand."

"So try me."

"No," he replied. "At least not yet. Here's what's going to happen. I need to make sure that you're not going to do anything stupid, and I have a tried and tested method for that sort of thing. Sure, it's a little harsh, but it gets the job done and it'll allow us to... spend more time together in a manner that's conducive to a proper discussion. You *do* want my help, don't you? I'm sure you want to become a better person. Isn't that what everyone wants?"

"I don't know what you -"

Suddenly he reached down and pressed the tip of the blade against the back of her ankle.

"Stop!" she gasped. "What are you doing?"

"It's going to hurt for a little while," he told her, "but you'll get over it, and then we can really get started. After all, you don't want to spend all your time tied to this bed, do you?" He glanced at her bloodied wrists. "Of course you don't," he added. "I can see that. You want to see the whole set-up I've got out here."

"No!" she shouted. "You have to -"

Before she could finish, he started cutting through the back of her heel, and Rebecca could only scream as she felt the knife scraping against bone.

\*\*\*

"There," Ted said a short while later, as he pulled the last of the cords away and stepped back from the bed, "now you can get around a little. That's going to feel good, don't you think?"

Letting out another gasp of pain, Rebecca threw herself over the side of the bed and landed on the hard, slightly splintered wooden floor. Her bloodied feet were still up on the mattress, with thick wounds cut into the backs of both her ankles where Ted had used the knife to gouge out chunks of flesh and bone. Now, unable to move her feet at all, Rebecca could only haul her legs down onto the floor. Her wrists were free now, so she immediately began to crawl forward, dragging herself to the door.

"You'll get used to that," Ted told her, observing her efforts with calm detachment. "You're probably stronger in your arms than you think you are, especially if you've got a baby."

Reaching out, she grabbed the bottom of the banister and pulled herself closer to the top of the stairs. She wasn't entirely sure where she was going, but she knew that she had to get as far away from Ted as possible. Even as she struggled to maneuver herself over to the top step, and as she felt the floorboards moving under her weight, she was filled with a desperate need to keep going. At the same time, she knew that there was no way Ted Armitage was going to let her leave so easily, and she figured that he must be playing some sort of game.

As she reached the top of the stairs and looked down, she heard footsteps making their way closer, and she turned just in time to see that Ted was now towering over her.

"Going down?" he asked with a faint smile. "That's what they all do, at least at first. Come on, seriously... what exactly do you think is going on here right now? How do you see this little escape attempt turning out?"

Determined to ignore him, she turned and began to crawl down the stairs. She knew she should turn around instead of going headfirst, but she didn't want to risk stopping; instead, she gripped the banister as hard as she could manage and tried to support her weight as she started slithering down toward the hallway below.

"That's an interesting approach," Ted mused, leaning against the wall as he watched her. "I'm not entirely sure that it's going to work, but it's certainly one way of approaching the problem. Have you considered -"

"Go to hell!" she yelled breathlessly, barely able to get the words out, but in the process she almost lost her grip. Steadying herself, she prepared once again to crawl down the stairs.

"Get on with it, then," Ted said, kicking the side of her leg. "You're taking your sweet time, aren't you? What exactly do you think is going to happen when you get down there, anyway?"

"I'm going to kill you," she muttered under her breath.

"What was that?" he asked. "I'm sorry, I didn't catch what you said."

Once again trying to ignore him, she resumed her painfully slow attempt to inch down to the hallway. Every time her ankles bumped against one of the steps, she felt a burst of pain, but she just about managed to keep from crying out. Already, she could see that there was some kind of hatstand by the front door, and she was starting to wonder whether she might be able to use that as a weapon and attack Ted. She crawled down a little further, and then she paused to steady herself now that she was almost halfway.

"Taking a breather?" Ted asked, stepping down to join her. "That's okay, I'd probably do the same in your situation. I'm not even -"

"Leave me alone!" she snarled.

"Or what?"

"You'll see," she added.

"Will I? Do you really think so?" He used his right boot to nudge the side of her face. "Don't take this the wrong way, but you don't seem very terrifying. In fact -"

"Go to hell!" she screamed again, and this time she turned and tried to grab his leg so that she could pull him down.

In an instant, Ted slipped free and stepped out of her reach. Rebecca turned and tried to grab him again, but at that moment she lost her grip; she tried to steady herself, but she was too late and instead she tumbled down to the bottom of the stairs, landing in a heap on the floor and letting out a terrified cry as she rolled onto her front. For a moment, convinced that she must have broken something, she didn't dare to move, but then Ted stomped down behind her and grabbed her by the shoulders.

"That was desperately unnecessary, wasn't it?" he muttered, before hauling her up off the floor. "Now that you've made it all the way down here, how about we try to have a nice civilized conversation?"

## CHAPTER NINE

"I'm always very careful to make sure that nobody can escape," Ted said calmly as he sat at one end of the table in the dining room. "Imagine if someone broke free and ran off after I'd tied them to the bed? They'd never see what I want with them. They'd probably think that I was some kind of..."

He paused, as if he was searching for the right word.

"Well," he added finally, "some kind of total lunatic!"

He started chuckling, as if the idea was completely ludicrous.

Sitting at the other end of the table, weak from having lost so much blood, Rebecca simply stared at him. She was struggling to remain conscious, but she knew that she had to stay awake. If not for herself, then for Chloe.

"Take a smell of this concoction," Ted said, getting to his feet and leaning across the table, then removing the lid from a large casserole pot.

Steam immediately began to rise from inside.

"Spaghetti bolognese," he said proudly. "Not your bog-standard type, either. I make mine from scratch. There's wine in there, and bacon, and carrots, and the whole thing takes around five hours to cook. A lot of people think the key is to smother the beef in tomato sauce, but what you want is a beef sauce and that isn't something you can just whip up in half an hour. Also, I like to leave mine to sit for twenty-four hours, because that's when it starts to taste really great."

After setting the lid aside, he slid a plate toward her.

"Home-made garlic bread, too," he added with extra satisfaction, before sitting back down. He waited a moment, as if he expected her to start making small talk. "You have to eat," he said finally. "You're going to need your strength. There's nothing in this meal that's going to upset your stomach, it's good old-fashioned grub, just the way it *should* be made. If you don't believe me, you'll soon see. I'm going to eat from exactly the same pot."

Looking increasingly pale now, Rebecca continued to simply stare at him.

"I know," he said with a sigh, "you're probably not best pleased with me, and I can understand that. You're only at the very beginning of your journey here." He paused. "What you have to realize is that nothing would give me greater pleasure than to eventually drive you home and drop you off so that you can resume that happy little life with your husband and daughter. I mean it, sincerely and from the bottom of my heart. I'm here to change your world. One day, you'll be on your knees thanking me."

Her eyes narrowed a little as she reached for the knife that had been left next to her plate.

"I mean it," he added. "One day, you'll -"

Suddenly Rebecca let out a cry of anger as she threw the knife at him. He ducked out of the way, but there'd been no need; the knife missed by a couple of feet, instead clattering into the wall and then dropping to the floor. She knew that, even if it had hit, it had been too blunt to really cause any damage.

"Well, that's okay," Ted said, clearly nonplussed. "That's a very honest reaction to the situation, although I hope you realize that there was no way it could possibly have -"

"Help me!" she screamed suddenly, gripping the sides of the table and looking up toward the ceiling. "You have to call the police!"

She waited, but all she heard – after a moment – was the sound of Ted laughing.

"We're miles from anywhere," he explained. "Who exactly do you think is going to hear you?"

"He's a maniac!" she shouted, still hoping that the other person in the house might come to their senses. "You can't let him keep doing this to people!"

"Are you religious?" he asked, with a hint of doubt in his voice. "Just who are you begging for help?"

She turned to him.

Getting to his feet, he stepped over to her and grabbed her plate, and then he began to dish up some food.

"I don't mean to hurt your feelings," he continued, "but I don't think any deity is going to help you right now. Nobody's watching over you, ready to step in and save you with some kind of miracle. Is that enough food or would you like more?"

He held the plate out to her.

"A little more, perhaps," he added, as he grabbed the ladle again. "There's no need to -"

Letting out a sudden cry of rage, Rebecca grabbed the casserole pot and threw it off the table, sending its contents spilling out across the floor.

Ted stared at her, as if he couldn't quite believe what he'd just witnessed, and then he slowly stepped around behind her and made his way over to the pot.

"Help me!" Rebecca screamed, once again looking at the ceiling. "Why won't you -"

Suddenly Ted slammed his elbow into her face, hitting her hard in the mouth and knocking her head to once side. Immediately tasting blood, Rebecca felt that one of her teeth was loose, and she began to cough and splutter as Ted grabbed the pot and set it back on the table.

"Well that's a new one," he said, clearly irritated. "I don't think anyone's ever been quite so ungrateful before. I can see that we're starting at a lower baseline with you than I'd anticipated, but that's all good. I've never shied away from a challenge."

"And what are you and your little friend going to do about it?" she sneered.

"I'm going to educate you in what's right and what's wrong," he replied, as he stepped over the mess of food on the floor. "By the way, I don't know what you're talking about, but I work alone. Always have, always will."

"You might want to remind your buddy upstairs about that."

He turned to her.

"Is he just as sick as you?" she asked, trying to hide the fact that she was shaking with fear. "I think I'm starting to understand now. You go out and get fresh victims, and you do all the torturing and he... I guess he watches, does he? Is that it? Does he prefer to watch from the shadows like some kind of pervert?"

"I have absolutely no idea what you're talking about," he told her.

"I heard him last night," she sneered. "Or her. I guess I shouldn't be sexist about this, it could just as easily by a woman. Don't think for one second that you can fool me. You're some kind of team, right? Do you get off on kidnapping women and torturing them to death?"

He hesitated, before making his way around the table and heading toward the kitchen.

"You must have hit your head," he said with a sigh. "You're not making a lick of sense."

She waited until he came back, and then she watched as he crouched down and started to scoop the spilled food into a bag.

"I didn't even see his face," she told him. "Or *her* face. Whatever. I heard them, though. Out there on the landing, loitering near the door, not daring to actually come into the room." She looked up at the ceiling again. "Hey!" she shouted. "Why are you still lurking up there? Even a coward should be able to show their face by now!"

She waited, but she heard nothing in reply.

Turning to Ted, she saw that he'd stopped cleaning up the mess and was simply staring at her.

"What's wrong?" she asked. "Aren't you going to go and fetch him?"

"This might come as a shock to you," he replied, "but I really *do* work alone. I can't say that any more clearly. Do you actually think that I come all the way out here into the middle of nowhere, only to turn around and invite some friend along for the ride?"

"I heard footsteps last night," she said firmly. "You might as well admit it."

"You *imagined* footsteps," he told her.

"You're pathetic!" she spat back at him.

"Really? I'm not the one who's trying to cause some kind of distraction by pretending to have seen or heard things." He got back to work, using the ladle to scoop as much of the food into the bag as possible. "I must admit, no-one's ever tried this particular approach before, so I suppose I should give you points for imagination. Then again, you lose points for making such a mess, so it all works out even. This was supposed to be such a nice lunch."

"I'm going to get out of here," she told him.

"I sincerely hope so."

"And I'm going to make sure you rot in jail. Both of you."

"For what? For trying to help you become a better person?"

"For taking me away from my daughter," she said firmly. "I don't know how many other women you've brought here, but I'm telling you right now that you've made a very serious mistake. You've kidnapped a woman who'll stop at nothing to get home. Do you understand me? Even if I have to kill you with my bare hands, I'm going to get out of here and I'm going to make sure that you never hurt anyone else ever again. And I'm going to see my daughter again!"

She waited, but for a few seconds he simply stared at her. And then, slowly, he began to laugh.

## CHAPTER TEN

The wheelchair bumped against a ridge of mud in the yard. Rebecca shuddered slightly, and she felt a tightening knot of dread in her chest as she saw that Ted was wheeling her closer and closer to the barn.

"Stop," she said suddenly.

"Why?" he asked, ignoring her command.

"I don't want to go in there."

"Well, I never particularly thought that you did."

"I want you to stop!" she shouted, and now she was starting to fill with panic. "Turn this thing around!"

"You really don't seem to understand the situation you're in," he replied. "I tried to feed you, and you turned that down. Now it's time to let you see exactly what's going on here. You need to understand that I'm really not trying to hide anything from you. Why would I? I want you to see the big picture here so that you realize you only have one option."

Stopping the wheelchair, he stepped around her and began to slide open a metal door on the side of the bar, revealing the darkness of the interior.

"And in order for you to truly comprehend the gravity of the situation," he added, turning to her again, "it's absolutely essential that you meet your predecessor."

\*\*\*

"Meet Emily," he said a couple of minutes later, as he wheeled Rebecca toward the far end of the barn. "Surname unimportant. What's important is that at one point she was right where you are now."

In the gloom, Rebecca was momentarily unable to make much out at all, but after a moment she realized she could see a naked woman hanging from chains. She immediately gripped the hand-rests of the wheelchair, but with each passing second she was rolled closer and closer and she began to see thick cuts and marks all over the woman's body. The stench in the barn, meanwhile, was overpowering, and she felt as if she might gag at any moment.

Just when she was starting to assume that the woman must be dead, however, she saw her head twitching slightly.

"Emily!" Ted called out. "Hey, Emily! You remember being in Rebecca's position, don't you? I thought you might like to offer her a little advice!"

He waited, and then he patted Rebecca on the shoulder.

"That was worth a try," he said with a sigh. "She's conscious, but I'm not sure that she's in much of a talkative mood. If you ask me, she's probably thinking about all the mistakes she's made while she's been here with me. And she's made a *lot* of mistakes, believe you me."

Too horrified to respond, Rebecca could only stare at the bloodied, emaciated woman who hung like a broken doll from rusted metal chains. Even in the gloom of the barn, she could see burns and cuts, and dark stains running down the woman's legs, and after a few seconds she realized that the faint humming sound in the air – a sound she'd noticed immediately but which she hadn't really registered properly – was being caused by the flies buzzing in the air and crawling on the woman's flesh.

"Emily had a little problem with professional honesty," Ted explained as he stepped around from behind the wheelchair and made his way toward a table in the corner. "She basically cheated her way up the ranks of the company she worked at, lying for things and sleeping around and doing whatever it took to get promoted. She had absolutely no shame at all."

He stopped and looked down at various tools on the table.

"Now, I have no problem with ambition," he added as he began to examine one particular knife. "I *respect* ambition. But Emily here was getting herself into positions for which she was wholly unsuited. And in the process, she was damaging her company's performance. I happened to be in a little cafe in Wakefield when I overheard her bragging about all of this to a friend, and I was horrified. She was dragging an entire company down, just because she thought she deserved to get fast-tracked up the corporate ladder."

He turned to Rebecca.

"I brought her here and tried to make her see the error of her ways, but I just couldn't get through to her."

Barely even hearing a word he'd just said, Rebecca continued to look at all the different wounds on the woman's body. She could tell that Emily must have been in the chains for some time, and after a moment she saw that the skin around Emily's wrists was worn almost to the bone. Looking down at her own wrists, she saw the marks left by her struggles to get free from the bed and she began to wonder just how many women before her had ended up at Ted Armitage's farm.

"Emily's problem now," Ted said as he wandered back over to the semi-conscious woman, "is that *you're* here."

"Let her go," Rebecca stammered, even though she knew he was never going to listen to her. "Please..."

"And now that you're here," he continued, holding the knife up and pressing the tip against the center of Emily's bare chest, "Emily suddenly becomes yesterday's news. I have a more exciting project." He leaned closer to Emily. "I warned you," he said eagerly. "I told you, you only have until the next lovely lady comes along and catches my attention. You've been on the other side of this situation, you've been where the lovely Rebecca is sitting right now, and you just didn't learn."

As the knife's tip ran along her flesh, Emily stirred. Lifting her head, she seemed to struggle to open her eyes for a few seconds; when she finally managed, she looked directly at Rebecca and began to try to say something.

"You need to speak up," Ted said firmly. "How can you expect Rebecca to understand what you're trying to tell her when you don't even raise your voice? Did I teach you nothing about the importance of proper elocution?"

Again Emily tried to speak, but all that emerged from her lips was a series of faint, guttural clicking sounds.

"You have to let her go," Rebecca said, watching as Ted continued to trace lines across the woman's chest with the tip of his knife. "If you get her to a hospital, she can still live."

"Oh, I know that," Ted replied, "but what would be the point? She hasn't learned. She feels sorry for herself, but deep down I know that she hasn't reached that moment of understanding. I brought her here for an epiphany and she failed."

He stopped the knife once the blade was pressing against Emily's belly.

"Her only value now is as an example," he added. "Look at her, Rebecca. This is what'll happen to you if you don't pay attention to what I'm going to teach you. If you fail, then in a week's time, or a month, or three months or whatever, you'll be hanging here like poor Emily, and *you'll* be just an example for whoever comes next. I'm begging you, just as I once begged Emily, don't make the same mistake that so many others have made."

"Please," Rebecca said, "just -"

Before she could finish, Ted plunged the knife deep into Emily's belly and immediately began to cut through the flesh. Instead of screaming, Emily could only manage a series of convulsions as blood began to pour from the wound, and after a few seconds Rebecca saw glistening intestines starting to tumble out.

Immediately squeezing her eyes tight shut and looking down, Rebecca tried to ignore what was happening in front of her. She could hear Emily's spluttering gasps, along with the sound of skin tearing open, and a moment later she also heard the squelching thud of something landing on the ground. In her mind's eye, she was already imagining the woman's guts spilling out, but she couldn't bring herself to look; instead, she tried to ignore the sound of Emily's dying groans, and the occasional shuffling footstep as Ted moved around the dying woman to get a better angle. Worst of all, however, was the sound of blood splattering against the concrete floor.

"You don't want to watch?" Ted asked merrily. "Well, that's fine. The sounds are probably just as bad. I'm sure you're still getting the message loud and clear."

With her eyes still shut, Rebecca heard the chains starting to rattle, and a few seconds later she heard the knife cutting through bone. A couple more thuds rang out as part of Emily's body fell to the floor, followed by a louder thud that she assumed must be the dead woman's torso. She felt something bump against her right foot, and she let out a cry of shock as she immediately tried to pull away. Metal clanged against metal, and now Ted was muttering something to himself under his breath as if he was struggling a little with some part of the grisly proceedings. Although she tried to push the awful noises out of her mind, Rebecca could still hear a scraping sound and she could tell that Ted was cutting through bone.

"Stop!" she screamed finally, squeezing her eyes tight until they began to hurt. "Leave her alone!"

## CHAPTER ELEVEN

The wheelchair bumped over another rough patch of dried mud.

Still keeping her eyes clamped tight shut, Rebecca felt a cool breeze blowing against her face. She hadn't dared to look at anything since Ted had started killing the woman in the barn, but he'd gleefully informed her of all the latest developments. Now she could tell that they were back outside again, and a moment later she felt the chair being maneuvered around a corner before finally coming to a halt.

"Despite everything I said just now," Ted muttered, "Emily did show *some* signs of progress. And she and I spent enough time together for me to consider her worthy of a place here at my monument."

He paused for a moment.

"Don't you want to see?" he continued.

Rebecca hesitated, before very slowly starting to open her eyes. As soon as she saw the heads on the metal pole, however, she looked down and closed her eyes again.

"This is a very important part of the farm for me," Ted explained. "You could almost call it the *most* important."

Rebecca waited, and then something was dropped onto her lap. Startled, she instinctively put her hands out to catch the object, but she was startled to feel what seemed to be hair. Her hands moved over the front of the object, and then she screamed as she felt a forehead and a nose on what was clearly a severed head. As she pushed the head away and let it fall to the ground, the fingers of her right hand briefly pressed against the bloodied meat of the neck area.

"Now that's not very polite," Ted said. "I only wanted you to hold her for a few seconds. Can't you be a little more respectful?"

She heard him picking the head up.

"You've seen my little tribute, I believe," he continued. "Only the best ones get to go on here, the ones whose heads deserve to have a place in the sun. I like to come here occasionally and look at them all, and I like to think of how close I've come to helping some of them. It's sort of a teachable moment for me, really. Each one of these heads represents someone who so nearly understood what I was trying to make them understand. I remember their names, I remember what happened and how I failed them, and how they failed me, and I feel hope for the future. Hope that soon I'll succeed. Maybe even with you."

Shaking with fear, Rebecca tried to turn away.

"Why don't you open your eyes and see the magnificence?" Ted asked.

She turned away even further.

"Okay, fine," he said with a sigh, and she heard him stepping past her. "I think you're being a little rude to your predecessors, but I suppose it's all part of the learning process. Let me just put Emily in place at the top of the column, where she belongs."

Although she tried to focus on something else, Rebecca soon heard a faint squelching sound, and she couldn't help but imagine the top of the post starting to dig into the woman's head. Sure enough, after a few seconds she heard the crack of breaking bone, and Ted was once again muttering under his breath. Moments later, bone cracked again, accompanied by an ear-piercing scraping sound, and then she heard footsteps making their way closer.

"There," Ted said, sounding extremely proud. "Do you still not want to take a look, Rebecca? This could be a really good educational moment for you."

Defiantly keeping her eyes shut and her face turned away, Rebecca focused instead on trying to make sure that she didn't vomit. She could feel nausea churning in her belly, but she told herself that she wasn't going to give Ted the satisfaction of letting her sense of horror show.

"It's so sad that she's ended up here," Ted said after a moment, before putting a hand on Rebecca's shoulder. "I really, truly hope that you're smart enough to avoid the same fate."

***

"Have you ever owned a drone?" Ted asked a short while later, as he took the machine from the back of his truck and set it on the grass near the house. "They're great. I've had a few now, I just can't help upgrading every time a new one hits the market."

Having finally dared to open her eyes now that she was away from the barn, Rebecca watched as he crouched down and began to examine the drone.

"I like to tinker with them," he added. "I bet you're impressed that this one could keep up with your car, even for just a few minutes." He turned the drone around. "Doesn't look like there's any real damage from the crash. Just a few cracks and dents on the casing, but that sort of thing doesn't really bother me. As long as it'll still fly, that's what matters."

He looked up at her with a broad grin.

"If you make it home," he continued, "you really should get one to play with. Or one might make a good gift for your husband. Does he have many hobbies?"

"What do you want with me?" she asked, her voice trembling with fear.

"You'll see soon enough," he replied. "I'm going to teach you to be a better person, Rebecca. I've seen all your flaws, and I want to help you eradicate them so that you're fit to go home and resume your life. Were you really happy living your little life with your husband and daughter?"

"I just want to go home," she told him.

"And you will, if you follow my course of tuition out here."

Getting to his feet, he set the drone back in the truck.

"We'll start this afternoon," he explained, "and I've got a really good feeling about you, Rebecca. I think you're going to respond very well to what I have to offer, and I genuinely believe that you have a chance of getting out of here. If I didn't think that, then I wouldn't be wasting my time with you. After all, my time is very valuable."

As Ted continued to talk, Rebecca looked over her shoulder and watched the farmhouse for a moment. After a few seconds, feeling a tingling sensation on the back of her neck, she looked up at the building's upper windows and she was surprised to see the faintest hint of a silhouetted figure standing at the window at the far end, seemingly staring back down at her. She couldn't make out any details of the figure, but it was clear enough for her to be certain that it was no figment of her imagination.

"What you have to understand," Ted said, as she turned back to him, and as he slammed the door shut on the back of the truck, "is that I'm in charge here. I'm in full control. And if you pay attention and you listen to me, you have every chance of walking out of this place."

Staring at him, she began to wonder whether she might have misunderstood what had happened to her during the night.

"When did you know I was gone?" she asked cautiously.

"Come again?"

"Last night," she continued cautiously, "after you brought me here, you went into the house."

"And?"

"And while you were in there, I got out of the truck and tried to escape."

"Honestly," he said, shaking his head, "you don't need to apologize. Anyone would have done the same thing in your situation."

"It's not that," she replied. "I just mean... When did you realize that I'd managed to get away from the truck?"

"I'm not sure that I follow."

She thought back to the moment in the night when she'd seen a figure staring out at her from the house's dark windows. At the time, she'd assumed that the figure had been Ted, but now she wasn't so sure.

"When did you realize?" she asked again.

"When do you *think* I realized?" he replied with a faint smile ."When I opened the truck up, you dumbass."

"So you didn't see me from the house? You didn't look out a window and see me climbing out?"

"No, I didn't," he said, and now he seemed a little irritated by her line of questioning. "What does that matter? I still managed to catch you again. I hope you realize that escape is completely impossible. No-one has ever managed to get away from me. Not even one person."

She hesitated, before turning and looking back up at the house. This time, the figure was gone from the window, but she was absolutely sure that it *had* been there, and that there was someone else at the farm aside from Ted and herself. She thought back to the sound of a person creeping about in the night, and she realized that whoever was in the house, they seemed determined to hide away and keep their presence hidden.

She turned back to Ted.

"And you live alone, right?" she asked.

"Why are you asking all these stupid questions?" he said with another sigh. "Do you think a guy like me really needs a roommate?"

She stared at him.

"No," she said finally, as she began to realize that he genuinely had no idea that there was something else in the house. "No, I don't think you do."

## CHAPTER TWELVE

"So this is another one I don't get," Ted said a couple of hours later, as they sat at opposite ends of a table in the front room of the farmhouse.

He turned the laptop around, showing Rebecca one of her own social media posts from a few weeks earlier. This particular post was a shot of a salad she'd eaten while out at lunch with a few colleagues.

"What's not to get?" she asked cautiously.

"It's your food," he continued. "That's all it is. It's literally just a load of salad leaves and a few other things, and I suppose some dressing and..."

His voice trailed off, and he seemed genuinely confused for a moment.

"It's just something you eat," he added finally. "Why would you post a photo of it? Why would you think that people care? If I want to see some salad, it's not going to take me very long to find all the photos I could ever want. Why would a grown woman, a wife and a mother, think that anyone has any interest in what you're having for lunch?"

She hesitated, trying to work out exactly how to answer. She hadn't been sure what to expect when Ted had told her that they were going to start an education session, but she certainly hadn't expected him to start going through her posts one by one, pointing out any flaws that he found and generally offering her tips on how he thought she should improve herself. Meanwhile she was trying to play along, hoping to unpick his motivation and try to figure out some what to get inside his head and influence whatever was going to happen next.

So far, he seemed to be completely crazy, but she knew there had to be more to him. There had to be some kind of trigger that made him who he was.

"I can't really argue with you," she told him. "You're right, it's just a bowl of salad, why would anyone who follows me on there want to see it?"

"That's what I don't understand," he replied, "and yet you have a couple of hundred people who presumably really thought that they might care about this stuff. And they don't seem to unfollow you, so it's not like they're annoyed by these posts. They just scroll on past. Some of them even leave comments."

"It must be a reflection of -"

"Listen to this," he continued, clearly warming to his theme. "Someone's written a comment about how great your salad looks. Who does that? Who takes time out of their day to type that out?"

"Is this what's bugging you?" she asked. "Posts about food?"

"It's more the whole culture around it," he replied, "and what that does to people." He looked across at her. "I think this sort of thing is at the root of all the problems you have in your life, Rebecca. You spend so much time posting pictures of inane things, you forget to take care of what really matters."

She swallowed hard.

"You might have a point," she said.

"No kidding."

"But it's not all like the salad picture," she added. "I try to post a few things that are relevant, too."

"Really?"

He clicked a couple of buttons, and the next picture in her feed showed several empty wine glasses in a restaurant.

"That was a night out for a friend's birthday," she said before he had a chance to make a comment. "It was her fortieth."

"Looks like you had a fun time. I guess you left your husband at home looking after the baby, huh?"

"It was one night out," she said through gritted teeth. "I was home by eleven. Believe me, my hedonistic days are way in the past."

"And this next one," he muttered, clicking through to yet another photo of a salad, "wow, you really do seem to have a thing about salads. Is that your way of showing people that you live a nice healthy lifestyle? Are you trying to show them that you don't rush down to the nearest fast food place and eat some burger that's full of chemicals?"

"It's just a salad," she replied, resisting the urge to scream.

"Ten comments and fifteen shares, though," he said, raising an amused eyebrow. "That seems like quite an extreme response to a salad."

"So's kidnapping someone."

He turned to her.

"Fair point," he added, "but if -"

Before he could finish, they both heard a low but clear creaking sound coming from the room directly above. They looked up, and after a moment Rebecca turned to Ted again.

"This is an old house," he told her, as he returned his attention to the laptop. He seemed completely untroubled by the noise. "You should hear what it's like in a storm."

"What do you do here when you're all alone?" she asked.

"What do you mean?"

Watching him, she realized that he truly seemed to have no idea that there was anyone else in the house. She hadn't even begun to figure out exactly what was happening, but as she looked at Ted's eyes and watched him scrolling through more posts on his laptop, she felt sure that he was genuinely oblivious to the mysterious third person. Sure enough, just a couple of seconds later she heard another creaking sound from upstairs and she saw that this time Ted didn't react at all.

"So do you have any family?" she asked.

"I don't see that my family, or lack thereof, is any of your business."

"Humor me," she added. "Do you live here all the time?"

"I really -"

"Because I get the feeling that maybe you don't," she said, interrupting him yet again before looking around the room. "I don't know why, exactly, but this place doesn't strike me as someone's permanent residence. I think maybe you come out here from time to time, maybe when you have an itch to scratch, and then you have some kind of normal life – well, as normal as it can be – that you return to."

She waited for him to answer. Although he was still pretending to be focused on the laptop, she could tell that he was hearing every word that left her lips. He seemed determined, however, to pretend that nothing she asked was important.

"I'm right," she added, "aren't I?"

"I'm sorry," he said, clearly lying, "I didn't catch any of that."

He looked at her again.

"This isn't about me," he told her firmly. "The fact that you're trying to distract me is a clear sign that you're not comfortable with the points that I'm raising."

"Untie me," she replied, pulling gently on the restraints that held her arms to the wheelchair, "and I'll show you just how comfortable I am."

"Resistance is to be expected," he continued, "and it's not necessarily a bad sign at this early stage, but you should be aware that we have a lot of work to get done before you're ready to go home."

"Do you think that somehow you're going to turn me into this... perfect person?"

"We should all strive for perfection."

"Do *you*?"

"I have my approaches to things," he told her. "Again, though, you're trying to distract me, and that's not going to work, not in the long run."

"Nobody can be perfect."

"You can be, Rebecca," he said. "I believe in you. I believed in Emily and the others too, and it's really not my fault that they fell short. One day, though, I'm going to help someone reach perfection, and I truly believe that person can be you."

He tapped at the laptop again, this time bringing up a photo of Chloe smiling as she sat on a picnic blanket in a field.

"Now this is quite wholesome and fun," he suggested, "although again, Rebecca, I've got to question your thought processes. Do you think your little girl would want to have all these pictures of herself online? They can never be entirely deleted, you know. And are you really doing it for her, or is this just another way for you to show off?"

"Leave my daughter out of it," she replied, gripping the sides of the wheelchair.

"Your daughter shouldn't be a prop," he muttered, shaking his head. "There's not much humility in these photos, is there? You're showing off, and that reflects very badly on your character."

"Don't look at her!" she snapped angrily. "Don't even talk about her! She's nothing to do with you!"

"But she has a lot to do with you," he pointed out, as he slid the laptop a little closer to her. "You get a lot of your sense of self-satisfaction from her, don't you? Your sense of superiority. And that, I believe, is central to the personality problems that you've been demonstrating. We're going to have to dig into those problems and bring about some real changes in the way your mind works, Rebecca." He looked at the picture of Chloe again. "And your daughter, I'd wager, is the best place to start."

## CHAPTER THIRTEEN

"You like sharing so much," Ted said later, as he set an open diary and a pen on Rebecca's lap. "Here you go. From now on, for as long as you're here with me, I want you to jot down all your thoughts."

Looking up at him, she realized that he was serious.

"Obviously I'll be reading them at regular intervals," he continued, "but I need to have an idea of how your mind works. More importantly, of how it's changing during the course of your stay here. I expect at least one entry per day, ideally three or more, and I'll be watching for signs that I'm finally starting to get through to you. Think of it as being like a social media page. The only difference is that you're writing for an audience of one."

"Do you seriously think that I'm going to do this?" she asked.

"Oh, I know that you are," he replied. "Even if it takes you a while to realize that this is what's best for you. You're clearly a woman of reasonable intelligence, you might even be above average, so I have no doubt that sooner or later you're going to start seeing things from my point of view."

"And you really think that eventually, at some point, I'll become this perfect person who you'll be happy to release back into society? Do you see me as some kind of animal that needs to be retrained?"

"I know you have it in you," he told her, leaning closer. "I can see it now. You'll be clutching my hands, sobbing with gratitude, telling me how much I've changed your life for the better. I know that might seem unlikely right now, but it's almost like... destiny." He reached down and took hold of her left hand. She tried to pull it away, but he gripped her too tight. "If you could see it happening already, then the journey wouldn't need to be made in the first place," he added. "This is what makes it all worthwhile."

"You want a diary?" she asked, feeling her blood starting to boil but determined to not give him the response that he wanted. "I'll give you a diary."

Grabbing the book, she quickly wrote two words and then turned it around so that he could see.

"Fuck you," he read from the page. He stared at the scribble for a moment, before looking her in the eye. "Fuck you? Really? Is that your level of sophistication right here in this particular moment?"

"You wanted to know what I'm thinking," she sneered.

"And I should have known that you'd resort to the kind of potty-mouth cursing that I really don't care for," he muttered. "Do you use that kind of language around your daughter?"

"I save it for psychopaths," she told him.

"Oh, right, okay," he said, nodding as if he understood. "That's a good point, and you've made it very well. I really appreciate your nuanced approach to this situation."

"Get over yourself," she told him. "I don't believe for one second that I'm the first person who's ever told you to go fuck -"

Suddenly he grabbed her by the throat and began to squeeze, using both hands to cut off her air supply. She reached up and tried to push him away, but she immediately found that his grip was far too strong.

"Should I take this approach instead?" he asked as she desperately gasped for breath. "Should I be a blunt instrument? Would you prefer it if I just went around killing people who displease me? Because I can do that, if you want. I can be just another in a long line of monsters who drag people off the roads and have their way with them."

Somehow, he managed to squeeze her throat even tighter.

"I can do that!" he shouted, and now he seemed to be losing control. "Anyone can do *that*! Anyone can become some kind of common or garden murderer who piles up the bodies! That's the easy part! The hard part is doing it for a good reason!"

"Please..." she gasped, as she felt herself starting to lose consciousness.

He squeezed even tighter for a moment, before finally letting go and taking a step back. As Rebecca desperately tried to get her breath back, Ted looked down at his hands and flexed his fingers a few times.

"You should probably," he said, also a little breathless now, "count your lucky stars that you were picked up by someone who has a modicum of restraint." He turned to her again. "We're at the start of a very long process. I can only hope that by the end of it all, you don't end up like poor Emily."

\*\*\*

"You're going to sleep in here tonight," Ted said as he wheeled Rebecca into one of the other rooms and parked her next to a desk. "There's no point lugging you up to the room and then back down in the morning, especially not when you've been so badly behaved. If you don't like it, you'll just have to lump it."

"You like reading," she said, looking around at the shelves that lined the walls.

"No, I hate reading," he replied. "I hate books, too. But I love knowledge, and learning things, and I suppose books are necessary for that."

He stepped around her.

"Don't try to be smart," he continued, "and don't try to psychoanalyze me, because it won't work. I'm impervious to that sort of thing."

"No-one's impervious to analysis," she told him. "Everyone can be studied."

"Spoken with true smug over-confidence." He checked his watch. "It's getting late and I have to do some work out in the barn. Seeing as how you were so rude when I tried to feed you last time, I don't see why I should bother tonight. You'll just have to be hungry until morning, and then maybe you'll be a little more grateful."

"I need the bathroom," she told him.

"Tough."

"But if -"

"You *earn* privileges in my home," he continued. "That's another thing you're going to have to learn. I'm not a monster, but -"

Before he could finish, a floorboard creaked in one of the rooms upstairs.

"I have to fix that some time," he said with a sigh, and now he sounded utterly exhausted. "I don't know if you've noticed, but this whole house is falling apart. One day a strong wind's going to come along and blow it away entirely."

With that, he turned and walked to the door. His shoulders were sloped now, as if the weight of the day's events had begun to drag him down.

"Can I have a drink?" Rebecca asked.

"No."

"Please."

He stopped in the doorway.

"I can get through the night without food," she continued, "but my mouth's so dry and I'm starting to get a headache, I think I might be dehydrated."

"You can go a little longer."

"I can't even think straight," she told him. "You want me to learn from you, right? I assume you want me to think things through tonight. How can I do that if all I can think about is the fact that I need water?"

She waited, and for a moment she felt as if she might actually have made him understand.

"Write it in your diary," he said finally.

"I -"

"Write down exactly how you feel," he continued. "Really try to put the suffering into words, so that when you read it back one day, you won't make the same mistake again. And there's one other thing that you need to remember..."

He paused, and then he turned to her fully.

"You're in my world now," he added. "My home. My land. My universe. I control everything here. Nothing's left to chance, nothing escapes me, nothing works against me or against my ambitions. This little patch of dirt belongs to me, and it's the one place on this miserable planet where I rule without interference. If you think you can change that – if you think you can change anything here – then you're going to learn a very hard lesson, and you're going to learn it fast. You'd do much better to accept the situation you're in, and adapt."

He stepped toward her and pressed a fingertip against her chest.

"Because I'm the top dog here," he said firmly, "and what I say, goes."

He stared at her for a moment, as if trying to intimidate her with the force of his glare, and then he turned and walked out of the room. As he left, he switched off the light, and then he did the same to the light in the hallway.

Sitting alone in the gloom, still tied to the wheelchair, Rebecca took a deep breath before looking up at the ceiling. She could hear Ted clattering about in one of the other rooms. A few seconds later she also heard a very faint, almost imperceptible creaking sound coming from the room above, as if an unseen foot had gently pressed against one of the floorboards.

## CHAPTER FOURTEEN

"Becky, it's okay," Phil said, gently tapping the side of her face to stir her from sleep. "Becky, can you hear me? It's all over now. You're going to be fine."

As her eyes flickered open, Rebecca tried to work out exactly what was happening. She could see her husband right in front of her, leaning close, but for a few seconds she didn't dare to believe that he was really in the room. And then, as she began to smell the cologne that she remembered buying him for Christmas, she realized that somehow – impossibly, miraculously – he'd come for her and he was going to take her home.

"That's better," he said, tilting his head slightly. "You've been so strong and so brave, but we've found you. Now you just have to do one thing."

"Phil?" she whispered, before leaning toward him, only to find that she was still tied to the wheelchair. "What -"

"Don't strain yourself," he continued, before taking a step back. "You're so nearly free. You just have to make it through one last part."

Before she could reply, he stepped aside and she saw Ted Armitage standing just a few meters away. In that moment, she realized that her arms were actually raised above her head, and she looked up to see that they were attached to thick chains that ran all the way up to the roof of the barn. Filled with panic, she looked down and found that she was hanging naked just above the ground, and then she turned to see Ted stepping forward with a large knife in his right hand.

"This is going to be nice and easy," Ted told her with a grin, as he pressed the blade against her belly. "All you have to do is listen to everything I tell you."

She opened her mouth to scream, but in that moment he plunged the knife deep into her body, until the tip pushed out the other side.

Startled, she jolted back, and she suddenly found that she was still in the wheelchair, in the dark office room at Ted's house. Realizing that the encounter with Phil in the barn had been just a dream, and that she must have nodded off for a few seconds, she took a deep breath and tried to calm her racing mind. The dream had seemed so real, she'd felt the blade slicing against her spine, and she could still smell Phil's cologne in the air. As tears filled her eyes, however, she realized that it had all been in her head. Already, the smell of cologne was fading away.

Closing her eyes again, she thought of her husband and daughter, and she knew deep down that they must be so worried.

"Please," she said out loud, "I just want -"

Suddenly she heard a bumping sound. Opening her eyes again, she looked over at the open doorway and saw the moonlit hall. A fraction of a second later she heard another bump, accompanied by a creaking groan, and she realized that somebody was making their way down the stairs. Her first thought was that Ted, who'd seemingly gone to bed several hours earlier, was up again, but then she began to wonder why he'd be sneaking about the house in the middle of the night. She listened, and she heard a faint shuffling sound, as if somebody was briefly brushing against a wall.

The footsteps – and she was increasingly sure that they *were* footsteps – began to move away, heading toward the kitchen.

"Hey!" Rebecca whispered, not daring to raise her voice too much in case Ted heard. "Wait! Come back!"

The footsteps stopped.

"I'm in here," she continued. "I don't know who you are, but please, I need your help. You have to get me out of this place."

She waited.

Again, she heard nothing.

"I'm begging you," she went on. "I have a daughter, she's only a year old and I have to get back to her. You can understand that, can't you?"

Silence.

A moment later, however, she heard the faintest shuffling sound somewhere near the doorway, and she saw what appeared to be a shadow falling across the floor.

"My name's Rebecca," she added. "You can call me Becky. If you -"

Before she could finish, she realized that someone was starting to peer around the edge of the door-frame. She held her breath and waited, and after a few more seconds she was just about able to make out the side of a face and a single eye staring straight at her.

"He doesn't know you're here, does he?" she asked. "I can't even begin to understand how that works, but somehow you're hiding from him. Is there some secret part of the house that he doesn't know about? Are you living in the walls or..."

Her voice trailed off as she began to realize just how absurd the entire situation seemed. She knew there was no way that somebody else could be sharing the house with Ted Armitage, and doing so without him even noticing, yet that appeared to be exactly what was happening. Whoever the person was, she — and she did appear to be female, although Rebecca couldn't tell for sure — was clearly extremely cautious, perhaps even filled with fear.

Reaching down, Rebecca began to wheel the chair forward, only for the figure to immediately pull away.

"No, wait!" she hissed, stopping the chair again. "I won't come toward you, I promise!"

She waited, and a moment later the face appeared again. Able to see a little more of the woman's features now, Rebecca could tell that she was terribly thin and emaciated, and covered in bruises and patches of discolored skin. She looked worse than a corpse, but at the same time Rebecca wasn't about to start believing that she was face-to-face with an actual ghost.

"We can help each other," she explained, struggling to keep her voice down. "Why don't you start by telling me your name? I've told you mine, I'm Rebecca. Please, call me Becky. What can I call you?"

As she waited again, she was almost able to feel the fear emanating from the woman. Although she knew she was most likely imagining that sensation, she still picked up on some kind of charge in the air, and for a few seconds she began to reconsider her early assumption. Given that many women had obviously died at the farm, wasn't it possible that the spirits of some of them might be lingering? Although she'd never believed in ghosts, Rebecca had to admit that if such things *did* exist, they were most likely to manifest at a place where so many people had been tortured and murdered.

"Can you come into the room a little more?" she asked. "At least let me see you. I'm on your side, I promise. We have a much better chance of getting out of here if we work together."

She desperately wanted to wheel herself closer to the woman, but at the same time she was terrified of scaring her away.

"Okay, here's an idea," she continued, "what if we -"

Suddenly she heard footsteps upstairs, followed by the sound of a door opening. The woman immediately pulled out of sight, and Rebecca listened with a growing sense of horror as the footsteps made their way down the stairs. A moment later, Ted Armitage stopped in the doorway and looked through to her.

"You're awake, huh?"

For a few seconds, she wasn't quite sure what to say. She had no idea how he'd managed to not see the strange woman in the hallway, although she figured that there must be some place to hide.

"You should try to sleep," he continued wearily. "Tomorrow's going to be a long day. The last thing I want is for you to start nodding off on me."

"I won't do that," she replied through gritted teeth. "You can count on it."

"I very much hope that I can," he said, before turning and sloping across the hallway. "Don't mind me, I just came down for a glass of water. And no, before you ask, you *can't* have one. Not until sunrise."

She listened as he walked away. Beyond the sound of him shuffling around in the kitchen, the rest of the house was completely quiet. Rebecca couldn't help thinking about the woman she'd seen, and wondering exactly where she'd gone. Although she still wasn't ready to believe in ghosts, she knew that it was very unlikely for a living, breathing woman to be able to survive in the house without being spotted by Ted, and for her to survive on scraps. At the same time, that was what seemed to be happening, and Rebecca was starting to think that she might have a way of escaping after all. She simply had to find some way to persuade the woman to help her.

First, though, she needed to stay alive for long enough to get another chance.

## CHAPTER FIFTEEN

"No, it's just going to be a few more days," Ted said as he stood at the kitchen window, looking out across the yard. "The weather's so great up here, I really think I'm going to have some luck if I'm patient."

Still in the wheelchair, still in the office, Rebecca listened to the conversation. Ted had phoned someone a few minutes earlier, and now Rebecca was trying to figure out a little more about the guy's background. She knew that even the tiniest scrap of information might help her to understand him a little more, and that in turn this understanding might help her to get free. Anything was better than nothing, as she tried to build up a better picture of the man who was holding her captive.

"Yeah, totally," he muttered, sounding a little tired. "You know, it is what it is. I'd love to show you, but I know how you feel about these things."

Another pause. He still hadn't said anything particularly revealing, but Rebecca was at least certain now that he had a family somewhere. A wife, or a child, or both.

"I knew you'd say that," he continued with a faint chuckle. "Okay, love you lots. Don't do anything I wouldn't do. Of course, I don't really expect you to listen to a word I say, but that's nothing new."

After a few seconds, Rebecca realized that he'd ended the call. Sure enough, he wandered through and stopped in the doorway.

"Who were you talking to?" she asked.

"That's none of your business," he replied with a faint smile, before stepping closer and placing a bottle of water and an apple on her lap. "Now how about you get those down you, huh? Because after breakfast, and before we get back to work, there's one other thing that I really want to show you."

She waited, but he simply stared at her.

And then, in an instant, he burst out laughing, causing her to flinch a little.

***

"I bought this farm about ten years ago," Ted explained a short while later, as he pushed Rebecca across the yard, taking her away from the barn this time. "An old fella by the name of Moses used to own it. Graham Moses, something like that, can you believe it? That's a name I can get behind. Anyway, he wanted to sell up and move on, and I wanted a place out in the sticks, so we came to an agreement."

Although she was trying to listen to him, Rebecca couldn't help but notice that she was being taken toward a section of the yard that was filled with what looked like a bunch of scrap.

"I don't get to come up here as much as I'd like," Ted continued, "but in a way that's not such a bad thing, because it means that I really appreciate the weeks when I can just squirrel myself away and focus on myself. Now, if that makes me selfish, then so be it, but I see the whole thing differently. I see it as a way of optimizing myself for when I go home and get back to my normal life. Even the best cars in the world need to get tuned occasionally, right? Same with pianos."

"And where *is* home?" she asked.

"I'm not going to tell you that."

"You've already told me a lot."

"Does that worry you?"

He parked her next to some barrels, and then he stepped around her and walked toward a large metal hatch on the ground. Crouching down, he began to fiddle with a padlock.

"You wouldn't tell me anything if you were planning to ever let me go," she suggested.

"That's where you're wrong," he told her. "You'll see. I have a -"

Suddenly he let out a gasp, and Rebecca saw that he'd managed to cut himself on the side of the padlock. He examined the wound and then sucked some blood away, before getting back to work.

"Occupational hazard," he muttered as he tossed the padlock aside and pulled a chain free, and then he opened the hatch. "Wow," he added, putting a hand over his mouth as he got to his feet and took a step back, "that's ripe."

Before she could reply, Rebecca realized that the most horrific stench was rising from whatever was under the hatch. Horrified, she turned away, and something about the rotten sweetness of the smell made her feel nauseous. Somehow she already knew that he smell could only be coming from something that was dead.

"Now," Ted said, stepping back behind her and grabbing the handles of the wheelchair, "I told you before that only the best get their heads on the monument. The rest, I'm afraid, have to be unceremoniously dumped down here with their heads still attached, where they become a kind of... soup, I guess."

He began to wheel her toward the edge of what appeared to be some kind of pit.

"No," she replied, turning the other way as the smell became stronger, "I really don't need to -"

"Of course you need to see it," he said, stopping her abruptly. "Come on, you're not going to chicken out and keep your eyes closed again, are you? I'll just leave you here until you get the guts to look. Is that what you want? Would you like me to set you right here and let you teeter on the edge all day and all night? Just look, and then it'll be over."

She hesitated, convinced that she'd vomit if she actually looked into the pit, but at the same time she had no doubt that he'd do exactly as he threatened. She took a deep breath, and she told herself that she just had to be strong for a few seconds, and then she forced herself to turn and look down.

What she saw was somehow – impossibly – even worse than she'd imagined.

At the bottom of the pit – about ten feet below ground level – several dead bodies lay partially submerged in brown, muddy water. One of the bodies, missing its head, looked fairly fresh, while the others appeared to be in various stages of decomposition. Although the water was murky, a few more corpses could just about be seen beneath the surface. Unable to look away, Rebecca realized that she could see at least a dozen bodies, some with heads and some without.

Suddenly the wheelchair lunged forward and began to tip into the pit. Rebecca was too late to react, and she slipped out of the seat, only for the restraints around her elbows to save her and hold her in place.

A moment later, Ted pulled the wheelchair back and set it down again.

"Sorry," he said with a chuckle, "I couldn't resist that."

As her heart pounded in her chest, Rebecca continued to look down at the corpses.

"I put a mixture in, every now and then," Ted said solemnly, "to try to minimize the smell. As you can tell, that only works to a certain degree. Long-term, I'm going to have to come up with some other approach."

"How..."

Rebecca's voice trailed off for a moment.

"How many?" she stammered finally.

"Nineteen," he told her. "The ones who don't earn a place on the monument are thrown in whole, while the others have their heads removed first. I like to keep this repository ticking over so that I can be reminded of all the work that I've put in so far. There's something almost hypnotic about looking at them."

He place a hand on her shoulder.

"You don't have to end up down there, Rebecca," he continued. "Really, you don't. I told them all the same thing, but I genuinely hope that you'll be the one who escapes this fate. It has to happen eventually. I know that I'm asking a lot, but one day someone has to respond to my attempts to help."

Still looking down into the pit, Rebecca couldn't help staring at one particular body. A face was visible just beneath the water's surface; locked in an endless scream, the woman seemed almost to be staring straight back up, although her eyes were nothing more than two dark smudges. Even from the edge of the pit, Rebecca could see that scraps of rotten flesh were hanging in the water, and she couldn't help but wonder how so many women could have gone missing without Ted eventually being caught.

Suddenly he pulled her wheelchair away from the pit, and then he headed back over to close the hatch.

"Congratulations," he said, "you just passed your first test."

"By not throwing up?" she asked, as a chill ran through her bones.

"By not trying to push me in," he said cheerfully. "Most of them do. I'm ready for it, of course, but it's always a good sign when someone doesn't make the attempt."

"I didn't think of it," she replied coldly, already ruing the fact that she hadn't tried.

"It's still a very good portent."

He closed the hatch and put the chain and padlock back into position, and then he made his way over to Rebecca again.

"Now you've seen what's happens to the people who fail out here," he said, "you know how high the stakes are. There's no middle ground, Rebecca. Either you end up going home to your family as a changed woman, or you end up down there with all the others. So... what's it going to be?"

## CHAPTER SIXTEEN

"Okay," Rebecca said with a smile, "you know what? You were right. I *am* enjoying this! I should have let you bring me here a lot sooner! What would I ever have done without you?"

As the video continued to play on Ted's laptop, Rebecca started laughing. A moment later, the angle of the video changed, looking up at her now as she stood in a field somewhere on a sunny day. A few seconds after that, a hand reached out holding a ring.

"Are you serious?" she stammered, clearly shocked. "Phil..."

"Rebecca," Phil's voice said, "will you do me the honor of becoming my wife?"

For a moment, the wobbly video remained focused on Rebecca's face, and she seemed almost lost for words.

"Yes!" she shrieked finally, bursting into tears. "Of course I will!"

For the next few seconds, the video was something of a blur. Phil stood up and put his arms around her, and she could be heard crying uncontrollably.

"I love you so much!" she gasped finally. "I never had any -"

Ted stopped the video and turned the laptop around, before looking along the table and seeing Rebecca – stony-faced now and with a faraway look in her eyes – sitting at the other end. Although he'd loosened the restraints around her arms, she'd made no attempt to get out of the wheelchair.

"Why would you do that?" he asked finally. "Why would you and your husband-to-be not only film that special moment, but then put it online for all the world to see? Don't you have any concept of a private life? He almost dropped the ring while he was holding the camera. Was the whole thing staged beforehand, just so that you could have a cute video to put online?"

"We wanted to share our -"

"You wanted to boast," he said, interrupting her. "That's what I see when I watch this video. I see two people who want to show off their perfect lives. Did you not realize how the video would come across? Are you really that incapable of self-reflection? There are people out there who are going through hard times. How do you think your videos make them feel?"

Rebecca opened her mouth to reply to him, but she found that she was unable to get any words out. Tears were brimming in her eyes, and all she could think was that she had to get back to Phil and Chloe.

"You need to show a little more humility," Ted said firmly. "Not everything has to be about chasing likes and comments. Believe it or not, there are other ways to achieve a sense of satisfaction. You don't see me posting videos of my work here, do you?"

"And how do you think people would respond if you did?" she asked.

"Fair point," he admitted, "but I'm sure there are a few souls out there who'd approve. Still, I choose to keep my private life private. I don't brag about having all this power and control."

"We just wanted to share our happiness," she told him.

"You wanted to rub it in everyone's face, you mean."

She shook her head.

"I heard you talking to your friend in that cafe," he continued. "Your marriage isn't in great shape, but you don't share *that* part with the world, do you?"

"That's private."

"So what's the difference? Do you just -"

"Leave me alone!" she screamed, gripping the sides of the table and trying to get to her feet, only for the wheelchair to slide back.

Unable to stand on her damaged ankles, Rebecca slammed down hard onto her knees, almost knocking her chin against the table in the process. She just about managed to remain upright as the wheelchair bumped against the wall behind her, and then she froze as she stared across at Ted. She tried again to stand, to show him that she wasn't entirely at his mercy, but she once again found that she was unable to support her own weight. Nevertheless, she kept trying, even though she knew that she looked ridiculous, until finally she used her arms to haul herself up; her feet, meanwhile, were barely any use at all, and she already knew that at any moment she'd have to fall back down.

"Impressive," Ted said calmly, "but ultimately futile. Real strength comes from within."

On the verge of collapsing, she gripped the table harder. Her arms were screaming with pain, but she was determined not to let him win.

"Okay," he said with a sigh, "enough of this nonsense. Sit down."

As her arms began to tremble, she kept her gaze fixed on him.

"Sit down," he said again. "Now."

Almost immediately, her arms buckled and she fell. Managing once again to keep hold of the table, she remained somewhat upright as Ted got to his feet and casually strolled over to the wheelchair. She heard him making his way closer, and she was too weak to resist as he hauled her back into the chair and then applied the brakes.

"I'm going to get something to eat," he told her. "I'll be back soon."

"I need to eat too," she replied, even though she hated to show any sign of weakness.

"Well, tough," he said as he headed to the door.

"Do you have a daughter?" she asked.

He stopped, with his back still turned to her.

"Or a wife?" she continued. "I don't expect you to tell me, but if you do, can you imagine what it would feel like if someone took them and did *this* to them?"

She waited, expecting him to simply walk away, but instead he lingered in the doorway.

"Are they perfect?" she asked. "If not, are you planning to bring them here and put them through your little program? Would you stick their heads on your big phallic spike if they failed?"

Again she waited.

"Or are you just another hypocrite who has one rule for other people and another for himself?" she asked, as her voice trembled with rage. "If you think there's something wrong with how the world works and you want to change things, wouldn't it make sense to start closer to home?"

She watched the back of his head.

"Or are some of the bodies in that pit from your own family?"

As those words left her mouth, she shuddered at the thought that this Ted Armitage guy – if that was even his real name – might be crazy enough and sadistic enough to torture and murder his own wife or daughter. After all, he hadn't denied her suggestion, and with each passing second she found herself wondering more and more whether he might be more unhinged than she'd already suspected.

Finally, without replying, he stepped out of the room and made his way through to another part of the house.

Leaning back in the wheelchair, Rebecca tried to figure out what she should do next. She knew she was running out of time to come up with a proper plan, and she worried that Ted might snap at any moment. Somehow she could still smell the bodies in the pit, as if their sickly stench had permanently lined her nose, and she shivered at the thought of so many corpses down in the cold, dirty water. A moment later, as she replayed the grisly scene in her mind's eye, she thought back to one particular body that she'd noticed; now, however, she imagined her own dead face staring up from the depths.

"I'm coming home, Chloe," she whispered, trying to scrape together a scrap of hope from somewhere. "Mummy's going to get out of here and hold you again, I promise."

She still couldn't help but think of her own corpse in the pit, and the image only left her mind when she realized that she could hear footsteps returning to the room.

Without saying a word, Ted set a plate on her lap, and she saw that he'd brought her a sandwich.

"I thought you said..."

Her voice trailed off as he turned and walked out of the room.

"I need to eat too," she remembered saying to him, just a couple of minutes earlier.

"Well, tough," he'd replied.

Why had he changed his mind? Reaching down, she carefully picked the sandwich apart, checking to make sure that there was nothing hidden inside; a razor blade, perhaps, or some pills. Finding nothing but some cheese and chutney, she realized that apparently he'd simply decided to feed her after all. She thought back to the questions she'd asked him about his family; although she wasn't entirely sure why or how, she realized that those questions seemed to have brought about a change, and she immediately tried to figure out whether she'd stumbled upon some kind of weakness in the man's psychological armor. By asking about his family, had she edged closer to what really made him tick?

Finally, unable to ignore the hunger in her belly, she began to eat the sandwich, while furiously trying to work out exactly how to get Ted Armitage to open up a little more. Her plan was working.

## CHAPTER SEVENTEEN

"Why do you do that like that?"

As she picked up the pen and prepared to write a note in the diary, Rebecca hesitated. She looked across the room and saw that Ted was standing in the doorway, watching her like a hawk. For a moment, somewhat startled, she struggled to work out exactly what he meant.

"That's the second time you've written in the diary today," he pointed out, "and both times, you balance it on your knees."

She swallowed.

"It would make more sense," he continued, "to wheel yourself over to the table and write there. It's not far, and you're more than capable."

"Well," she said cautiously, "I think -"

"Because it's obviously inconvenient for you to do it the way you're doing it," he added. "Also, your handwriting suffers. I don't understand why an intelligent woman would inconvenience herself like this."

She opened her mouth to reply, but she really wasn't sure what to say. A moment later he stepped across the room and grabbed the chair from behind, before wheeling her over to the table. He took the diary and placed it in front of her, and then he stepped back.

"See?" he said. "That'll be better."

"It probably will," she replied, before turning to write something in the diary. "Uh... thank you."

"Your posture's no good."

She froze.

"Did no-one ever teach you how to sit properly?"

She took a moment to adjust her position in the chair.

"That's a little better, but it's still not good," he told her. "You're going to damage your back, you're going to end up with all sorts of spinal problems and pains as you get older."

"I..."

Her voice trailed off.

"Probably, yes," she said, adjusting herself again. "I'm sure you're right."

She waited, in case he said anything else, and then she began to write a few notes. She wanted to show him that she was cooperating, because she felt that cooperating was the only way she might be able to get him to drop his guard.

"Why do you breathe like that?" he asked suddenly.

She turned to him.

"I'm sorry?" she asked.

"I noticed it earlier," he continued. "You sometimes hold your breath for a few seconds."

"I do?"

"There are courses you can take," he told her. "Breathing has all these techniques that you can learn to master." He made a show of taking a couple of big, deep breaths. "Like this, see?" he continued. "Breathing properly can really help you to access your potential. This is all linked to your posture problems, by the way. These difficulties you're experiencing aren't isolated, they're part of a chain that's restricting you and holding you back."

Making his way behind her again, he put his arms around her and pulled her back in the chair, and then he placed a hand on top of her head and adjusted her sitting position. She flinched, but she knew that resisting would only make him angry.

"Do you feel that?" he asked. "It's such an improvement already."

"I feel it."

"Are you sure? Or are you just saying that?"

"No, I'm sure," she said, bristling at the fact that he was touching her in so many different places at once. She could even feel his breath on the side of her neck. "I should try to sit better."

She waited for him to let go, but instead he simply continued to hold her. Although she hated him, she had to admit that in that moment there was something strangely tender about his touch, as if he genuinely cared.

"Why haven't you tried to kill me?" he asked.

"I'm not sure that I -"

"I kidnapped you from the side of the road," he continued, "after sabotaging your car. I injected you, I brought you here, I made you witness awful things. I threatened to kill you, I made it very clear that you could end up becoming just another one of my victims. In the past, the women in your position have always screamed a lot more, and made more attempts to run. Even after I damaged their ankles, some of them tried to crawl away into the woods. I've sort of come to know what to expect, but you..."

He paused, and she could tell that he was studying her with great intent.

"You're not reacting properly," he said finally.

"How do you want me to react?"

"It doesn't matter how I *want* you to react," he told her. "You should have cried more by now."

"I guess I'm trying to hold it together," she replied.

"Sure, but there's a limit. No-one should be able to hold it together as well as you're managing. I can't help wondering whether this strength might in some way be a character flaw."

"I study people for a living," she pointed out. "I analyze them and I try to get into their heads."

"Is that what you're doing?" he asked. "Are you analyzing me?"

"I'd like to know a little more about you."

"I would never tell you *anything* about me," he countered. "You must have realized that by now."

"I can scream if you want me to scream."

Again she waited. Looking down at the pen, she wondered what would happen if she tried to stab him in the neck, or maybe in the eye. All she needed to do was immobilize him for a moment, and then she might be able to get the upper hand. At the same time, she knew that the consequences of a failed attempt would be severe, and that she might very quickly end up chained in the barn. Even as her hand twitched slightly, she told herself that she had to be patient until a better opportunity came along.

"You're an odd bear," he whispered. "You're doing this whole prisoner thing... wrong."

"Sorry about that."

"Huh."

He hesitated, before letting go of her head and stepping away from the chair.

"Write in your diary," he told her, "and remember to work on your posture. I've got things to do. You're free to wheel yourself around in the house, but don't try to go outside. You won't get far, and you'll only end up pissing me off. Is that understood?"

She looked at him for a moment, before nodding and then turning back to the notebook.

"I guess you just don't care enough," he added. "You haven't done enough screaming about missing your little girl."

She flinched again.

"How much screaming *should* I be doing?" she asked.

"You've screamed for a total of two and a half hours since you got here," he told her. "I keep track of these things. By now, you should have screamed for at least ten hours, maybe twelve. I find that very telling. And you should have made some big, botched attempt to escape by now. Don't take this the wrong way, but as a kidnap victim, you're kinda of..."

She waited for him to finish that sentence.

"Underwhelming," he said finally. "You're reacting all wrong."

"Sorry about that," she murmured, not quite daring to look over at him again.

A moment later she heard him walking out of the room. She waited until she was sure that he was gone, and then she sighed and leaned back in the wheelchair. She was pleased to find that she'd managed to get under his skin, although she still wasn't quite sure how best to take advantage of that fact. Although she knew she was making progress, she also knew that she had to find some way of making Ted feel more unsettled. And if she could do that, she might actually have a chance of incapacitating him properly so that she could get away.

\*\*\*

"Okay," he said a few hours later as he wandered back through after cleaning up in the kitchen, "I think tonight you deserve a proper bed, so I'm going to carry you upstairs."

"No," she replied, turning away from the window. "I'm okay down here."

"Are you sure?"

"If you carry me up, you'll just have to carry me back down in the morning," she pointed out. "You said it yourself."

"Sure, but..."

He hesitated, and then he shrugged.

"Suit yourself," he muttered. "I hope you're not thinking of trying anything stupid."

"I wouldn't dream of it," she told him.

"Do you at least need to use the toilet?"

"No, I'm fine," she told him, fully aware that he seemed a little more considerate this time around. "I'm exhausted. I'll be okay right here."

He stared at her for a moment, before taking the diary from the table.

"I'm going to have a little bedtime reading before I turn in," he said, waving the diary at her. "Tomorrow we're really going to ramp up the work. I want to get into your mind, Rebecca Ballard, and see what makes you tick."

"Ditto," she almost said, but she managed to hold back.

Instead, she watched as Ted turned and headed out of the room, and she listened to the sound of his footsteps as he made his way upstairs. She was somewhat amazed that he was simply going to bed, and she had to acknowledge that if she was an unusual prisoner, then he was something of an unusual captor. She felt fairly certain that he had some hidden way of making sure that she wouldn't get far if she tried to escape, but that was fine; she was already planning to try something else entirely, something he couldn't possibly predict. In fact, she'd been slowly and carefully working on a plan all day.

She listened as the house fell silent, and then she slowly looked out toward the hallway.

## CHAPTER EIGHTEEN

Sitting in the dark kitchen, several hours after Ted had gone upstairs, Rebecca continued to wait. She'd positioned herself just inside the entrance to the room, where she wouldn't be seen by anyone approaching from the bottom of the stairs, and she was starting to wonder whether she might have drawn a blank. After all, the clock on the wall showed that the time was a little after one in the morning, and she felt that something should have happened already.

A moment later, however, she heard the telltale sound of a creaking step on the stairs, and she immediately leaned back in the wheelchair and waited.

For the next couple of minutes, she listened as somebody crept closer to the kitchen. She was certain that Ted was still upstairs, hopefully fast asleep, and sure enough she finally saw a figure stepping into the room. For the first time, she was able to make out the mysterious woman in much more detail, and she saw that her bare skin was covered in wounds that were in most cases only partially healed. Festering, infected cuts were dotted across her back and she moved stiffly, as if her bones had never quite recovered from whatever injuries she'd suffered.

The woman took a shuffling step toward the fridge, and Rebecca seized her chance. Reaching out, she grabbed her by the wrist.

Startled, the woman immediately turned and tried to pull away.

"Don't!" Rebecca hissed firmly, tightening her grip on the woman's arm. "If you try to run, I'll scream and wake him up. And even if you manage to hide, I'll tell him everything about you and he'll track you down! Is that what you want?"

The woman froze, her eyes filled with terror.

"We're going to sit at that table," Rebecca continued, somewhat amazed that her little plan had worked so perfectly, "and you're going to tell me exactly who you are and what you're doing here."

\*\*\*

"Cally," the woman said finally, after Rebecca had asked several times for her name. "I... I'm... Cally Rogers."

"Hi Cally," Rebecca replied, keeping her voice down as they sat at the kitchen table, "it's nice to meet you properly."

She paused, momentarily struck by the woman's emaciated state. Terribly thin and covered in wounds, Cally looked almost as bad as the corpses out in the pit. Although she hadn't really wanted to admit it to herself at the time, Rebecca knew that deep down she'd initially been worried that this woman was going to turn out to be some kind of ghost. She didn't know whether to be relieved or appalled that she was a real, live person apparently living in secret in Ted Armitage's farmhouse.

"I'm going to hazard a guess here," Rebecca continued, "that you were once where I am now. So what exactly happened? How come you're not dead like all the others? And how the hell are you lurking in this house without him knowing that you're here? What kind of person doesn't notice that they're sharing their home with someone else? Even if you're really careful, he has to be aware that something's going on!"

"Please," Cally said, her voice trembling with fear, "if he finds us down here..."

"You're going to talk to me or I'll scream," Rebecca reminded her. She felt bad for issuing threats, but she knew she had no choice. "Try to understand."

She waited, and she could see that Cally was starting to shiver.

"He's deaf."

"I'm sorry?" Rebecca replied.

Reaching up, Cally touched her left ear.

"Here," she explained. "I realized it quite early on. He's deaf in his left ear. I think his right one's okay, but the left..."

Her voice trailed off.

"Okay," Rebecca said, nodding slowly, "that might be useful to know. I hadn't noticed."

"I used to work in a care home," Cally explained. "I worked with..."

Again, she hesitated.

"That doesn't matter now," she added. "He also doesn't have great sight."

"How do you mean?"

"I mean that he doesn't always see things that I think he *should* see. I noticed the signs every so often, he has to physically turn to look sometimes. I think it might be both sides, it's probably something like glaucoma. I haven't been close enough to him lately to see whether it's getting worse, but he tries to move very slowly and deliberately. Not that he'd ever admit any of this, of course. He's probably too proud."

"That might explain a few things," Rebecca admitted.

"He also takes pills to help him sleep. I think he had medication for his heart, as well. I've seen a lot of pill boxes up by his bed, but I haven't had a chance to examine them properly. I actually think he might be in pain quite a lot of the time. When he thinks no-one's watching, he rubs the side of his belly, and he has ankle mobility problems as well."

"How long have you been here?" Rebecca asked.

"I don't know."

"Did he kidnap you from the road, like he did with me?"

Cally paused, and then she nodded.

"Okay," Rebecca said, "and -"

"Christmas," Cally whispered.

"Christmas?"

"It was the week before Christmas," Cally continued. "That's when he picked me up. I was driving home for Christmas, and I took the road through this Twist Valley place because there were some jams on all the other roads. Not the last Christmas, because I know that happened while I was here. The one before."

"It's July now," Rebecca told her. "Are you telling me that you were kidnapped more than a year and a half ago?"

Cally nodded.

"You must have family out there," Rebecca said. "Friends. Colleagues. People who miss you."

"They probably think I'm dead by now."

"Why has no-one come looking for you? Why has no-one come looking for *all* the women he's murdered?"

"He told me that the farm isn't on any maps. Something to do with someone building it illegally years ago. And he takes steps to keep it hidden, I don't exactly know what, but obviously it works. He says this place is very out of the way. I'm not certain, but I suspect that he might pay people off to make sure that no-one digs around too much. He told me quite a lot before he..."

She paused, and then she looked down at her scarred belly.

"He told me that I screamed too much," she added. "That I screamed way more than any of the others and that it was off-putting, that I should have moved on to the next phase sooner. That I should have begged him more. He didn't put me in a wheelchair, though. I think he likes to change things up with each victim."

"This whole thing is insane," Rebecca pointed out. "I keep wondering whether I'm suddenly going to wake up and find that it was all a dream. It's almost impossible to believe, but I *do* believe you. And he brought you here, and I'm guessing you went through pretty much what I'm going through now." She looked down at Cally's belly and saw several particularly thick scars. "I'm also guessing that you might have ended up further along in the process. He chained you up in that barn, didn't he?"

Cally nodded again.

"So how are you still alive? I've seen what he does to those women, he cuts off their heads sometimes, and he guts them."

"He panicked," Cally explained. "I don't know exactly how I survived, but I did. He told me I didn't deserve to be on his sick monument, and that he was just going to kill me and throw me down with his other victims. But then..."

She paused, as if she was reliving that awful day.

"Then a car arrived," she continued. "It just pulled up right outside. He gagged me so I couldn't cry out, and he went to see who was in the car. I heard them talking, it was two men from another farm, they wanted to know whether they could borrow some equipment."

"Didn't you try to get their attention?"

"I couldn't," she replied. "I was barely conscious anyway. They left after a couple of minutes, he didn't have what they wanted, but he was really spooked. He kept going on about how no-one ever turned up at the farm like that, and he started getting paranoid that someone was onto him. I think that's why he rushed everything. He stabbed me instead of ripping me open, and he didn't check that I was dead before..."

Rebecca waited for her to continue.

"Before..."

"Before what?" Rebecca asked finally. "Please, Cally, I want to help you. I think we can help each other. We have to hurry, but first I need to understand... what exactly happened to you? Why are you still here?"

## CHAPTER NINETEEN

*19 months earlier...*

Crashing down into the murky water at the bottom of the pit, Cally Rogers finally let out a gasp of pain. As she hit a wet, rotten corpse, she rolled into the depths, quickly sinking beneath the surface. Naked and bleeding, almost sent into shock by the cold, she spluttered and reached out, quickly finding the side of the pit and hauling herself up. She lifted her head above the water and spat out a mouthful of foul, discolored water as the hatch slammed shut above her and the pit fell into darkness.

"Damn it!" she heard Ted shouting in the distance, and he continued talking to himself as he walked away.

Barely able to see a thing, since only a single crack at the edge of the hatch allowed any light into the pit at all, Cally pulled back against the wall and looked out across the array of corpses floating in the water all around her. She could taste the foul soupy liquid in her mouth, but she knew she couldn't make too much noise as she began to try to figure out how she was going to escape.

Wincing, she felt under the water and touched her belly, and she realized that somehow the blade of Ted's knife seemed to have missed any vital organs. Her blood was starting to color the water, however, and she knew that she was guaranteed to get an infection, so she turned and tried to climb up the muddy wall, only to find that it was far too steep.

Looking back across the pit, she saw that the opposite wall was a little rougher and more sloped, and she immediately understood that there was only one way she might ever be able to climb out. She began to clamber across the corpses, pushing several of them deeper into the water, and once she reached the other wall she immediately tried to climb. To her surprise, she found that she was able to make progress, and she could only pray that in his panic Ted might have neglected to put the padlock back in place.

***

Staggering away from the hatch, having put it back in place, Cally stumbled several times as she desperately looked around and tried to work out which way to run. She'd seen no sign of Ted since climbing out of the pit, but she knew that he must be around somewhere, and a moment later she heard the sound of something heavy falling in the shed.

She turned and looked over her shoulder, but Ted was still nowhere nearby, so she hurried to the side of the house and took shelter for a moment. Desperately out of breath and still bleeding, she felt as if she might pass out at any moment, and then she glanced to her left and saw the forest. She knew that she was many miles from civilization, but she figured that her only chance was to run as far away as possible and hope for the best.

Setting off, however, she stopped as she suddenly remembered Ted's words from a few days earlier.

"Do you think I don't have ways of monitoring my own land?" he'd asked with a grin. "A sparrow can't fart out there in that forest without one of my sensors picking it up."

Staring at the trees, she realized that there were likely hundreds – if not thousands – of devices hidden all around. She imagined herself trying to get away, but deep down she knew that she wouldn't manage to run very far, and that Ted would certainly catch up to her and finish her off. She briefly considered screaming, but she knew that this too was never going to work. All she could hope was that the men with the car would return; until then, she needed to hide away and fix herself up.

Looking down, she saw the thick cut on her waist.

"Damn it!" Ted shouted in the distance.

Peering back around the corner, Cally saw that he was storming along to the other end of the barn. He seemed to be very busy, and she realized after a moment that he might well be away from the house for quite some time. She considered her options again, and then she crept around to the back door and pulled it open, before stepping into the house and hurrying up the stairs to find the bathroom. Although she was terrified that Ted might appear at any moment, she figured that he must have a medical kit somewhere, and once she was in the bathroom she began to carefully look through the cabinets.

Finally, with trembling hands, she took out a green bag and set it on the toilet, and she was relieved to find various bandages and solutions inside.

After looking out the window and seeing that Ted was still busy in the barn, she set to work cleaning her wound and trying to find some way to fix it up, at least temporarily. She thought back to her training, and soon she'd managed to put a bandage in place. She knew that she'd need proper medical treatment soon, but for now she carefully put the medical kit away and then took a few steps back. Her mind was racing and she was starting to wonder whether she might be able to find the keys to Ted's truck and drive away.

Suddenly she heard a banging noise, and she realized that he was back in the house.

Trying not to panic, she listened as he stomped through to the kitchen. Heading out onto the landing, she looked down and saw that the front door was open, but she told herself that it was too soon to try to run. She needed to come up with a better plan, and when she looked back across the landing she saw a door that appeared to lead up into the attic. Sure enough, when she hurried over and pulled that door open, she saw a set of steps leading up into the darkness. She briefly tried to figure out whether there might be any other option, and then she began to limp up the stairs in the hope of finding a place where she could hide.

At least for a few minutes.

\*\*\*

"No, I'm going to be here a little longer than planned," Ted said, pacing about in the room below as Cally sat shivering in the attic. "There's always so much to do here, and I really don't want to let that hole in the barn's roof get any bigger."

She heard him making his way across the room.

"Monday, I think," he continued. "Tuesday at the latest. Listen, I'll keep you updated, but I've been neglecting a lot of things out here that need doing, and I'm worried that it's all going to snowball eventually if I don't get a move on."

Holding her breath for a moment, Cally continued to listen.

"Exactly," Ted added. "Thanks for being so understanding about this, I just really need to get on top of it all. I'll make it up to you when I get home, I promise."

After a few more seconds, Cally realized that the call seemed to be over. She listened as Ted's footsteps headed out onto the landing, and then she heard him stop abruptly. Terrified that he might be about to make his way up into the attic, Cally kept her eyes fixed on the darkness ahead and prayed that a patch of light wouldn't suddenly appear. She had no idea whether Ted used the attic regularly, although so far she'd seen nothing up there other than a few boxes. With each second that passed, she simply hoped that she wasn't about to be discovered.

Finally she heard footsteps heading downstairs, and she allowed herself to breathe a sigh of relief. And then, hearing the front door slam shut, she crawled across the attic as quietly as she could manage and she peered out through a small hole in one of the walls.

Ted was making his way back across the yard, and she watched as he disappeared into the barn.

For a moment, she considered going back downstairs and trying to find some way to escape, but she decided instead to wait and come up with a better plan. She knew that if she set off any of the sensors in the forest, she'd be quickly tracked down and killed; she also knew that, at least for a while, she was safe so long as she remained undetected in the attic. The thought of that safety was the only thing that gave her any hope whatsoever, and she told herself that she had to be absolutely certain of her next move before she tried to get away from the farm. She'd come up with a good plan, she was certain of that, and she simply needed to give herself a little more time.

"I'm going to go home," she whispered to herself, as she began to gently rock back and forth. "I'm going to figure this out, and then I'm going to go home."

## CHAPTER TWENTY

*19 months later...*

"And you've been here ever since?" Rebecca asked after a moment, barely able to believe what she was hearing. "Seriously?"

"I sneak down at night and take food from the bin. That way he won't notice. I never take anything from the fridge, even if the bin's empty. I can't risk doing anything that might attract his attention."

"You just sneak about, night after night?"

"He's not always here," Cally explained. "He comes for a week or two at a time, then he'll go away for a couple of weeks, then he'll come back. I can never really predict when he'll arrive, I just have to be careful. When he's away, I spend a little more time downstairs, and I manage to put aside some extra scraps of food so that I've got something for those longer periods. Then, when he comes back, I go up into the attic again and..."

Her voice trailed off.

"I hear the screams," she continued. "I think I heard you screaming the other day. Sometimes I think I should try to do something, but I can't, I just..."

She hesitated for a moment.

"I just can't do it," she added finally. "It doesn't work like that. The worst time is the first night, because he always ties them to the bed in that room, and I have to be extra careful. I don't think you're the first one who's noticed me. I should have been more patient, but I hadn't eaten for almost a week and I knew there'd be something in the bin."

She paused again.

"There was a lot of bolognese yesterday," she added. "Most of it had been thrown away. It's been a long time since I ate that well."

"I don't get how he never notices you."

"I'm careful," Cally said firmly. "I know what works and what doesn't. I don't ever do anything risky."

"Does he never go up into the attic?"

"Not once," she replied. "I don't know why, but I guess maybe I've just been lucky. Every time I think I should try to escape, I just know that..."

Her voice trailed off.

"He has all these devices in the forest," she continued finally. "He told me about them and -"

"And you believe him?"

"How do you know it's not true?"

Rebecca thought about that question for a few seconds.

"I don't," she admitted finally, "but I'm not convinced that he's some kind of tech-savvy mastermind. To completely monitor the forest, he'd need to have a hell of a lot of sensors."

"He has gadgets," Cally told her. "He has a drone."

"Yeah, I've met his drone," Rebecca muttered. "Listen, I'm not saying that he definitely *doesn't* have sensors out there, but that doesn't mean that we have to just sit around here." She paused. "We outnumber him. He has no idea that you're still alive. That has to count for something, right? We can get a jump on him."

Cally shook her head.

"I'm not staying here!" Rebecca hissed.

"You can't make me do anything," Cally told her. "Ted told me, back when I was his prisoner, that I'm not very smart, and he was right."

"You really don't have to listen to anything he says."

"No, it's true," she stammered, "I think I knew it already, but he helped me to understand. Whenever I'm under pressure, I always make the wrong choice. That's why I never dare to leave the attic for long. At least while I'm up there, I know that I'm safe. I've developed a system and it works. Even if he ever goes up there, I know where I'm going to hide and I don't think he'll find me."

"You're living in fear," Rebecca pointed out. "And filth!"

"Just until I come up with a foolproof plan," Cally countered. "One that can't fail."

"You're never going to find a plan that can't fail. Listen, we have to find a way to work together and bring this bastard down. I know you're scared, anyone would be after what you've been through, but he's going to notice you eventually. Please, I'm begging you, you have to help me get us out of here." She waited for a response, and as she stared at Cally's eyes she began to feel as if she might be getting through. "Think of your family," she added. "You want to get back to them, don't you?"

"More than anything in the world," Cally sobbed.

Rebecca hesitated, before reaching over and putting a hand on the woman's knee. Cally flinched, but she didn't quite pull away.

"I'm going to get you away from here," Rebecca said firmly, "and I'm going to make sure that you go home. This whole nightmare is going to end very soon."

Cally opened her mouth to reply, but at the last moment she hesitated.

Suddenly they both heard a thud from upstairs followed by footsteps.

"It's him!" Cally gasped, as a door opened somewhere near the top of the stairs.

"I'll scream!" Rebecca hissed. "If you hide again, I'll tell him about you!"

Hurrying away, Cally disappeared into the next room, leaving Rebecca sitting all alone as Ted's footsteps clomped down the stairs. Although she desperately wanted to call out to Cally, Rebecca simply turned and watched as Ted stepped into the room, and then she squinted as he turned on the light.

"What the -"

Clearly surprised to see her, Ted stared for a moment.

"You nearly gave me a heart attack there," he said finally, clearly flustered. "What are you doing in here, anyway?"

Rebecca looked over at the other chair and saw that it was away from the table, but then she turned and saw that Ted was already making his way to the fridge.

"I'm getting old," he continued. "I rarely make it all the way through the night without having to get up and pee. Sometimes twice."

"You told me I could explore the house," she replied. "I can't sleep, so I rolled myself through here."

"Suit yourself," he muttered, before grabbing a carton of milk and pouring himself a glass. "I hope you're not thinking of doing something foolish like trying to steal a knife, though. If you think I haven't secured these drawers, you've got another thing coming."

"The thought hadn't occurred to me," she told him, before looking over toward the hallway as she heard the faintest sound of a creak on the stairs.

For a moment, she considered crying out and calling for Cally to help her. She knew that'd force the issue, and that Ted would be momentarily confused, but at the same time she also worried that Cally would simply try to run. Far better, she told herself, to wait and talk to Cally again, and to try to persuade her that they needed to work together properly.

"This is an old house," she said.

"Huh?"

Ted turned to her, and she thought back to Cally's claim that he was deaf in his left ear.

"I didn't catch that," he told her.

"I just said that this is an old house," she replied. "It must get quite spooky being here all by yourself."

"Not really," he said with a shrug. "I'm not given to imagining that things are going bump in the night, if you catch my drift. That kind of thing's for fools and simple folk."

"You're lucky," she suggested. "A lot of people would start thinking that they can hear things."

"Well, a lot of people are idiots," he replied as he made his way back across the room. "I only deal in straightforward matters, as you might have noticed. There's enough horror and pain in the world, without imagining that people hang about after they're gone." He reached out to the light switch, and then he turned to her. "When someone's gone, they're gone, and that's the end of it. You'd do well to reflect on that fact before we get started again in the morning. Light on or off?"

She thought about that statement for a moment, and she realized that he genuinely had no idea that one of his former victims had not only survived, but was living some kind of terrified existence hidden away in his attic.

"Off," she said finally. "Please."

"Suit yourself."

He flicked the light off, and then he headed to the stairs.

"Get some sleep," he called back to her. "Tomorrow's going to be a long day, and I want you to have as much of your strength as possible. I want you to really start showing me what you're made of!"

Once she was alone, Rebecca realized that she was going to have to think of some other way to get through to Cally. After all, the poor woman was clearly far too terrified to confront Ted, even if – deep down – she had to understand that she couldn't spend the rest of her life living in the man's attic. Although Rebecca knew that a year and a half's worth of terror could never be undone so quickly, she also told herself that she didn't have time to gently coax Cally out of the shadows.

"I'm getting out of here," she whispered to herself as she heard Ted's bedroom door swinging shut upstairs. "Tomorrow."

## CHAPTER TWENTY-ONE

"Isn't this just a lovely sunny day?" Ted said, beaming from ear to ear as he wheeled Rebecca out into the yard. "Take a deep breath of that air. Don't you ever worry about raising your daughter in the middle of a town? Think of all that pollution getting into her lungs."

"What about *your* children?" she asked. "Did you raise them here?"

"Nice try, but you know I'm not going to break that easily," he told her as he pushed her past the truck, the door of which he'd left open. "Today's going to be all about -"

Stopping suddenly, he looked over his shoulder and stared at the house for a moment.

"What is it?" Rebecca asked after a few seconds. "Is something wrong?"

"You know what?" he said with a sigh. "I just realized I'm a complete idiot. I need to move some equipment that's in the barn, but for that I need to have the right keys for the drill and the -"

He hesitated again, before letting out a heavy sigh.

"Okay," he continued, "I'm just going to have to leave you here for a few minutes while I go and root around for some old keys that I haven't seen in the best part of a year. I think they're in the office somewhere, or maybe the kitchen." He paused. "I can trust you out here, can't I?"

"Yes, you can trust me," she said wearily.

"I'll be back before you even have time to miss me," he replied, turning and hurrying into the house. "I must have had a little bit of a senior moment just now. How could I have come out without the right keys?"

Rebecca turned to watch him go, but at that moment she spotted something glinting in the truck. Looking through the open door, she was surprised to see that Ted had left the keys in the ignition. She froze, realizing that there was nothing to stop her trying to climb into the truck; although she could barely use her feet for anything, she figured that she'd at least be able to apply pressure to the gas pedal, and that she wouldn't need to think about the brakes until she was a long way from the farm.

Glancing back across the yard, she saw the rough road that led off into the distance. Suddenly freedom seemed so attainable, and potentially so easy to grasp. She just have to be brave, and yet...

And yet it seemed almost too easy.

She looked at the keys again, and she couldn't help but notice that Ted had positioned her in the perfect spot. A few feet forward or back, and she'd never have spotted the keys at all. On top of that, he'd left her very close to the truck, so that she'd be able to reach out and haul herself inside. He'd also failed to tie her back into the wheelchair after letting her out earlier to use the toilet; she'd noticed that at the time and thought that it was odd, but now she was starting to wonder whether she was being subjected to some sort of test.

Slowly, after looking at the house one more time, she began to reach out toward the truck.

***

"Well," Ted said a few minutes later as he wandered back out into the yard, holding up a set of jangling keys, "they were in the last place I looked. I mean, of course they were. It's not like I would've carried on looking for them after I found them, is it?"

Stopping next to the wheelchair, he smiled as he looked down at Rebecca.

"Why so glum?" he asked.

She looked up at him.

"Huh," he continued, before looking into the truck and seeing that the keys were still right where he'd left them. "Well, what do you know? You passed my little test."

He turned back to her.

"Or was it too obvious?" he added. "Hell, I suppose I'm not quite as subtle as I'd like to think. I just made it all look a little bit too easy, didn't I?"

"I don't know what you're talking about," she replied.

"I know that you do, but that's okay." He swung the door shut and then grabbed the wheelchair's handles. "I'm honestly pretty chuffed. You're the very first person who's ever passed this particular test. You should've seen the rest of them, always clambering into the truck and trying to start the engine." He chuckled. "Then there was always the moment when they realized I'd left it disabled. That was usually the beginning of the end for them, but not for you, huh?" He patted her on the shoulder. "No, you showed remarkable restraint, and that suggests to me that you're starting to learn. I think you're actually listening to me."

He pushed her toward the barn.

"This changes things," he explained. "I assumed that I'd have to spend the rest of the day punishing you. I even thought it might be time to move on to the ultimate stage, but now it looks like we can get on to something more enjoyable."

He stopped her once again, right in front of the barn's metal door, and then he stepped around and crouched down to start fiddling with a padlock down near the bottom.

"This damn thing's getting rusty," he muttered, struggling with the key. "Sometimes I think that if I didn't have bad luck, I'd... well, you know how the saying goes, right?"

With his back to her, he continued to fiddle with the padlock.

Slowly, Rebecca reached behind her back and pulled out the spiked metal object that she'd found under the front seat in the truck. It was the same object that had ruined her tire on the road, and now – as she turned it around in her hands – she realized that one swift strike could send the metal barbs straight through Ted's skull. She adjusted her grip slightly as he continued to work on the padlock, and then she held the metal chunk up and leaned forward slightly, ready to bash his brains out.

"Of course," he said, stopping suddenly with his back still turned to her, "I suppose there's a possibility that you only *think* that you passed the test. What if I was subtle after all?"

He half turned, but he still wasn't looking directly at her.

"What if," he continued, "it wasn't the keys that you were supposed to notice?"

She stared at the back of his head. Part of her still wanted to attack him, but now she was starting to worry that she might miss, or that he might be able to fight her off.

He turned to her, and after a moment he looked at the metal object in her right hand.

"It was originally part of a pulley system," he explained, "but I added the little spiked parts myself. I'm kind of handy like that. I've developed a way of hiding it next to the tire using magnets, and then I can remotely set it to detach and shred the carcass when the driver's at a nice isolated part of the road. It's very good at its job, but I imagine it'd be equally good at cracking a man's skull open and bashing his brains out."

He waited.

"Is that what you're going to try to do, Rebecca?" he continued. "Is that your big plan?"

She hesitated, and then – realizing that she most likely wouldn't be able to knock him out – she tilted her hand forward and let the piece of metal fall to the ground.

"Wise choice," Ted said, nodding approvingly. "I might be getting on, but I still know how to defend myself. Better than some out-of-shape suburban mother, at least."

"You can trust me," she replied through gritted teeth, already regretting the fact that she hadn't struck instantly. "See?"

"Well, that's a complicated point," he said as he picked the metal chunk up and got to his feet. "I bet you're just about starting to regret your choice there, aren't you? And there's the little fact that you still concealed it in the first place."

"But I didn't use it," she pointed out.

"Oh, Rebecca," he said with mock sadness, "that isn't the test. The test is whether or not you take the damn thing out of the truck in the first place."

"No, the -"

"I set the test," he said firmly, as he turned and began to slide the door to the barn open, "so I'm the one who gets to say when you've failed. And I'm afraid to say that after a promising start there, you *have* failed."

He stepped aside, and she saw the chains dangling in the gloom.

"That means," he added, "that it's time for your punishment."

"No!" she shouted, as he took hold of the handles and began to pull the wheelchair into the barn. "You can't do this!"

Reaching out, she grabbed the side of the door and held tight, desperately trying to keep him from taking her anywhere near the chains.

"This behavior is beneath you," he told her. "Rebecca, please, don't make this any harder than it has to be. You can still get through today, but only if you take your punishment properly."

"I'm not going in there!" she shouted. "I passed your stupid test!"

"And I'm telling you that you didn't," he said, leaning over her and starting to prise her fingers away from the frame. "This only has to be as difficult as -"

"Cally!" she screamed, looking back toward the house. "Help me!"

## CHAPTER TWENTY-TWO

"What did you just say?" Ted asked, letting go of her hands and taking a step back. "Who the hell are you talking to? Who's Cally?"

Staring at the house for a moment, Rebecca watched for any sign of movement. She knew that Cally must have heard her, but after a few seconds she imagined the poor woman shivering with fear in the dark attic. She opened her mouth to call out again, and then she slowly turned and looked up at Ted.

"Who's Cally?" he asked again, before tilting his head slightly. "I haven't heard that name in a long time, but there *was* a Cally here once, for a while."

He paused, clearly suspicious.

"Why did you call that name out just now?"

"It's my daughter," she stammered, hoping against hope that she might be able to put him off the scent. The last thing she wanted was to give up the element of surprise, or to expose Cally's position. "My daughter's name is Chloe, I was just... calling out to her."

"You said Cally."

"No, I said Chloe."

She waited to see his reaction. She knew that her lie was somewhat tenuous, but after a moment she saw that Ted was furrowing his brow.

"Well, that doesn't change anything," he told her, once again reaching past and trying to pull her hands away from the frame. This time he succeeded, before she had a chance to stop him. "Your husband and your daughter are hundreds of miles away and there's absolutely nothing that they or anyone else can do to help you. You're going to take your punishment properly, and then we'll see where we are by the end of the day. Did you really think that a baby was going to come to your rescue?"

"You can't do this," she replied, turning and trying to climb out of the chair. "It's not fair!"

"It's completely fair," he replied, grabbing her around the waist and hauling her back. "And even if it wasn't, you're really in no position to argue."

Knocking the wheelchair over, he began to drag Rebecca into the barn, holding her tight even as she tried to struggle. He quickly managed to get her all the way over to the chains, and then – a little breathless now – he dropped her onto the floor and took a step back.

"You could do with losing a stone or two, do you know that?" he muttered. "What happened, did you never quite lose all your baby weight? Have you spent months and months eating bad food while grumbling about your expanding waistline to anyone who'd listen? I bet you don't post anything about *that* on your stupid social media pages, do you?"

"I passed your test!" she sneered.

"No," he replied, shaking his head, "you really didn't."

Stepping around her, he began to adjust the chains.

"Do you want to know something strange?" he asked. "I actually began to think that maybe, just maybe, I'd never get to this stage with you. I thought that by some absolute miracle I'd finally chanced upon a subject who was responding perfectly to my teaching. You should be proud of yourself, in a way. That still puts you in a very good light, even if you then made a little mistake. I still believe in your potential, Rebecca."

Looking around, she tried to spot something she could use as a weapon.

"I hope you understand that I won't enjoy this," he continued. "In fact, I blame myself for having not drummed a few things into your head sooner. Now, let me be honest, no-one has ever made it out of these chains alive, but that doesn't mean that it can't be done. Despite this little slip-up, you're still ahead of every other candidate who's ever been my guest here at the farm."

He turned and looked down at her.

"Doesn't that make you feel -"

Before he could finish, she screamed and tried to stab him in the leg with the small trowel that she'd found on the floor nearby. When that failed, she reached up and tried again, but this time he grabbed her arm and pulled the trowel away with ease, before putting her hand against the floor and then slamming his foot against her wrist.

She cried out as she felt the bone break.

"What was *that* all about?" he asked, moving his foot away. "Are you just losing your goddamn mind today? Are you determined to undo all your good work?"

She reached out and tried to grab the trowel again, before slumping down as she realized that she was too late. She knew that she should have hit him with the metal object earlier, and that she could be on her way to freedom by now, and she silently vowed that she'd never miss another chance again. She was going to stop over-thinking things and start striking as soon as she saw an opportunity.

"Up you come," he said, grabbing her by the shoulders and lifting her off the ground, then turning her around and grabbing one of the dangling chains. "You've got a lot to think about, Rebecca," he added as he began to slip her broken wrist through one of the looped sections. "You really need to start thinking about a long-term plan here. You need to understand the benefits of cooperation."

He stepped around her and smiled.

"Violence," he added, "is tantamount to failure."

As pain burned in her damaged wrist, she opened her mouth to tell him what she really thought of him. At that moment, however, she spotted movement in the darkness nearby, and she was shocked to see that Cally was slowly making her way up behind Ted, holding a large spade. For a moment, she didn't even dare to believe that what she was seeing could possibly be real.

"Violence," Ted said firmly, grinning at her with smug satisfaction, "never solved anything."

"You know," Rebecca whispered, watching as Cally raised the spade up high, "I'm not sure that you're entirely right about that."

She saw the very beginning of a quizzical expression on Ted's face, but this was interrupted as Cally let out an agonized scream and smashed the head of the spade against the side of his skull. Immediately crumpling to the floor, Ted groaned and reached up to touch the spot where the spade had hit him, but Cally smacked it against his head again, this time knocking him out cold.

As her damaged wrist slipped out of the chain, Rebecca dropped to her knees. For a moment she felt as if she was about to pass out and topple over, but somehow she managed to remain upright. Looking down at Ted, she told herself that there was no way she was willing to give him the satisfaction.

"I'm sorry," Cally stammered, trembling with fear as she continued to hold the spade up, "I should have come sooner, but I..."

Her voice trailed off.

"I did it," she continued, her voice filled with shock. "I actually did it. I just wish he'd seen my face before I knocked him out, so that he knew it was me. I wish I'd been able to make him suffer more."

"It's okay," Rebecca said, struggling to get her breath back as she looked down at Ted's unconscious body. "You're here now. It looks like you got him pretty good."

She let Cally help her up, and then they began to limp together toward the door. Barely able to put any weight on her ankles at all, Rebecca felt as if she might collapse at any moment, but Cally was strong enough to support her and they reached the door relatively quickly, at which point they both stopped and looked back.

Ted was still on the ground.

"Should I kill him?" Cally asked. "I don't... I mean, I'm not a killer but..."

"We should tie him up," Rebecca told her, "and make sure that he faces justice. Killing him's too easy. I want the police to tear this place apart and make sure that he pays for every life he ruined."

"I'll wrap him up in those chains," Cally said as she helped her over to the truck. "I think we should just leave him trapped here and then tell the police all about him. I can't believe he managed to go undetected for all these years."

She set Rebecca on the truck's passenger seat, and then she looked back toward the barn.

"You saved me," Rebecca told her. "I thought... I didn't actually think you were going to come."

"I nearly didn't," Cally replied, still watching the barn as tears ran down her face. "For a moment, it was almost as if my body wouldn't let me go into the barn again."

"We can go back in there together, if you like," Rebecca continued. "If it's too much for you, I -"

"No, I'll be fine. It shouldn't even take too long. I want to make sure that bastard gets everything that's coming to him. He deserves to rot in a jail cell for the rest of his miserable life."

She hesitated, and then she stepped away from the truck.

"I won't be long," she said as she walked back toward the barn. "Then we can get out of here. I'm finally going to go home."

"We both are," Rebecca whispered as she leaned back and took a deep breath. Her ankles hurt and her broken wrist was throbbing with pain, but all she could think about was the fact that she was going to see Phil and Chloe again. "And I'm never going to let either of them out of my sight again."

## CHAPTER TWENTY-THREE

"Becky, wake up," Phil's voice said firmly. "Becky, you're not safe yet."

Startled, she sat up and realized that she'd begun to pass out. Still in the passenger seat in the truck, she looked around and saw that Cally wasn't back, and when she looked over at the barn she realized that she wasn't quite sure how long she'd been unconscious. Had she simply dozed off for a moment, or had she been out for longer?

"You need to keep running," she heard Phil's voice whispering, already fading away to nothing. "You can't trust anyone."

"Hold it together," she said, taking a deep breath, although she could already feel herself starting to slip back under. Although her mind knew that nothing was set in stone, her body seemed to be reacting to the fact that Ted Armitage was now a prisoner, and she had to really focus in order to stay awake. "Not long now..."

As those words left her lips, she saw movement in the barn, and a moment later Cally stepped out into the sunlight. Rebecca waited for her to come closer, but as soon as she saw Cally's face she realized that something was wrong. She told herself that she was worrying over nothing, that Cally was understandably and justifiably traumatized, but deep down she couldn't help worrying that there was some other problem.

"Are you ready?" she shouted, leaning out of the truck. "Did you tie him up?"

She waited, but Cally said nothing. Instead, seemingly frozen, she hesitated for a few seconds before finally starting to make her way forward.

"Is he awake?" Rebecca asked, but she was becoming increasingly concerned about the way Cally was behaving. "Hey, are you okay? Did you manage to tie him up so that he can't get away?"

Again, she waited for an answer.

"You didn't kill him, did you?" she added cautiously. "He needs to stand in a courtroom and pay for every single life he took."

"He told me it's a test," she replied.

"What?"

"He told me he's known that I was hiding all along," she continued, as her voice began to break, "and that this is... it's another test. It's another chance for me to prove myself to him."

"No," Rebecca replied, shaking her head, "you can't listen to him. You tied him up, right? Tell me that you tied him up!"

"He told me that I have one more chance," Cally said, as fresh tears began to roll down her cheeks. "He says that if I pass, I might be able to get out of here. He might let me go home if -"

Suddenly a gunshot rang out and one side of Cally's head exploded, showering Rebecca with blood.

Pulling back, Rebecca watched as Cally's body fell to the ground, and then she looked over at the barn just in time to see that Ted was making his way out with a rifle in his arms.

"No!" she gasped, grabbing the keys and turning them, starting the truck and then pulling the door shut.

She somehow managed to clamber into the other seat, and then she forced her legs down into the foot-well and used her hands to shift her feet until they were in position. Despite the agony, she managed to press against the gas pedal, and then she put the truck into gear and began to drive forward across the yard, turning right to avoid the barn and starting to aim for the dirt road. The truck bumped against a ridge of dirt, but she kept her foot down and focused on trying to get away as fast as possible.

Suddenly the truck slammed to halt with such force that Rebecca was sent crunching forward into the steering wheel. She let out a cry of pain as her head hit the windscreen, and then as she slumped back in the seat she felt for a moment as if she was once again going to pass out. Blood was running down her face, and a fraction of a second later the truck somehow switched into reverse and began to drive slowly backward across the yard.

Forcing herself to stay conscious, Rebecca reached down and tried to put the vehicle back into first gear, only to find that for some reason the stick wouldn't move. She tried a couple more times, as the wheel turned and the truck drove slowly around the side of the barn.

Looking out the window, she saw Ted watching from a distance, and she couldn't help but notice that he was tapping at his phone. In an instant, she realized that somehow he'd taken control of the vehicle.

"No," she said firmly, convinced that there had to be a way for her to override whatever he was doing. "Come on, you can't do this to me."

She reached for the stick again, but at that moment the truck bumped over something on the ground. Even before she looked out the front, Rebecca had a sickening fear that she knew what had caused the bump. Sure enough, the truck reversed a little further and she saw Cally's crumpled body on the ground, partially crushed into the mud.

She looked at Ted.

He was grinning.

Before she could react, the truck lurched to one side and picked up speed, racing backward around the other side of the barn. Grabbing the steering wheel, Rebecca tried to figure out what she should do next, but the truck was picking up speed now and she knew that trying to jump out would be suicidal. She also knew that even if by some miracle she survived, she'd have no way of escaping, so instead she turned and looked over into the truck's back seat and tried to figure out whether there was anything she could use as a weapon.

She saw a bunch of bags, and when she opened them she found that they contained various different tools. She quickly pulled out a large wrench, but she knew that trying to smack Ted on the side of the head would be difficult. The drone was also within reach, but again she had no idea how that might be useful. Finally, spotting a hefty-looking hammer, she reached for that and told herself that if she was going to go down, she was at least going to go down with a fight.

She looked out the window again, and she could just about see Ted over on the far side of the yard, still controlling the truck with his phone.

"Okay then, you bastard," she muttered, tightening her grip on the hammer, "let's see what you're made of. You're not taking me alive. Not again."

She waited as the truck reversed at speed around the house, but she knew that at some point Ted was going to have to make a move for her. Sure enough, the vehicle finally came to a shuddering halt right outside the front door, and Rebecca found herself staring out at Ted through the window as he stood just a few meters away.

The truck's engine was still running.

"Poor Cally," Ted said, unable to hide a faint smile. "She really thought I had no idea that she'd made it out of the pit. Sure, I have a few problems with my hearing and whatnot, but did she genuinely believe I didn't know she was here? For that matter, did *you* believe it?"

He let out a little chuckle.

"I didn't plan for her to survive the pit," he continued, "but when she did, I thought there was an interesting opportunity to give her one final chance. Of course, she failed that when she tried to help you, but there was something endearing about her desperate attempts to get me on her side."

"Bullshit!" Rebecca snapped, still holding the hammer out of sight, waiting for him to make his way closer. The truck was rumbling as its engine continued to turn over. "You make all these rules up as you go along!"

"You've got me there," he admitted. "To some degree, at least. But the overarching theme of helping you to overcome your imperfections is genuine."

"You shot her in cold blood!"

"I don't like using guns," he replied, "but sometimes they're the best way to tidy up a messy situation. That poor girl really believed me when I told her that I'd let her take your place. I almost feel sorry for her."

"So what's next?" Rebecca asked. "I'm pretty sure I've failed your latest test."

"Oh, that's an understatement."

"So come and get me, then," she continued, and again she changed her grip on the hammer. She was trying to work out how he'd approach, and how best to attack.

He stared at her, as if he was trying to reach into her mind.

"You look like a woman with a plan," he said finally.

"I'm not in much of a position to fight back."

"You never were, but you've made it this far." He paused, before tapping at his phone again as the truck's engine continued to run. "If there's one thing I've learned, it's to never underestimate a woman who's fighting for her life. You can still walk out of here, Rebecca, even if you've made some bad choices over the past hour or so. You just need to be punished first."

She swallowed hard.

"Come and punish me, then," she said firmly.

She waited, but he simply tapped again at his phone.

"Did you mother never tell you," he said finally, "to always buckle up when you get into a vehicle?"

She opened her mouth to ask what he meant, but in a split second she understood.

Before she had a chance to grab the seat belt, Ted sent the truck lurching forward, forcing it to quickly build up speed before hitting the brakes. Thrown forward, Rebecca again hit her head on the windshield, and this time she felt several ribs cracking on her left side as she crunched against the steering wheel. Almost immediately, the truck switched into reverse and raced back across the yard, before coming to a halt and then racing forward again. Reaching down, Rebecca tried to grab the seat belt, but she was too late.

The truck slammed to a halt and she was thrown against the windshield, and this time she let out a brief, agonized scream before the impact knocked her out cold.

## CHAPTER TWENTY-FOUR

"Becky," Phil said as he reached through the shattered window and grabbed her arm, "listen to me, you're going to be okay."

As she began to open her eyes, Rebecca realized that the world seemed to have fallen silent. The truck's engine was no longer running, and after a moment the only sound she could hear was birdsong coming from the forest. She looked around, stunned, and then she turned back to her husband.

"Don't panic," he told her. "Don't fight it. Everything's going to be fine now."

"Where's Chloe?" she stammered, before hearing a gurgling sound.

Turning, she saw to her astonishment that her daughter was on the seat next to her, laughing despite the fact that she was resting on a sea of broken glass.

"What are you doing here?" Rebecca asked, scooping Chloe up and brushing shards away from her leggings. "Phil, why did you bring her to this awful place?"

"You're going to be in peace now," he replied.

"She might see something awful!" she told him. "She might smell that pit! What were you thinking?"

She turned to him, and in that moment she realized that something was still terribly wrong.

"You don't need to fight anymore," he said calmly. "You've already fought so hard and so long. This guy's never going to let you go. You saw what he did to Cally. That'll be you one day. Just stay here with me and Chloe. I'm begging you, Becky. Don't keep fighting. Don't go back there. If you stay here, you don't have to know how he kills you."

\*\*\*

Letting out a pained gasp, Rebecca opened her eyes and immediately felt a burning sensation in her arms. She twitched, and then she looked up and saw that her arms were raised high above her body, attached to thick metal chains that hung from the roof of the barn.

Looking down, she found that she was naked, and she saw that the concrete floor all around was stained dark with what she could only assume was the blood of all the other women who'd been in the same position before. She instinctively pulled on the chains, but she could already tell that they were far too firmly wrapped around her arms; she tried again, filled with panic, until she felt as if she might be about to tear her shoulders away from her body.

Hearing a faint shuffling sound, she looked straight ahead and realized that she could just about make out a figure in the darkness.

"You're awake," Ted said, stepping closer until she could see his face. "That's good. For a moment there, I thought you maybe weren't going to make it. You took quite a battering but, hey, I found the hammer you were going to try to use on me. That was a decent, if rather desperate, little plan. You might have actually succeeded. Fortunately, I was pretty sure that you had something up your sleeve. You're not the best liar in the world."

"What are you going to do to me?" she asked, unable to hide the fear in her voice.

"I think -"

"Are you going to kill me?" she continued. "Like you killed that other woman in here? Because if you do, you might as well just get on with it."

"I might well end up killing you," he replied, "but only if one of two things happened."

He made his way closer.

"If you fail and I consider you to be beyond salvation," he said calmly, "then there'll be no point continuing, and I'll put you out of your misery. The other risk, as far as you're concerned, is if I become distracted by another potential target. That happens more often than I'd like to admit, really. I'm working on one person, and then my head gets turned by another and I just can't help myself."

He reached out and ran a finger against the side of her face. She flinched and pulled away, but she was powerless to stop him as he tried again.

"Your predecessor was unlucky," he continued. "She might have been given another chance, if I hadn't happened to overhear you talking to your friend about your marital problems. You captured my interest in that moment, Rebecca, which meant that poor Emily's time was up. If I were you, I'd hope and pray very hard that I don't run into anyone soon who takes my fancy."

"Just get it over with," she sneered.

"It's understandable that you're feeling dispirited," he explained. "Anyone would in your position, but you have to focus on the positives. How many times do I have to tell you?"

He clapped his hands together.
"You."
And again.
"Can."
And again.
"Still."
And again.
"Make."
And again.
"It."
And again.
"Out."
And again.
"Of."
And again.
"Here."
He grinned.

"You can still make it out of here," he said again, before poking a finger at the center of her forehead. "Do you get it now, dummy?"

"I don't believe you."

He tilted his head.

"You just tell people that because you like torturing them," she continued. "Maybe you even fool yourself into believing it, but there's zero chance of you ever letting anyone go."

"You're wrong."

"Because as much as you try to act like you're above it all, at the end of the day you're just another sadistic bastard who likes kidnapping women and doing nasty things to them. That's a story that's as old as time itself."

"I'm trying to help you."

"Why am I naked?"

He opened his mouth to reply, but then he hesitated.

"Why do I need to be naked for this part, huh?" she continued. "You haven't got an answer, because there *isn't* an answer."

"I need to expose your vulnerability," he replied. "Your fragility. I need you to be stripped down to your basic animal level."

"I think you just get a little buzz out of seeing a woman's body," she snarled. "What's wrong? Is this the only way you can do that?"

"You should be thanking me," he told her. "I'm revealing your soul here."

"Rubbish!" she shouted angrily, as she pulled on the chains again. "That's the biggest load of crap I ever heard in my life!"

"You don't understand," he said, shaking his head. "They never do, not really. It's one of the main parts of the test that they always fail."

"The only one who's failing any tests here is you," she told him. "It doesn't matter how you dress it up, you're just another sadistic bastard who goes around hurting people. You fail the test of being a decent human being, and all the other crap that comes out of your mouth is just nonsense that you use to fool yourself."

"Absolutely not," he said, shaking his head again. "You couldn't be more wrong if you tried."

"You're just -"

"I'm trying to help you!" he shouted, leaning so close that she could feel his breath on her face. "Why can't you get that into your thick head? You have so much potential but you're ruining it all with these faults that you let run rampant through your life. Even now, when you should be begging me to show you some mercy, you're choosing to waste your time with all these nasty little insults. You don't even listen when I explain how I'm going to help you, and it's that pigheadedness that's going to trip you up."

He took a deep breath.

"I don't care for your tone," he added.

"I don't care what you care for," she told him, "and I will never, ever listen to you. So you can save all your attempts to fix me, and you might as well skip straight to the end. We both know what that's going to be, anyway."

She waited, but for a moment he simply stared straight at her. Although she'd meant every word of what she'd just said, she was starting to wonder whether he might take her literally. She flinched slightly, half expecting to feel a knife slicing into her gut, but instead Ted continued to keep his gaze fixed on her, almost as if something deep inside his mind had suddenly broken.

"Do you know why no-one has ever completed your little training program?" she asked. "It's because no-one can. Even if they could, you move on to your next victim before they have a chance."

Again she waited, but she wasn't sure whether he'd even heard her. For a moment, she felt she could see the cogs turning behind his eyes, and she worried that she might have been a little too successful at getting under his skin.

"Well," he said finally, "you've certainly given me a lot to think about."

He took a step back, and for a few seconds he seemed genuinely shaken.

"I have to take a little trip for a couple of days," he continued. "I'll give you food and water before I go, and then you'll just have to wait for me to get back."

"You can't leave me like this!" she snapped.

"I'll be two days," he replied. "You can handle two days. Don't worry, I've made sure that there's zero chance of you escaping. When I get back, we can move on to the next stage of my plan to educate you on living better. I'll prove to you that I have a system that really works, and I'll make an extra effort to show you the benefits as we go along. All that cynicism is going to get swept away, Rebecca, and it'll be replaced by genuine appreciation for my efforts. I *will* get through to you."

With that, he turned and began to walk away.

"You can't leave me like this!" she shouted again, as she started pulling harder and harder on the chains. "Stop! You can't do this! Come back!"

## CHAPTER TWENTY-FIVE

"Yeah, I'm just picking up some supplies," Ted said the next evening, as he stood outside a restaurant a few hundred miles from his farm. "Did you ever notice how I say I'm going to the farm to relax, and I end up doing more work than ever?"

As a tinny voice replied to him over the phone, he took a few steps across the car park and watched traffic passing on the street. The lights of the cars were so bright, reflecting in the lenses of his sunglasses, and he watched the world going by as he listened to the voice in his ear. Taking a deep sniff, he noticed the smell of grass and damp cement.

"A real holiday?" He chuckled. "Yeah, that'd be nice, but you know I don't have the time. You should go on one, though. I'll even pay for the damn thing. You deserve one, after putting up with me for so long."

He smiled as he listened to the reply.

"Well, think about it," he added. "Seriously. Old Ted'll put you up in a hotel somewhere for a week. Room service, spa treatments, a minibar, all the luxuries. You just name it, and I'll book it." He checked his watch. "But now I need to get going, because I'm starving and I've still got a long drive ahead of me. When I get back to the farm..."

His voice trailed off for a moment, and he watched another line of passing cars. Their lights were filling his sunglasses more than ever.

"Well, when I get back to the farm I've really got to throw myself into some good old-fashioned hard work, that's all," he explained with a faraway look in his eyes. "I think it's going to be make or break for a few things."

\*\*\*

"And here's your pasta," the waitress said as she set a plate down in front of him. "Is there anything else I can get you? Some cheese, maybe?"

"No, that's fine," Ted replied. "Thank you."

As the waitress walked away, Ted took a deep breath and reminded himself that he had to eat. In truth, he'd somewhat lost his appetite over the previous few days, and he couldn't help but feel that this was all Rebecca's fault. She'd stood up to him in a way that no-one had ever stood up to him before, and more than anything he wanted to prove her wrong. She was a tough case, that much was certain, but he'd never shied away from a challenge and he wasn't going to stop now. She was certainly very special.

Picking up his fork and spoon, he began to eat.

"You're going to kill me."

He froze, and then he looked across the table and saw Rebecca – beaten and bloodied, and still naked – sitting in the opposite chair. He knew that she wasn't really there, of course, but he was somewhat surprised to realize that he was hallucinating. That hadn't happened for a while.

"You know it," she continued, "and I know it. You never see things through to the end. You just toss us all aside when you get to the hard part."

"That's not true," he wanted to reply, although he knew he'd look like an absolute lunatic if he started talking to himself in the middle of the restaurant. "You don't understand."

"I'm you," she replied. "Remember? The real Rebecca's hundreds of miles away in the barn. I, on the other hand, am a manifestation of your subconscious mind, and I'm the one who's telling you now... You're not going to complete your work. Rebecca's going to end up in that pit like all the others."

Ignoring her, he looked down at his food. When he glanced across the table again, he was relieved to see that the hallucination was now gone. He looked around, worried that she might be somewhere else nearby, and then he took a deep breath and tried to pull himself together.

"I hate it when people dress up as cats," a guy at a nearby table was saying, his voice almost impossible to ignore since it was so grating. "You know when they have a leotard and fake ears, and a fake tail, and then creep about and make cat noises? I hate that. Like, it makes my skin crawl."

Rolling his eyes, Ted tried to focus on his food.

"And spoons dressed as people," the guy added. "Why do some people get a kick out of putting little faces on spoons and holding them up like they're puppets? What kind of mind would enjoy something so stupid?"

Ted had to hold himself back from turning to the guy and asking him to keep his voice down. The last thing he wanted was to make a fuss in the restaurant, so he forced himself to hold his tongue and he tried to focus on what he was going to do to Rebecca once he got back to the farm the next day.

"Do you know what freaks me out the most?" the guy continued, apparently not done with his inane observations. "Child actors. Like, children should *not* be good at acting. At all. Whenever I see a child in a film or a show who's really good at acting, I just wonder what the hell is going on there. Like, how did that happen?"

"I'm really sorry," a female voice replied, "but I..."

She hesitated.

"My head's really not in a good place tonight," she added.

That was no wonder, Ted figured, since she was on a date with a loud, obnoxious guy who seemingly couldn't shut up for five seconds. Then again, he quickly reminded himself that the guy might simply be babbling because he was nervous, in which case wasn't it the woman's job to try to make him feel more at ease? In an instant, his opinion on the situation changed and he felt as if the guy wasn't getting a fair crack of the whip.

"I'm so sorry," the woman at the next table continued. "I was looking forward to this date all week, and then, to tell you the truth, my mum called me yesterday and she lives hundreds of miles away and she lives alone and she had a fall and because of work I can't go to her until tomorrow and so here I am sitting here trying to be a good date but my mind..."

She sighed.

"I completely understand," the guy replied.

"I'm so, *so* sorry."

For the next few minutes, Ted found himself listening to more and more of their conversation. Something about their interaction was strangely compelling, although Ted could feel his blood boiling as he realized that the woman had completely mishandled the situation. In fact, she'd been extremely rude, and he was tempted to turn around and say as much right to her face. After a moment, however, he reminded himself that he needed to stay calm. He'd let his anger boil over a few times in the past, and that had never gone well. The last thing he wanted was to make a scene in public.

"It's happening again," Rebecca said, and he realized that the hallucination had returned. "You're finding a new one, aren't you?"

"No," he whispered. "It's not that."

"I should have canceled," the woman at the next table said finally. "I nearly *did* cancel, but then Hayley called and told me I'd be fine, and I listened to her. Since she's the one who set us up in the first place, I figured she knew what she was talking about."

"In the ten years I've known Hayley, her longest relationship has been about a month."

"Yep, me too." She paused. "You seem like a really nice guy, Richard, and I'm sorry for wasting your time like this."

"You haven't wasted my time. And, hey, when you get back from your mum's, we can always try again. Right?"

Try again?

Why would he ever give her another chance?

Once again, Ted wanted to turn around and tell the woman exactly what he thought of her, but he somehow managed to restrain himself, even as the date ended and the couple arranged to pay.

"It's just like I told you," Rebecca said, watching Ted from across the table, "you never finish a job, because you always prefer to start a new one instead. That way you never have to face up to the fact that you're on a hiding to nothing. You never have to admit that you're one big, stinking, sloppy failure."

The man and woman at the next table got to their feet and began to head to the door, still talking about the failure of their date. Ted kept his eyes fixed firmly on the hallucinated form of Rebecca, and he felt a flicker of anger as he saw the smirk on her face. Part of him wanted to throw the table over and scream at her that she was wrong, but once again he managed to restrain himself. He was going to prove to her that she was wrong, and he was going to start by heading back to the farm and starting a new training session. That bitch was going to learn that she was nothing special.

Getting to his feet, he set some money down on the table – more than enough to cover his half-eaten meal – and then he turned to leave, only to stop as soon as he saw the couple from the next table. They were over by the door now, and something about the woman immediately caught his attention.

She was perfect in every way.

## CHAPTER TWENTY-SIX

"Chief Inspector Noad? Can I grab you for a second?"

Having been going through a pile of papers on his desk, John Noad turned just in time to see Detective Inspector Warren Pacey standing in the doorway. Although he'd wanted to just swing by and grab a few things, Noad had fully expected that one or other of his colleagues would try to stop him for a quick chat.

"Make it quick," Noad muttered. "I'm supposed to be on sick-leave, remember?"

"There's another missing woman," Pacey explained. "I only found out about it just now, she lives a couple of hundred miles away. Her name's Rebecca Ballard, the police in her local area have been looking for her for a few days but they've found nothing apart from her abandoned car. It looks like she was in some kind of accident, but so far they've had no luck working out where she might have gone after the car went off the road."

"Why are you telling me this?" Noad asked, although deep down he already knew the answer to that question.

"I know you've been working on some theories, Sir," Pacey continued, "and... I might be imagining it, but some aspects of this case seem to fit that stuff you were going on about a while back, about there maybe being a serial killer at work in the Twist Valley area."

"You said this woman was in a car crash, right?"

"By all accounts, her vehicle was pretty badly wrecked. I'm waiting to get some images through now."

"All the other missing women have left perfectly undamaged cars."

"I know, but..."

"Why would he suddenly start changing his methods?"

"I suppose I just thought that this might still be worth looking into. I know you've been trying to get people interested in your theories, and I wanted to let you know that this case might be relevant."

Noad opened his mouth to tell him that he had better things to be getting on with, but then he hesitated as he thought about exactly what Pacey had just told him. He looked down at his papers, and he knew that he should be getting home, but a niggling little sense of doubt was warning him that he shouldn't dismiss Pacey's new lead too quickly. Even before he was willing to admit the truth to himself, some part of him already knew that he was going to be late leaving.

"Okay," he said finally, "you've got ten minutes. Tell me everything."

\*\*\*

"She disappeared here," Pacey said a short while later, as he pointed at one particular spot on a large map that covered a wall in the office. "That's just past the marker for Twist Valley, so technically she's within the zone that you identified."

"She certainly is," Noad muttered.

"She would have been coming from this direction," Pacey explained, pointing at another section of the map. "She'd been to lunch with a friend, and then she'd done some more work before heading home. I remembered that you thought meals might be relevant somehow. Didn't you suggest that all the victims had eaten in a public place before they disappeared?"

"That's far from conclusive."

"Sure, but there's a definite pattern emerging. Sir, I know I told you before that I was never quite onboard with your theory, but it's getting harder and harder to ignore."

"You're not the only one," Noad muttered grimly. "I've been trying to persuade people for years that someone's up to no good in Twist Valley, and all my suggestions fall on deaf ears. Sometimes I even wonder if someone higher up in the chain of command is trying to protect the culprit."

"You don't seriously believe that," Pacey said, before hesitating. "Do you?"

"Relax, I stopped thinking it might be an inside job a long time ago," he replied, before stepping back and taking a broader look at the entire map. "Twist Valley is huge. It's certainly the place I'd pick if I wanted to disappear. Or to make other people disappear."

"But there have been searches, right?"

"I got a couple up and running, but I never managed to persuade anyone to give me all the resources I needed. I have absolutely no doubt that someone could be hiding out there, covering their tracks and keeping a low profile, and just generally getting up to no good. It's really the perfect place for that sort of thing."

"This Ballard woman has been missing for a few days now."

"What about her background?" Noad asked. "Has she ever disappeared like this before?"

"I don't believe so."

"And everything's alright at home?"

"As far as we can tell. She and her husband had a child last year, and by all accounts Rebecca's a devoted mother. Everyone our officers have spoken to say that it's completely out of character for her to run off like this."

"It's always out of character until it happens," Noad said sniffily.

They stood in silence for a moment, still looking at the map. Noad had previously marked out the spots where several women had disappeared. Although nobody else had ever taken much of an interest in his theories, he'd continued to carry out work on the side, gradually building up a collection of evidence so that he'd be ready to hit the ground running if the day ever came. He'd told himself many times to give up and stop wasting his time, but deep down he'd never been able to let the case go; he knew that he probably never would, not until his dying day.

"Go down there and talk to this woman's husband," he said finally.

"Don't you want -"

"I'm sending *you*," he added. "What's the matter, don't you think I can trust you with this?"

"Of course you can." Pacey hesitated. "I guess I'm just... honored, Sir."

"Find out everything you can and report back to me," Noad continued. "I'm too old and grouchy to go running up and down the country after every possible tip. If you uncover anything that looks genuinely interesting, that's when I'll step in and take charge of the investigation. And whatever you do, don't tell anyone that you're there on my behalf, okay? Over the years I've developed a reputation as something of an idiot. There are plenty of people who are only too happy to explain that I'm chasing shadows."

He let out a heavy sigh.

"I mean it," he added. "If people know you're working with me, they'll treat you different. Like you're just another crank, infected by my stupid theories."

"I can be there first thing in the morning, Sir," Pacey told him, "and I should have a report for you by tomorrow evening."

"That'll do just fine. No reports, though. Keep it unofficial for now."

Again, they stood and looked at the map.

"Well?" Noad said after a moment. "What are you waiting for?"

"Of course," Pacey replied, turning and hurrying to the door, "I'm sorry."

Stopping just as he was about to leave the room, Pacey hesitated for a moment before turning to look back toward his boss. He looked for a moment at the map, and at the array of other evidence that Noad had – over the years – pinned to various noticeboards, and he felt a shudder pass through his chest as he considered the possibility, however remote, that they might be on the brink of uncovering something significant. He opened his mouth to ask Noad if he was sure he didn't want to tag along, but he quickly reminded himself that his boss wasn't the kind of man who liked to be asked the same question twice.

"How big is Twist Valley?" he asked again.

"Huh?" Noad turned to him. "A couple of thousand square kilometers."

"That's pretty massive."

"It certainly is. By the standards of our little land, at least."

"And a lot of it's just... forest, right?"

"Indeed. There are houses out there, although they're not all on the grid, if you know what I mean. I've tried looking into the tangled mess of land ownership covering that place, and it's not easy."

"So I guess it's almost like outlaw country."

"That might be taking things a step too far," Noad replied, "but... there's certainly enough room for the odd lunatic to get about without anyone noticing."

"And do you really think that..."

Pacey's voice trailed off for a moment.

"Do you really think that some guy could have been out there, snatching people and doing all sorts of things to them somewhere in Twist Valley, without anyone ever noticing?"

"*I* noticed."

"Sure, but..." He hesitated again. "It's just a lot to get my head around."

"Mary Walsh was the first," Noad told him. "At least, the first on my radar. Twenty-five women have vanished in and around Twist Valley in the decade since Mary went missing. The area's so vast, and the creep covered his tracks so well, that I'm the only person who's seriously put in the work to connect them all together. All women, all adults, all seemingly snatched from their cars. No bodies have ever been found."

"How can this not be a bigger story?" Pacey asked.

"I've spent a long time trying to make it the biggest story in the country," Noad replied, "but certain people just don't want to know. In a way, it's a good thing that this Ballard woman's a mother. That might help get her story onto a few front-pages. I shouldn't have to think like that, but I do. Now get out of here and find Mrs. Ballard's husband. Make sure you call me tomorrow, as soon as you know what's going on down there. Move!"

Without another word, Pacey turned and hurried away.

Left all alone, Noad looked back at the map. He tried once again to tell himself that everything was going to be okay, but he couldn't shake a sense of dread that was slowly rising through his chest. He'd developed a decent instinct over the years, and he was starting to wonder whether the disappearance of the Ballard woman might finally get things moving. If that happened, whole teams of officers could be sent to search key areas of Twist Valley, and there was a chance that they just might find something significant.

"Don't get too comfortable," Noad whispered as he continued to look at the map, and as he imagined some crazed killer lurking somewhere in the forest. "You can't stay hidden forever."

## CHAPTER TWENTY-SEVEN

"She's seen you, you know," Rebecca said, standing next to Ted a couple of hours later as he watched the figure in the window. "She saw you earlier, in the car park, and she's *definitely* seen you now."

"Shut up," he replied, keeping his eyes fixed on the window. He could see the woman's silhouette, and she certainly seemed to be looking back down at him as she spoke to someone on the phone. "I don't need you in my ear all the time."

"It's already begun," she continued. "While the real me is probably desperately trying to get out of those chains, you're already eyeing up my replacement. This is all so pathetically predictable, Ted Armitage."

"You have no idea what you're talking about."

"Then walk away. Stop researching her and stop going through her social media pages. Forget that she even exists. It's pretty easy for you to show me that I'm wrong about all of this. You could do it in a flash."

Reaching out, she snapped her fingers in front of his face.

"Don't do that!" he hissed.

He wanted to tell her that he was merely taking an interest in the woman, but deep down he knew that it was more than that. Charlotte – he'd learned from some sleuthing that her name was Charlotte Walker – seemed full of potential, and he was certain that he could put her back on the right path. She was beautiful and smart, and he felt sure that she just needed a gentle nudge. Suddenly Rebecca didn't seem so important; suddenly Charlotte was the future.

"Please save me!" Rebecca screamed suddenly, dropping to her knees and grabbing the front of Ted's shirt. "I'm begging you, you were right all along! I see that now!"

"Of course I was right," he replied, "but -"

"I'll do anything you want," she continued, clutching his shirt as tears rolled down her cheeks. "I didn't see it until now, but it finally all makes sense. Everything you told me was true, I just needed time before I could see it. Please, Ted, help me be a better person. I'm entirely in your hands, I won't resist, not again. I need you to save me."

Staring down at her, he realized that she was sincere. He could see the desperation in her eyes, and he knew that she wasn't lying. She'd finally come around to his way of thinking, and she was willing to open herself completely to his teaching. He just had to decide whether he was still willing to come to her aid, or whether she'd pushed him away one time too many.

"Please," she sobbed, as she leaned forward and pressed her forehead against his belly. "Help me."

He opened his mouth to reply, but a moment later he realized that she was starting to laugh. Confused, he watched as she looked up at him, and in a flash he saw that her tears were now tears of laughter.

"You fool," she said, barely able to speak at all. "That's really what you want, isn't it. It's what you think might happen."

"You disgust me," he sneered.

"Even your fantasies turn against you in the end," she pointed out. "You want to talk about disgust? When I see you, I see a man who does everything in his power to pretend that he's not just another murderer. Look at you, skulking about at night, stalking someone, having a conversation with an imaginary friend based on the woman who's hanging in your barn. Don't you think that maybe you're not quite right in the head? Don't you think that beyond all the death and murder and pain, this is rather..."

She paused, trying to find the right word.

"Sad?" she suggested finally.

He looked down at her, and in an instant she blinked out of existence.

"I'm starting to think," he said after a moment, "that maybe I was wrong about you after all. It's Charlotte. She's the one who's going to be special."

\*\*\*

The following day, as soon as Charlotte had made her way into the service station's food court, Ted hurried away from his truck and walked briskly toward her car.

Reaching into his pocket, he took out the spiked metal object and crouched down next to the side of the car, before reaching past the tire and carefully attaching the object to the vehicle. He took a moment to make sure that it was firmly in place, and then he got to his feet and headed back to his truck. Glancing around, he was relieved to see that he hadn't been spotted.

Everything was ready.

\*\*\*

Sitting in his parked truck at the side of the road, Ted stared down at his phone and watched as the tracking beacon blinked on the screen. The beacon hadn't moved for quite some time, and he knew that meant that his plan had worked perfectly. Charlotte's car was now crippled, and he just had to wait a little while longer so that he could turn up and offer to save the day. She was only a short way along the road, past a couple of turns, and he could feel a knot of anticipation tightening in his chest.

Soon.

"Poor bitch," Rebecca said, sitting in the passenger seat. "She's about to go through what I went through, isn't she? Unless she manages to escape, that is."

"No-one's ever escaped," he replied, keeping his eyes fixed on the beacon.

"Not yet, maybe."

"It's impossible," he continued. "I have so many sensors around the farm, it's impossible for anything to move out there without me knowing."

"There *are* one or two gaps," she pointed out.

"It's fine," he said firmly. "Everything's under control."

"And the cycle begins again. Why are you wearing that hat, anyway? And what are those sunglasses about? Why do you always wear those when you meet a new one?"

"You're starting to irritate me," he said through gritted teeth.

"I *am* you," she reminded him. "What do you think the real Rebecca's doing right now, back at the farm? Do you think she's still trying to escape? I've got to admit, I'm surprised you were willing to leave her alone like this. What if some random person stumbles across the farm?"

"They won't."

"But what if they do?"

"They won't."

"But -"

"They won't," he said for a third time, turning to her. "The place is hidden away. You know I have my methods."

"This can't last forever, though," she told him. "Nothing can. Sooner or later something's going to happen and your little fun will all be over. The only question is whether or not you'll let them take you alive."

"The police are idiots," he replied. "I know how to keep off their radar."

"And what about -"

"I have my methods."

"But what if -"

"I know what I'm doing!" he said angrily, as he put the truck into gear and began to set off after Charlotte's stranded vehicle. "I didn't get to where I am now by making mistakes. And why are you asking me all this stuff, anyway? If you're just a figment of my imagination, why are you constantly asking me questions that I already know the answer to?"

"You might well wonder," she said with a smile. "Are you starting to get that tingling feeling again? The one you always get when you're about to snatch a new victim from the road? Did you get that with me, when you plucked me from safety the other day?"

Ignoring her, he focused on the road ahead.

"Give it a week," she added, "and Charlotte Walker will be old news. You'll have yet another exciting new project."

"Charlotte's going to be the one," he replied, even though he knew that there was no need to rise to her bait. "I can feel it in my gut."

"That's probably just an ulcer."

He opened his mouth to reply, but at that moment he saw Charlotte's car up ahead, and he breathed a sigh of relief as he spotted her. Although he'd been determined to wait a while before showing up, he'd worried that she might set off to find help, which would have meant driving a little further to find her. Fortunately, she was already climbing out of her car, and she waved at him as he pulled over and cut the engine.

"Good girl," he muttered under his breath.

"You're so excited," Rebecca said as he opened the door. "It's almost cute."

"Well, hello there," he said, ignoring her as he removed his hat and sunglasses and began to make his way over toward Charlotte, "what seems to be the problem?"

"My wheel's wrecked, I think," she replied. "I've got no signal, I was sitting here and waiting, hoping that someone would come by who might give me a lift to the next town."

"I can do better than that," he told her, even as his heart pounded in his chest. "My name's Ted Armitage and I happen to know my way around a car. I've even got a load of tools with me. If you like, I can take a look at the damage and hopefully get you back on the road in no time."

"That'd be amazing," she said with a big sigh. "Thank you so much. You're a lifesaver!"

## CHAPTER TWENTY-EIGHT

As he stepped out of the truck, Ted looked over his shoulder and stopped to watch the barn. He listened for a moment, but he heard no sounds at all.

No screams.

No cries.

No clanging of chains.

He waited a few more seconds, before telling himself that Rebecca Ballard would still be right where he left her. Assuming she was conscious, she'd have heard his truck arrive, and the last thing he wanted was to give her the satisfaction of rushing straight over to check on her. Far better, he decided, to let her stew a little while longer. After everything she'd said to him during the day, he wanted to make her suffer.

No.

That wasn't her.

He had to remember that.

The hallucination had been a product of his imagination, and he knew that it wouldn't be fair to blame the real Rebecca for anything that had happened during his travels. Still, he didn't feel like seeing her just yet, so instead he made his way around to the rear of the truck and looked inside. Sure enough, Charlotte Walker was still unconscious, and he was keen to get her up to the room and tie her to the bed. Then again, he knew that once he did that, there'd be no chance to bring her back down before...

Before.

"You're still zonked out, right?" he said cautiously, watching Charlotte's face in case there was any hint of consciousness. "Hey, if you can hear me, now's the time to speak up. I don't take too kindly to people trying to deceive me, so let's start on the right foot here."

He hesitated, and then he looked back over toward the barn.

\*\*\*

Pushing the wheelchair through the open doorway, with Charlotte slumped in the seat, Ted felt an immediate rush of relief as he saw Rebecca still hanging from the chains. Although he'd been confident that there was no way she could have escaped, a part of him had still been aware that leaving her alone for two days had been something of a risk.

Now, however, he allowed himself to grin again as he wheeled Charlotte over to the far end of the barn and stopped just a few feet from Rebecca. He could see fresh blood caked on her arms, and when he looked up at her wrists he was immediately able to see that she'd tried again and again to break free; she'd managed to tear the skin around the top of her hands, and he wasn't certain but he felt that her left wrist looked slightly elongated, as if it had perhaps become dislocated.

He waited, but so far Rebecca seemed to be unconscious.

"I'm back," he announced.

No reply.

"Hey, I'm back," he continued, before clearing his throat. "Come on, I know you're still alive. I brought something for you to see. Seriously, you won't want to miss it."

He waited.

He furrowed his brow.

Making his way over to her, he nudged her shoulder. He could hear a series of rasping breaths now, but when he pushed her shoulder a couple more times he found that he still couldn't rouse her. The tops of her arms seemed distorted somehow, as if she's almost pulled them out of their sockets. Finally he patted the side of her face with his hand, hoping to make her stir.

After a moment, Rebecca let out a faint groan and lifted her head. She had trouble opening her eyes, and more trouble focusing as she tried to look at him, but finally her gaze slipped down until she was looking directly at Charlotte.

"Her name's Charlotte Walker," Ted explained, stepping aside so that she could see properly. "I wasn't planning to pick anyone up during my travels this time, but she more or less just fell right into my lap. You wouldn't believe some of the things I heard her saying, and I just felt compelled to bring her here so that I could try to help her. I really, truly believe that I'm the right person to make her see the error of her ways."

"My..."

Rebecca's voice trailed off for a moment.

"My replacement," she managed to whisper finally.

"Don't look at it like that."

"You're not going to work on... two of us at the same... time."

He opened his mouth to reply, but then he hesitated. After all, she was right, even if he hadn't quite admitted that to himself yet.

"A lot of things are still up in the air," he said cautiously. "It wouldn't be fair to rush to any kind of judgment. I had to take Charlotte when the opportunity presented itself, otherwise she'd have been lost. And there's just something about her..."

Reaching down, he brushed the hair from one side of Charlotte's face and looked at her features.

"There's something about her that gives me a really good feeling," he continued. "It's in my gut, this belief that I know exactly what she needs and that I'm the only person who can give it to her." He stared for a moment, almost mesmerized. "She's a good person, she just needs someone to steer her back onto the right path, that's all. She did wrong by this guy she was meeting for dinner last night, but at least she had the good grace to *admit* that she was wrong. That shows a level of self-awareness that some people – present company included – can be lacking from time to time. I've really got to hone in on that and -"

Before he could finish, Rebecca started laughing. Startled, Ted looked over at her and watched as her body twitched and jerked as she hung from the chains. Her laugh almost wasn't a laugh at all, it was almost some kind of spasm. He wanted to ask her what was so funny, but he knew that to do so would be to admit that he didn't understand, and the last thing he wanted was to look stupid. He also didn't want to let her see that she was getting a rise out of him.

"I should take her inside," he said, as he began to turn the wheelchair around. "I just thought you might like to meet her, that's all."

"How long before she ends up hanging here like me?" Rebecca gasped.

"Hopefully, that won't happen," he replied, stopping and looking back at her. "She won't be a disappointment."

At this, Rebecca laughed again.

"I wouldn't do that in your position," Ted said firmly. "You're making a really big mistake. You're not endearing yourself to me one bit, and I shouldn't have to remind you that endearing yourself to me might be a very good idea right now."

As she continued to laugh, he felt his anger starting to rise, and finally he let go of the wheelchair and stormed back over to Rebecca. Grabbing her throat, he squeezed tight and choked the last of the laugh out of her.

"You think you're so smart," he sneered, looking into her terrified eyes, "but you're not! Do you think I care about all that crap you were going on about in the restaurant yesterday? Do you think it bothers me at all? You think you've got me all figured out, but you don't understand me at all! Every word you said to me last night was a lie! You were so pompous and smug, telling me all about how my mind works, but how clever do you feel right now, huh?"

He glared at her, enjoying her fear.

"What restaurant?" she asked finally. "I was here last night."

He opened his mouth to reply, but then he hesitated for a moment.

"You know damn well what I mean," he added after a few seconds, somewhat shaken by the realization that he'd managed to get the real Rebecca and the fantasy version confused. "Don't try to be smart with me. I'm going to go and attend to Charlotte, and that'll take me a little time, but I *will* be back for you tonight, and that's going to be your moment of reckoning. Until then, I'd suggest that you think long and hard about whether you're going to blow your last chance to accept my help. You still have hope, Rebecca, but it's running out. For the sake of your husband and your daughter, I'd like to think that you'll do the right thing."

With that, he turned and started pushing the wheelchair out of the barn.

"Come back here, you bastard!" Rebecca shouted, pulling on the chains. "You can't leave me here again! I won't let you ignore me!"

He was already gone, however, and she could do nothing more than try yet again to pull free. She twisted in every possible direction, but her wrists were secured too tightly and she knew that she had no hope of escaping using brute force alone. With no other ideas, however, she couldn't stop herself trying over and over again, pulling so hard that after a few seconds she began to think that her hands might end up getting torn clean away from her wrists.

## CHAPTER TWENTY-NINE

Several hours later, standing in the kitchen and eating a sandwich, Ted looked out the window and watched the barn. Bathed in moonlight, the barn seemed somehow to be calling to him, although he knew that it was a little too early still to go over there. He wanted Rebecca to really think about what she'd done wrong, he wanted her to twist and writhe in agony and fear.

"You still have a chance," he whispered, as much to convince himself of that idea. "You don't realize it, but you can still make it out of here. You just have to do the right thing."

He took a bite of the sandwich he'd prepared, although in truth he wasn't really hungry.

Hearing a creaking sound, he looked over his shoulder. There was no sign of anyone else in the kitchen, and he knew that Charlotte Walker was still unconscious on the bed upstairs; in fact, he expected her to remain unconscious for quite some time to come, at least a couple more hours.

A moment later, however, he heard another floorboard creak, and he turned to look to his left.

"You're going to kill me," Rebecca's voice said, and now Ted realized that he could see a silhouette in the darkness. "Just admit it," she continued. "This is all just a pantomime that you're keeping going so that you can convince yourself that you gave me a fair shot, but tonight or tomorrow you're going to kill me and the only question is whether or not I get to go on your little monument of heads."

"Absolutely not," he replied.

"You're lying to yourself."

"No, I'm telling the truth," he said firmly. "I've given you so many chances. All I ask now is that you submit to my methods and let me guide you to where you need to be. The truth is, until the moment I kill someone, they're never entirely out of luck. There's always a chance to turn things around."

"There's never a chance," she told him. "From the moment they arrive here, they're all doomed. Even that new one upstairs right now. You're going to lead her through the same song and dance and then you're going to hang her up in that barn and then..."

Her voice trailed off for a moment, as a smile spread across her face.

"You're going to do the same thing to her, that you've done to..."

Again, she paused, and then she held her hands up and clapped them together.

"All."

And again.

"Of."

And again.

"Us."

He opened his mouth to reply, but in that moment he heard the sound of a floorboard creaking over his shoulder. He froze, worried that Charlotte might have somehow managed to break away from the bed, but in that instant he heard another floorboard, then another, and he realized that he could smell something rotten. The smell was familiar, but it took a few more seconds before he was willing to admit *where* he'd encountered it before.

The pit.

He began to turn and look, but he stopped as soon as he spotted multiple silhouettes in the darkness. A flicker of fear began to burn in his chest, and somehow he was unable to shake the feeling that this had all happened many times before.

"They all know that I'm right," Rebecca said firmly. "They all know, because they're all like me. And very soon, I'm going to be joining them, aren't I?"

Before Ted could react, several of the figures stepped forward. As soon as he saw their faces, he recognized them as the women from the pit, as the women he'd killed over the years. More of them made their way toward him, and he instinctively began to back away until he bumped against the sideboard. For a moment, too horrified to even begin to cry out, he could only watch as the women continued to advance, and he soon began to notice the cracking sounds coming from their dead bones.

"It's so cold down there," Sylvia Reynolds said, her face partially missing after years spent down at the bottom of the pit. "Don't you want to join us?"

"You're not real," he sneered.

"You told me I still had a chance to survive," Cally reminded him as she edged closer. "You lied to me. You told me I had a chance, I did exactly what you asked, and then you shot me in the back of the head."

"You deserved that!" he stammered. "You tried to hide in my house! You actually thought I wouldn't notice!"

"You lied to all of us," Lydia Cole said, as several of the dead women stopped in front of him. "You brought us here and murdered us like common animals."

"And you still think there's something noble about what you do," Lizzy Burnett added. "Even after all these years. How long has it been now since the first victim?"

"No," he sobbed, sliding down onto the floor, looking up at the women as they stood around him in various stages of decomposition, "you don't understand."

"Let's ask her," Andrea Souvelli suggested, and after a moment the women all stepped aside. "Your very first victim, all those years ago... Let's see whether *she* understands your sick, twisted mind better than the rest of us."

"No, please," he whimpered, but he could already see a shadowy figure limping toward him from the far end of the kitchen. "Why do you always do this to me?"

Unable to turn away, he watched as the rotten, almost skeletal corpse of Mary Walsh – the first woman he'd dared to pluck from the side of a road, almost a decade earlier – limped but surely toward him. Her flesh was horribly discolored, with pieces of bone poking through, and her legs were barely strong enough to carry her. Ted would have been more shocked, but in truth he'd witnessed the same vision many times before, even though he knew that Mary's body remained firmly at the very bottom of the pit, weighed down by all the other corpses.

"Don't," he stammered, with tears running down his cheeks as he looked up at Mary's face. "Please..."

Opening her mouth, Mary let out a faint groan as gray water dribbled from her lips. As she began to crouch down, her bones clicked loudly, and a moment later she reached out and placed an icy hand on the side of Ted's face. He could only stare back at her with a growing sense of horror as he saw that thousands of tiny holes had been dug into her face, perhaps by worms or other parasites that lived in the depths of the pit. Her eyes were pale and glassy, although something dark was squirming about deep in one of the balls, just about visible.

"This happens every time, doesn't it?" Rebecca said calmly, clearly enjoying Ted's suffering. "This is why you do it, isn't it? Every time, for the same thing. This little reunion with all your victims. This is what gets your rocks off."

Mary leaned closer to Ted.

"This is what it's all about," Rebecca added. "Enjoy."

Ted screamed.

***

Sitting all alone on the floor, surrounded by darkness and silence, Ted tried to get his thoughts together. The phantom version of Rebecca had been right: he'd imagined all the women standing around him so many times, although that didn't make it any easier each time it happened.

Finally, getting to his feet, he picked up the sandwich again. His hands were trembling, but he told himself that he'd have to eat before going back out to Rebecca.

Suddenly he heard a muffled voice from upstairs. At first he assumed that he was imagining the sound, but after a few seconds he realized that Charlotte must have woken up. He listened, and sure enough he could tell that she was trying to get off the bed, so he made his way through to the hall and looked up the stairs.

He hesitated, and then he walked up to take a look. He'd been planning to go straight out to Rebecca and see whether she was finally ready to do the right thing, although in truth he was glad of a distraction. As he approached the door to the second bedroom, he allowed himself a faint smile as he listened to the sound of Charlotte wriggling and trying to get free on the bed.

"Ah, there you are," he said finally, as he leaned against the side of the door. "You woke up a little faster than I expected, but not a great deal. It's all good. You must be a little heavier than you look."

"What do you want from me?" she asked.

"Well, first I'd like you to chill out a little," he explained, before taking a bite from his sandwich. "There's no need to be rude just because you've found yourself taking something of an unexpected diversion. The truth is, I knew you'd never reach a town if you just went wandering off. You'd most likely have died of exposure, so I very kindly decided to bring you back to my place."

## CHAPTER THIRTY

Letting out a pained gasp, Rebecca twisted her arm and pushed against the base of her hand, and finally she applied enough pressure to break her own thumb. She screamed, but in that moment she forced herself to start pulling. After a few seconds, her wrist slipped out of the chain and she realized that was at least partly free.

Reaching up, she began to work on her other hand. She had to twist the thumb back, but this time she was more determined than ever to escape. She took a moment to gather some more strength, and then she snapped the thumb and forced her hand back through the chain until it came loose, at which point she slumped down onto the concrete floor and rolled onto her side.

Struggling to get her breath back, she realized that she was finally free. She'd beaten him. Somehow, her body wasn't even registering the pain as anything more than a dull ache.

She sat up and tried to figure out which way to go next. She still couldn't walk, and the wheelchair was nowhere to be seen, and she knew that she'd never survive if she tried to escape through the forest. Even if Ted somehow didn't manage to track her down, she'd die of exposure, which meant that she only had one option.

Attack.

Looking around, she tried to spot something that she could use as a weapon. She knew that she'd most likely only get one shot at Ted, which meant that she had to make it count. Barely able to even pull herself forward on her elbows, she nevertheless managed to drag herself over to the legs of a workbench, and then she carefully clambered up onto her knees and started looking through the various tools. Any one of them seemed like a decent choice, but she was more worried about whether she'd have the strength to strike him with enough force. Finally, she settled on a large knife and -

"Got you!"

Suddenly Ted grabbed her from behind. She tried desperately to snatch the knife, but she was too late and Ted quickly began to drag her back toward the chains. She struggled, but he quickly reattached the chains to her wrists and hauled her up, and then he stepped over to the side of the barn and flicked a switch, activating an arc light that almost blinded her with its intensity.

"You're proving to be a slippery customer tonight, aren't you?" he muttered as he made his way back over to her. "All those high hopes that I had for you are lost now, replaced by a genuine and very honest sense of what could have been. You haven't angered me, Rebecca, and you haven't hurt me. All you've done is disappoint me."

Pulling frantically against the chains, she twisted in every possible direction as she tried to escape. The chains were tighter this time, however, and after a moment she saw that Ted was picking up the very same knife that just a moment ago she'd planned to use against him. He turned to her, and she saw that something had changed in his eyes. He looked like a man who was ready to kill.

"No!" she screamed. "Please, don't do this!"

Filled with panic, she pulled again and again on the chains. Whereas before she'd always tried to think her way out of danger, now she was resorting to sheer force. Some kind of primal terror was taking over, to the extent that she could barely think properly at all. All she knew was that she'd been so close to escaping, and now that last brutal sense of hope was being snatched away.

"Why are you doing this to me?" she sobbed, even though she knew she'd never get a proper answer. "Just let me go. Please, I'm begging you, I have a husband and a child, you have to let me go..."

She pulled on the chains again, more out of desperation now than any belief that she might – for a second time – find some way to escape. All she needed was one sliver of hope, one last chance.

"What do you think that's gonna achieve, huh?" Ted asked. "I already told you, I've got your replacement lined up. We both knew this day was going to come. And you have to admit, you've caused me a fair old bit of trouble lately."

He stepped toward her and held up a large knife with a rusted serrated edge. Turning the blade for a moment, he let it glint in the light, and then he moved it down and drove it straight into Rebecca's belly.

"No!" she screamed, but she could already feel him starting to cut through her guts as blood splattered down against the floor.

"Don't feel bad," Ted told her. "You were good. She's just better, that's all. I think she and I are going to have a lot of fun."

He stepped around her.

"When I'm done here," he continued, as he reached up and loosened the chains around her wrists, "I'm going to go and start her first lesson. Ordinarily I'd wait until morning, but tonight I'm just so fired up to get going."

As soon as the chains were gone, Rebecca began to slump down, only for Ted to catch her from behind.

"Not so fast," he said, turning her around and starting to drag her out of the barn. "There is *one* scrap of good news for you. As you know, some of my guests are simply thrown into the pit and left to rot, but some get the privilege of a spot on my monument. And you, Rebecca, have certainly earned that privilege. And then some."

Barely conscious, Rebecca felt herself being dragged outside and around to the barn's far side. Her bare, battered feet bumped against the grass, until Ted stopped and turned her around, forcing her onto her knees. At that moment, she saw the spike of heads in the moonlight and she instinctively turned and tried to crawl away.

"It's too late for that," he sneered, pulling her back and then shoving her down so that she was flat on the ground. Turning, he set the knife aside and picked up an ax that had been left leaning against the barn. "I've learned a lot from you Rebecca. Really, I mean that. And I'm going to apply everything that I've learned to Charlotte. Think of her up there in the room, waiting for me, not knowing the amazing opportunity that's about to be dropped into her lap. She and I are about to set out on a beautiful journey. I hope you envy her. You certainly should."

She let out a faint, gurgling groan, but already she was thinking of her daughter. In her mind's eye she could see Chloe laughing in her crib, and she tried to focus on that image as she waited for the end to come. With one side of her face pressed against the grass, she felt the ground shudder as Ted stepped around her, and then she allowed herself a faint smile as she remembered what it felt like to hold Chloe after bath-time. The smell of the talcum powder. The light in Chloe's eyes. The sound of her laughter.

In a flash, Ted brought the ax crashing down, slicing straight through Rebecca's neck with one swift blow. After tossing the ax aside, he picked up her severed head and looked at her face, and her mouth twitched slightly as if – deep inside – some final part of her soul hadn't quite departed.

"Enjoy," he said, before reaching up and placing her head on the top of the spike, then forcing it down until the spike's tip burst out through the top of her skull.

Rebecca's eyes opened wide. One pupil expanded, the other contracted, and her mouth opened as she let out one last gasp.

And then she was gone.

Dropping to his knees, next to Rebecca's headless corpse, Ted looked up at her face and felt a strange sense of calm wash through his body. He knew that he'd failed with Rebecca, but he was far more interested in the fact that he had a nice fresh student waiting on the bed in the spare bedroom. He took a deep breath, reflecting upon everything that had happened, and then he got to his feet and dragged Rebecca's body across the grass.

"You were good, I'll give you that," he told her. "It's not your fault that I happened to bump into Charlotte. If that hadn't happened, you and I might have had a lot more time together. It's just that Charlotte's so special."

He opened the hatch and threw Rebecca's headless body down, and he watched as it splashed against the other corpses and then slithered down into the cold water.

"Goodbye, Rebecca," he said calmly. "No hard feelings. Things just didn't work out. If it's any consolation, I think I might actually miss you a little."

After closing the hatch, he headed back into the house and took a moment to freshen up, and then he headed upstairs and through to the spare bedroom. He already had quite a spring in his step again as he contemplated all the exciting work that lay ahead.

"Okay, Charlotte Walker," he said with a smile, "it's time to -"

Stopping in the doorway, he was shocked to see that the bed was empty, and that one of the slats in the headboard had been broken away. For a few seconds, he was too shocked to react, and he simply stared at the scene as he contemplated the reality that for the first time ever one of his guests had not only escaped from the bed but might actually have made it away from the farm itself.

"Well," Rebecca's voice whispered, right behind him in the darkness, "now you've got a chase on your hands, haven't you?"

# EPILOGUE

*Several days later...*

"So is that your real name?" Charlotte asked.
"Is what my real name?"
"Ted Armitage."
He glanced at her.
"Why wouldn't it be?"
"And why do you do what you do?" she continued. She looked outside again, and she saw that John was still working. "I mean, no-one kidnaps and murders people unless they've got a good reason."
"Are you sure about that?"
"Did someone hurt you?"
"Save the psychological investigation," he replied, as he checked under one of the sofas. "You don't know anything about me, and you don't *need* to know anything. As far as you're concerned, I'm just someone you had a little run-in with, and soon I'll be out of your hair. I'm not some puzzle, waiting to be solved."
"But what about -"
"I know what you're doing," he added, as he went out to check the hallway. "You want some more information you can pass on to the cops when you eventually go and tell them everything. Relax, don't deny it, I already know that's what you're planning to do. The truth is, I'm not too worried. Sure, it would have been fun to get to know you a little better, but I honestly don't think you pose much of a threat."

She looked out at John to make sure he was still working, and then she turned back to Ted.

"Once we say our goodbyes," he continued, "that'll be the end of it. It'll be as if I just vanish into the forest. I've been doing this for long enough to know how not to get caught. I'd sure appreciate it if you don't tell anyone about me, but to be honest I doubt you'll be able to contain yourself. Honestly, it's no biggie either way."

"So kidnapping me was just completely random?"

"I'm not getting into a deep conversation about this," he replied, before stepping back into the doorway and looking at her, "unless..."

"Unless what?"

"Well..." He took a step toward her, and for a moment he saw Rebecca smiling at him from the corner of the room, right behind Charlotte. "I do sometimes open up to people, about my background and so on, but only in very special circumstances. I happen to have had quite a lousy few days before I met you."

Book Three

# THE GREAT BEYOND

## PROLOGUE

"You don't have to do this," Noad said firmly, staring at the barrel of the gun and trying very hard to remain calm. "Think about your legacy."

"My legacy?"

Ted hesitated, before starting to laugh.

"I don't care about my legacy," he explained. "I don't *have* a legacy. This has always been about two things, and two things only. First, there's my desire to help people. I only succeeded once, but that's not too bad, not when you factor human nature into the equation. And second, there's always been a battle, hasn't there? You and I have always been aware of one another, always fighting to come out on top."

"I'm not sure that I'd put it quite like -"

"That battle ends today," Ted said firmly. "After all this time, I've finally come out on top, and there's nothing you can do about that."

"I don't think you really believe it's over," Noad told him.

"It doesn't matter what you think," Ted replied. "But if you don't believe me, then there's really one very easy way to prove my point."

"Listen to me," Noad said, holding his hands up, "I only want -"

Before he could get another word out, Ted pulled the trigger, firing a single shot that immediately sent Noad crumpling down to the forest floor.

## CHAPTER ONE

*Several days earlier...*

Out on a remote road in the heart of Twist Valley, with only a vast and ancient forest surrounding them for miles and miles in every direction, two figures stood between their vehicles.

"I'm sorry," Wendy said, "what did you just..."

Her voice trailed off.

"It's just something that's been bugging me," Ted Armitage said, as he removed his sunglasses. "I happened to be in that cafe yesterday. You know, the one with the big glass windows overlooking a car park outside the -"

"I know what cafe you're talking about," she said cautiously, before swallowing hard. "That's not what I meant. I just don't quite understand why *you're* asking me about a private conversation I had there with a friend. Do you know Debs?"

"Oh, I was just in there minding my own business," he explained, "and suddenly I noticed your voice. It's a little problem I get now and again, someone's voice drifts into my head and..."

He hesitated, and then he offered a nervous smile.

"Anyway, that's by the by," he continued. "The point is, I overheard you telling your friend – Debs, right? - that you were thinking of breaking up with your boyfriend when you go back to university in September, and I couldn't help thinking that it sounded a little like you were... I don't know, stringing him along."

Staring at him, Wendy seemed momentarily dumbstruck.

"Especially," Ted added, "since you acknowledged that he's paying for you two to go to some music festival next week. Tickets, camping, travel, the works. I just think that if you're going to break up with the poor guy, you should maybe do it *before* you take advantage of his generosity. That just seems like basic human decency to me."

He waited.

"You know what?" Wendy said after a moment. "I think I'm just going to wait in my car for someone else to come by and help me with my tire."

"Oh, no, I'm still more than happy to do that for you," he said, stepping toward her.

Flinching, she immediately pulled back and bumped against the side of her stricken car.

"It's okay," Ted said, stopping again and holding his hands up, "I'm just a friendly passing mechanic. I reckon I can have that tire sorted in no time, although there might be some damage to the wheel itself. It's hard to know until I get a proper look." He waited for her to reply. "Do you mind if I get in there and see what I'm dealing with?"

"Like I said," she replied, "I think I'm going to be happier waiting for someone else."

He stared at her.

"Is there something wrong with me?" he asked cautiously.

"No offense, dude, it's just... you're a little..."

Again, she hesitated for a moment.

"Thanks again," she added, before turning and opening the car door, "but -"

Suddenly hearing his footsteps hurrying closer, she turned just in time to see that Ted was holding a syringe. For a fraction of a second she watched as he raised the syringe to her neck, and then – at the last possible moment – her training from an old self-defense class kicked in and she swung the car door open until it slammed against his chest, knocking him back.

Letting out a loud gasp, Ted fall down onto the tarmac, dropping the syringe in the process.

"Get away from me!" Wendy shouted. "Don't you fucking dare come near me!"

Muttering something under his breath, Ted grabbed the syringe and stumbled to his feet. Before he could turn to Wendy again, however, she smacked him in the chin with a powerful undercut that sent him staggering back and almost knocked him straight back down.

Sitting up, Ted felt as if his skull had begun to vibrate.

Turning, Wendy tried to climb into the car, but she almost immediately heard Ted rushing up behind her. This time, she turned and saw that he was holding a large knife with a serrated edge. Immediately stepping out of the way, she managed to avoid the blade by just a few inches as Ted lunged at her. The knife hit the side of the car instead, and in that moment Wendy grabbed Ted's arm and smashed his wrist against her knee.

"What the -"

Trying to pull away, Ted managed to drop the knife, but Wendy kept hold of his arm and shoved him against the car before putting an arm around his neck and pulling him back.

"Oh, you picked the wrong fight here," she sneered, before slamming a knee into his leg, causing him to cry out in pain.

Shoving him back, she slipped a foot between his legs, sending him clattering once more to the ground. Slightly out of breath, she reached down and picked up the knife, and then she turned to see Ted staring up at her with a shocked expression.

"You want a piece of me?" she asked, holding the knife up. "Is that it? Are you some kind of psycho pervert who preys on lone women out here on the road?"

"Let's not get carried away," Ted replied as he began to get up. "I'm only -"

"No!" she screamed, flashing the knife close to his face. "Stay down there!"

"Okay!"

He held his hands up once more in surrender.

"This isn't the time to do anything hasty," he continued. "We both need to keep cool heads."

"My dad's one of the top cops in the country, asshole," she sneered. "All those self-defense classes I hated so much are really paying off now, huh?"

"Listen, I -"

Without letting him get another word out, she kicked him hard in the face, sending him crashing back down until he rolled onto his side and spat blood out onto the tarmac.

"You're a real piece of shit," she continued, stepping around him, still holding the knife. "Look at you. As soon as someone pushes back, you crumple like a cheap suit." She adjusted her grip on the knife. "I bet you thought I was gonna be easy pickings, huh? I bet you thought my panties'd fall right off and you'd be slithering all over me. I've met guys like you a million times, and I'm more than ready to teach you a lesson. How do you like that?"

She waited for him to reply, and then she slammed a knee against the back of his head.

"Huh?" she shouted. "Give me one good reason why I shouldn't cut your heart out!"

"I don't think you're the kind of girl who cuts hearts out," he replied breathlessly. "You might *break* a few but that's something else."

"Do you think you're charming?" she asked. "I don't think you're charming."

"I don't think I'm remotely charming," he told her, keeping his eyes fixed on her face while making sure to retain awareness of where she was holding the knife. "I think maybe I've got the gift of the gab, especially in tight situations, but that's only of limited benefit." He took a moment to clear his throat. "Listen, I think we've gotten off on the wrong foot, and there's been something of a misunderstanding. How about we each head off on our separate way? What do you say to that idea? Let's just wipe the slate clean and never see each other again."

"What was in that syringe?"

"I don't -"

"What *exactly* were you planning to do to me?"

"Well, that's complicated," he replied, unable to hide a faint smile.

"You think this is funny?"

"No, I don't" he told her, trying to push the smile away. "I just think that I don't need this hassle in my day, and I'm sure you don't either. Let's let bygones be bygones, let's admit that we reached an impasse, and let's get on with our lives." He hesitated, as if he expected her to simply shrug and walk away. "You've made your point," he added, as he wiped blood from his lips. "Lesson learned. Now, I don't think you want to escalate this any further and risk turning it into something that it doesn't need to be."

"Risk escalating it?" she replied, and now she was the one with a smile. "What are you, some kind of comedian? You can't come at a woman with a syringe, then with a knife, and expect to laugh the whole thing off. Sorry, mate, but you're gonna stay down there until I can get the police here."

"Right," he replied, "and how exactly are you going to do that, considering the fact that there's no phone service out here?"

She hesitated for a moment.

"Well," she said cautiously, "I'm going to start by checking your truck to see if you're operating some kind of jamming device."

"How would that fit in a truck?"

"For all I know, you're some kind of tech -"

Suddenly he grabbed her legs and pulled her down, while pushing her arm away and slamming her wrist against the ground. Before she had a chance to react, the knife fell from her hand and Ted placed an arm against her throat, pushing hard.

"Don't feel too bad," he hissed as he kicked the knife further away. "I'm going to take you back to my place, and I'm going to help you become a better person. By the time we're done together, you're going to be so grateful." He licked his lips. "I think you're finally the one. After searching for so long, I've finally found the soul I'm going to save."

"You forgot one thing," she gasped.

"And what's that?"

"You're not the only one who carries a knife."

He opened his mouth to reply, but at that moment he realized that she seemed to be reaching for something around her waist. He looked down, just as she let out an ear-piercing scream and plunged a pocket-knife straight into his gut.

## CHAPTER TWO

"You stupid bitch!"

Stumbling to his feet and stepping back, Ted reached down and grabbed the knife's handle. He began to pull it out, only to remember at the very last second that the knife might very well be the only thing that was keeping him from bleeding out. A moment later, hearing a scuffling sound, he turned to see that Wendy had reached over to grab the other knife.

"You don't like a taste of your own medicine, do you?" she snapped, lunging toward him and slashing the knife at his face.

Pulling out of the way just in time, Ted shoved her in the back and then turned to limp over to his truck. He winced as he felt the blade sliding in his belly, but now he was holding the handle in a desperate attempt to keep the knife from falling out. As he reached the truck, however, he heard footsteps racing up behind and he turned just as Wendy rushed at him again.

This time she slammed against him and pushed him onto the truck, before holding the other knife up to his face.

"You don't get away that easily," she sneered, her eyes filled with blood-lust. "I've changed my mind about handing you over to be questioned by the cops. I might as well just kill you right here and *then* call them. After all, it's blatantly self-defense. I just wonder what the police are gonna find when they start looking into your history. I'm not the first woman you've come after, am I?"

"You're making a very big mistake," he told her.

She moved the knife closer to his face.

"Am I?" she asked, as she pressed the blade against his left cheek. "Do you really think so? Because someone here's made a mistake today, but I'm not entirely sure that it's me. The thing is, Ted – that *is* what you called yourself just now, isn't it? - you're way out of your depth. How old are you, anyway? Mid-fifties? Older? You're clearly in no condition to be getting in fights with people, especially not when they're not much more than a third of your age."

"You've more than made your point."

"You want to talk about making points?"

She moved the knife down until the blade's tip was pushing against his belly, just a few inches from the first wound.

"I can make points all day," she told him. "I can make points until you beg me to stop. You see, that's the thing about me. I'm pretty chilled most of the time, but when someone really pisses me off, I tend to go a little overboard with the whole revenge thing." She leaned closer. "It's a bad habit that I just can't shake, although I try my best. Tell me, though, what's your deal? Somehow I think this isn't your first indiscretion. Are you some kind of serial killer? Do you drag women back to some lair and do awful things to them? To be honest, you've got that whole serial killer vibe that I -"

Suddenly he slammed his head against her face, sending her stumbling back, and he followed that with a swinging punch that instantly broke her nose and sent her crumpling to the floor.

"Damn you," Ted stammered, leaning against the side of the truck for a moment and taking another look at the knife in his gut. The blade had sliced a little further, and he knew that he needed to fix the wound before he lost too much blood.

Turning, he opened the truck's door and began to climb inside, only for the door to suddenly crunch against him as Wendy threw her weight against the window.

"Stop!" Ted yelled, struggling desperately to get free.

"You fucking psychopath!" she screamed, with blood pouring from her smashed nose. "I'm gonna make sure you never get a chance to hurt anyone ever again!"

Still pinned in the door, Ted reached into the truck and tried to find something he could use as a weapon. Quickly grabbing a knife that he'd left on the dashboard, he turned and tried to reach out to Wendy, only to find that he couldn't squeeze his arm through the gap. Reaching down, he lowered the window in the door, and then he drove the knife straight into her belly.

Crying out, she stumbled back, releasing the door and letting Ted clamber into the seat.

"Dumb bitch," he muttered as he started the engine.

He leaned back in the seat for a moment, trying to ignore the pain in his gut, and then he looked over at Wendy and saw that she was still on the ground. Although he just wanted to get as far away from her as possible, he knew that he couldn't leave loose ends, so he took a deep breath before starting to climb back out of the truck.

"You want to try again, huh?" she snarled, holding the knife up toward him. Her hand was trembling, but already she was starting to get to her feet. "Bring it on!"

Ted hesitated for a moment, before climbing back into the truck and swinging the door shut. With the engine already running, he began to drive away, only for Wendy to scream and rush at him. He ducked to the side as she tried to climb through the open window, and he was powerless to stop her as she clung to the side of the truck and started slashing the knife at him. The blade caught his hands several times as he tried to push her away, but all he could do was floor the gas pedal and then swing the car around, hoping to dislodge her.

Still screaming, Wendy tried to stab him in the neck, but this time Ted managed to shove her back hard. Hanging from the window as the car raced along the road, Wendy tried again to climb inside, but Ted slammed his fist against her hand. With one final cry, she tumbled away from the window.

Looking in his rear view mirror, Ted saw her rolling violently across the tarmac until she came to a juddering stop at the side of the road.

He slowed the truck, wondering whether he should go back and finish her off, but at that moment he saw that she was already starting to get up again. Although he considered the possibility of simply driving away, he knew that she was still a danger, so he put the truck in reverse and drove back toward her at full speed.

"You -"

Before she could get another word out, he slammed against her and she disappeared under the truck's wheels. The entire vehicle shuddered as it drove over her, and then Ted looked out the front and saw her crumpled body on the ground.

He stopped the truck for a moment, before snarling as he changed gear and drove forward again. He saw Wendy trying to get up, but he quickly drove straight over her. This time he heard an anguished cry that was cut brutally short as her bones splintered. He drove on a little further, before stopping and looking back.

Wendy was in the middle of the road, bloodied and broken but somehow – by some infernal miracle – she was still just about alive.

"Oh, I'm going to finish you close up," he muttered, reaching for the knife again, "and then -"

Suddenly he spotted movement in the distance, and he saw to his horror that a van was trundling along the road. He watched as the other vehicle passed Wendy's car, and then as it ground to a halt just a few meters beyond the woman's shaking body. Frozen in place for a few seconds, Ted kept his eyes fixed on the van, but he could already see that there were at least two people in there, if not more, and he knew that he was in absolutely no shape to take on anyone else.

A door opened on the side of the van, and a man climbed out, clearly shocked by what he was seeing. Tall and broad-shouldered and clearly in good shape, the man took a step toward Wendy before stopping and looking directly at Ted.

Turning, Ted floored the gas pedal and began to drive away, even as the pain in his gut became stronger. He knew there was no way he could ever explain what had happened, so all he could do was get as far away as possible and hope that he was never linked to the dying, hopefully soon dead, woman on the ground. At the same time, she'd claimed to be the daughter of some high-ranking cop, and he knew that if this was true then there was no way her death wouldn't attract a serious amount of attention.

"Ungrateful idiot," he muttered under his breath as he struggled to keep his trembling hands on the steering wheel. "Why couldn't you just accept that I was trying to help you?"

## CHAPTER THREE

As soon as he stopped the truck outside his farmhouse, Ted leaned forward and rested for a moment. He'd barely made it back, but he knew that the hard work was only just beginning. Blood was soaking through the front of his shirt, and he realized that he was going to have to make his way all the way upstairs to the bathroom.

"You can do this," he whispered, even as he felt himself getting weaker by the second. "You're not going to let some stupid little whore take you out this easily."

\*\*\*

A short while later, sitting on the edge of the bath with his shirt off, Ted continued to examine the wound in his belly. He was fairly sure that he'd been lucky and that nothing major had been damaged, and he'd promised himself that there was no need to go to a doctor. Sure, he knew that he might be wrong about that, but any attempt to get help would be too much of a risk. He'd just have to trust his instincts.

Instead, he began to sew the wound shut, wincing at the pain but promising himself that it would all be over soon.

\*\*\*

Stepping out the front door, Ted stopped for a moment and looked across the yard. So far, everything seemed to be in order, and he tried to tell himself that there was no need to panic. He watched for a moment longer, just in case, and then he crouched down and set his latest drone on the ground.

"Okay, my friend," he muttered as he wiped some dust from the engines, "you're just going to check the perimeter. We've done this before a million times. It's going to be a nice gentle reconnaissance flight for you, and you'll be back home before you know it."

He took a deep breath, which he instantly regretted as he felt a sharp pain in his belly, and then he got to his feet. Taking his phone from his pocket, he brought up the app for controlling the drone and then he tapped to start the engines running.

On the ground, next to his feet, the drone shuddered to life, although after a moment one of the engines sputtered and stopped again.

"Come on," Ted said, tapping a few more times as he tried to figure out what was wrong, "don't do this to me, not today. I just need you to work. I fixed your casing, didn't I?"

The drone began to lift slowly from the mud, although one of the engines was still shuddering. In normal times, Ted would have taken the damn thing inside and fixed it properly, but he was struggling to ignore a sense of panic and all he could think was that he *had* to send the drone out as an early warning device. There'd be time to fix any lingering damage later; at that moment, he switched the engines to their highest setting and watched as the drone slowly rose above his head.

"That's right," he said, looking up as the drone hovered against the dull afternoon sky, "you can -"

Before he was able to finish, the drone suddenly dropped a couple of feet, although its damaged engine quickly began to surge and it managed to stay in the air.

"Come on," Ted said, as the drone once again began to rise. "You're a plucky little thing, aren't you? Show me what you're made of."

This time the drone managed to go a little higher, but the fourth engine was clearly still struggling. After a moment the drone began to fall again, and Ted instinctively reached out and tried to push it back up.

"Failure isn't the Armitage way," he said firmly. "We don't do failure round here, remember? Now you're going to pull yourself together and get out there."

He watched the drone, hoping that in some way his little pep talk might actually have helped.

"That's better," he continued, as the drone managed to stay up in the air. "Now we're going to take it nice and gentle, okay?" He tapped to send the drone a little higher. "There you go," he added with a grin. "You're such a star."

Although somewhat wobbly, the drone continued its ascent, until finally it was almost clear of the farmhouse's roof.

Suddenly Ted heard a whooshing sound, and a moment later a helicopter roared into view, racing across the yard before heading out across the trees; turbulence sent the drone crashing against the side of the house, which cut the four little engines and left the machine clattering to the ground.

Stunned that he hadn't heard the helicopter's approach, Ted quickly told himself that it had simply approached from the side of his bad ear and that most likely it was off on some random mission. A moment later, however, the helicopter began to turn around, and Ted felt a tightening sense of dread in his chest as he saw the vehicle return to the yard and start hovering above the house.

Somehow he immediately knew that it was a police helicopter.

Turning, he hurried around to the other side of the house, almost tripping over his damaged drone as he rushed toward the kitchen. He grabbed a mask and slipped it over his nose and mouth, and then he took his rifle from the cabinet and made his way back outside. His hands were trembling more than ever, but he forced himself to stay focused as he loaded the rifle and then aimed it up toward the helicopter.

Almost immediately, the helicopter turned and began to fly away.

"Not so fast," Ted sneered, before pulling the trigger.

To his surprise, he missed the departing helicopter. He aimed again, determined to succeed with his second attempt, but his hands were trembling violently and the second shot was no better than the first.

"Damn it!" he snapped, throwing the rifle hard against the ground as the helicopter took up position much further away.

Staring at the helicopter, Ted realized that he could no longer deny the obvious. In the fifteen or so years since he'd bought the farm, he'd never once seen anything fly over. A few hours had passed since he'd left Wendy dying on the road, and he figured that was enough time for the alarm to have been raised. Now, as the helicopter hovered in the distance, he realized that backup was almost certainly on the way and that – at the very least – the idiots from the local station would want to go over the farm with a fine-toothed comb.

"It's over," he whispered, as the truth finally dawned on him. He stepped back, and as he did so his right foot crunched against the drone, smashing one of its engines. "All of it..."

***

Standing at the edge of the pit, Ted poured more gasoline down onto the bodies at the bottom. He knew he wouldn't be able to burn them all, but he wanted to at least buy himself some more time. He watched as the gasoline splattered against the bodies that were poking above the surface, and then he grabbed the rags from the ground and held them out.

"I'm sorry, ladies," he said, before taking a deep breath. "We all knew this was going to have to end one day."

He hesitated, before setting fire to the rag and then letting it fall. As soon as the burning rag landed at the bottom of the pit, flames began to roar across the corpses, and Ted stared down for a moment before turning and starting to make his way toward the barn. Glancing over his shoulder, he saw that the helicopter was still hovering in the distance, and he knew that scores of police officers would already be on their way.

"You won't find much when you get here," he said firmly, as he made his way around the barn and then stopped to look at his monument of heads.

In that moment, he felt a profound sense of sadness. A dozen heads were arranged on the metal spike, and each of them reminded him of a particular time in the past. He saw Anita's skull near the bottom, and he remembered the way she'd screamed for forgiveness as she'd died; he saw Carolyn's head, with some flesh still clinging to the bones, and he thought back to her desperate attempt to offer him anything he wanted; he saw Rebecca's head, still very much recognizable after five years, and he smiled at the memory of her final moments; and he saw the head of Suzie, his most recent victim, still fresh near the top of the spike.

"I think we'll leave you as you are," he told them. "It wouldn't feel right to burn you or do anything to damage your beauty."

Stepping closer, he reached out and ran a hand down the heads, touching them one by one as tears filled his eyes.

"I had such high hopes for each and every one of you," he continued. "Some of you came so very close to getting out of here, but the important thing is that I learned from all the failures. And I need to learn, because Jane..."

He hesitated, trying to delay the inevitable, and then he took a couple of steps back.

"Goodbye, ladies," he added. "God bless you all. I will never, *ever* forget any of you."

He paused again, before turning and forcing himself to walk away, heading into the forest. Each step felt so heavy and difficult, but finally he stopped and looked back between the trees. As he slipped his phone out of his pocket, he reminded himself that he'd always known that the end – when it came – would be sudden. In some strange way, he almost felt relieved, since he'd been living under something of a cloud for more than a decade. He'd long prepared for the final moment, although that didn't make it any less bittersweet as he brought up the app and tapped the green button on the middle of the screen.

Immediately, a huge explosion ripped through the house and the barn, sending debris crashing out into forest. Turning away from the immense heat, Ted felt the ground shake violently as he took refuge behind a tree, and when he dared to look back he saw that his entire farm was now nothing more than a field of flames.

Realizing that he had no time to lose, he turned and began to limp away through the forest.

## CHAPTER FOUR

"Thanks for the lift, my friend," Ted said several hours later, as he stepped out of the man's white van and turned back to him. "You're a real lifesaver."

"Are you sure you want to stop here?" the man asked, clearly a little puzzled.

"As long as that motel's got a phone," Ted replied, "I'll be just fine. All I need is to call someone and arrange for them to go and fetch my broken-down truck in the morning, and then I'll get myself a room for the night. This time tomorrow, everything'll be good. Thanks again for stopping to pick up a poor, humble hitch-hiker such as myself, though. I really didn't fancy walking all this way."

"Good luck," the man said. "Maybe bump into you again some time."

"Maybe," Ted muttered, stepping back as the van drove away. "You never know."

He watched as the van rejoined the flow of traffic, and then he turned and began to limp across the car park, heading toward the motel's reception area. As he walked, he sniffed his jacket a few times, just to make sure that he didn't smell of gasoline; he figured that the guy in the truck might have mentioned something about that, but he quickly told himself that he was probably just being paranoid. Glancing over his shoulder, however, he realized he could just about see smoke rising into the sky on the horizon, which he figured meant that the farm was still burning.

Stopping at a window, he took a moment to make sure that he looked presentable, and then he forced himself to smile as he stepped through into the motel.

"Hi there," the woman at the desk said, looking up at him, "how can I help you?"

"Well," he replied, as he slipped his sunglasses off and removed his hat, "the truth is, I just need a room for the night."

\*\*\*

"No, I'm fine," he said half an hour later, as he sat on the edge of the bed in room 119 and looked down at the wound on his belly. "I'll be home soon, I promise."

As a voice spoke to him through the phone's speaker, Ted reached down and touched the stitches, although he winced as he felt a sore, burning pain at the edges. Although the wound didn't look particularly swollen or discolored, he couldn't help but worry that he might be developing the early signs of an infection. If that was the case, he'd have to get someone to take a look, although he figured that he'd be able to come up with some kind of cover story. For now, he'd just have to deploy some good old-fashioned fortitude.

"Huh?" he said after a moment. "Oh, no, I'm just tired, that's all. I'm turning into an old man now, remember? This rundown body of mine is starting to complain more and more about all the time I spend on the road."

He hesitated for a moment, thinking back to the sight of flames engulfing the farm.

"It might be time for me to settle down a little soon," he continued. "Don't die of a heart attack, but I'm actually thinking about the 'r' word."

He listened as she asked him if he was serious, and then he chuckled.

"Everyone has to retire at some point," he pointed out. "Don't worry, I've got plenty of hobbies, it's not as if I'd just be sitting around all day doing nothing."

Glancing over his shoulder, he looked at the muted TV and saw that it was still running commercials. He looked back down at his wound, and he began to wonder whether at some stage he might need to redo the stitches. Already, smeared blood around some of the home-made stitches suggested a certain amount of leakage.

"Honestly, there's nothing to worry about," he said with a chuckle. "You're making me out to be some kind of cliched old fart who doesn't know when it's time to stop."

He looked at the mirror and saw his own tired face, and for a moment he found it hard to believe that he was so close to turning sixty.

"I'm not scared of getting old," he continued. "I don't necessarily like it, but I can meet it head on. And the last thing anyone needs is to have some old-timer blundering around, refusing to admit that his way belong in the past. I can -"

Suddenly he felt a spark of pain in his wound, and he let out a startled gasp as he leaned forward.

"No!" he blurted out. "It's nothing! I just... I stubbed my toe, that's all."

He listened as she asked if she was sure it was no more than that, and then – looking over at the TV again – he saw that the news report had finally begun. He froze as the screen showed images of flames rising high above the forest.

"I have to go," he told her. "I love you. I'll talk to you soon."

Without waiting for her to reply, he cut the call and then shuffled around on the bed until he was looking directly at the screen. Reaching out, he grabbed the remote and quickly unmuted the show.

"- tonight at the scene of an almost unimaginable horror," the reporter, a man identified by the onscreen graphics as a reporter named Seth Warner, told viewers. "This farm, deep in Twist Valley, is now the focus of a massive police investigation as investigators seek to discover just what happened here and whether it's connected to the disappearances of a number of women in the area."

The image changed and Ted saw another shot of the forest with smoke rising above the trees. He figured that the fire would be out by now, and that the farmhouse and the barn would be little more than piles of ash.

"The investigation began after tourists encountered a grisly scene while driving home," the reporter continued. "Wendy Waller, a twenty-one-year-old student and the daughter of local police chief Michael Waller, was found badly injured in the middle of the road. Although she was rushed to hospital, sadly Ms. Waller was pronounced dead on arrival, and police are now urgently working to identify a man who was seen driving away from her body at speed."

The image changed again, this time showing the man Ted had seen climbing out of the other vehicle.

"He was old," the man explained, "like sixty or more than that, and -"

"Go to hell," Ted muttered darkly.

"I didn't get a good look at him really, but I think he might have been hurt," the man continued. "I don't know, it's just a hunch, but I don't think he was doing too well."

The reporter appeared back on the screen.

"Police remain tight-lipped about the exact sequence of events," he explained, "and they've refused to comment on rumors that the suspect might have been briefly spotted by a helicopter crew before opening fire and forcing them to retreat to a safe distance. They're also refusing to comment on reports that Ms. Waller's death might be linked to a series of disappearances stretching back over more than a decade. Tonight, the family of one missing woman – fitness instructor Mary Walsh, who vanished on a drive home in the summer of 2006 – have called on police to accept an independent investigation into claims that these disappearances weren't given enough attention."

Suddenly breaking into a coughing fit, Ted leaned forward and tried to clear his throat. Each cough brought a fresh burst of pain to the skin around his stitches, but a couple of minutes passed before he was able to get his breath back. Sitting up straight again, he wiped spittle from his lips, and he was starting to wonder whether he was running a temperature. Touching his forehead, he found that he was indeed a little clammy.

"So what we're looking at," a different presenter on the news show said, pointing at a map of Twist Valley, "is a number of women who've gone missing in and around this area over a period of at least fifteen years. Now, police sources say that until tonight there has been no reason to believe that any of these cases might be linked. They point to the distances between them, and the ruggedness of the terrain, and they insist that each case was individually investigated with full resources. But the discovery of this farmhouse, and the rumors about what might have been found there, suggests that there's a real chance something has been missed."

"And that some kind of serial killer has been operating in the area?" one of the other presenters suggested. "If that's the case, how worried should members of the public be tonight?"

"The police are stressing that people should go about their normal business," the first presenter explained. "However, if anyone sees anything suspicious or out of the ordinary either in Twist Valley itself, or in the surrounding area, they're encouraged to call the phone number at the bottom of the screen and let investigators know."

Ted turned and looked over at the window. He could see cars racing past the motel on the main road, rushing to get home in the night.

"Because if this killer exists, he's still out there, right?"

"There's certainly no indication that anyone has been apprehended as of yet," the reporter replied. "There have been reports of an explosion at the farm where he lived, in which case he might have activated some kind of exit strategy."

"You're saying that he might have expected he was going to get caught?"

"If he did, then there's no telling where he might might be now, or what he might be planning as his next step."

Hearing a buzzing sound, Ted turned and looked at his phone, and then he let out a heavy sigh.

"Great," he groaned. "What *now*?"

## CHAPTER FIVE

As morning light streamed down through the treetops, Detective Inspector Warren Pacey stopped for a moment and watched as a team of officers continued to examine the pit at the far end of the yard.

Slowly, two of those officers were reaching down to take something that was being handed up from the bottom of the pit. Even before he saw the dark bag, Pacey knew that yet more human remains had been recovered. He still hadn't been able to ascertain how many bodies were down there, but the process of sorting through the burned bones had already begun and Pacey was sure that there must have been at least two dozen. Swallowing hard, he watched as the latest bag was carried away toward a waiting van, and then he looked over his shoulder as he heard the sound of an approaching car.

"Finally," he said with a sigh, as he saw a black vehicle pulling up near the smoking remains of the farmhouse. "The big man's here."

***

As the car stopped, Chief Inspector John Noad felt every muscle in his body tighten. He'd sat in silence on the long journey out to Twist Valley, but now the moment had arrived and as he peered out the window he saw not only the smoking hulk of the farmhouse, but also the barn a little further away. He felt a sickening sense of dread in the pit of his belly, although he knew that he couldn't turn back now.

After all, he'd been waiting more than a decade for this moment.

Grabbing his walking stick, he opened the car door and began to climb out. Unsteady on his feet and already wishing – as his feet pressed into the mud – that he'd brought sturdier shoes, he immediately noticed a foul, acrid stench in the air, which he assumed was the result of one or other of the fires that had ravaged the entire site. He stopped and looked around, and a moment later he saw the annoyingly perky face of Detective Inspector Pacey, who was already on his way over.

"I'm glad you could make it," Pacey said as he reached Noad's side. "You're not going to believe some of the stuff we've found here."

Noad watched as officers worked at various spots all around the site, and then he turned to Pacey.

"On the contrary, young man," he said, with heaviness in his voice, "I not only believe it, I *anticipated* it. Remember, you're talking to the one person who suspected all along that something like this might be happening."

"If there's -"

"Show me the worst," Noad added. "Let's start with the worst and work out way back from there."

"Well..."

Pacey's voice trailed off, and then he gestured for Noad to follow him.

"This way," he said cautiously, making sure to not walk too fast as Noad limped along at his side. "It's difficult to know exactly what counts as the worst here. We've got men removing bodies from that pit. Most of the bodies are burned, and it's certainly going to take us a long time to start identifying any of them."

Noad looked over at the pit, and he saw that smoke was still rising from the bottom.

"That was the main building," Pacey continued, pointing in the other direction, toward the ruins of the farmhouse. "The same accelerant was used across the entire site. Forensic teams are looking through what's left of the house now, but we're not expecting to find anything useful. This guy doesn't strike me as someone who'd accidentally leave anything behind."

"That's no reason to stop looking," Noad muttered.

"Of course not," Pacey added, correcting himself. "And over here, you'll see the barn."

"So this was a working farm of some sort?"

"Not that we can see so far," Pacey explained. "The barn actually suffered less damage than the house, we've been able to identify an area at one end with chains attached to the ceiling, and we're working on the theory that the suspect might have used the barn as some sort of torture chamber."

"Did you find any traces of blood?"

"We believe so, yes. On the concrete floor, mainly."

"Get that analyzed. Leave no stone unturned."

"Absolutely."

Reaching the entrance to the barn, Noad looked through and saw more officers combing through the wreckage. He watched their silhouettes, and after a moment he realized that he could just about see the chains that Pacey had mentioned. For a moment, in the back of his mind, he could almost hear agonized screams ringing out from the barn as terrified victims cried for help that was never going to come. Some of that horror and anguish seemed somehow to be hanging in the air.

"No-one would have heard anything," he murmured.

"I'm sorry?"

"You could scream your lungs out," he continued, "and there'd be nobody for miles around in any direction to hear."

"This place is completely isolated," Pacey said, nodding in agreement. "I hate to phrase it quite like this, but it's pretty much perfect as a place to bring people and murder them. It's ideal."

Noad turned to him.

"If you were that way inclined," Pacey added, correcting himself.

"I asked you to show me the worst," Noad reminded him. "Somehow I get the feeling that a burned-out barn with some bloodstains isn't going to be the worst thing here."

"There's one more thing we've found so far," Pacey replied, and now he seemed a little uncomfortable. "It's, uh..."

His voice trailed off.

"It's round the corner," he added finally, "and it's not really... I mean, it's..."

Again, he was unable to complete the sentence.

"Show me," Noad said firmly.

Pacey hesitated, before starting to lead him toward the far corner. Each step made him feel a little more nauseous; he knew he should start to prepare Noad for the horror he was about to witness, but at the same time he couldn't even begin to put the situation into words.

Finally, stopping at the corner, he saw that several officers were still examining the heads that had been left on a metal spike. The explosion at the other end of the barn had left the spike still standing, although the subsequent fire had burned the flesh away from most of the heads, leaving twelve charred skulls arranged vertically. For a moment Pacey could only stare at the awful scene, before turning as Noad stepped around him.

"And what do we have here?" Noad asked, leaning on his stick as he limped over to take a closer look at the heads. "Our mystery man certainly appears to have had an eye for the theatrical."

"Some of the bodies in the pit are missing their heads," Pacey told him, "but others... still have them."

"This was some kind of ritual," Noad suggested. "It's also notable that the explosion didn't damage this thing, as if our perpetrator couldn't bring himself to destroy what he considered to be the most important part of the place."

"You think he left it intact deliberately?"

"I think everything here was very carefully planned," Noad replied, as he looked up at the highest head on the spike. "This man had a system, right to the bitter end. He's intelligent, and he'll have left behind precisely what he wanted to leave behind, which means that we're wasting our time here."

Pacey turned to him.

"Sir?"

"This is all a distraction," Noad explained. "He wants us combing methodically through the ashes, because that gives him time to get further and further away, and time to cover his tracks. By the time we're finished cataloging every flake of burned wood out here, he'll have used that time to disappear into thin air."

"We can't just leave it, though," Pacey pointed out. "We have to look."

"Of course," Noad replied, "but we can leave that to the rank and file. I'm going to be of more use out there on the road, tracking this man down. And for that, I'm going to need an assistant." He turned to Pacey and looked him up and down for a moment, taking care to let his disdain show. "I suppose," he added, "*you'll* have to do."

"Absolutely," Pacey replied, taking care to not look directly at the severed heads. In truth, he was relieved at the thought that he wouldn't have to spend much longer at the farm. "Should we get going?"

"We're going to track this bastard down," Noad told him, with a hint of grit in his voice. "I've been waiting so long for this chance, and I'm not going to fail, not now. I'm an old man, and in all honesty I should have retired a few years ago, but I've hung on because I was certain that eventually I'd get this chance. Now that it's here..."

He paused, and then he turned to look back at the heads as they stood high against the afternoon sky.

"I'm going to get this monster," he said firmly, "even if it's the last thing I ever do."

## CHAPTER SIX

"Wow," Pacey said later that afternoon, as he stood in the doorway and looked through at Noad's office, "when you said you'd been preparing for this moment, you really weren't kidding."

"I know you've been here before," Noad muttered as he limped around to look at the piles of boxes next to the desk, "but all you saw then was a fraction of the material I've gathered over the years. I arranged for the rest to be brought out of storage this morning, and now I have to sort through it all and try to figure out exactly what's going on in this man's mind."

He looked at the boxes.

"The answer's in here somewhere," he added. "I know it. Some shred of information, some little connection that I've missed, is all it'll take for the whole damn thing to make sense. When that happens, I'm going to be kicking myself for not having caught the bastard sooner."

"I'm waiting to hear back about the preliminary findings from the site," Pacey told him, "and I've also got someone running searches on the property, that sort of thing. Unless this guy is a complete ghost, we should have a good lead on him within twenty-four hours."

"I wouldn't be so sure about that," Noad said as he reached down to pick up one of the boxes, only to wince as he felt a sharp pain in his leg.

"Let me do that," Pacey said, hurrying over and lifting the box, then setting it on the desk.

"I've identified thirty-eight missing women who could conceivably be linked to this killer," Noad explained as he removed the lid from the box. "Some of them undoubtedly will prove to be unconnected, but the majority are almost certainly this man's victims. There has to be some other link between them, other than their ages and the fact that they all broke down somewhere in or within reach of Twist Valley."

"What about that woman who claimed to have escaped from some killer in the area?"

"You're talking about Charlotte Walker," Noad replied. "We're going to need to talk to her and take her to that farm so she can confirm that it's the same place. She's the only person we know who might have been face-to-face with this guy and survived, so it's vital that we go and see her as quickly as possible. Even after all this time, it's still more than possible that she might remember something useful, even if it seems insignificant. Can I rely on you to get an address?"

"On it."

"And I want us to talk again to the families of each of the women I've singled out," Noad added. "All of them. There might be some link that we've overlooked so far."

"I'll get the details ready."

"The severed heads are our best bet right now. Put a rush on the tests. I want to know the names and backgrounds of those women before the end of the day. I want photos of them lined up on my wall."

"Of course," Pacey replied, as his phone buzzed to indicate a new message.

"The net's closing in on this guy," Noad said. "I can feel it in my gut. We've never been this close."

"We just got a lot closer," Pacey told him as he read the message on his phone. "We've identified the owner of the land out there in Twist Valley." He turned to Noad. "Does the name Alan Baxter ring any bells?"

\*\*\*

"Nobody move!" one of the officers shouted as he and his colleagues surrounded the bungalow, all with their guns aimed at the various doors and windows. "Come out with your hands up!"

"It can't be this easy," Pacey whispered, watching from a safe distance, before turning to Noad. "Can it?"

"Charlotte Walker gave us a name five years ago," Noad replied, watching the front door carefully, waiting to see who – if anyone – was going to emerge. "Ted Armitage. Edward. I ran that name through every system I could, and I didn't come up with a single person who could have been the guy who abducted her. The few Ted Armitages I discovered were easy enough to rule out. To be honest, I was never entirely sure whether Charlotte was a reliable witness. Even if she was, Ted Armitage was certainly a fake name."

As the front door of the house opened, a startled-looking elderly woman stepped out with her hands partially raised in front of her chest. She stumbled a little on the step, and one of the officers immediately grabbed her by the arm, pulling her out of the doorway and then forcing her down onto her knees.

"Mike Walton was the guy who dealt with Charlotte at the time," Noad continued. "I don't know if you ever knew him, but he was a good guy. Died tragically young, left a wife and two kids behind. He wrote her off completely, he said although she'd obviously gone through something traumatic, her recollections couldn't be trusted. It all got mixed in with the John Harrison stuff, to the extent that Mike thought..."

He watched as the elderly woman desperately tried to ask what was happening, while several armed officers hurried into the bungalow.

"Mike thought that the stress of the situation with Harrison had caused Charlotte to hallucinate," Noad added. "He thought she'd imagined this Ted Armitage guy."

"Do you think it's possible that whatever happened to Charlotte Walker was somehow unconnected to all of this?"

"It's possible, but I'd d say it's very unlikely."

"I've got an address for her, she lives down in Cornwall these days. I've tried calling but I haven't managed to actually speak to her so far."

"Then you need to go and see her in person," Noad replied. "I can't make a trip all the way down there, so I need you to go and bring her back here so we can take her to that farm. Bundle her into the car if you have to, it's essential that we find out if that's really where she was held. First, though, I want her to give another description of the place, to see whether it matches what we've seen. We need to rule out the possibility that she's being influenced by what we tell her."

"She described the heads on a spike, didn't she?"

"She did," Noad said darkly, as he watched the officers leading an elderly man out of the bungalow. "Come on, this is a waste of time, that's clearly not the guy we're after. He's ninety if he's a day."

"He still -"

"He can barely walk!" Noad snapped. "Run his details, but you won't find anything useful."

"Should we go over and talk to him?"

"You go," Noad replied. "Find out if he knows how a tract of land hundreds of miles away ended up registered in his name. I strongly suspect you're going to learn that he has absolutely no idea about any of this."

He flinched as the armed officers yelled at the elderly couple. Although he wanted to go over and tell them to calm down, he knew that they had to be allowed to go through the motions, even as he saw tears in the eyes of the man and the woman as they lay on the ground. He knew full well that they were being put through hell for nothing, but at the same time he supposed that they'd get over the shock soon enough.

"This is just another distraction," he continued after a moment. "We're still letting Armitage, or whatever the hell his name really is, dictate our actions. What we need to do is break that cycle and start making genuine progress."

"How do you propose we should do that?"

Noad thought for a moment.

"We're still getting push-back from higher up the chain of command," he explained. "Certain people don't want to admit that mistakes have been made in this case, because they know there'll be demands for heads to roll. Pardon the metaphor. Armitage probably anticipated all of this, and he's relying on us still being so pathetically slow to react. Instead of running around scaring old people in their homes, we need to be doing something that lights a fire under this bastard. You never know, we might be able to force him into a mistake."

"What do you suggest?"

Noad watched as one of the officers pushed a gun into the elderly lady's face, and then he slowly turned to Pacey.

"You're a photogenic young fellow," he said, with a glint in his eye. "Do you happen to have the number for the department that arranges press conferences?"

"Of course, but -"

"Good. Throw it away." He smiled. "And then fetch your best tie from home."

## CHAPTER SEVEN

"Of course," Noad said later, as he stood in the park opposite the local police station, with a phone against one side of his face, "I'm in complete agreement. Sir, you don't have to worry, we're going to do this by the book."

"I don't want the public to be alarmed," Commissioner Prentiss replied. "We're already facing a crisis of trust. We have to be very careful how we feed out any information. Over the next few hours, I'm going to get a team together to discuss when to hold a press conference and how it should be handled."

Before he could reply, Noad saw that Pacey had stepped out of the station and was heading toward the gathered pack of reporters, who were already calling out questions.

"This could get so much worse if we're not careful," Prentiss continued.

"If I might be so bold," Noad replied, "I *did* suggest that something might be happening out there at Twist Valley. I brought up -"

"This isn't the time to be claiming that you're some kind of damn prophet!" Prentiss snapped.

Noad watched for a moment as Pacey spoke to the reporters.

"I didn't mean it like that," he said finally. "I have a lot of information to hand, though, and I think that should give us a certain jump on the killer."

"If you think you're going to be leading this investigation," Prentiss replied, "you've got another thing coming. I need someone who's good with the press, someone who can put on a decent smile and try to fix this screw-up."

"Sir, I couldn't agree more."

"I don't want you, or anyone you're working with, to talk to the media," Prentiss added. "Is that clear?"

Noad tilted his head slightly as he saw several more journalists thrusting their microphones into Pacey's face.

"Wouldn't dream of it," he said with a grin.

"And one more thing," Prentiss continued, "if you -"

He stopped suddenly.

"Noad," he added after a few seconds, "what's this I'm seeing right now about a press conference with one of your officers?"

"That'd be young Mr. Pacey," Noad replied. "I told him to brief the gathered reporters about the state of our investigation."

"But you just told me that you -"

"I was lying," Noad said, interrupting him. "Sir, please, you must have been lied to before. There's really no need to get all hot under the collar. Anyway, the signal's breaking up, and I should get going. I'll call you in a few days."

"What the hell are you doing? You have to stop this -"

After cutting the call and then setting his phone on silent, Noad began to make his way cautiously toward the back of the gathered pack of journalists. As he got closer, he was finally able to hear what Pacey was telling them, and he smiled as he realized that the young chap was managing to stick very closely to their pre-arranged script.

"All I can tell you right now," Pacey explained to the journalists, "is that we're making headway with multiple avenues of investigation, and that we expect to make a significant breakthrough within the next few hours."

"Do you have a suspect?" one of the reporters called out.

"Why has it taken fifteen years to link all these cases together?"

"How many of the victims have you identified so far?"

"If we can just handle this one at a time," Pacey replied tactfully, "that'd really help. In terms of a suspect, I'm not at liberty to divulge that sort of information. In terms of the timeline of our investigation, I can only assure the public that each and every one of these disappearances was thoroughly looked into at the time."

"How dangerous is this man?"

Noad smiled. Finally he'd heard the question that he wanted, and he knew that Pacey was fully primed to give a perfect answer.

"We believe that this man is not that dangerous at all," Pacey explained, although he glanced briefly at Noad for reassurance. "Our preliminary attempts to understand his actions suggest that everything he did was focused on this one location. By destroying the facilities he used for his crimes, we believe that he was in some way attempting to draw a line under it all, and he probably hopes that he can now walk off into the sunset and face no consequences. I'm here today to tell you all that he's wrong about this, and that he'll soon face justice for his many crimes."

"Would it be fair to say," one of the reporters asked, "that you know a lot more about this individual than you're perhaps willing to admit right now?"

"You might think that," Pacey replied, "but it really wouldn't be appropriate for me to comment at this stage."

*\*\*\**

"You did a great job up there," Noad said a short while later, as he and Pacey made their way to the car. "You were word-perfect."

"I still don't quite understand why you wanted me to lie like that. Do you really think that this Armitage guy is going to start panicking just because I hinted that we're close to catching him? Why would he even believe me?"

"It's not about that," Noad explained, "it's about shifting the narrative and making him question certain things. I want to undermine his confidence."

"Everyone's going to be looking for him now," Pacey pointed out. "I'm not even sure that this press conference was a good idea. If people start panicking, we're going to end up getting so many false leads, we'll be completely oblivious if any genuine information comes in."

"Don't worry about that," Noad replied. "That's for the people running the main investigation to sort out, but we're doing our work on the side."

"We are?"

"We are, and that means that we want to keep Prentiss and his team out of our way as much as possible. There's no harm in tying them up in a whole load of other work for a few days."

"Just a few days?"

"We should have Armitage by then."

"Hang on," Pacey said as he checked his phone, "I've got about thirty missed calls from the last ten minutes alone."

"Speak of the devil, that'll be Commissioner Adrian Prentiss right about now."

Stopping at the car, Pacey turned to him just as all the color drained from his face.

"Why would Commissioner Prentiss want to talk to *me*?" he stammered. "I'm just... I mean, I'm only... I..."

He hesitated.

"Sir," he added cautiously, "you *did* clear the press conference with him like you said you would, didn't you?"

"You're going to Cornwall," Noad said, patting him firmly on the back. "I'm not sitting around waiting for Charlotte Walker to pick up the phone, so I want you to go down there and fetch her. I don't care what you have to do, just make sure that she comes back with you. Remember that she went through an extreme ordeal five years ago, one she barely survived. She's likely to be suffering from some kind of trauma, but you need to get through to her. She could be the key to identifying this Ted Armitage guy."

"Okay," Pacey said cautiously, "we can get going immediately."

"I'm not going all the way down there," Noad replied dismissively. "I already told you that. Instead, I'm going to look into some of the other victims and their families. I want to know every last thing about them, even down to what color underwear they were wearing on the day they disappeared." He paused for a moment. "There has to be something that links every one of these women together. We just have to figure it out."

"What if Charlotte Walker refuses to come with me?"

"She's not allowed to refuse."

"Well, she... I mean, she *is* allowed to refuse. Technically."

"You're going to get her here one way or the other," Noad said firmly. "Frankly, I don't care if you have to tie her up and throw her into the trunk of your car, this is too important and too many lives are at stake. If she really resists..."

His voice trailed off for a moment.

"Tell her he might kill again," he added finally. "Tell her he's more dangerous than ever now that he's cornered, and that he might very well be planning to abduct another woman."

"Do you think that's true?"

"I think it should be enough to make her see that she has a duty to help us," he replied. "From what I remember reading, Charlotte Walker seemed like a decent enough person. If she can be coaxed into getting over her fears, I'm sure she'll come back and do whatever she can. Just don't be afraid to lay it on a little thick if she needs some extra persuasion. Remind her of the horrors out at that place." He paused again. "Tell her she has no choice. Tell her she has unfinished business in Twist Valley."

## CHAPTER EIGHT

"What?"

As soon as his eyes opened, Ted Armitage knew that something was wrong. He was on his side in the motel room, but his body felt heavy and he realized after just a few more seconds that he seemed to be running a fever. He began to sit up, only to find that the side of his belly was stuck to the bed-sheets; looking down, he saw that the wound had begun to leak again in the night, and he took a moment to reach down and carefully pull the fabric aside.

"That settles that, then," he said with a sigh. "I definitely need to see a doctor."

He turned to climb out of bed, but in that moment he suddenly saw a naked woman sitting next to him. She was looking over at the window, but even from behind Ted could already tell that he recognized her from somewhere. He sat up and pulled back a little, and then – as the woman slowly turned to look at him – he realized exactly where he'd seen her before. Although he told himself that he had to be wrong, that the strange visions had ended as soon as he'd left the farm, he couldn't deny what he was seeing now.

"Monica," he whispered. "Monica Potter."

"Help me!" he remembered her screaming in the barn, as he'd cut her gut open with a knife. "Somebody help me!"

Sitting in silence now, Ted continued to stare at her as she turned a little further and looked directly at him. All her marks and cuts were gone; her flesh was as fresh and unharmed as it had been on the day ten years earlier when he'd first taken her to the farm. He still remembered the sight of her body, with its head attached, crashing down into the pit. All his work, all his careful teaching, appeared to have been undone: in death, she'd fully recovered.

"You're not really here," he told her. "Don't think for one second that you can fool me."

"You're just relieved that I'm the only one," she replied, her voice sounding strangely flat and emotionless. "Which I am. For now."

"I -"

"I can't promise that the others won't show up soon, though," she added. "All those other ghosts are still out there, and they still want to make you suffer."

"You're not a ghost," he said firmly. "You're just a figment of my imagination."

"Does that make me *less* scary," she asked, "or more?"

"I don't have time to sit around talking to you," he muttered as he turned and began to clamber off the other side of the bed. "I only needed a short nap. It's time for me to hit the road again."

As soon as he was standing, however, he realized that he felt strangely dizzy. Reaching out, he leaned against the wall and waited as the sensation began to pass. Glancing over his shoulder, he saw that Monica still appeared to be sitting on the bed, and he felt a flash of pride as he forced himself to stand up straight; he knew that it was foolish to worry about what a hallucination might think of him, but he still wanted to look his best.

"How bad is it?" she asked.

"I'm fine."

"That's a lie."

"I told you I'm fine!" he snapped, even though he knew that there was no point being angry with a ghost. No, not a ghost; a hallucination. He had to remember that key distinction. "Stop nagging me all the time."

"It's over, you know," she said calmly.

"I don't need a lecture from you."

"I know you don't. I just wanted to remind you. You've spent fifteen years doing your thing out at that barn, but now it's at an end. The only question is where you end up. Will it be a jail cell?"

"Home," he told her, gritting his teeth. "I'm going home."

\*\*\*

"Nice car," Monica said a while later, standing right behind the salesman at the rental agency. "Something of an upgrade on that rickety old truck you insisted on driving for so long."

"I don't know if you're interested," the salesman continued, oblivious to her presence, "but for just a small amount extra each day, I can upgrade you to -"

"No, this'll be fine," Ted replied. "All I need is a set of wheels that'll get me home. I've got no interest in the latest fancy gadgets."

"If you want a car with -"

"This one will be fine," he said firmly, forcing a smile, hoping that this time the salesman would get the message. "I want this one, and only this one. No fancy extras, no high-tech radios or anything like that, just a set of wheels that'll get me to where I need to be."

"Alright, then," the salesman replied, looking down again at Ted's driving license, "Mr. -"

"Can we hurry this along a little?" Ted continued. "I'm sorry, I don't mean to be rude, but I'm in a hurry. I've been away on a business trip for a couple of weeks and I'm really looking forward to getting home and putting my feet up. I'm sure you know how it is, sometimes a man's just tired and -"

Before he could finish, he felt a sudden, sharp pain in his gut, as if some of his stitches had begun to come loose. He tried to hide his reaction, but when he looked at the salesman he realized that he was already too late.

"Cramp," he explained, once again managing to somehow conjure a smile. "I'm getting old."

"I'll just go and sort out the paperwork," the salesman replied, somewhat awkwardly, "and then we can get you on your way. How about that?"

"All I could ever ask for," Ted said as the man headed back into the office.

"You're not fooling him," Monica pointed out. "What if he calls the police?"

"He won't."

"But -"

"He thinks I'm a little odd," Ted continued, "but that doesn't mean he thinks I'm a killer. Besides, I'm immune to all that suspicion." He turned to her. "And you know why."

"That's only going to get you so far."

"I don't have far left to go," he reminded her.

"And you really just want to go home and settle into a quiet life?"

"That's what I told you, isn't it?"

"I'm just having a hard time believing that you'll be happy," she replied. "The great Ted Armitage doesn't seem like the kind of man who could ever be content in retirement. No offense, Ted, but you really didn't achieve what you set out to achieve at the farm, did you?"

"You don't know *what* I set out to achieve there."

"I know about that nasty little underground chamber. I know about -"

"I'm going to get exactly what I want," he added, interrupting her, even as he felt another rumbling pain in his gut. "I've known all along that this day was coming. Do you think those explosives just dropped into my lap at the exact moment I needed them? Of course they didn't. I set them up years ago, ready to be activated at the push of a button. I'm prepared, and so far everything's going more or less to plan."

"Apart from the hole in your belly."

Turning to look over at the office, Ted saw that the salesman was still tapping away at a computer.

"He's taking a long time," Monica pointed out. "What if he's noticed something amiss? For all your claims to have the situation under control, you can't account for the human mind. What if he was watching the news last night and his head was already filled with the horror of Twist Valley before you even showed up? What if he's stalling while he waits for the police to get here?"

"I'm not worried about that."

"You should be."

He turned back to her.

"They're not going to stop until they've got you," she told him. "And what if they find your last big secret? After all, the fire will only distract them for so long."

"You're forgetting my secret weapon," he replied, allowing himself a faint smile. "The police aren't going to get me now, for the same reason the police never even got a sniff of me over the past decade and a half. I've always been able to cover my tracks, because I -"

Before he could get another word out, he heard a door swing open nearby, and he turned to see that the salesman was making his way out from the office.

"All done for you," the man said, holding out the license and a set of keys. "You're ready to roll."

"Thank you very much," Ted replied, and he couldn't help but smile. "It's good to know that some things in this life still run smoothly. And don't worry," he added, glancing briefly at Monica, "I won't put a scratch on her."

## CHAPTER NINE

"Chloe, can you pick these up before we go inside?" Phil asked as he watched his daughter heading to the front door. "Hey, Chloe, remember what we talked about."

Turning, the little girl began to gather the dolls she'd left on the lawn. Phil watched to make sure that she didn't leave anything behind, and he allowed himself a faint smile as he realized that she was taking great care.

"Philip Ballard?"

He turned to see a man limping toward him from a car that had pulled up just a moment earlier. He'd noticed the car, barely, although he'd given it no real thought.

"Who wants to know?"

"I'm Chief Inspector John Noad," the man said, stopping on the other side of the fence and holding a hand out for him to shake. "I'm sorry to take up your time, but I'm afraid I need to ask you some questions about your wife."

"My wife's at work," Phil said cautiously.

"Right," Noad replied, nodding slowly. "I'm afraid I don't mean your current wife, Mr. Ballard. I mean your first wife, the one who went missing five years ago. I'm here to ask you about Rebecca."

*\*\*\**

"I never intended to get married again so quickly," Phil explained a few minutes later, as they sat in the kitchen. "To be honest, I didn't think I'd ever get married again at all. Then I met Karen and..."

His voice trailed off, and for a moment he looked almost guilty. A few seconds later, Chloe stepped into the room and grabbed one of her toys, before hurrying back through to the front room.

"She looks like her mother," Phil continued. "I see it more and more every day. It's as if Rebecca's blossoming inside her. Sometimes it's so good to see a little part of her showing through, and then other times it just reminds me of what we've lost."

Noad turned and watched as Chloe sat on the carpet in the front room and resumed her game.

"She doesn't remember Rebecca, of course," Phil said, as Noad turned back to him. "We haven't had to have a big conversation about her, or about what happened, although that day'll come eventually. I don't quite know what I'll tell her. The truth, I suppose. With the internet these days, she's bound to get all the details. This might make me sound crazy, but I really miss the days when we could just hide things away."

"I'm here this morning," Noad replied, "because we might have made a breakthrough in the hunt for the man who abducted your former wife. In fact, we might have made a breakthrough in something that's much bigger than just the disappearance of one woman. Mr. Ballard, I know this might be very difficult for you to hear, but I have to be honest with you. I'm of the opinion that Rebecca was just one of a number of victims of a very dangerous man."

"You mean a serial killer?"

"I'm expecting to find that he had at least thirty victims over the space of ten or fifteen years."

Phil stared at him for a moment.

"Have you found her body?" he asked finally.

"We've found a number of bodies," Noad explained, "and we're in the process of identifying them now. Since we already have Rebecca's D.N.A. on file, I'm expecting a confirmation one way or the other within the next twenty-four hours." He paused again. "Mr. Ballard, you should probably prepare yourself for some shocking news. If Rebecca is one of the victims of this man, and I think that she is, then you're going to hear details of what likely happened to her after she was kidnapped and..."

His voice trailed off.

"You might want to be ready," he added finally, "that's all."

"Who is he?"

"I'm not at -"

"Tell me!" Phil said through gritted teeth. "I have a right to know!"

"And you *will* know, just as soon as there's anything to share."

"What aren't you telling me?"

"There's a process that we have to go through before we -"

"What did he do to her?"

Noad opened his mouth to reply, but the words hung in his throat.

"You have no idea what I've imagined over the years," Phil continued. "Some nights I can't sleep, and I just think of the most awful things that this monster could have done to Becky. I'm ashamed that my mind is even capable of imagining such disgusting acts, but it's like they rush into my mind and I can't keep them out. I'm not talking about dreams. I'm wide awake when this happens. In my mind's eye, I see him skinning her alive, or doing things to her sexually, or cutting her with all these awful knives and machines while she's screaming. I can't help myself. I just keep thinking of these things."

"Mr. Ballard -"

"Sometimes I go online and search for videos," he added. "Not of Becky, obviously, but of things people have done to other victims. You can find a lot of nasty stuff once you learn how to search on the dark web, you know. I watch videos of... eyes being plucked out from the sockets of people who are still alive. People being burned alive. People being lowered into acid as they scream. I know I shouldn't be looking at any of these things, but I can't stop myself. And the worst thing is, in the back of my mind I'm always wondering whether one day, by sheer chance, I'll load up one of these videos and it'll be... her."

"I understand that this must be very difficult for you."

"I have more than twenty-three thousand videos on a hard drive that I keep hidden in the garage."

Noad stared at him, not quite knowing what to say.

"There's one," Phil continued, "where this guy took this woman's labia and -"

"I don't need to know about that," Noad said firmly, keen to end that side of the conversation. "Please, Mr. Ballard, let's..."

His voice trailed off as he tried to think of a way to phrase his request.

"Let's just stick to the subject," he added finally.

"We had a great marriage," Phil continued, with tears in his eyes. "It was perfect, really. Obviously I love Karen, that's beyond question, but there'll always be a part of me that wonders what would have happened if Becky had taken a different route home. I don't even know what she was doing out there in that Twist Valley place, I'd never even heard of it before."

"It's a little out of the way," Noad admitted, before hesitating for a moment.

"You've found her body, haven't you?" Phil replied.

"I can't -"

"It's okay, I can see it in your eyes. Did he... did he film it?"

"We have no reason to believe so."

"That's a relief," Phil said, although at the same time he sounded almost disappointed. "I want you to catch him," he continued after a few seconds. "Don't let him die, don't let him take the easy way out. I want you to catch him so that one day I can look him in the eyes."

"We have every intention of taking him alive," Noad replied.

"Just give me five minutes with him," Phil added. "Less, even. One minute would be enough. I can make him suffer in one minute."

"I won't be able to do that," Noad explained. "There are processes. Procedures."

"Thirty seconds."

"I'm sorry," Noad said, shaking his head, "but -"

"I'll rip his eyes out," Phil said, interrupting him, "and then I'll peel his skin off piece by piece while he's still alive. I'll make him scream more in one minute than he ever made Becky scream." He paused. "Are you sure he didn't film what he did to her? There has to be a chance, doesn't there?"

"Mr. Ballard, I -"

Before he could finish, he and Phil both heard footsteps outside, and they both turned just as the door opened and a heavily-pregnant woman stepped into the house.

"Oh, sorry," she said, clearly taken aback, "I didn't know that you had company."

"This is just an old friend," Phil said, getting to his feet and turning to Noad with a pleading expression. "He just dropped by to say hello, but he's on his way now."

"That's right," Noad replied, figuring – as he struggled to stand – that there was no need to cause any trouble. "I'm afraid I have a lot to do and I'm already running late." Leaning on his cane, he began to make his way to the door. "I'll be in touch, Philip, when I have more news."

"Make sure you are."

Opening the door, Noad turned to him.

Stepping behind his new wife, Phil made a point of placing a hand on her swollen belly, just as Chloe ran through and gave the woman a hug.

"I'm a man who protects his family," he told Noad. "I don't know if you realized that about me, but it's pretty much all I live for. If anyone lays a hand on someone I care about, they'd better be prepared for me to come at them and come at them hard. I'm like a ninja, I don't forget."

"I think that's elephants," Noad replied, before stepping out onto the porch. "As I said, I'll be in touch."

With that, he shut the door and turned to make his way down the steps. He struggled a little, but finally he reached the path and began to make his way back to the car. As he reached the gate, he glanced back at the house and saw Philip Ballard with his wife and daughter, and he felt a flicker of dread as he realized that soon Mr. Ballard was going to find out everything that had happened to his missing wife Rebecca. He wouldn't get to exact his revenge on the killer personally, of course; he wouldn't get close, so what would happen instead to the man's rage? After all, his anger wouldn't simply disappear; instead, it would have to find some other way out.

After stepping onto the pavement and carefully shutting the gate, Noad turned and made his way to the car.

## CHAPTER TEN

Seagulls screeched all around as Detective Inspector Warren Pacey stepped out of the fish and chip shop and looked across the quay. He'd arrived in the Cornish town of Falmouth just a short while earlier, and he'd decided to get something to eat before heading off to find Charlotte Walker. Spotting a bench in the distance, he began to make his way across the car park, as his tie flapped in the wind.

Suddenly something slammed into him from above. Stunned, he stepped back and fell, landing hard on the ground as a seagull flapped its wings furiously in his face. Before he had a chance to react, he saw the bird flying away with his battered cod in its beak, and he looked down to see that his chips were scattered on the ground all around.

"They do that," an old man said as he shuffled past, grinning from ear to ear. "They can recognize a newcomer from a mile away. Try to look more confident next time, and they might leave you alone."

"Thanks for the advice," Pacey, brushing feathers from his jacket as he got to his feet, and quickly seeing a ketchup stain on his tie. "I think maybe I'll find somewhere to eat inside."

\*\*\*

Standing at the door to a cottage, up a side-street not far from the town's center, Pacey listened to the sound of someone sliding a chain across, followed by the sound of a key turning. After hearing the same thing for a few more seconds, he realized that the quaint little cottage seemed to be heavily secured.

Finally the door opened, and a middle-aged woman with dark hair peered out through the crack.

"Can I help you?" she asked.

"I'm looking for Charlotte Walker."

"She's not here at the moment," the woman replied. "I'm a friend of the family. What do you want with her?"

"Do you know where I might be able to find Charlotte?" he continued, before taking his badge from his pocket and holding it up for her to see. "I'm Detective Inspector Pacey, I've tried to contact Ms. Walker several times over the past few days without success. I came all this way to see her in person, so -"

"She's not around at the moment."

"Is she in town?"

"She comes and goes a lot," the woman explained. "I'm sorry, is she in some kind of trouble?"

"Not at all," Pacey replied, "but I -"

"Then I really can't help you."

The woman shut the door abruptly, leaving Pacey standing all alone in the sloping street. He reached out to knock again, and he could already hear the woman putting all the chains and bolts back in place. Sighing, he took his phone from his pocket and brought up a photo of Charlotte Walker. As he looked at the image, he tried to work out whether she might be the woman he'd just encountered; there were certainly a number of similarities, although the picture was five years old and he really couldn't be certain that they were the same person.

He knew he couldn't simply walk away, however, so he decided that he was going to have to try a different tactic.

***

"Don't you dare," Pacey said firmly as he sat on a wall at the edge of the car park, trying once again to eat fish and chips. "If you come any closer, I'll kick you in the beak."

A solitary seagull had begun to approach, although it backed away again as soon as it realized it had been seen. Turning and starting to walk away, the bird stopped after a few paces and turned partly back to look at Pacey, and then it let out a brief squawking sound.

"I mean it," Pacey continued. "You're not exactly being subtle."

He watched the bird, and then he looked down at his food, only for the seagull to immediately start approaching him again.

"Stop it!" he snapped.

The seagull immediately began to back away once more.

"How do you think this is going to work?" Pacey asked, somewhat exasperated by the fact that the wretched creature still hadn't given up. "I'm not going to change my mind and decide to give you my food. For all I know, you're the same one that had my first lunch. Go on, hop it, or I'll nick you for loitering."

He waited, and then he leaned toward the bird, causing it to immediately back away even further. Its beady black eye remained fixed on him, however, and Pacey knew full well that the bird was up to something.

"I mean it!" he said angrily. "Go to -"

Suddenly something slammed against him from the side, and a rush of white feathers immediately began to beat against his face. Panicking, Pacey got to his feet and turned just as another seagull took off with his half-eaten piece of battered cod. Reaching out to grab the bird, Pacey managed to drop the box of chips, and then he looked down to see that the first seagull was gulping them down.

"Get out of here!" he shouted, kicking the bird and sending it scurrying away. "Are you serious? Do you work in teams now?"

Realizing that his second lunch was now ruined, Pacey let out a heavy sigh and turned to make his way back down the hill; at the last moment, however, he spotted movement in the distance, and he saw that the woman was now emerging from her cottage.

Stepping back, Pacey waited until the woman had made her way past him. For a moment he wondered whether he should just leave her alone; after all, if she *was* Charlotte Walker, she'd clearly chosen to hide herself away from the world, and he knew that he had absolutely no right to insist on her return. At the same time, he desperately needed to get her help, and he hoped that with a little nudge she might be willing to do whatever it took to bring Ted Armitage down.

"Charlotte?"

"Hmm?"

The woman turned, and for a few seconds she seemed utterly shocked.

"It *is* you, isn't it?" he continued, stepping toward her. "Ms. Walker, I can't even begin to imagine what you went through five years ago. I know the basics of the case, about this Ted Armitage guy and about John Harrison as well. I don't blame you for wanting to hide away like this, but the truth is that we've made a huge breakthrough in our investigation. Well, the breakthrough is that there's an investigation at all now. You might have seen it mentioned on the news. I'm so sorry that you maybe weren't believed at the time, but I really need you to come with me so that we can try to track this man down now."

He waited, but she seemed almost frozen in place.

"We've found the farm," he explained, taking another step forward. "The one where you were held at the beginning, I mean."

"I don't know what you mean," she said stiffly, although there was fear in her eyes.

"You mentioned a pole with some heads on it. We've found that too."

She shook her head.

"It's by far the most shocking thing I've ever seen in my career," he continued. "I don't mind telling you, I've had nightmares about that thing."

"I really don't know what you're talking about."

As those words left her lips, tears began to fill her eyes.

"We're so close to nailing this guy," he continued, "but we need you to help us. You're the only person who saw his face properly and who lived to talk about it. I get that you chose to hide yourself away down here, but please, help us take this man off the streets. He's on the run now and we're closing in, but we still have to do things by the book. If we get him and you identify him, that's basically game over."

She hesitated, and then she took a deep breath.

"I'm sorry," she said, as her voice trembled with fear, "but as I already told you, I'm not Charlotte Walker and I have no idea when she'll be back. In fact, as far as I know, she might not even come back at all. I haven't heard from her in a long time. You're wasting your time here."

Turning, she hurried away down the hill.

Pacey opened his mouth to call after her, but she quickly made her way around the corner and he sighed as he realized that running after her would do no good at all. Still, he was sufficiently convinced now of her identity, so he took a card from his pocket and scribbled a quick note, asking her to reconsider and call him. He slipped the card through the cottage's letterbox, and then he began to wander back down toward the fish and chip shop.

The two seagulls were well advanced with their attempt to clean up all the spilled chips.

"Enjoy it while you can," Pacey muttered at them darkly. "That's the last you're going to get from me."

## CHAPTER ELEVEN

"I've identified all twelve of them," Doctor Zinovik said as he glanced down at his clipboard. "We had material on file for all the victims, even going back a decade and a half. I suppose we can start informing the families."

Barely even hearing a word, Noad stood in the lab and stared at the dozen severed heads laid out in a row on the counter. They'd been placed in date order, with the oldest on the left and the newest on the right; somehow they seemed to represent the slow change of human flesh over the years, with some skulls almost entirely devoid of meat and others covered in charred remains. A few of the fresher heads even retained some of their hair.

"Which one is Rebecca Ballard?" Noad asked.

"Ballard?"

Zinovik checked his notes, before pointing at one of the newer skulls.

"That's her."

Noad peered down at the face of the dead woman. Although she was by no means recognizable from the photos in her file, she nevertheless still retained certain features and Noad couldn't help but think of her husband. Eventually he'd have to be informed that the head had been recovered, and most likely the body had been found in the pit, so at least some kind of funeral would be possible. As he looked at Rebecca's face and saw that her mouth was slightly open, as if she'd been in the process of screaming as she died, he felt a shudder run through his chest.

"He's a monster," Zinovik said.

Noad turned to him.

"You know me," Zinovik continued, "I don't usually use that sort of emotive language, but this man... he's almost not a man at all."

"Oh, he's a man alright," Noad replied. "That's almost the scariest part of all. He's a man, like either of us, except something has driven him to do these despicable things. It's almost as if something inside him just... broke, and after that he felt no remorse for his actions."

"I've examined the bodies, and body parts, from his farm," Zinovik explained. "There are exactly thirty women. Eighteen still had their heads attached when they were thrown down there, while the other twelve were decapitated first."

"The ones in the pit were discarded," Noad muttered. "He had no use for them, he just wanted them out of the way as quickly and as conveniently as possible. For some reason, these twelve were different. These twelve were deemed worthy of being put up as some kind of display, almost a monument."

"There's no sign of anything sexual having been done to any of the victims."

"Of course there isn't," Noad replied, still staring at the heads. "This isn't about sex, it's about control. It's as if he was trying to do something with these women, or to them, and he retained the heads of the ones who were successful, or the ones he liked the most. He wanted to be reminded of some little victory they'd helped him achieve."

"Seems like you're getting into the profiling business there."

"I'm trying to understand the man's mind," Noad admitted, "and calling him a monster doesn't help with that. I want to know who he is and what drives him. I want to peel away the layers until I get to his center. That's where we'll find the real Ted Armitage. I feel as if..."

His voice trailed off for a moment as he continued to stare at the heads.

"I feel," he continued finally, "as if he's hiding just out of sight."

\*\*\*

"And you're sure it's her?" Noad said later, as he stood in the car park at the front of the station. "You're positive that the woman you met is Charlotte Walker?"

"Pretty much," Pacey replied, his voice coming over loud and clear from the phone's speakers. "She really doesn't want to help, though. I'm thinking I might as well turn right around after I've had my lunch."

"No, stay a little longer."

"But -"

"One night," Noad added. "I might be wrong, but I think Charlotte Walker might just need more time to think about things. Your arrival today must have been a shock. I wouldn't be at all surprised if you get a call back from her this afternoon." He waited for the other man to reply. "You wouldn't want to have to drive all the way down there a second time, would you?"

"I hope you're right," Pacey said, "but I don't share your confidence. You didn't see the look in her eyes. I think she wants to pretend that none of this ever happened to her."

"Well, she can't," Noad said firmly. "None of us can. We can't turn away from our experiences and pretend that they haven't changed us. Sooner or later, that woman is going to have to be a little brave and do the right thing. It might not be easy, but it's the only way she's ever going to be able to sleep at night."

"You've got more faith in people than I have."

Just as he was about to tell Pacey that his attitude was more about hope than faith, Noad spotted a figure hurrying his way, and he turned to see that Inspector Jannings from the station was approaching with a thunderous look in his face.

"Pacey, I'll call you back," Noad muttered as he ended the call. He already knew that he was about to -

"What the hell are you playing at?" Jannings snapped as he stopped at the foot of the steps. "I've had Prentiss on at me all morning, demanding to know why one of your lackeys staged a press conference yesterday."

"I wouldn't know," Noad replied. "You'd be better off speaking to the man himself."

"Which I'd have done by now," Jannings continued, "except he hasn't answered any of my calls. And apparently he's buggered off to Cornwall or Devon or some other shithole part of the country."

"He's his own man," Noad said, nodding sagely. "And I might add, there's nothing wrong with Cornwall and Devon. I've been there myself numerous times, in fact I've often thought about retiring to Cornwall and living out my final years in a pretty little cottage somewhere far away from people."

"You're up to something," Jannings said firmly, wagging a finger in his face, "and I want *you* to know that you're treading on very thin ice. I know you've always had an interest in this Twist Valley nonsense, and -"

"I'd call it more than mere interest."

"Don't split hairs with me! You think everyone else is stepping on your turf, but this is much bigger than one man. If you interfere in this case one more time, I'll make sure that you're shut down permanently."

"What's wrong," Noad asked, "are you scared of getting another bollocking from the scary Mr. Prentiss?"

"You've been warned. Cross me again, Noad, and there'll be hell to pay."

With that, Jannings turned and stormed away, clearly in the belief that he'd managed to get his point across. Noad, for his part, watched his superior's departure with an expression of amused detachment, before tapping at his phone and bringing up Pacey's number. Letting out a weary sigh, he glanced up at the sky for a moment and saw that there seemed to be a threat of rain in the air.

"Sorry about that," he said as soon as Pacey answered, "I just had some paperwork to get on with."

"I got another missed call from Commissioner Prentiss," Pacey said cautiously. "Sir, are you sure I shouldn't give him a call back, just to check that -"

"I already told you," Noad replied, "that's just his office attempting to cover their tracks. They want to be able to claim that they tried to stop you giving any more press conferences, even though they're actually fine with it. They've specifically asked me to make sure that you don't pick up any time they call. You wouldn't want to make me look bad, would you?"

"No," Pacey said, although he sounded far from convinced, "it's just that... well, he's the boss, right? I mean, you're *my* boss, but he's the boss of everyone. It feels a little odd to be ignoring him."

"Get yourself a room in a nice little bed and breakfast for one night," Noad continued. "Worst case scenario, you get a short break you can charge to expenses, but I've got a hunch that you'll be hearing from Charlotte Walker before too long. When you do, it's imperative that you get her into your car and take her to the farm in Twist Valley. Let me know when you're on the way, because we need her to confirm beyond all doubt that we're dealing with the same person."

"Fine," Pacey replied, "as long as you can spare me for twenty-four hours. I don't mind -"

Suddenly Noad heard an almighty crashing sound coming from the phone, accompanied by a series of thuds and what seemed to be a startled squawk.

"It's the same bloody one each time, I swear!" Pacey shouted. "I'm inside this time! They're not supposed to come inside!"

## CHAPTER TWELVE

As he pulled the car over and parked on the side of the road, Ted had no choice but to lean against the steering wheel. Letting out a pained gasp, he waited for the latest bout of discomfort to pass, and for a moment he felt as if his belly might be about to split open.

"Not far now," he muttered, wiping sweat from his brow. "You'll be home before you know it."

This time, however, the pain lasted longer than before; so long, in fact, that he began to wonder whether it was ever going to ease. The swelling sensation became stronger and stronger before finally starting to fade a little, although he knew with absolutely certainty that it'd soon be back.

"That's all you've got to do," he continued. "Get home."

He took a series of deep breaths, just as another vehicle trundled past and then pulled over a little way along the road. Watching the vehicle with a sudden sense of concern, Ted saw that a man was stepping out, and he immediately sat up straight and tried to smile as the man approached. He knew that he had to appear normal, that anyone who'd seen the news over the previous twenty-four hours would be on the lookout for anyone behaving suspiciously.

"Are you okay there?" the man asked as Ted wound down his window. "Have you broken down?"

"I'm fine, thanks," Ted replied.

"I just saw you parked here and -"

"I'm stopped for a rest, that's all."

"Okay, no worries," the man said. "I wouldn't normally ask in a situation like this, but I know this road pretty well and I know there's no phone signal for a couple of miles."

"Is that right?" Ted asked.

"If you broke down here," the man continued, "you'd really be stuck unless someone happened to come across you. If you set off to walk, you'd be going for hours before you reached a town."

"Good job I *haven't* broken down, then."

"As long as you're okay, I'm just sorry to have bothered you. Have a nice day!"

The man turned and headed to his car, leaving Ted to let out a sigh of relief. He knew that the man had only wanted to help, and he felt bad for being so annoyed. As he watched the man driving away, however, he couldn't help but wish that busybodies would simply leave him alone. Even as the man's car disappeared around the next corner, Ted felt as if his privacy had been invaded.

"You're dying."

Startled, he turned and saw a woman sitting in the back seat. He blinked a couple of times, shocked that he couldn't remember her name, although he vividly remembered the sight of her hanging from chains in his barn. He also remembered her screaming as her guts had spilled out from her belly; ordinarily he'd have had no trouble recalling all her details, but somehow his mind felt a little muddied, as if he was finding it harder and harder to settle on the details. Almost as if...

"Louisa," she reminded him.

"I knew that!" he lied.

"You're dying, Mr. Armitage," she continued. "You know I'm right."

"Everyone's dying."

"Not as quickly as you are. Not with their gut slowly leaking out into their shirt."

"I've made it this far!"

"And you should be commended for that," she told him, "but these home-made remedies will only last for a short while. You're really just delaying the inevitable."

Looking down, he realized that she was right. Clear liquid was staining a large patch on his shirt and running down onto the top of his trousers. He could feel a burning pain around his stitches, and he knew that he was long past the point at which he should have gone to the hospital; at the same time, going to a hospital would inevitably arouse suspicion, and he couldn't afford to do anything that might lead to people asking questions. He told himself that the stitches would most likely hold for at least another twenty-four hours.

"I'll be fine," he murmured, even though he didn't believe that himself. "I'll get home and I'll be fine."

"What do you think comes next?"

He turned to her.

"For a man like you, I mean," she continued. "Do you think the great beyond is the same for everyone, or is there some kind of -"

"There's nothing after this," he replied, interrupting her. "We die, and that's it."

"I don't think you really believe that."

"You don't know what I believe!"

"You're scared," she told him. "All your life, you've assumed that there's no grand day of judgment at the end of it all, but what if you're wrong? What if, after you breathe your last breath, you have to stand in front of some heavenly figure and account for your life? I think we both know that you'd have trouble with that. It's one thing for you to come up with these long, meandering explanations for your crimes when you're talking to your victims, but I imagine a higher power would take issue with at least some of your activities."

"I can defend myself," he sneered.

"You're a murderer. A mass murderer. A serial killer."

"Those women -"

"Those women didn't deserve to die. They might not have been perfect, but they should have had the chance to live their own lives."

"Then they should have listened to me," he said firmly. "They should have let me help them, instead of fighting back all the time. I told them how it was supposed to work, all they had to do was listen."

He waited for Louisa to reply, but at that moment he heard his phone starting to buzz. He knew full well, without even looking at the screen, who was trying to get through.

"Are you going to answer?" Louisa asked.

"I..."

His voice trailed off.

"What if she hears it in your voice?" she continued. "She's your daughter, she knows you better than anyone. What if she realizes that something's wrong? In fact, what if she realizes a lot more than you ever could have imagined? What if..."

She paused, before leaning toward him.

"What if she knows what you are?"

"She doesn't."

"But what if the -"

"She doesn't know anything!" he shouted angrily, turning to her as the phone continued to ring. "She has no idea! She thinks I'm working, or she thinks I'm on holiday, and that's the end of it! She doesn't have a clue about the rest of it!"

"She will," Louisa said calmly, "if you get caught. What do you think that'll do to her?"

Hesitating, he waited for the phone to stop ringing, but the buzzing sound went on and on.

"She just wants to talk to her daddy," Louisa continued with a faint smile. "How old is she now, anyway? Twenty-three? Twenty-four? I bet she still idolizes you so much. I bet she thinks there's no-one in the world who's as wonderful as you."

"She'd be right," he said through gritted teeth.

A moment later, the phone stopped ringing.

"She'll try again soon enough," Louisa pointed out. "Are you just never going to talk to her again?"

"I'll talk to her when I get home."

"*If* you get home."

"And will you tell her everything?"

"That way, she'll have to understand," he muttered. "I could explain it to her, so that she hears it properly instead of getting the whole thing second-hand through the media. She's a smart girl, she has to realize that I've only ever done the right thing."

"You killed more than two dozen women over fifteen years."

"For the right reasons."

"She'll never see it like that," Louisa told him. "She'll be horrified. She'll think that you're a monster and she'll never want anything to do with you again. Her life will be ruined when she finds out what her daddy's been doing."

"I'll make her see it from my perspective."

"You're a miserable failure. You never succeeded in helping any of those women! Not even the ones who mattered most."

"Everything's going to be fine," he said firmly. "You don't understand me. No-one does. I'll handle whatever happens next."

"Or what?" She smiled. "Will you tie *her* up too?"

"Don't be disgusting!"

"Time's running out," she said as she leaned between the seats and reached down toward his belly. "How long do you think you can survive like this? A day at most?" She paused, before gently pushing a fingertip against the stained part of his shirt. "Maybe less," she purred. "This time tomorrow, you'll most likely be a corpse, and then everything will be out of your hands. Still, at least the pain will be over."

Before he could reply, he felt her pushing harder against his gut. Her finger broke through the fabric of his shirt and sliced straight into the wound, tearing the stitches apart. Although he tried to push her away, Ted found that he was powerless to resist and – as her finger dug deep into the cut left by the knife – he could only lean back in the seat and scream.

## CHAPTER THIRTEEN

"What?"

Startled, John Noad opened his eyes and rolled onto his back. He blinked a couple of times as he tried to remember exactly where he was, and then he realized that he'd checked into a motel. He'd knocked back a bottle of wine and then he'd read some notes for a while, and now he found himself in the dark room; all he could see, aside from the faintest outline of the curtains, was the blinking red light of a fire alarm directly above the bed.

Feeling somewhat dazed, Noad sat in silence for a moment. Although the clock on the nightstand showed the time as only 2am, he felt as if he was about to be interrupted. Indeed, he was reasonably certain that he'd heard a noise just a moment ago, something that had stirred him from sleep, although he wasn't entirely sure what the noise had been or where it had come from. He checked his phone and saw no missed calls or messages, and then he turned and sat on the side of the bed for a moment.

He needed to go to the bathroom anyway, although he was delaying the trip. Still, the static charge in the room seemed to be rising, almost as if -

"He's about to talk to you."

Startled, he looked over his shoulder. In the darkness, he could just about make out the shape of a naked woman sitting on the far end of the bed, with her back to him.

He opened his mouth to ask who she was and what she was doing in his room.

Suddenly his phone began to buzz. Turning, Noad saw that an unrecognized number was trying to get through. He reached over and took the phone, and he hesitated for a moment before answering and tentatively raising the phone to the side of his face.

"Hello?" he said cautiously.

"Chief Inspector John Noad," a slightly whiny male voice replied, "I'm sorry about the late hour, but I thought it might finally be time for us to talk."

"Who is this?" Noad asked, still feeling slightly groggy.

"Oh, I think you know," the voice said. Whoever he was, the man sounded very pleased with himself. "For now, you can stick with the name you've been using for me recently. Call me Ted Armitage."

"Ted -"

Noad hesitated.

"How did you get this number?" he asked cautiously.

"The same way I covered my tracks for fifteen years," Ted replied, "and the same way I kept my little farm hidden, and the same way I slipped away even when your men were closing in."

"Where are you?" Noad asked, getting to his feet and switching on the bedside light. Turning, he saw no sign of anyone, not even the naked woman.

"Relax," Ted said, "if I wanted to talk to you face-to-face, I'd be doing that by now. The truth is, I just thought I should touch base and let you know that you need to stop chasing me. Now."

"That's never going to happen, Mr. Armitage," Noad replied. "Not until you've been caught. Why don't you give yourself up? You must know that we're getting close to tracking you down. Wouldn't it feel better to surrender, rather than letting yourself get hunted like some kind of animal?"

"We're all animals, Chief Inspector Noad," Ted pointed out. "I don't feel the need to elevate myself above anyone or anything else. I called you because I want you to know two things. First, I'm not going to kill anyone else. Not ever. When my farm went up in flames, that was the end of the line. I had a plan, and I failed to execute that plan fully, but I'm a big enough man to accept that failure. At least I tried."

"So are you suggesting that I should just let you walk away?" Noad asked.

"I am, as it happens. That's the second thing I wanted to tell you. Just leave me alone. You won't catch me. I'm already a long way from Twist Valley and I'm going to keep on going, and I've made sure that there's no way you can identify me. You don't even know which direction I'm heading in, so do everyone a favor and accept that this is over. I'm sorry you won't get your big moment in the sun, your chance to be a hero, but that's just the way things go sometimes. I've accepted that my time is up. Now you have to do the same."

"That's not how it works," Noad told him.

"You'll never take me alive," Ted replied, "I'm too -"

Suddenly he let out a pained gasp.

Noad listened, acutely aware now that the man on the other end of the line was in serious discomfort.

"I can get you the help you need," he told Ted. "Physical help, psychological help, whatever you want. Hell, you can even plead insanity and try to get yourself a nice cushy little stay in a hospital. You have options and -"

Before he could finish, he heard Ted starting to laugh through the pain.

"If you didn't want to hear what I have to say," Noad continued, "you could have hung up by now. I don't think you called just to gloat. I think you're out of luck and you still haven't quite decided what to do. Tell me about your family, Mr. Armitage. What do you think would be best for *them*?"

He listened, but the laughter continued.

"I saw your collection of heads," he added. "That was a nice little flourish, wasn't it? Everything else at the farm was rather mundane. Even that pit was more about function, but the heads on the stick, those were impressive. What was it about those particular women, anyway? Why did they get to go on the -"

"Don't try to understand me!" Ted screamed suddenly.

Noad instinctively moved the phone away from his ear.

"You never will!" Ted shouted. "One day I'll be standing over your cold dead body and I'll know everything about you and you won't know a thing about me, and that's how it was always meant to be!"

"Mr. Armitage, I -"

"Because you're pathetic," Ted continued, "and you've always been pathetic, and I've always been several steps ahead of you. You were never able to catch up to me, Chief Inspector Noad. It wasn't even a fair fight. I crushed you a long time ago, and you never even noticed."

"Mr. Armitage," Noad said firmly, "I think you -"

Before he could finish, he heard a brief crackling sound, and then he looked at his phone as he realized that Ted had ended the call. He tapped to ring back, only to find that for some reason his phone had been unable to track the number. He checked a few different menus, but the number simply hadn't been recorded anywhere on his device. Figuring that Ted was obviously more technologically sophisticated than he'd realized, he set the phone down and let out a long sigh, and then he hauled himself to his feet. He knew he should report the call and see if anyone from the station might be able to pull up the details, but first he needed to get to the bathroom.

"He's coming for you," a female voice said.

Noad froze, and then he turned to see that the naked woman was sitting on the end of the bed again, still shrouded in darkness. After a moment, however, he realized that this was a different woman, and that she wasn't alone. Another woman was standing by the window, and another was next to the wardrobe. In fact, as he turned and looked all around the room, he saw that there were several women, some of them just a few feet away, all staring straight at him. And they all had their backs to him.

"Who are you?" he stammered, although deep down he already knew that they must be the women from the farm.

From the pit.

"You're not really here," he told them, although he was aware of a hint of uncertainty in his own voice. "You're all hallucinations."

"Of course we are," one of them said, and he turned to see that she was standing right behind him now, still facing the other way, "but that doesn't mean that we're not real, or that we're wrong."

He opened his mouth to reply, but no words left his lips.

"Not long now," the woman added.

He blinked, and in that instant all the women disappeared. Turning and looking around once more, he was relieved to find that he was alone again, although he was somewhat startled by that fact that he'd hallucinated in the first place. Realizing that he was letting the stress of the case get to him, he headed through to the bathroom and then, once he was back over at the bed, he took a seat and switched the light on. He knew there was no point trying to sleep, so instead he grabbed his notebook and began to jot down anything from the conversation with Ted Armitage that seemed even remotely relevant.

"I'm coming for you," he whispered. "You might think you're smart, but I'm smarter. By the time this is over, I'll have you rotting in a cell."

## CHAPTER FOURTEEN

"We're not exactly rushed off our feet," Mrs. Pearson said as she set a rack of toast on the breakfast table, "so if you *do* need to stay another night, it won't be a problem."

"That's very kind of you," Pacey replied, "but I'm not sure how it'd go down in the office. I'm going to be heading off when I'm done here. Thanks all the same."

As Mrs. Pearson left the room, Pacey tried to focus on his meal. He'd slept fairly well, but he knew that he faced a long drive back up the country. Although he understood why Noad had sent him all the way to Cornwall, he couldn't help but feel that his trip had been a waste of time, and he was worried that he must have missed some vital part of the investigation. Deep down, he also couldn't help but wonder whether Noad had sent him on the trip because he considered him to be somewhat inessential. Couldn't anyone else have been sent on a two-day wild goose chase?

Hearing his phone buzz, Pacey glanced at the screen, and he saw that an unrecognized number was trying to get through. He considered not answering, but then – worried that perhaps something important might have happened – he tapped at the screen.

"Detective Inspector Pacey," he said as he began to open a small packet of butter.

"Mr. Pacey?" a woman's voice replied, sounding somewhat nervous. "It's Charlotte Walker. I'm sorry about yesterday. What exactly do you want from me?"

\*\*\*

"I still have nightmares about it," Charlotte explained an hour later, as she and Pacey made their way slowly past Gyllyngvase Beach. "About all of it. That room at his house. The barn. Running through the forest. Then everything that happened at John's place..."

"I read the case files again last night," Pacey replied, "to remind myself of the details. You went through three or four days of absolute hell."

"The worst part is when I think about all the stupid decisions I made," she continued. "You know when you watch a film and you think the characters are doing really idiotic things? When I look back at what happened, I can't believe some of my choices. Why did I let Ted Armitage get a jump on me at the beginning, when I was still right by my car? I always thought I was pretty smart, but he grabbed me without any trouble at all."

"It seems he'd had a lot of practice," Pacey pointed out. "You shouldn't worry about that."

"It happened twice," she told him. "First Ted Armitage, then John Harrison. They were two very different men, but..."

Her voice trailed off as they walked past the cafe.

"After I escaped," she added, "I was determined to track him down. I think I was in shock after having killed John, but I set out to find Ted Armitage's farm. I shouldn't admit this, but I drove up and down the roads out in Twist Valley. I was convinced that I'd spot something familiar, but there was nothing. It was as if the land had simply swallowed the farm up, as if it had disappeared."

"You went out there alone?"

"I had a gun."

"You -"

"Don't worry, it was all legal," she said, cutting him off. "I told myself that I was ready, that I'd be able to handle myself if I saw him again. That might have been a load of rubbish, but it's what I believed. And the strange thing is, I knew he was still out there somewhere. His body wasn't found in the truck, and I just felt like he was the kind of slippery bastard who'd get himself out of any tight situation."

"Hopefully his luck has run out."

"Eventually I had what I suppose you'd call a breakdown. My mother died, and I started to get really paranoid that I was going to answer the door one day and..."

Her voice trailed off for a moment.

"That's why I came down to Cornwall," she added finally. "I figured that this was as far as I could get from Twist Valley without leaving the country. Plus, Cornwall isn't on the way to anywhere, so I told myself that there was no way he'd end up here by accident. I tried to go completely off the grid. I hid myself away and I pretended that it was all over. I figured that I could handle the nightmares, just so long as there was no chance of him knocking on my door one day."

They walked on in silence for a moment.

"Have you been watching the news?" Pacey asked.

"Not at first. After a while, though, I realized that I had to."

"We've got men crawling all over his farm," Pacey continued. "The thing is, we need to put all the pieces together and make sure that everything's connected that *should* be connected."

"Where do I come in?"

He opened his mouth to reply, but he hesitated for a moment as he wondered how best to broach the subject. Before he could continue, his phone buzzed and he saw that Noad was trying to get in touch, but he told himself that his boss could wait a little while longer for an update. He'd already let him know that he was going to meet Charlotte, and he figured that the most important thing was to try to get her onboard.

"I know this is a big ask," he said cautiously, "but I need you to come with me to Twist Valley."

She stopped and turned to him.

"I need you to come back to the farm," he added.

"You can't be serious."

"You'll be completely safe. In fact, you'll be safer there than -"

He stopped himself just in time.

"Safer than what?" she asked. "Safer than here? You really don't have a clue where Ted Armitage is right now, do you?"

"We're working on it."

"He could be anywhere in the country," she continued, clearly starting to become agitated, "and you wouldn't have the first clue. Do you know his real name?"

"We have a number of leads."

"You don't even know his name," she added, "and now you've come here and you've probably made it more likely that he'll be able to track me down. What if he followed you?"

"No," he said firmly, shaking his head, "that's completely impossible. You have to understand, Ted Armitage is most likely running scared right now, which means that he's focused solely on the need to save his own skin. He'll be putting his plans into action and trying to keep his head down. The last thing he'd want to do now is come looking for you. He must know that we'd be expecting that."

"So have you come here to act as some sort of bodyguard?"

"I've come to ask you for your help," he told her. "I can't force you, but if you really want this guy brought to justice, please consider coming back with me. This is the one thing you can actually do right now that'll help put this bastard behind bars."

He waited, watching her face for any hint of her decision. He could see tears in her eyes, but he told himself that she seemed like a good person and that hopefully she'd be able to get past her fears and recognize the need to cooperate. Although he wanted to say something else that would make her feel better, he forced himself to stay quiet so that she might eventually make the right decision.

"You said yesterday that you found the... heads on the pole," she said, and now her voice was cracking with fear.

"That's right, we did."

"Am I the only person who ever escaped?"

"We're not aware of any others."

"So I should have..."

She took a deep breath.

"I should have been on that pole, shouldn't I? My head, at least."

"Some of the bodies were thrown into the pit with their heads still attached."

"What pit?"

"I -"

"Never mind," she added, before taking a deep breath, as if she was trying to summon a little extra courage from somewhere. "If I come with you, I need you to promise me two things."

"Name them."

"First, I need you to promise that you'll catch him."

"I'm absolutely certain that we'll have him within the next day or two."

"And second..."

She paused again, as a solitary tear rolled down her cheek.

"You have to promise," she continued finally, "that there's no chance that I'll see him again. Not even after he's been caught. I want to know that he's in jail, or that he's dead, but I don't want to see him. Promise me that, and I'll come with you."

Pacey hesitated for a few seconds.

"I promise," he said, trying his best to sound comforting. "There's zero chance that you'll ever come face to face with Ted Armitage again."

## CHAPTER FIFTEEN

"Chrissie, I told you, I just got delayed," Ted said as he continued to drive along a narrow country lane. "I'm heading home right now, I had to get a rental car. When I tell you about the last few days, you're not going to believe the bad luck I've had."

He listened to her reply as he kept his eyes on the road ahead. The signal was weak and her voice was starting to break up.

"Yeah, I know," he continued. "I stopped off for a few hours during the night, but I set off again first thing this morning. You wouldn't want to know some of the crazy stuff that's been going on up here. I just want to get home and put my feet up and -"

Before he could finish, he saw that there was a car pulled over on the side of the road, with the hood up. He immediately slowed down, and as he drove past he saw a young woman – no more than twenty, maybe twenty-five years old – looking at a smoking engine.

"I'm going to have to call you right back," he said, parking his car and switching the engine off. "I'll call you later, Chrissie. Sorry, something's just come up."

He cut the call, and then he looked in the mirror and saw that the woman was waving more smoke away. Whatever had happened to the engine must have been pretty catastrophic, but Ted briefly considered simply setting off on his way. After all, he was in a hurry and he was in pain, and he was certainly in no position to actually help the woman. Nevertheless, he felt that he couldn't possibly leave her stranded, so finally he unfastened his seat belt and climbed out of the car. After all, old habits were difficult to shake.

"Hey there," he said with a smile, as he adjusted his sunglasses, "what seems to be the problem?"

\*\*\*

"It's totally busted," he muttered a short while later, as he took a step back and watched more smoke rising from the engine. "I know a few things about fixing cars, but this is way out of my league. Sorry."

"Thanks for trying," Vicky muttered as she waved her phone in the air again. "I don't have any signal out here, either. Can you believe that?"

"Mine was getting patchy just before I stopped," he told her. "Listen, I think I saw that there's a town about ten miles up ahead. If you want, I..."

His voice trailed off as he began to consider the absurdity of the situation. After everything that had happened, was he actually about to offer to genuinely help someone? Sure, in the old days he'd have jumped at the chance, and he'd have marveled at the fact that a new subject had dropped into his lap so easily; now, however, with nowhere to take the girl and with several serious wounds, he knew that he needed to be far more careful.

"I mean," he continued, "I could drop you off. At the town. If you want."

She checked her phone again, before turning to him. For a moment, she seemed almost to have not really heard his offer.

"I'm not getting in a car with you," he expected her to say. "I've seen the news, I know there's some psycho on the loose. Do you think I'm an idiot?"

"Would you mind?" she asked instead. "I've been camping in the middle of nowhere for the past week, and the thought of having to walk another few miles makes me want to scream. Plus, my feet are covered in blisters."

"Step this way," he replied, gesturing toward his car, even though he was worried he might be making a mistake. "Honestly, it'll be my pleasure."

\*\*\*

"So are you heading anywhere special?" Ted asked as he drove the pair of them along the road. "You said you'd been camping, right?"

"Yeah, just for a week," she replied, as she checked her watch yet again. She seemed nervous, as if she was worried about being late for something. "To tell you the truth, I..."

He waited for her to continue, but after just a few seconds he realized that she seemed to be holding something back. There was something very fidgety about the girl.

"It's okay," he said, "I'm a good listener."

"I'm kind of running away," she told him.

"From what?"

"From who, more like," she admitted. "I don't even know why I'm telling you this. You're a complete stranger. I'm sorry, I'll shut up."

"No, it's fine. Honestly."

He felt a flicker of pain in his gut, but he forced himself to keep smiling.

"I'm getting married tomorrow," she said suddenly.

"I'm sorry?"

"It's kind of an unconventional set-up," she continued, "but basically I'm marrying my childhood sweetheart tomorrow morning at St. Vincent's Church about twenty miles from here. That little camping trip was supposed to be my last chance to get away from all the madness. I know it's not exactly normal behavior for a soon-to-be-bride, but I had to clear my head. It seemed like a good idea at the time, except while I was alone I started to think..."

Once again, she seemed hesitant.

"I'm not going to show up," she said finally.

"I beg your pardon?"

"I can't tell him to his face that I'm not marrying him," she explained, "so I'm going to take the coward's way out and just skip town. Actually, I'm going to skip the country. I've booked a little place in France and I'm going to stay there for a couple of weeks with my phone off, and I'm just going to pretend that everyone here won't be going absolutely nuts. Obviously I'll let them know that I'm okay, but other than that I'm just going to detach myself from the whole mess."

"Isn't that a little..."

He paused.

"I know," she replied, "I'm a bad person. You don't need to tell me."

"I wasn't going to."

"You were thinking it, though."

He took a deep breath.

"I suppose I was," he admitted finally. "Are you really going to just vanish and leave everyone in the lurch? Don't you think you should at least talk to them all?"

"I can't."

"But -"

"I just can't!" she said firmly, clearly on the verge of a full breakdown. "It's too complicated to explain, but I can't face them. Believe me, it'd take more than a short car ride to explain every bad choice I've made in my life. The truth is, I've got myself into this situation and I've just got to get out before it all snowballs to hell." She paused for a moment. "They'll thank me later. It might take a few years, but eventually they'll all realize that I'm doing this as much for them as for me."

He glanced at her, wondering whether she really believed what she was saying, but he was immediately struck by the realization that she seemed to be genuinely traumatized by her decision.

"It's the best for everyone," she added, clearly trying to convince herself. "I'm actually doing the right thing for once."

"If you don't mind a little advice," he replied, "the best thing in any situation is always the same. You should talk to the people involved."

"I can't."

"Why not?"

"I just can't. You don't understand."

"But if -"

"You don't know what I've done!" she snapped, briefly allowing her anger to bubble up. "Sorry, I don't mean to be rude, but I'm not a good person. I've hurt a lot of people and I don't want to do it again. If I'd just made this decision sooner, they'd all be fine by now."

"I'm sure they love you very much."

"They think they do, but they don't know the real me. They think I'm some virtuous, perfect girl who never puts a foot wrong. They don't know about the lies, and the cheating, and the bad thoughts that are always running through my head. You have no idea what it's like to hide your real self from the people you love the most."

"Oh, you might be surprised," he told her with a faint, wry smile.

"I've fought it long enough," she continued, looking straight ahead, watching the road. "I've tried to be a good person but it's time to admit that I'm just bad at heart. I should just be myself instead. At least that way nobody else gets hurt. I don't mind screwing up my own life, I've got plenty of experience with that and I don't feel guilty, but too many other people have suffered because of my stupidity and I refuse to let that happen again."

"You shouldn't give up on yourself just yet."

"That's easy for you to say," she muttered. "Is that the place up ahead?"

Spotting a service station and some other buildings in the distance, Ted realized that they might be a little further from the town than he'd realized.

"That's not the town I was thinking of," he told her. "They might have a mechanic, though. And at least they should have phone signal."

"Do you mind if we stop there?" she asked, turning to him. "I don't want to put you out any more than I have already. And the sooner I get to France, the sooner I can put my old life firmly in the past."

## CHAPTER SIXTEEN

"Oh, hey, you're back."

As he leaned against the car and looked out at the road, Ted realized that he recognized the voice. Turning, he was surprised to see a familiar-looking man wandering over, although for a moment he couldn't quite work out where he'd met him before.

"You rented this beauty from me yesterday," the man added, patting the front of the car.

Startled, Ted looked toward the building and realized that he was at the same showroom. For a moment, that simple fact didn't compute; he felt as if the entire world had gone wrong, as if he'd driven miles and miles and somehow a glitch had deposited him right back where he'd started.

"I thought you were heading south," the man said as he raised a hand to shield his eyes a little from the sun.

"I was," Ted replied. "I mean, I am. I mean..."

He hesitated as he tried to figure out exactly what had happened. Since pulling up in the car park and telling Vicky that he'd wait around to see whether she needed more help, he somehow hadn't noticed that he was right back at the beginning of his journey.

"I guess I just had a few things to do in the area first," he said cautiously. "I must have just... driven round in a big old circle. Funny how that sort of thing can happen, isn't it?"

"Huh."

The man stared at him, but something about his expression seemed a little odd, as if he was concerned.

Ted looked toward the far end of the car park. Vicky had disappeared into one of the other buildings, hoping to find a mechanic, and she'd been gone for at least ten minutes. Although he'd allowed his thoughts to drift, Ted realized now that he'd let his guard down a little, and that he was in danger of sleepwalking into danger. He looked around, to make sure that there was no sign of Vicky anywhere, and then he turned to see that the car dealer was taking a couple of steps back.

"Are you okay there, Doug?" Ted asked, peering at the man's badge. "You look a little... nervous."

"I'm fine," Doug blurted out, before forcing the least genuine smile Ted had ever seen in his life. "I just have to get back inside now. Sorry, I..."

He mumbled something under his breath, and then he turned and almost ran back toward the showroom. There was no escaping the man's sense of sheer panic.

Ted watched him for a moment. He tried to tell himself that there was no need to worry, but deep down he could tell that Doug was onto him. After looking around one more time to make sure that Vicky was still otherwise occupied, he turned and made his way toward the showroom's front door.

"Man," he muttered under his breath, "do I not need this right now."

\*\*\*

"Can I help you?" Doug asked, holding his phone and turning to look as Ted stepped into the reception area. "I'm just -"

He froze as soon as he saw Ted.

"I didn't get to come in here earlier," Ted mused, looking over at the cars and then spotting an escalator leading to the upper floor, where a balcony offered a chance to get a bird's eye view of the vehicles. "You've got a pretty grand set-up here. Do you work all on your own?"

"Nancy's at lunch."

"Nancy?"

"She's my..."

Doug hesitated.

"Secretary."

"Nice cars over there," Ted said, looking once more at the sports cars parked over by the windows. "I'm only just starting to appreciate what you've got going on here. You must be doing pretty well for yourself, Doug."

"I guess so," Doug replied, before hesitating for a moment. "Listen, I really need to make this call."

"Go ahead. I just want to look at those beautiful cars."

"I..."

Again, Doug seemed lost for words.

"I'll just go upstairs," he stammered finally. "I don't want to disturb you, so I'll go upstairs and make the call, and I'll leave you in peace down here."

He turned and hurried toward the escalator.

Letting out a faint sigh, Ted immediately set off after him. By the time he reached the bottom of the escalator, Doug was a few steps further up and had already started to rise toward the first floor. Ted watched him for a moment, before stepping onto the escalator and joining him on the slow journey.

"I thought you wanted to look at the cars," Doug said, and now the fear in his voice was impossible to miss.

"I do," Ted said calmly, taking another couple of steps up, until he was right behind him. "I feel like getting an aerial perspective. You don't mind, do you?"

"No," Doug replied, although now he looked white as a sheet.

Glancing down at the man's left hand, Ted saw that the number 999 was showing on his phone's screen, and that it'd only take one more little tap to connect the call.

"I just wanted to check something," Doug explained, clearly aware that the number had been spotted. "Honestly, it's no big deal."

"I'm sure it isn't," Ted said as they reached the top of the escalator.

Doug stepped off, and Ted quickly joined him.

"Feel free to take as long as you like," Doug told him.

"Oh, I will," Ted replied, adjusting his sunglasses for a moment. "There's just one other thing, though."

Doug swallowed hard.

"What's that?"

Ted paused, and then he smiled.

"I -"

Before Doug could get another word out, Ted grabbed him by the throat and slammed a hand over his mouth, before spinning him around and shoving his head against the wall. As Doug's knees buckled, Ted turned and began to stamp hard on the top of the escalator, and then he reached down and carefully opened the service hatch, revealing the slowly turning mechanism beneath.

Ted carefully leaned the unconscious Doug against the wall, before reaching into the hatch. He could see the elevator's belts running in the narrow space, and he watched as the steps trundled down and disappeared from view. A smile began to cross his lips as he thought about what would happen to a human body if it ended up getting jammed into the heavy, grinding machinery.

"Oh, this isn't going to be pretty," he muttered, shaking his head, "but it certainly should be convenient. This thing's nothing more than a big old meat grinder."

Taking a pen from his pocket, Ted slipped it into the machine, and he watched as the plastic casing immediately snapped.

"Okay," he said, grabbing Doug and pulling him closer, then starting to turn him around, "I don't have long, so this is going to be a little quicker than I'd otherwise have liked."

"Wait," Doug murmured, as he slowly began to stir, "what are you doing?"

"I'm putting you out of your misery, my friend."

He adjusted his grip on Doug's shoulders, before shoving his feet down through the open hatch.

"Stop!" Doug shouted. "Let me go! I'll do anything you want! I won't tell anyone!"

"Sorry, but I really don't think I can trust you to keep your word on that."

"Help!" Doug screamed. "I'm -"

Ted clamped a hand over his mouth again, and then he began to feed the man's legs into the escalator's belt system. Doug's body began to shudder violently as his feet were crushed, but Ted kept a hand over his mouth and began to push down harder.

"You know," he sneered, as Doug struggled violently, "I always had this idea in the back of my head as something I'd like to try some day, but I never thought I'd actually get a chance. Funny how the word works, huh?"

He shoved Doug down even harder as blood began to splatter around the edges of the hatch. Doug reached out with his left hand, making a hopeless attempt to hit the emergency button up by the handrail, but he had absolutely no chance of getting close. He still tried for a few more seconds, before his body lurched deeper into the guts of the escalator and he let out another pained cry. Blood was starting to burst from his mouth.

"I've got to admit," Ted continued, "this isn't quite as nasty as I'd imagined. Then again, I *do* have quite a vivid imagination. I suppose all the blood and pieces of bone are gathering underneath, waiting for some poor technician to find them, huh?"

Doug's body was shuddering wildly now as Ted shoved his head into the jaws of the escalator mechanism. As the man's skull crunched open, Ted got to his feet and carefully replaced the panel, and then he took the stairs back down. With each step, he was able to hear a grinding sound coming from the escalator, although this sound was starting to fade as he got to the bottom. Looking down at the escalator, he saw that although there was already *some* blood circulating on the steps, there wasn't as much as he'd expected, which meant that the man's disappearance might not be noticed immediately.

"Rest in peace," he muttered, before turning and heading to the door, whistling as he walked back out into the sunshine.

## CHAPTER SEVENTEEN

"You're back," Ted said a few minutes later, as he waited next to the car and saw Vicky approaching. "Did you manage to find someone to fix your car?"

"No, I..."

Her voice trailed off, and she seemed a little troubled. She turned and looked over her shoulder, back toward the far end of the car park, and then she turned to Ted again.

"Don't worry about me," he told her, "I was fine here. I kept myself busy."

"I've been thinking about what you said," Vicky told him. "Damn it, an hour ago I was so sure that I knew what I had to do, but what you said has really got into my mind. I'm starting to think..."

Her voice trailed off.

"*What* are you starting to think?" Ted asked.

"I think you might be right."

He raised a skeptical eyebrow.

"I'm going to do what you suggested," she continued, before taking a big, deep breath as if she was trying to find a little extra courage. "I'm going to go and talk to James. That's my fiancee. I'm going to talk to him, and to my family, and I'm going to do something I've never done before in my life. I'm going to be completely open and honest about everything I've been thinking."

"That's... good," Ted replied, somewhat shocked that she seemed to have taken his advice onboard so fully.

"I said I'd tried everything, but that's not true," she added. "Honesty isn't just about telling people all the facts. It's about sharing what you really, truly think, and the time has come for me to step up. Sure, it might all go horribly wrong, but I won't regret it, and do you know why?"

"Why?"

"Because deep down I know that it's the right thing to do," she said, and she took another deep breath. "Now I just have to find a mechanic, because I don't have much time. I need to get home before it's too late."

"You can call a mechanic when you get there," he replied. "Jump in. I'll take you wherever you need to go."

***

"You live *here*?" he asked as he brought the car to a stop outside the gates of a large country house. He stared for a moment, before turning to her. "Are you..."

"My dad's in banking," she told him. "He's kind of a big deal."

Looking past Ted, she watched the house for a few seconds, and she was unable to hide a sense of dread that began to creep across her face.

"They don't know that anything's wrong," she continued. "They're going to be so excited for the big day, and I have to go in there and break the news to them that it's not happening." She hesitated. "I've changed my mind. I'm going back to my first plan. Take me somewhere else. Anywhere. I need to get to an airport, or a ferry terminal, or -"

"You don't want to run away," he told her.

"I'm not brave enough to do this."

"Of course you are," he replied. He waited for her to realize that he was right, but he quickly understood that she needed another little nudge in the right direction. "I give advice quite often," he said cautiously, "and to be honest with you, that advice is rarely taken. And the consequences of people ignoring my advice... well, it's not pretty. To be honest, no-one has ever taken it all the way, and I just think that's a terrible shame. Now, I can't force you to listen to me, but I have a feeling that deep down you know I'm right."

She turned to him.

He blinked, and in an instant he imagined her tied to the bed in the farmhouse, struggling desperately against the restraints. As soon as he blinked again, he saw her hanging from the chains in the barn, naked and bloodied, begging for her freedom. He knew that in normal circumstances he'd have drugged a girl like Vicky by now, and that he'd be taking her back to the farm, but those days were over and he felt strangely at peace. At the same time, he knew he was on the verge of his first success story.

"Okay," she said finally.

"Okay?"

She nodded.

"You're terrified, huh?" he asked.

"More than terrified," she replied, as she opened the door and stepped out of the car. "I can't believe I'm actually doing this, but I guess I just know somehow that you're right."

"And you won't chicken out before you get in there?"

She thought about that question for a moment, and then she shook her head.

"Then I wish you all the luck in the world."

"Thanks," she replied. "I'm just so lucky I met you today. You've changed my life."

She hesitated, before suddenly leaning back into the car and giving him a kiss on the cheek.

"What was *that* for?" he stammered.

"For being a cool guy," she said, standing up again and taking a step back. "Do you have any kids?"

"I..."

He hesitated as he tried to work out how to answer that question.

"Sure," he said finally. "Yeah, I do."

"They're so lucky to have a dad like you," she continued. "I hope they know that."

With that, she swung the door shut and then made her way past the gates and along the driveway. She glanced back for a moment and waved, but she didn't stop, and Ted realized after a few more seconds that she was actually taking his advice. With each nervous, hesitant step that she took toward the house, it was clear that Vicky had really listened to what he'd said to her, and that she was determined to change her life for the better.

"You finally succeeded."

Turning, he saw one of his older victims – Natalie Pressman – sitting on the back seat. Unlike some of the other hallucinations, she was fully clothed and unharmed, and he remembered that she'd spent a long time tied to the bed before he'd eventually had to take her through to the barn. She'd been one of his most promising captures, although ultimately her head hadn't made it onto the monument. There had been some... disappointment concerning her final actions.

"How do you feel?" she asked. "Vindicated?"

"I feel sad," he told her, "that there are so many people out there in the world who need help, and that I won't be able to get to all of them."

"One's more than your deserve."

"She was smart. That's why she listened."

"Are you sure it's not the fact that you didn't kidnap her?" Natalie replied. "You might have missed your calling, Ted. In another life, you could actually have done some good in this world."

"I've done plenty of good," he muttered. "Even away from the farm. Do you know how many bad people are -"

"How's your wound?" she asked suddenly, interrupting him.

Looking down, he saw that blood was already soaking through his new shirt. He'd managed to hide his discomfort from Vicky, but that had come at a cost; now he could feel a rush of pain spreading throughout his body, and he knew that time was running out. He began to pick the shirt open, only to stop as soon as he felt some kind of clear, sticky liquid bleeding through the fabric. The pain in his gut was starting to throb, and he was becoming increasingly convinced that he was running a temperature.

"The life is leaking out of you," Natalie observed, as she leaned over from the back seat and took a closer look. "Drop by drop, it's leaving you and it can't ever be replaced. You can't hide the truth forever. Soon you'll be a lifeless corpse, and your blood will be nothing more than a stain."

Ted looked toward the house, just in time to see Vicky stepping inside.

"So where are you going to die?" Natalie asked. "Right here, slumped in your car like some kind of moron?"

"No," he said through gritted teeth.

"You've been driving in circles," she continued, "so I think we both know you can't and won't go home."

"That's where you're wrong."

"You'd never make it in time."

"You'd be surprised how fast a man can drive when he's motivated," he said as he put the car in gear and began to speed away from the gates.

"Sure," Natalie said, "but miracles aren't -"

Suddenly Ted turned the car around, and he quickly set off back the way he'd just come.

"Aren't you going the wrong way?" Natalie asked.

"Hell, no," he replied, pushing the pedal to the floor as he began to race along the country road. "I told you I'm going home, and I meant every word. In fact, I never should have *left* home in the first place."

"But you're -"

Natalie fell silent for a moment.

"Ah," she added finally, "I think I understand now."

"I'm going to Twist Valley," he said, gripping the wheel tighter than ever as he raced toward the distant forest. "I achieved everything I ever wanted to achieve, so I'm going back to my farm. I'm going to my real home!"

## CHAPTER EIGHTEEN

"Okay, I'll tell her," Pacey said, before cutting the call and turning to look back into his car. "Chief Inspector Noad's running a little late, but he'll be here soon. He wants us to start without him, so if you don't mind taking a look around with me..."

His voice trailed off as he saw Charlotte's terrified face. As she peered out at the burned farmhouse, she seemed to be in some kind of catatonic state, and Pacey realized after a moment that she probably hadn't heard a word he'd just said to her. He wanted to gently wake her her daze, but at the same time he worried that he might cause some harm. Better, he reasoned, to let her come around in her own time.

Turning, he looked once again at the farmhouse, and then at the barn. The various investigative teams had pulled out for the day, leaving just a few guards they'd passed on their way up; with the time approaching 5pm, the sun was starting to set and Pacey knew that he and Charlotte only had a couple of hours before they too would have to head off for the night. He could only hope that Noad would arrive before darkness fell.

"This is the place," Charlotte said.

He turned to her.

"This is it," she continued, and now all the color had drained from her face. "It's different, obviously, but I'd recognize it anywhere. I've seen it in my nightmares so many times."

"Most of it's been on fire," he pointed out, somewhat unhelpfully.

"I remember running across there," she said, before turning and looking at the burned-out barn, "and stopping over there."

She paused, as she remembered the screams of the woman who'd been chained up inside the barn.

"He killed a woman," she continued. "I was going to help her, but I didn't get a chance. He gutted her right in front of me, although he didn't know I was watching. At least, I don't think he knew. She told him she had a husband and a kid, and he didn't care. He murdered her anyway."

"We're still working to build up a final list of all his victims," Pacey mentioned.

"And then the heads..."

She looked toward the far end of the barn.

"Are they still there?"

"No," Pacey told her. "They've been removed for further examination. Eventually they'll be reunited with their bodies and then they'll be released to the families for burial. Some of those families have been waiting fifteen years for the chance to do that. I can't even begin to imagine how they must be feeling right now."

"Is that all you need from me?" she asked, looking up at him. "I've told you that it's the same place."

"Chief Inspector Noad wants you to take a look around," Pacey replied. "He's aware that your claims five years ago were perhaps not investigated as fully as they might have been, and he thinks that you might have more information buried in your memory. I know it sounds silly, but sometimes people *do* turn out to know more than they realized."

He waited, but he could tell that she was reluctant to leave the safety of the car. After a moment, however, she opened the door and got to her feet, while looking around as if she still expected to see Ted Armitage leap out from somewhere.

"He's so far away from here by now," Pacey told her. "I promise."

"You can't promise that."

"I'm pretty sure I can in this instance," he continued. "He damn near blew this place sky high. He wouldn't have done that if he intended to ever come back."

She looked around for a moment longer, and then she turned to him again.

"Can I be alone for a little while?" she asked.

"Are you sure that's a good idea?"

"You want me to see what I remember, and I won't be able to do that if you're watching me the whole time." She paused, clearly scared. "Please. I need to do this. I need to prove to myself that he's really gone."

\*\*\*

Half an hour later, as he peered into the ruined barn, Pacey heard the sound of a car approaching. He turned, just in time to see that Noad had finally made his way back, so he wandered over to greet his boss and explain the latest developments.

"Where is she?" Noad asked as he climbed out of the car.

"Out there," he replied, turning and nodding toward the forest.

"Out there?" Noad said, furrowing his brow. "What do you mean by that?"

"I mean she wanted to take a look around on her own," he explained. "In the circumstances, I didn't see the harm. Sir, she's clearly traumatized by what happened, but she's pushing herself to help us. I think we just need to give her a little more time."

"I want to talk to her."

"She went out into the forest. I asked her if she wanted someone to go with her, but I think it's important to her that she does it by herself. She told me she wouldn't be long."

"She'd better not be," Noad muttered as he looked around for a moment. "I just got off the phone from a long conversation with Commissioner Prentiss. He wanted to tell me all the things I've done wrong, but I could tell from his tone of voice that he's starting to panic."

"Panic?" Pacey replied. "Why would he panic?"

"Because the media will soon start asking why there hasn't been an arrest," Noad told him. "This case is stalling, just as I predicted, and it's stalling because the people in charge don't know what the hell they're doing. Meanwhile the newspapers are filling up with shots of photogenic young women who haven't been seen for years. Fortunately, you and I are busy getting the actual work done. When Prentiss finds out what we've been up to, he'll have to admit that we were right."

"But if he..."

Pacey thought about that suggestion for a moment.

"Wait," he said cautiously, "does Commission Prentiss not know what we're doing? I thought we had some kind of plan that he understood and -"

"Ms. Walker!" Noad shouted suddenly, cupping his hands around his mouth in an attempt to make his voice travel. "Where are you? I need to talk to you! It's urgent!"

"I haven't seen her for a while," Pacey admitted. "She'll be back soon. She promised."

"That's all well and good, but we're running out of daylight."

"She's already confirmed that this is the place where she woke up five years ago."

"How sure is she?"

"Completely."

"Then that's something," Noad said with a sigh. "When the truth about this Armitage guy gets out, there's going to be hell to pay. Prentiss knows full well that his neck's on the chopping block. Of course, if they'd listened to me, we'd have been investigating Ted Armitage a long time ago."

"Did no-one *ever* think that you were right?"

"There were some nibbles occasionally," Noad explained, "but for the most part I was written off as some kind of dumb old crank. I suppose it was easier for them to do that, instead of actually considering the possibility that I was onto a serial killer. After a while, it became too embarrassing to listen to me. No-one wanted to be seen in my company." He paused for a moment. "I was shunned," he added finally, with a hint of bitterness in his voice, "and laughed at, but they're not laughing now. Now they're just trying to work out how to admit that I was right without losing face."

"I'll go and find Charlotte," Pacey said, stepping past Noad.

"No, wait," Noad replied, grabbing his arm, "let her be. Just for another half hour or so, at least. I want to go and check something nearby anyway before I talk to her, and I want you to look around for any sign that there might be more of those pits."

"More pits?" Pacey asked. "Why would -"

"Call it a hunch," Noad said firmly, "but I have a sneaking suspicion that we still haven't see the full picture about this place. Ted Armitage, or whatever his name was, seems to have been something of a slippery character. I hope I'm wrong, but it wouldn't surprise me at all if there's something else lurking around here. Check the ground. Look for anything that the others might have missed."

"Sure," Pacey replied, although he was still somewhat puzzled by the order. "If there's anything else here, I'll find it."

"There's something else," Noad muttered, as he looked out toward the forest. "It's right in front of us, and yet we're not seeing it. And I have a feeling that when we *do* see it, it might be too late for us to do anything about it."

## CHAPTER NINETEEN

*Scrambling down a steep hill in the dark, struggling to keep hold of the ax while remaining upright, Charlotte felt as if she was about to slip in the wet leaves and tumble down the rest of the way. Somehow she made it to the bottom of the hill, and then she turned and looked back up, terrified that at any moment she was going to see Ted Armitage coming after her.*

Now, five years after that desperate scramble for freedom, Charlotte Walker stood alone in a small clearing – a little way from the farm – and listened to the silence of the forest.

For a moment, she felt all the memories rushing back. She'd tried her best to forget the details of her frantic escape, but the truth remained buried somewhere in her mind.

The barbed wire.

The drone.

The waterfall.

The drone again.

John Harrison's cottage.

That wretched, infernal drone.

She flinched as she thought about her younger self racing desperately through the forest. After a moment she set off again, making her way down the muddy slope, and then she slowed her pace as she saw something ahead. Sure enough, she realized that she'd found the fence, the same one that had caught her in the darkness, the one that had damn near torn her body apart. The one that had almost cost her an eye. Reaching out, she touched one of the spikes.

*Throwing herself forward, she immediately felt barbs cutting into her belly and waist, but this time she was determined to keep going. Even as her clothes tore, and as she felt blood bursting from wounds all over her lower body, she scrambled through into the darkness, screaming as she clawed at the ground and tried to drag herself free.*

"Yeah," she muttered now, "that was... an experience."

Hearing a rustling sound nearby, she looked over her shoulder. She half expected to see Detective Inspector Pacey making his way through the forest, but instead she spotted a small bird hopping across the dead leaves on the forest floor. She allowed herself a faint smile, and then – figuring that there was no way she wanted to try to climb through barbed wire for a second time – she began to make her way along the path of the fence, following its line around what she assumed must be the perimeter of Ted Armitage's property.

"Hello, Charlotte."

Startled, she turned and saw Ted standing just a few feet away, as if he'd just stepped out from behind one of the trees.

"Long time," he continued with a faint smile. He looked exactly the same as before, as if no time at all had passed. "I hope you've been keeping well."

She froze, not even daring to breathe, but she already understood that she wasn't really seeing him at all. With his big sunglasses and his stupid fishing hat, he was just a hallucination. She'd encountered him in her nightmares so many times, and she was determined to make sure that she didn't succumb to madness. After all, she'd escaped from Ted five years earlier, and she refused to let herself fall victim to his memory.

"You're not real," she whispered.

"What was that?" he asked, cupping a hand next to his ear. "I didn't quite hear you."

"You're not real," she said again, as she clenched her fists.

"I'm not?" He furrowed his brow. "You thought I was real five years ago."

"That's because you *were* real then," she replied. "Don't try to confuse me. I know my own mind."

"Are you sure about that?" he asked. "I'm not trying to be rude here, Charlotte, but you look pretty scared right now. In fact, you look like you might be about to faint."

"You have no power over me," she said through gritted teeth. "Not anymore."

"Is that right?"

He hesitated, before stepping toward her.

She immediately flinched, but she somehow managed to stand her ground, even as he made his way closer. After a couple more paces he was standing just inches away, staring down at her as she looked up and saw her own face reflected twice in the lenses of his sunglasses.

"You've had nightmares about this moment, haven't you?" he asked with a grin.

"I'm not scared of you."

"Then prove it. Touch me. Prove to yourself that I'm not really here."

She knew it should be easy to do what he asked, but she couldn't quite bring herself to reach out and try to touch his chest. Although she could tell that she was playing right into his hands, she lacked the strength to do the one thing that would settle the argument forever, and she knew that each moment of doubt allowed little cracks to spread through her resolve.

"There," he purred, "I knew it. You're nothing but a scared little woman who doesn't have the guts to put her money where her mouth is."

"Oh yeah?"

"Yeah."

She hesitated for a moment longer, and then she finally reached forward. As she did so, she blinked, and in that instant the image of Ted Armitage vanished into the evening air.

Letting out a huge sigh of relief, Charlotte stepped back until she bumped against a tree. Her heart was pounding, and she could finally admit that – deep down – there had been a part of her that had worried Ted might have been real. As tears filled her eyes, she slid down until she was sitting on the forest floor and she put her head in her hands. Frustrated by her own foolishness, she realized that she'd spent fifteen years trying to put Ted Armitage in the past, only for him to have turned her into a wreck once again.

"Damn you!" she snarled, hoping to find some courage from somewhere. "When will you learn?"

For the next few minutes, she could only sob quietly. She was glad that she'd taken Detective Inspector Pacey up on his offer, and that she'd returned to the farm in Twist Valley, but she was disappointed that her mind had weakened so easily. The worst part was that she knew now how easily Ted could reappear, and that most likely he'd be part of her forever. Finally, wiping her eyes, she told herself that she had to somehow force herself to keep going, and she thought back to the moment when – clinging to the wet rocks as she'd tried to climb down the waterfall – she'd somehow found the anger that she'd needed.

"Go to hell!" she remembered screaming as the yellow drone had made its way down and hovered just inches from her face.

"Go to hell," she whispered now, as she slowly got to her feet and wiped away more tears.

She looked around, and all she saw was the forest stretching out in every direction. She knew that she needed to get back to the farm, but there was one other thing she wanted to do first.

"Go to hell!" she called out.

Still not loud enough.

"Go to hell!" she screamed, as loud as she could manage, and this time she figured that she might even have been heard all the way back up at the farmhouse.

Taking a deep breath, she turned and began to make her way back up the slope. With each step, she felt more and more determined to help catch Armitage and then to get back to her little cottage in Cornwall, and to put the misery of Twist Valley firmly in the past. In fact, in some strange way she was starting to feel better about the future, and she told herself that – in time – she might eventually come to view her return to the farm as some important cathartic moment. As she continued to hurry up toward the ridge, she barely even noticed the sound of a second set of footsteps approaching, until a moment later a twig snapped nearby.

Turning, she was horrified to see Ted Armitage again.

"It won't work this time," she said firmly.

"Charlotte," he replied, tilting his head slightly, "was that little performance for my benefit?"

"Sorry," she said, "but..."

Her voice trailed off as she realized that something was different this time. For one thing, Ted looked older now, slightly plumper and a lot more scruffy; for another, his clothes were torn in places, and when she looked down at the front of his shirt she saw that he seemed to be bleeding from a wound in his belly.

She looked at his face again.

"Go to hell," she said firmly, before turning to walk away.

Suddenly a rock slammed against the back of her head. Letting out a gasp, she crumpled unconscious to the floor, landing in front of Ted and then rolling down until she bumped against his feet.

"How many times have you told me to go to hell since we first met?" he asked, as he dropped the bloodied rock next to her face. "It's so good to see you again, Charlotte. You're the one final loose end I was hoping I'd get a chance to wrap up."

## CHAPTER TWENTY

"Something isn't right here," Pacey muttered as he stopped next to the burned farmhouse and took another look around. "Something's..."

His voice trailed off as he tried to figure out exactly why he felt so uncomfortable. Even since Noad had headed off into the forest, he'd been dutifully searching for more hatches in the ground, but the task had begun to seem increasingly pointless. There were still some patches of land that he hadn't managed to check, but deep in his gut he was starting to realize that there was nothing left to find. In which case, he was starting to wonder why his boss had set him to work on such a thankless task.

Feeling a vibration in his pocket, he slipped his phone out and saw that someone from the station was trying to get through.

"Pacey," he said as he answered, "what -"

"Where are you?" Sergeant Whitloss asked before he had a chance to say more.

"I'm out at the farm with Chief Inspector Noad," he explained. "We're just -"

"You need to get out of there," Whitloss said firmly. "We've got a team heading out to you right now, but we have reason to believe that Ted Armitage might be on his way."

"What..."

Pacey hesitated for a moment.

"Why would Ted Armitage be coming back here?" he asked cautiously.

"I have no idea," Whitloss replied, "but there's been an incident at a car showroom about sixty miles from your location. One man's dead, and we believe we've caught this Armitage guy on camera. It's hard to make him out, he's got a hat on and sunglasses. We've run A.N.P.R. on the vehicle he's driving and it looks like he's heading straight back to the farm."

Turning, Pacey looked around, but so far there was no sign of anyone. In fact, for a moment the entire scene seemed completely peaceful and serene.

"I'm going to send the details of his vehicle over," Whitloss continued, "but it's likely that he'd choose to park some way from the farm and approach on foot. Like I said, we have a team heading out there right now but they won't be there ahead of him. You need to get Chief Inspector Noad and leave the area immediately."

"I'll have to find him first," Pacey said, looking the other way and still seeing no sign of either Noad or Charlotte. "Okay, I'd better get off the line and contact them. I'll be in touch once we're away from the site, but you've got to promise me that you're sending enough people to grab this guy once and for all."

"There's a veritable army heading your way," she told him. "Hurry."

\*\*\*

Stopping for a moment as he reached another clearing in the forest, Noad listened to the sound of the forest all around. He could hear leaves rustling at the tops of the trees, but something else had caught his attention, something that didn't seem quite right. He listened for a moment longer, before turning to look back up the slope.

A moment later he heard the telltale sound of a twig snapping.

He turned the other way, and then he took a couple of steps forward, only to stop again as soon as he saw a figure slumped on the ground. Hurrying over, he propped his cane against a nearby tree and then slowly, painfully got down onto his knees. Reaching over to the figure, he moved matted hair from across her face, and he immediately recognized the bloodied features of Charlotte Walker.

"No," he muttered, checking for a pulse and – to his relief – finding one, "Ms. Walker, I -"

"I owe you one," a voice said suddenly.

Noad turned and saw that a man was standing just a few feet away, leaning against a tree.

"You brought her right back to me," the man continued. "Straight into my clutches, so to speak. I never would have managed to catch up to her otherwise."

"Ted Armitage," Noad whispered, as he looked at the sunglasses that hid the man's eyes. "It *is* you, isn't it?"

"It's only appropriate that we finally come face to face," Ted replied, wincing slightly. "You've been onto me for a long time, Mr. Noad, haven't you? Tracking me. Keeping notes. Waiting for the day when someone else would take your suspicions seriously."

Reaching into his jacket, he slowly pulled out a gun.

"Let Charlotte Walker go," Noad said firmly. "If you have an issue with me, then we can talk it out, but this young woman has been through more than enough."

"You know it doesn't work like that," Ted told him. "Of all the guests I brought to my farm, she was the biggest failure. By running, she proved that she didn't even deserve to be there in the first place. I made a rare mistake."

"You need to give it all up," Noad replied, as he slowly began to get to his feet. "You know you can't keep running."

"Can't I?"

"Where would you go?"

"Wherever I like," Ted said with a grin. "You don't even know my name."

"We're closing in on you."

"But what's my *name*, Mr. Noad? I know who you are. Believe me, I know a hell of a lot about you, but after all this time you still know next to nothing about me."

"I -"

"What's my name?"

Noad opened his mouth to reply, and then he hesitated.

"Say my name," Ted continued. "My real name."

"I'll find it out soon enough."

"I think you know," Ted replied. "Deep down. You just can't quite bring yourself to say it."

"You're nothing but a deranged killer."

"And yet I let a girl go just this afternoon," Ted told him. "She was a pretty little thing, she'd have looked great strung up in my barn. Or I could have just killed her in the car. But I didn't, and do you know why? Because I'm not a monster. I always said that I was trying to help the women I took, and I was true to my word. I finally found one who was willing to listen to me."

"That's wonderful," Noad said, "but -"

"Of course, the idiot at the car showroom deserved to die. I'd never killed a man before, but I suppose it was only a matter of time. I'm always -"

He winced again, and this time he couldn't help but clutch his belly.

"You're sick," Noad said firmly. "Do you want to die out here like a wild animal? There's no dignity in that. Let me help you, Mr. Armitage. I can tell that you're an intelligent man. While I don't condone your actions, I can tell that you had the best of intentions. Come with me and I assure you that you'll be treated properly. You'll have an opportunity to explain yourself and to tell the world why you did what you did. Isn't that what everyone wants? A chance to be heard?"

"You make a good point," Ted said cautiously.

"I have my moments," Noad told him. "I've studied you, Mr. Armitage. From afar, but still... I've tried to understand you, but that hasn't been easy. It would be the greatest honor of my life to be able to work with you now, to learn from you and to see the world through your eyes."

"Are you trying to flatter me?"

"I'm trying to appeal to you. We're both smart men, and we both know how the world works. We both know that there are only so many ways that this evening can end for you."

Ted hesitated for a moment, mulling those words over, before slowly aiming the gun.

"You don't have to do this," Noad said firmly, staring at the barrel of the gun and trying very hard to remain calm. "Think about your legacy."

"My legacy?"

Ted hesitated, before starting to laugh.

"I don't care about my legacy," he explained. "I don't *have* a legacy. This has always been about two things, and two things only. First, there's my desire to help people. I only succeeded once, but that's not too bad, not when you factor human nature into the equation. And second, there's always been a battle, hasn't there? You and I have always been aware of one another, always fighting to come out on top."

"I'm not sure that I'd put it quite like -"

"The battle ends today," Ted said firmly. "After all this time, I've finally found a way to push you down forever, and there's nothing you can do about that."

"I don't think you really believe it's over," Noad told him.

"It doesn't matter what you think," Ted replied. "But if you don't believe me, then there's really one very easy way for me to prove my point."

"Listen to me," Noad said, holding his hands up, "I only want -"

Before he could get another word out, Ted pulled the trigger, firing a single shot that immediately sent Noad crumpling down to the forest floor.

## CHAPTER TWENTY-ONE

"Did you hear the crap he came out with?" Ted muttered a few minutes later, as he continued to drag Charlotte's unconscious body through the forest. "That Noad fellow really was a piece of work, huh? He really thought he could get inside my head and figure me out. I'm sure glad I won't have to hear from him again."

As he reached the barbed wire fence that marked the edge of his property, he let go of Charlotte and took a moment to wipe sweat from his brow. Reaching down, he touched the wound on his belly and he immediately realized that more blood had leaked through onto the shirt. As he felt a fresh wave of weakness filling his body, he knew that time was running out, but he told himself that he still had a chance to deal with a few final loose ends.

He looked at Charlotte, before nudging the side of her face with his boot.

"Are you awake down there?" he asked, before nudging her again. "Hey, wake up. I'm sick of dragging you around, it's time for you to start walking."

He waited, and then he crouched down and pressed the barrel of the gun against her temple.

"I mean it," he continued. "You're not exactly the lightest woman on the planet. Come on, let's be having you, get up."

He waited again, and then he sighed as he checked her head wound.

"I suppose I might have given you more of a wallop than I intended," he added, as he found blood on her scalp. "That's too bad. I had a big speech lined up, I was going to tell you my whole plan before I popped a bullet into your face. There's no point doing that now, not if there's no-one around to listen, so that means it's time to do what I should have done five years ago. Apologies for the fact that you didn't get to go through my whole training system, but you've only got yourself to blame for the fact that you ran away."

He carefully adjusted the position of the gun.

"Goodnight, Charlotte Walker," he said with a faint smile. "Enjoy your -"

Hearing a shuffling sound, he looked over toward the trees. He saw no sign of anyone, but he instinctively got to his feet and stepped over Charlotte before stopping next to one of the trees and taking a moment to listen. He knew there shouldn't be anyone nearby, but he remained vigilant for a few seconds before turning back to Charlotte.

"I -"

"Die!" she screamed as she slammed a broken branch into the side of his face, sending him thudding back against the tree with such force that the gun fell from his hand.

Before he could react, she hit him again, this time knocking him down onto the ground, and then she kicked him hard in the chest.

"You piece of shit!" she yelled, hitting him with the branch again and again, battering him as hard as she could manage.

Desperately trying to get free, Ted began to crawl away and reach for the gun. Charlotte immediately kicked him hard in the face, but this time he was prepared and he managed to steady himself before trying to get to his feet. He let out a faint gasp and crashed against one of the trees, and then he turned to find that Charlotte was now holding the gun, with the barrel pointed directly at his face.

He waited for her to pull the trigger.

"You wouldn't," he told her. "You don't have the balls to kill me. You probably believe all that nonsense about how you'd be just as bad as me, about how you don't want to lower yourself to my level."

"Not really," she replied, before lowering the gun and firing, shooting him in the left leg.

Letting out a cry of pain, Ted dropped down, clutching his leg as he leaned back against the tree.

"There," Charlotte said, her voice trembling with fear, "that should keep you in one place while I go and get the police. Believe me, I want to kill you, but I also want you to pay for what you did. I want you to get dragged through the courts, I want you to hear what everyone says about you, and I want you to spend the rest of your life knowing that you're a monster. That's the only reason why you don't already have a bullet between your eyes."

Turning, she began to run back up the hill.

"Get back here and finish me off!" Ted snarled, trying to get up but quickly slumping back down. "I dare you! Don't be a coward, Charlotte! You must have had dreams about this moment! Kill me or you'll always know that you failed!"

Stopping suddenly, she kept her back to him.

"You know I'm right," he sneered. "What's wrong with you? Are you a complete moron?"

Charlotte hesitated, and then slowly she turned to him.

\*\*\*

"Have you seen anything unusual?" Sergeant Doyle asked as he stepped out of the first patrol car, while four other cars pulled up nearby.

"If you mean Ted Armitage, then no," Pacey replied. "Chief Inspector Noad went out into the forest a while ago and I haven't managed to get hold of him, and there's also a witness out there, her name's Charlotte Walker."

"We've got teams trying to track down the car Armitage was last seen in," Doyle continued, "but so far there's no sign of it having been abandoned anywhere in the area. There's no way he'd just drive straight up to the farm, though. He has to be coming on foot."

"Are we really sure he's coming *here*?" Pacey asked. "Of all the places..."

"There's nothing else for miles around," Doyle pointed out. "Right now, this is the best lead we've got."

"Sir," Constable Jones said as he made his way over to join them, "we've been running A.N.P.R. checks but it's hopeless, there are no cameras anywhere in Twist Valley. Once he entered the area, he could have gone anywhere."

"Keep looking anyway," Doyle told him. "You never know, we might get lucky."

"There's nothing here," Pacey said with a sigh. "Noad just had me searching the entire site to see if there might be anything hidden, but I drew a complete blank. There's nothing more than a bunch of burned buildings. He seemed to think there might be another pit or a hatch or something, but if there is, I can't find it."

"Armitage might be getting sentimental, then," Doyle suggested, "in which case -"

Before he could finish, they all heard a gunshot out in the forest.

"Noad and Charlotte are still unaccounted for," Pacey pointed out, before hurrying around Noad's car and starting to make his way across the yard. "We have to get to them."

"I want armed officers out in that forest now!" Doyle shouted, just as a police van rumbled to a halt nearby. "The suspect has a gun and he's extremely dangerous!"

"Which way did it come from?" Pacey asked, stopping next to the burned barn and looking out into the trees. "It seemed to almost echo all around." He cupped his hands around his mouth. "Sir! Chief Inspector Noad! Charlotte! Where are you?"

As he waited for an answer, he heard footsteps nearby and he turned to see that several armed officers were making their way down the slope that led into the forest. For a moment he felt completely helpless, but he quickly set off after them.

"Pacey, wait!" Doyle called out. "You need to let them do their job!"

"Charlotte Walker's here because of me," he replied, not even stopping to look back. "I won't let anything happen to her."

"This isn't the time to be getting in the way!" Doyle yelled, but he could tell that he was already too late.

As Pacey disappeared into the forest, rushing after the armed officers, Doyle turned and headed back to one of the vehicles. He grabbed his phone and brought up the number for Commissioner Prentiss, but a moment later he heard someone hurrying up behind him and he turned to find that Constable Jones was approaching.

"Anything?" Doyle asked.

"Sir, I -"

"It's an easy enough question to answer!" Doyle snapped. "Did the A.N.P.R. system throw anything up?"

"No," Jones replied, staring at the screenshot on his phone, which showed Armitage's car passing a camera a few hours earlier, "but... I don't quite understand."

"What don't you understand?"

Jones hesitated, before holding the phone up.

"That's the rental vehicle Armitage was driving, right?"

"I know that."

"But are we really truly *sure* that it was Armitage in that car?"

"Of course we are. We've got footage of him getting in on that forecourt."

"Okay," Jones said, "but in that case..."

He turned and held the phone up again, so that the image was adjacent to the car parked over near the burned farmhouse.

"It's already here," he pointed out. "Armitage's car, I mean. It's parked right there. Why didn't Detective Inspector Pacey say anything?"

Doyle hesitated, staring at the screen for a moment before looking at the identical car parked about twenty feet away.

"Because," he said cautiously, as he tried to understand what was happening, "that's Chief Inspector Noad's car."

## CHAPTER TWENTY-TWO

"Sir!" Pacey yelled, rushing over to Noad and dropping to his knees. "Are you okay? What happened?"

"That idiot shot me!" Noad replied, clutching his injured leg.

"Who?"

"Armitage! I've been trying to get up for the last twenty minutes!"

"Twenty minutes?" Pacey hesitated. "Sir, I heard the shot just a couple of -"

"Are you going to help me or not?" Noad asked, reaching out and grabbing Pacey's arm. "I saw a bunch of armed morons heading down to the south. Do they seriously think that Armitage went that way?"

Pacey took the older man's weight and helped him up.

"Sir, have you seen Charlotte Walker?" he asked. "She's out here somewhere, and I'm worried that Armitage might be after her. We know he's in the area and -"

"I know he's in the bloody area!" Noad snapped angrily. "I've got a bullet in my leg to prove it."

"And if -"

Before he could finish, Pacey noticed that Noad was also bleeding from some kind of wound in his belly. He moved the edge of Noad's jacket aside and saw thick blood caked all over the fabric.

"Sir, what happened?" he asked. "How did you get this? Have you been stabbed?"

"That's none of your concern," Noad replied, pushing him away and taking a moment to lean against the nearest tree. "While those grunts are chasing after Armitage, we need to focus on finding Charlotte Walker. Pacey, I hate to say this, but we can't trust a word that woman says."

"I'm sorry?"

"She's working *with* Armitage," he continued. "I don't understand exactly what they're doing together, but he seems to have her under his spell and I worry that she'll do whatever he wants."

"No," Pacey replied, "Charlotte would never do that. She hates Armitage. Believe me, I've talked to her about him and there's no disguising the fact that she wants that man behind bars." As his phone began to ring, he pulled it from his pocket and tapped to answer. "You must have misunderstood something," he added. "Whatever else might be going on here, Charlotte Walker would never do anything to help Ted Armitage."

"Detective Inspector Pacey?" Doyle said, his voice sounding very tinny over the line. "I'm not quite sure what's going on here, but we think we've found Ted Armitage's car."

"Where is it?" Pacey asked.

"That's the thing," Doyle continued, "it's right -"

Suddenly Noad snatched the phone from Pacey's hand and cut the call.

"Sir?"

"I need you to listen to me and trust me," Noad said firmly. "You know that I'm the one person who's been onto Ted Armitage from the beginning, don't you?"

"Yes, but -"

"And you also know that I've faced opposition all through the ranks. So many people have tried to stop me investigating this man, to the extent that I've begun to wonder whether somebody's protecting him."

Pacey opened his mouth to reply, but then he hesitated.

"I can't go into all the details right now," Noad continued, "but I have reason to believe that certain people within the force have been working extremely hard to protect Ted Armitage. Those same people, even now, are working to facilitate his escape and I have no doubt that he'll slip through our fingers if we let them dictate what happens here today."

"But -"

"Ted Armitage told me something," Noad added, cutting him off. "I think he was planning to execute me, but he got scared away, and I'm certain I know where he went. If we want to catch him, we're going to have to go after him alone."

Pacey paused, clearly struggling to understand exactly what was happening.

"This way," Noad said, grabbing his shoulder and then leaning on him as they began to walk down the slope, heading in the opposite direction to the armed officers. "He thinks he's managed to get away from us, and we're going to use that fact to our advantage. His luck's going to run out this evening, and with any luck you and I are going to be the heroes of the day."

***

"Help!" Charlotte shouted as she finally scrambled up the slope and found herself next to the burned-out barn again. "He's here! Ted Armitage is here!"

Dropping to her knees, she struggled to stay conscious as she heard footsteps racing in her direction. As several police officers reached her, she set the gun down on the ground and took a series of deep breaths, although in her mind's eye all she could see the moment when she'd aimed the gun at Ted and pulled the trigger. She replayed the moment again and again in her mind, each time wondering whether she should have done something different, whether she should have shot him in the head. Instead, she'd backed down at the last moment and lacked a killer instinct.

And then she'd run.

"Are you Charlotte Walker?" Sergeant Doyle asked. "Where did you get that gun?"

"He had it," she said breathlessly. "Ted. I shot him with it, in the leg. Then I chickened out of finishing him off."

"You're safe now," Doyle told her, as he helped her to her feet. "We've got armed officers swarming all over the forest, and the perimeter of Twist Valley is being secured as we speak. He can't get away, not again."

"You don't know him," she replied darkly.

"He -"

"He wasn't supposed to be here in the first place," she added. "I was told over and over again that this was the last place he'd ever be!"

Doyle hesitated, before taking his phone and bringing up a photo of Chief Inspector Noad.

"I know this might seem like an odd question," he said cautiously, as he turned the phone around so that she could see the screen, "but is this the man you know as Ted Armitage?"

She peered at the screen, and although her initial instinct was to say that he was wrong, she realized after a moment that the man in the picture *was* Ted. Sure, he was cleaned up and he looked professional, and a little younger, but she recognized the grin.

"This man is Chief Inspector John Noad," Doyle explained, "and it's starting to look like..."

His voice trailed off.

"The police?" she whispered, keeping her eyes fixed on the screen for a moment before turning to him. "Are you telling me that Ted Armitage is a police officer?"

"I'm telling you that everything's up in the air right now," he replied, "but at the moment -"

"He's one of you?" she sneered through clenched teeth, before shoving Doyle hard in the chest. "He's been a cop all along?"

"Calm down," he replied. "Please, it's as much of a shock to us as it is to anyone. Then again, it might explain how he's managed to keep under the radar all these years. We need to capture him alive, so we can figure out exactly how he managed to do all of this, but for now it at least looks like he didn't have any help. He was able to do this all by himself. What you have to understand is that John Noad is one of the most respected men in the force. I don't think there's a single person who doesn't look up to him. I mean, sure, he's considered to be a kind of crackpot, but that's hardly a crime."

"And you've just let him do this to people for fifteen years?" she asked.

"Nobody *let* him do anything, but no-one ever had any reason to doubt him. I'm telling you, I personally would have trusted John Noad with my life."

"That makes you a complete idiot," she replied.

"Noad's always been odd," he explained. "Confrontational. Strange. The guy's got a hell of a reputation in the force, some of it positive and some of it... Well, let's just say that a lot of people try to avoid him. To be honest, most of us just assumed it was because of what happened to his family."

"What family?" she asked.

"He lost his wife and daughters a long time ago," he continued. "Almost twenty years, in fact. His youngest daughter died in a freak accident, and then his other daughter and his wife vanished not long after. At the time, everyone assumed that some vengeful criminal had kidnapped them, but they were never found. Noad damn near lost his mind, but in many ways he was an inspiration to us all." He paused, before reaching out and taking her hand. "Charlotte, it's not safe for you to be here. I have to get you away from Twist Valley."

"But -"

"No arguments," he added. "We're onto him now, and pretty soon there's going to be nowhere left for him to hide. Please, you have to come with me. I'm going to make sure that you never have to see Ted Armitage ever again."

## CHAPTER TWENTY-THREE

"Sir, where exactly are we going?" Pacey asked, as he and Noad continued to make their way through the forest. "I think maybe we should get back to the others."

"It's not far now," Noad replied. "It's just up ahead."

"What is?"

"Home," Noad replied breathlessly. "His home. You'll understand when you see it."

"Can I at least have my phone back?" Pacey asked. "I really should check in."

"It's too risky. I told you, Armitage has allies in the ranks, and we have no idea who we can trust. That's why I didn't want you to talk to Prentiss. I think Prentiss might be in on it. For now, we have to stick together and make sure that we nail this bastard once and for all." Stopping, he looked down at the ground, and then he kicked some leaves aside to reveal a metal ring.

"What's that?" Pacey asked.

"It's..."

Noad's voice trailed off. He knew he'd seen the ring before, but he couldn't quite remember when or how.

"Open it," he said finally. "I don't... just open it."

Stepping closer, Pacey looked down at the ring.

"Sir, what's going on here?"

"Armitage gave me just enough information to let me figure out the location of this thing," Noad explained finally, although he sounded a little uncertain. "This is his deepest, darkest secret. It's the one thing he wants to keep hidden from the rest of the world at all cost. He tried to run away from it, but he couldn't, not in the end." He paused for a moment as he stared down at the ring, and then he took a step back. "Open it, man. If you want to understand Ted Armitage, you need to see what's down there."

Pacey hesitated, but deep down he trusted Chief Inspector Noad more than he'd ever trusted anyone, and he told himself that he shouldn't expect to fully understand the great man's mind. Stepping forward, he leaned down and took hold of the ring, and he was surprised to find that the hatch opened fairly easily. He had to maneuver himself to the other side, but he soon had the hatch open all the way and he looked down to see a set of rickety wooden steps leading down beneath the forest floor.

"What's down there?" he asked.

"You go first."

Pacey turned to him.

"Sir, how did you know this would be here?"

"Don't be afraid," Noad continued. "The truth is what's waiting for us down in this chamber, and I for one have never turned away from the truth in my life. Have you?"

"No," Pacey said awkwardly.

"Then go first," Noad said, before taking a flashlight from his pocket and handing it over. "And take this. You'll need it."

Pacey looked down at the flashlight, but he knew he was stalling. Something still didn't seem right about what was happening, but he reminded himself once again that Noad was beyond reproach, so finally he stepped back around to the other side of the opening and he began to make his way cautiously down the steps.

"It's cold," he said, as he switched the flashlight on. "It's really cold down here."

"Yes, it is," Noad muttered under his breath, watching as Pacey disappeared into the depths. "*She* always used to complain about that too."

\*\*\*

"There's not much clearance!" Pacey called out as he ducked down and continued to walk along the narrow passageway. "Sir, I don't know what this place is, but it looks like someone carved it out of the ground with their bare hands!"

"Something like that," Noad replied, as he finally reached the bottom of the steps. Wincing, he leaned against the wall for a moment and told himself that he only had to ignore the pain for a little while longer.

"The smell's incredible," Pacey continued. "Sir, I think something's rotten down here."

Noad watched as the flashlight's beam moved further along the tunnel. He could feel himself getting weaker by the second, but he knew that the past fifteen years had been building to this moment. He wasn't entirely sure how he'd known about the hatch, or about the chamber under the forest floor, but he was certain that it all had a lot to do with Ted Armitage, and that he was about to get the answers to all his questions. Somehow, he could tell that two worlds were about to collide.

*She always used to complain about that too.*

He suddenly wondered what he'd meant by that sentence, which had slipped out so easily. For a few seconds, he felt as if some other memory, some other mind, was starting to bubble up from the depths of his consciousness; the sensation passed quickly enough, but he still couldn't help worrying that he'd forgotten something important. He tried for a moment longer to remember, and then he began to set off after Pacey, determined to see exactly what was waiting at the other end of the passageway.

"Sir," Pacey said suddenly, his voice filled with a fresh sense of urgency, "you need to get in here. Now."

Noad forced himself to hurry, even as he felt as if his leg might be about to give way. He had no flashlight of his own, so he could only follow the light up ahead, even if he felt deep down that the corridor seemed strangely familiar. He told himself over and over again that he'd never been to the place before, yet he found himself anticipating each twist and turn, as if some part of his body was following a long-established muscle memory. Finally, as he reached the end of the corridor and found himself standing in the entrance to a low-ceilinged chamber, he somehow knew what he was about to see.

"How long do you think they've been dead?" Pacey asked.

Noad felt a shiver pass through his chest as he saw the two human figures hanging from chains, their partially-rotten features picked out in the flashlight's harsh beam. From what was left of the meat and muscle, he could tell – just – that the bodies belonged to two women, and as he took a step closer he realized that one of them appeared to have been much older than the other. Dark stains had been left on the rough concrete ground beneath the women, and over by the far wall a table had been left decked out with various knives.

"We need to get a forensics team in here right now," Pacey said, taking a step back. "Sir, we mustn't touch anything."

"I know that," Noad muttered, keeping his eyes fixed on the older woman.

Pacey stepped toward one of the women and reached out to touch her, although after a moment he held back.

"They *are* dead, aren't they?" he whispered.

He peered more closely at the woman's face. Although he could barely believe that she could possibly be alive, he couldn't help but wonder whether...

"Don't touch her," Noad said firmly.

"What is this?" Pacey asked, turning to him. "We know he was torturing women in his barn, but we didn't have any idea about there being another location."

He paused for a moment, before turning to Noad.

"Sir, how exactly *did* you know about this chamber?"

"I'm not entirely sure."

"Did Armitage tell you about it when you encountered him in the forest?"

"That would seem to be the most likely explanation, but..."

Noad's voice trailed off, and for a few seconds he felt as if he recognized the two women. He could hear screams echoing in the back of his mind, along with the sound of the chains rattling loudly.

"It's been a while since I was down here," a voice said.

Turning, Noad saw Ted Armitage standing in the corner, watching him with a broad grin.

"I suppose I wanted to seal them away and forget about my failures," Ted continued. "I've been coming down every so often, just to tend to them. They really should have listened to me, but every time I offered to help, they laughed in my face."

"Who are they?" Noad asked.

"Sir?" Pacey looked over toward the spot where Ted was standing, and then he turned to Noad again. "Who... I'm sorry, Sir, but who are you talking to?"

"I tried to make them understand," Ted added, taking a step forward, "but they always thought they knew better than me. Until I brought them down here, at least. Then they started taking me seriously, but by then it was too late. I tried to train them, but I could see from the look in their eyes that they were just saying whatever they thought I wanted to hear. Can you believe that? My own wife and daughter, and they wouldn't even take me seriously until I forced them to listen."

"Your wife and daughter?" Noad whispered, before turning to look again at the women. "I..."

"Sir?"

Pacey watched Noad for a moment, before glancing toward the corner. He saw no sign of anyone, and he was starting to wonder whether his boss was experiencing some kind of hallucination.

"Sir," he said cautiously, looking back over at the two women, "I think we really need to get some backup down here."

"You don't want backup here," Ted gloated. "Come on, Mr. Noad, be serious for one minute. Everything falls apart once the backup arrives."

"You don't get to tell me what to do," Noad murmured as he picked up one of the knives and examined the blade. "This is a police investigation and the entire location is going to be examined and -"

"Big mistake," Ted said, sounding much closer now.

"You're going to answer for your crimes," Noad said firmly, as he held the knife up. "I'm an officer of the law and I won't rest until you've paid for what you've done."

"You're not -"

Before Ted could get another word out, Noad turned and thrust the knife straight into his belly, before shoving him hard against the wall. As the other man tried to push him away, Noad twisted the knife, and then he froze as he heard laughter coming from over his shoulder. He turned, and to his horror he saw that Ted was now standing all the way over on the other side of the chamber.

"Maybe you *should* call for that backup after all," Ted chuckled. "I imagine they'll be mighty interested in what's been going on here."

Slowly, Noad turned to look down at the knife, which was still embedded deep in a man's belly. And then, as he looked up, he realized that he'd plunged the blade into Detective Inspector Pacey.

## CHAPTER TWENTY-FOUR

"He's out there somewhere," Charlotte said as she looked out the car's window and watched the forest flashing past. "I can sense him."

"You don't have to worry about that," Doyle replied, keeping his eyes on the road. "You have no idea how many armed officers are in the area right now. There's no way this guy can get away, not again."

"You'll have to forgive me if I don't immediately believe you," she said, turning to him. "I thought Ted Armitage was long in the past. I thought I wouldn't ever have to even think about him, but here I am almost..."

Doyle waited for her to continue.

"Almost what?" he asked.

"It's almost like I'm right back where I started," she said after a moment. "I got away from him, but somehow he ended up dragging me to this place again."

"You're here to help."

"I shouldn't have come."

"You don't mean that."

"I do," she said firmly. "I'm an idiot. I should have told Detective Inspector Pacey that there was no way I was coming to help out. I thought I made some dumb choices five years ago, but none of that compares to the fact that I willingly walked straight back into the lion's den. And now it looks like I -"

Suddenly one of the tires exploded, and Charlotte screamed as Doyle struggled to bring the vehicle under control. As the car spun around and slid backward off the road, Doyle finally managed to hit the brakes, and the rear bumped simply nudged one of the nearest trees.

"What the hell was that?" Doyle said breathlessly.

"It's him!" Charlotte shouted. "Hurry! We have to get out of here!"

"Calm down," he replied as he unfastened his seat belt and opened the door, "I'm just going to -"

"Don't go out there!"

"Ms. Walker, I -"

"Do you have a gun?" she asked.

"No, I don't have a gun."

"Get the car going again!" she snapped. "Please, you have to trust me, I know how he works! He's doing this to us!"

Doyle hesitated, before climbing out of the car.

"You're falling right into a trap!" Charlotte hissed, watching as he walked around to check the rear tires. "How can you not see this? I know how he works!"

She looked out toward the road, convinced that at any moment she was about to see Ted's truck pull up. Failing that, she also looked up into the trees, terrified that his drone might be about to return. Deep down, she knew he was close.

"He's coming," she whispered, looking all around now, worried that Ted could appear from any direction. "This is what he does, he strands people and then he shows up to get them."

"Looks like a boring old blowout," Doyle said as he made his way back around to the driver's seat and leaned into the car. "The timing couldn't have been worse, huh?"

"Why won't you listen to me?" she asked, as tears began to fill her eyes.

"There's no phone service round here," he told her, "so we only have one option. We have to walk. Fortunately, I happen to have spent a lot of time studying a bunch of maps of this area over the past few days, so I've got a pretty good idea of where we are." He turned and looked into the forest. "We'll save a lot of time if we just cut through there. We should meet the main road after just a couple of hours."

"It's going to be dark soon!" she hissed.

"Would you rather stay here all night?" he replied, before reaching into the glove compartment and taking out a flashlight. "Ms. Walker, I can assure you that I recognize a blown tire when I see one, and I really don't see how this Ted Armitage guy could have arranged for it to happen. Not when he's probably got a lot more on his mind right now."

Staring at him, Charlotte realized that he seriously wanted her to follow him out into the forest.

"Please," she sobbed, "don't make me go through this again. I escaped once already. Don't make me have to escape again."

"You're completely safe," he said firmly. "Think about it, though. If Armitage *is* out there somewhere, do you really want to sit around like this? Wouldn't you rather get going? We don't even have too far to walk." He waited for her to answer, and then he smiled. "Come on. Let's just get this over with."

\*\*\*

"It's too dark now," Charlotte said a short while later, as she and Doyle made their way between the trees. She couldn't help looking around, watching in case there was any sign of Ted. "It's getting cold. We shouldn't be out here."

"I agree with you on that point," Doyle muttered, aiming the flashlight straight ahead, "but I really don't see that we have any choice."

"He'll be able to see the light for miles," she continued. "He'll come straight for us!"

"I'm sure he's been caught by now. You really need to have more faith in the police, Ms. Walker. We might have dropped the ball on this before, but we're all over it now. Ted Armitage's days are very much numbered."

"Yeah, I'm sure you really think that," she replied, still looking around, "but that doesn't make it true. You have no idea how slippery this guy is. For all we know, he could be watching us right now."

"And why wouldn't he have made his move?"

"He's insane," she told him. "I don't think you get that, do you? The guy is completely out of his mind, but he's also smart. He's manipulative. He plans ahead."

Suddenly Doyle stopped and turned to her, shining the flashlight's beam straight into her eyes. Startled, Charlotte had to hold her hands up in front of her face.

"You really have some trust issues, don't you?" he asked. "I get that you went through a lot five years ago, but doesn't there come a time when you have to sort of... let it go?"

"What do you mean?" she asked, still shielding her eyes from the flashlight. "Do you mind lowering that thing for a minute?"

"Have you spent the past few years living in fear?" he continued. "Seriously, did you just decide to hide yourself away down in deepest, darkest Cornwall in the vain hope that somehow you could spend the rest of your existence under a rock, not being noticed?"

"I -"

"You said earlier that you didn't believe me," he added. "I told you not to worry, and you flat out replied that you think I'm wrong. Naive. An idiot. Doesn't that strike you as being a little rude, Ms. Walker? Don't you think that makes you a nasty piece of work?"

She opened her mouth to reply, but she hesitated as she realized that she recognized something about Doyle's tone. As the light continued to fill her eyes, she began to worry that Doyle actually reminded her of Ted Armitage; sure, they clearly weren't the same person, but his tone was awfully, terrifyingly familiar.

Slowly, he lowered the flashlight.

"We're nearly there," he told her.

"Where?" she asked cautiously.

"I told you, I'm taking you to the road, and we'll be able to get help from there." He paused. "Although, there's one place I want us to stop at first."

"Out here in the middle of nowhere?"

"Humor me," he said firmly. "There's someone who's really going to want to see you. In fact, he's hopefully there already, although if not we'll have to wait a while. He taught me everything I could ever have wanted to know, and in return I've... helped him out on a few occasions. Just when he really needed a hand. After all, despite his greatness, he couldn't get *everything* done all on his lonesome. Even the gods need the help of lesser mortals from time to time."

"I'm not entirely sure what you're talking about," she told him, as she took a step back, "but I think I want to head back to the road. Someone might -"

"No-one's coming to help you, Charlotte," Doyle said flatly. "You realize that, don't you?"

"Sorry," she replied, as she turned to run, "but -"

Suddenly he grabbed her from behind and clamped a hand over her mouth. She immediately began to struggle, but he began to pull her between the trees, and a moment later he turned her around and shoved her to the ground. She tried to get up, but he kicked her hard on the side of the face, sending her crashing down again.

"That's not how this is going to work," he said breathlessly, as he stood over her and watched her struggling again to get up. "I'm sorry, Ms. Walker, but you've got an appointment with someone who hates to be kept waiting."

## CHAPTER TWENTY-FIVE

*Sixteen years earlier...*

"Come on, you know I hate to be kept waiting."

"Dad, you complain *all* the time," Jane said with a heavy sigh as she hauled her backpack out of the car. "Do you realize that you left us waiting for almost an hour earlier, while you got everything ready for this trip?"

She looked past him and saw the farmhouse over on the far side of the clearing, and she was unable to hide the sense of disappointment that she was feeling.

"This place looks... old," she added.

"It has history," John Noad replied, as his wife stepped out of the house and stopped at the top of the steps. "What about you, darling? What do you think of my little hideaway?"

"You actually paid money for this place?" she asked. "*Our* money?"

"It's a complicated situation," he explained. "There are some irregularities with the deeds, so the whole thing had to be done in cash, but that's how I managed to get such a big plot of land at a great price. Anyone else would have ended up paying ten times what I paid. Aren't you at least a little proud of me for getting a good deal?"

Janice hesitated for a moment, but – as she looked across the yard and saw the old barn – she couldn't help but purse her lips. She was fully accustomed to her husband's unusual holiday choices each year, but even by his standards this latest trip was rather unusual. He'd promised that the family would be able to get away from civilization and embrace the natural world for a week, so she'd expected at least a nice lake or perhaps some rolling countryside; instead, all she saw was a tatty farm and an even tattier-looking forest, and she wasn't sure she could drum up much in the way of enthusiasm.

Finally, she turned to him.

"It looks lovely, darling," she said kindly. "Will we be going on lots of long hikes?"

Before John could reply, they both heard the sound of footsteps running through the farmhouse, and they turned just in time to see their other, younger daughter racing out onto the steps.

"What do *you* think, Chrissie?" Janice asked, as she put an arm on the girl and pulled her closer. "You're the most important member of the family. Do you like it here?"

"It smells funny," Chrissie said, wrinkling her nose.

"I bet someone died here," Jane said, tramping up the steps and then pushing past her mother as she carried her backpack inside. "Man, it sure smells like that. The whole place smells of old man farts."

Chrissie started to giggle.

"You're going to love it here," John told Janice, "I promise. There's so much land to explore. Honestly, after two weeks, you're going to feel so refreshed. You'll never want to leave."

"Two weeks?" Janice felt her heart sink. "I thought we were only staying 'til next Monday?"

"I think we should stay for a fortnight," he replied. "Come on, embrace the opportunity. This is a chance for the whole family to disconnect from the crazy modern world and enjoy some nature for a change." He made a show of taking a big, deep breath. "Man, can't you feel the difference in the air?"

*\*\*\**

"John, are you coming to bed?"

"Mmm?"

Unable to look away from his laptop, John hesitated for a moment before tapping at the keyboard.

"Soon," he murmured. "You go without me. I'll be up in five minutes."

"We're supposed to be on holiday," Janice pointed out. "Don't you think that for once you could not sit up all night on that thing?"

"It won't be all night," he told her, as he continued to type. "Just go to bed and I'll be up real soon."

Engrossed in the comment he was carefully wording, John didn't even notice as his wife stepped up behind him. Instead, he deleted a couple of lines and typed them out again, taking care to phrase them so that they'd have the maximum possible impact. He wanted to really make his point this time.

"Who's Ted Armitage?"

"What the -"

Slamming the laptop's lid down, he turned to find that Janice was towering above him.

"John?" She raised a skeptical eyebrow. "Who's Ted Armitage?"

"He's no-one."

"Were you using a fake -"

"Can I just have a little privacy?" he asked, trying not to sound too flustered. "I was driving all day, and then I had to get this place set up once we arrived, and now I just want to unwind for a few minutes before I go to bed." He waited for her to answer. "Can I please be allowed to do that?"

"You can do whatever you want," she replied, leaning down and kissing the top of his head, "but promise me you won't stay up for hours, arguing with people on the internet. It's a complete waste of time, you're never going to change anyone's mind." She turned and headed back to the hallway. "Besides, what does it matter if some idiot on some website is wrong about something? You need to learn when to let things go."

"People talk such crap," he muttered as he opened the laptop again. "They sit there typing away, pretending that they know how the world works when the truth is, they don't know anything."

Sure enough, one of his new online foes – a coward who identified herself only as CustardyDanglyBits – had already posted a response to one of his earlier messages:

*SMSL your so full of shit!*

John winced, not only at the typo 'your' but at the complete failure to engage with the point he'd been trying to make. He wanted to reach through the laptop's screen and grab CustardyDanglyBits by the throat and beat some sense into her, although he knew that she was probably far too stone-headed to learn.

He started crafting his comment again, determined to prove a point to someone who'd written a lengthy critique of a recent police case. He knew he couldn't use his own name, so he'd come up with a pseudonym for his online work. The name Ted Armitage didn't actually mean anything; his grandfather had been named Ted, and Armitage was simply something he'd plucked out of thin air. He'd made sure to cover his tracks so that the fake name could never be traced back to him, and now he was finally able to say what he really thought. All he hoped was that eventually people would listen to him.

"You should be grateful for my advice," he whispered, as he posted his latest comment and waited for the replies to arrive. "If you've got any sense, a few of you might even start paying attention."

\*\*\*

Five hours later, exhausted and simmering with anger, John began to make his way up the stairs. He knew he'd stayed up far too late again, but he'd started arguing with several morons who's not even *tried* to understand what he'd been telling them. Finally he'd stepped away in disgust, although he was already wondering whether he should go back down and send one last message, just to underline a few of his points.

He stopped at the top of the stairs and turned to go back down, and then he hesitated as he realized he could hear a whispered voice coming from one of the bedrooms. Checking his watch, he saw that it was almost 4am, but Jane seemed to be awake. He made his way over to her door and listened for a moment, and now he could tell that she was definitely talking to someone on the phone.

"It's not even a holiday," he heard her complaining, "it's just Dad dragging the rest of us around as usual, not giving a crap about the fact that we're all bored out of our minds. Mum's used to it, she's obviously found some way to cope with being married to the dullest man in the world, and Chrissie's too young to really notice. Which leaves me as the only member of this family who's fully aware of how much we're being tortured."

Feeling a flicker of anger, John reached for the door handle, only to stop himself at the last moment. He knew that there was no point igniting a blazing row, although he was shocked by his daughter's extreme lack of gratitude. Did she not respect him at all?

"I can't wait to come over to your place when I get back and just hang out and smoke and not have to pretend that I don't hate everything in my life."

Again, John desperately wanted to push the door open and tell his daughter that he'd overheard everything, but he was just about able to hold back.

"For real," Jane continued. "I'm just counting the seconds while I endure the moron's so-called holiday. I know I shouldn't say this, Jason, but I hate him. I really, truly despise him."

Before he could stop himself, John reached up and knocked gently on the door.

"Jane?" he called out. "You shouldn't be up this late. Get some sleep, so that you're ready to come out on a hike with the rest of us in the morning."

He waited, but he heard no reply. Still, at least she'd stopped talking, so he told himself that she'd listened. He hesitated for a moment longer, and then he turned and made his way through to the master bedroom. As he stepped into the darkness and saw Janice sleeping soundly, he realized that his hands were trembling with rage.

## CHAPTER TWENTY-SIX

"Come on!" John shouted the following day, stopping in the yard and turning to look back at the house. "I want to show you the route down to the river! It's so beautiful, it really has to be seen to be believed!"

Chrissie immediately ran out from the house and hurried over to her father, and she quickly put her arms around him and gave him a big hug. She was wearing her favorite yellow and red sweater.

"Will you carry me?" she asked.

"We're both too old for that," he replied as he saw Janice making her way out onto the steps. "Don't worry, it's a nice gentle hike. You'll have a great time."

He watched the front door, and to his disappointment he realized that there was still no sign of Jane.

"Where -"

"She's gone to her room," Janice said wearily, having evidently anticipated his question. "Please don't make a fuss, John. She's a teenager, all she wants to do is sit around feeling sorry for herself, and there'll only be an argument if you try to stop her. Let's just give her some space. She's got her laptop."

"It's not healthy to be so insular," he pointed out. "It's a proper addiction, too. She's constantly on that computer."

"I wonder where she gets it from."

"Hey, I'm doing work stuff," he replied. "I'm doing important things."

"Just let it be," Janice replied as she stepped past him. "You've got Chrissie and me, that should be enough for you. Let's get going and find this river. I want to be back in time to get cracking with dinner. Something tells me that there aren't any takeaway places that'd deliver all the way out here."

Watching the house for a moment, John once again felt a rising sense of anger as he thought of Jane slouching on a bed in one of the upstairs rooms, no doubt complaining to another friend about her awful life. He wanted to go storming in there, to grab her by the scruff of the neck and haul her out, but deep down he knew his wife was right; besides, did he really want to drag a recalcitrant, sarcastic girl out into the forest, just to hear her grumble about everything? He looked at the upstairs windows for a moment longer, and then he turned and followed Janice and Chrissie out into the forest.

*\*\*\**

"It's certainly very pretty," Janice said later, as she stood with her hands on her hips and looked at the river. "I'm not sure I'd want to go out on it in a boat, though."

"There's a waterfall a little way along," John told her, as he watched Chrissie throwing rocks into the water. "I find great peace in the natural world. I love coming here and just listening to the river as it flows."

Janice turned to him.

"If I didn't know any better, John Noad," she said after a moment, "I'd be starting to think that you're getting a little soft in your old age."

"I'm only forty," he pointed out. "That's hardly old."

"Forgive me," she said with a faint smile. "So should we head back now?"

"Don't you want to come for a little stroll along the bank?" he asked, disappointed by the fact that she seemed somewhat uninterested in the beauty of the world around them.

"My legs ache," she told him, "and I've got so much to do in the kitchen when we get back. You and Chrissie can go for a walk if you like, and we can meet back at the house later. Don't worry, I remember the way."

John watched as she walked away. Although he wanted to call her back and make her take time to appreciate her surroundings, he could already tell that she was completely uninterested. He hadn't expected undying gratitude for the trip, but he'd assumed that she and the rest of his family might at least show some kind of awareness of the fact that he'd made an effort. As Janice disappeared into the distance, John had to force himself to keep from showing his displeasure.

"Where are the fish, Daddy?"

Turning, he saw that Chrissie was climbing over the rocks next to the river.

"Be careful," he said quickly, although she wasn't too close to the edge. "I don't know what the fish situation's like round here, but I'm sure you'll at least spot a few tiddlers. Just make sure you don't fall in, okay?"

"I can't see any."

"I'll help," he replied, smiling as he made his way over to join her. At least one member of the family was bothering to take in their surroundings. "There's another spot further down where -"

Before he could finish, he felt a buzz in his pocket, and he pulled out his phone. Seeing a text message, he took a moment to open it up, and then he froze as soon as he saw the words:

*Your still a moron, Ted Armitage. Online, offline, wherever.*

He hesitated, but deep down he could tell – from the tone, and from the poor spelling – that somehow CustardyDanglyBits had managed to obtain his phone number. He glanced over at Chrissie, and then he turned away and began to type a reply:

*You've made a big mistake. I can have this number traced. Now I can really teach you a lesson in decorum.*

Once he'd sent that message, he waited for a reply. He told himself that CustardyDanglyBits was a coward who'd probably shrink away at the first sign of trouble. He was surprised, then, when he quickly received another reply:

*LOL get over yourself. Have fun at your stupid farm.*

A shudder passed through his chest as he realized that somehow CustardyDanglyBits had acquired not only his number, but also his location. He knew that shouldn't be possible, and that he'd covered his tracks perfectly, but a moment later another message arrived and confirmed his worst fears:

*See you around, John.*

He immediately began to type a reply, but he forced himself to hold back. Clearly he was dealing with someone who knew their way around technology, and after a moment he glanced around and watched in case anybody might be nearby. Satisfied that he was alone, he looked back down at the phone and tried to think of some way he might scare the crap out of CustardyDanglyBits, but he worried about just how much information she'd managed to uncover. He knew that silence would make him seem weak, but he told himself that he was going to take his time and make sure that when he struck back, he'd take the bitch down.

And he'd make her suffer.

In his mind's eye, he imagined her begging for mercy while he held her down. He wasn't entirely sure what he'd do to her, but he imagined her wetting herself with fear as he held a knife against her face. At first he told himself that he wouldn't *really* hurt her, that he'd just scare her a little, but then he realized that he could use her as an example to all the other morons in the world. All the anger he felt online was finally breaking through into the real world.

"Please, Ted Armitage!" he imagined her screaming. "Let me go!"

He imagined himself cutting her head off. The idea shocked him, but at the same time it seemed like the only way to shut her up properly. Whoever she was, she clearly had nothing to contribute to the world beyond venom and hatred, so would it really be so bad if he dealt with her properly? He fantasized for a moment about ripping her head away from her shoulders, and he thought of the shocked expression on her face as she finally understood that he'd been right all along.

Blinking, he remembered that he should probably calm down a little.

"Chrissie?" he said, turning to look over at the river. "What -"

Stopping, he realized that she was nowhere to be seen. He looked around, and then he made his way to the rocks and checked that there was no sign of her in the water.

"Chrissie?" he called out, while telling himself that there was no need to worry. "Hey, listen, let's go downriver a few miles and we'll have a better chance of spotting some fish. You'd like that, wouldn't you? No promises, but your old daddy's got a hunch and, well, my hunches usually play out pretty well."

Again he waited, and again there was no sign of his daughter. He looked toward the forest, but he knew deep down that Chrissie wasn't the kind of girl who'd simply wander off.

"Chrissie?"

Although he could feel the panic starting to rise in his chest, he told himself that his smart, precious little girl would never get too close to the water's edge. Sure, the current was fairly strong, but Chrissie was an intelligent child and he'd taught her over the years to always be respectful of the natural world, including its dangers. In fact, Chrissie – far more than Jane – reminded John of himself, to the extent that he sometimes found himself wondering if his soul had somehow been replicated in the girl's body.

"Chrissie!" he shouted, cupping his hands around his mouth, desperate to make himself heard over a greater distance. "Chrissie, where are you? Hey, kiddo, get back here!"

He listened for a reply, but all he heard was the sound of the river. Looking back down at the water, he tried to imagine what would have happened to his daughter if she's fallen. She was a reasonable swimmer, but the rocks were just beneath the surface and he worried that she might have been knocked unconscious.

"Chrissie!" he yelled, as he began to make his way along the riverbank, following the flow of the water. "Chrissie Noad! Christina! Where are you?"

As he continued to call out, his voice could be heard far and wide, ringing out between the trees of the immense, rolling Twist Valley forest.

## CHAPTER TWENTY-SEVEN

*One year later...*

"Are you sure you want to do this?"

Feeling a flicker of irritation in his chest, John focused on packing the last few items into his bag. His hands were trembling slightly, and deep down some part of him knew that he was being irrational, but at the same time he'd been planning the trip for a while and he wasn't going to let anyone deter him. Not even his own wife. Hell, why wasn't she packing a bag too?

"It's a long way to go just to..."

Her voice trailed off. For a moment, she simply stood in silence, watching as John prepared for his trip. She'd been trying to find some way to dissuade him, and in truth she'd assumed that ultimately he'd see for himself that the whole thing was pointless. Now she realized that he was serious, and that he intended to drive all the way up the country and spend a week searching the forest. The thought of him out there all alone, calling Chrissie's name over and over, was enough to make her heart break.

"She's out there," he murmured.

"You don't know that."

"I feel it," he said firmly, turning to her and then tapping his chest, right above his heart. "In here. Chrissie's still out there somewhere in Twist Valley and I'm going to find her. I don't know what state she'll be in, I don't know how she'll be when we're reunited, but she's there somewhere and I'm not going to rest until I'm holding her in my arms again."

Janice opened her mouth to reply, but then she hesitated. Tears were dancing in her eyes, and as she stood in the kitchen doorway she looked for all the world like someone who was on the verge of giving up.

"What's *that* thing?" she asked, looking at a large contraption that John had placed on the table. She peered at the little propeller blades, but she had no idea what she was seeing.

"It's a drone," he told her wearily. "Ex-military. I pulled some strings. I can use it to cover a lot of distance, especially parts of the terrain that are difficult to reach. There's a camera, and I can download the footage to my laptop."

"Sounds high-tech."

"It is."

"John, this isn't going to help," she replied. "Chrissie's gone. You have to see that."

"I'll drive up tonight," John explained, as if he hadn't heard her, "and then I'll start searching tomorrow and hopefully by the end of the -"

"They searched that forest a year ago," Janice reminded him. "They went through it so carefully, John, and there was no sign of her."

"So what are you suggesting? That she just disappeared into thin air?"

"No, but -"

"Or that some monster took her?"

"Again, no." She paused. "I just don't see what you're going to get out of this trip."

Before he could answer, John heard his phone vibrate and he looked down to see that he'd received another message. He bristled for a moment, before picking the phone up and taking a look. Sure enough, his old friend CustardyDanglyBits had sent him a few more words of wisdom:

*Your pathetic. You couldn't even keep your daughter safe. She died because of you.*

He felt another rush of rage, but he managed to keep his emotions in check. CustardyDanglyBits had spent the previous year upping her campaign, deluging him with messages, and despite his best efforts he'd been unable to track her down. He'd never been able to figure out how she kept up with his movements, but somehow she seemed to know so much about him.

"John, please don't go," Janice said suddenly.

"She's your daughter too," he replied, turning to her. "Why aren't you coming up there with me? Why isn't Jane coming?"

"Because we both know that..."

Her voice trailed off.

"She could still be alive," he said, as his phone buzzed again. "It's not unheard of. People can survive in the wilderness and -"

"She's an eight-year-old child."

"She'd be nine by now."

"So what do you think happened here, John?" she asked sounding exasperated now. "Do you think she pulled a Tarzan and she's been living in the wilderness all this time?"

"Don't be ridiculous," he muttered as he checked the latest message:

*Poor little Christina. Dead and rotting somewhere, just because her father's a loser.*

As much as he wanted to scream and throw the phone across the room, John managed to stay somewhat calm. He told himself that there was no way he was willing to rise to the bait.

"When are you finally going to let her go?" Janice asked. "We both know she's dead and -"

"We don't know that!" he snapped.

"We do, John," she continued, as a tear ran down her cheek. "You know it too, if you're really honest with yourself. The most likely explanation is that she had an accident, it was no-one's fault, it just happened and her body just got missed by the search parties. I don't know how they didn't find her, but it's not completely beyond the realm of possibility. She just..."

Her voice trailed off.

"I've got to go," John said, grabbing his bag and pushing past her, heading through to the hallway. "I'll be back in a week. Maybe sooner if I have a little luck."

"John..."

He opened the front door, and then he stopped and turned back to look at his wife, just as his phone buzzed yet again.

"I'm going to bring our little girl home," he said, and now he too had tears in his eyes. "One way or another, she's not spending another year out there in the cold."

He looked at his phone, and he saw yet another message from CustardyDanglyBits. He almost didn't bother to read her latest attack, but the first few words caught his attention so he read on:

*I was just texting Dad. The asshole's going up to look for C again. He's deluded. I hope he dies. I hate him so much.*

He read the message several times, struggling to understand what it meant. He double-checked, but the message had been sent by the same number, yet it seemed markedly different to all the rest. Finally, as the awful truth began to dawn, he slowly looked toward the stairs.

***

"Hey!" Jane yelled angrily as John pushed open the door to her room. "What the hell are you doing?"

Without answering, he stormed over to the bed and grabbed her by the throat, before swinging her around and slamming her hard against the wall.

"Dad -"

"Did you think that was funny?" he snarled, leaning close to her terrified face. "Did you think you'd get a kick out of terrorizing me for the past year? What part of your sick brain did those messages come from?"

"I don't know what you -"

"You sent that last message to the wrong number," he sneered, holding his phone up so she could see what he meant. He immediately spotted the recognition in her eyes, followed a moment later by fear. "It's been you all along," he continued. "You're the one who's been sending me those messages the whole time, taunting me about the death of your own sister!"

"Dad, you're hurting me!" she gasped, struggling to breathe as he squeezed her throat tight. "You've lost your mind!"

"All those disgusting things you said!" he continued, as his voice shook with anger. "All that poison! All those lies! All the -"

"You *did* kill her!" Jane shouted suddenly. "The only reason you're so angry is you know I'm right! If you'd been paying attention instead of worrying about your stupid Ted Armitage crap online, she'd still be here!"

"Shut up," he said firmly.

"Why? Because you don't like the truth?" She tried again to get free, and then she simply stared at him for a moment. "I know I've been mean to you," she continued, "but everything I said was completely true. You're such a big, tough man when you're Ted Armitage online, aren't you? But when you're pathetic John Noad, a run-of-the-mill cop who can't even keep his family together, you're nothing. Sorry, but it's the truth."

She waited for him to reply.

"And now you're going up to look for her again," she continued. "What do you think you're going to find? The absolute best case scenario is that you end up holding her bones. Will that really make you feel better? Will it make the guilt go away, Dad?"

Again she waited.

"Or," she added, "should I call you Ted?"

Letting out a sudden cry of anger, John swung her around and slammed her head against the other wall, knocking her out instantly and sending her crumpling down to the floor. At that moment, Janice stopped in the doorway and saw what had happened, and she froze for a moment before rushing over to her daughter.

"Leave her," John sneered, before furrowing his brow. "So many spelling mistakes in those messages. I never knew she lacked such basic skills."

"What the hell did you do?" Janice stammered, as she rolled Jane over and saw a patch of blood on the side of her head. "John -"

"I said leave her!" he shouted, grabbing his wife and shoving her against the desk, only for her head to crack against the corner.

As Janice slumped down against the carpet, John stood over the pair of them, trying to contain the anger that was rising through his chest. Over the previous year, he'd learned to keep that anger pushed down, but this time something was different. This time he could feel the anger spreading, filling his bones, changing him so much that he started to question whether he was still himself.

"You think I'm pathetic, huh?" he muttered, staring down at Jane's unconscious body. "Fine. Then I guess it's time for me to show you just what a pathetic man can do."

## CHAPTER TWENTY-EIGHT

Slowly, as she finally emerged from a long, deep sleep, Janice Noad began to open her eyes. She immediately realized that something was wrong, and that her head felt extremely heavy. She blinked a couple of times, hoping that the grogginess would pass, and it was at that moment that she realized she was in one of the bedrooms at the farm in Twist Valley.

She immediately began to sit up, only to find that her wrists were tied firmly to the headboard. Startled, she tried to pull free, but the ropes were too tight and she knew that brute force was never going to work. At the same time, as she looked round, she realized that she was supposed to be at home hundreds of miles away, and that she wasn't quite sure what had happened.

"John?" she called out cautiously, as she began to notice a throbbing pain on the side of her head. "John, are you here?"

She tried not to panic, and a moment later she heard the sound of someone making their way up the stairs. She pulled on the ropes again, and then she saw John stepping into the doorway.

"John, what's going on?" she asked. "John you have to untie me. I don't know what this is about, but you're scaring me."

She waited, but he simply stared at her, and after a moment he took a bite from a sandwich he'd brought up from the kitchen. He seemed utterly relaxed, as if nothing was wrong in the whole world.

"Is this some kind of sex thing?" she asked.

He furrowed his brow.

"John, did you knock me out and bring me all the way up here?" she continued, as she began to remember the incident in Jane's bedroom. "Did you drug me? John, where's Jane? Tell me where Jane is."

"Jane's fine."

"I want to see her."

"That's a little tricky at the moment."

"John, I want to see her so that I know she's not hurt."

"She's a little wounded," he explained, "but it's nothing that won't heal. Actually, she's feeling very sorry for herself at the moment, and I'm waiting for her to calm down a little. Fortunately one of the outhouses that came with this place is underground, out in the forest, so she can scream and scream to her heart's content and I can wait around here until she's mature enough to engage in a proper conversation."

He took another bite from the sandwich.

"She needs to learn a few lessons," he continued, speaking with his mouth full, "but that's okay, I'm a good teacher."

"John -"

"And you need to learn a few as well," he added, spraying a few crumbs onto the bed in the process. "You haven't exactly been the wife of the year, and frankly I think you share some of the blame for our daughter's poor behavior. Now, I'm confident that you'll come around to my way of thinking pretty easily, but I have to warn you that there'll be consequences if you don't. You never know, you might even end up joining Jane out there."

"John, I need you to untie me right now and take me to Jane," Janice said firmly. "I don't know exactly what you're thinking here, but this all has to stop. Are you not feeling well, John? Is that what's going on? Are you struggling with what happened to Chrissie? I told you, you should have seen someone to talk about it. There's no shame in that, and it's never too late to start."

John popped the rest of the sandwich into his mouth, and then he stepped out of the room.

"Come back!" Janice shouted, pulling once again on the ropes. "John, you can't leave me here! John, we have to talk about this!"

\*\*\*

Reaching down, John Noad grabbed the metal ring and pulled the hatch open, revealing a set of steps leading down into the darkness beneath the forest.

"Help!" Jane shouted, her voice ringing out from far below. "Somebody help me!"

John hesitated, before feeling a tear running down his cheek. Surprised, he reached up and wiped the tear away, and then he began to make his way down the steps as Jane continued to scream.

\*\*\*

"Dad, what are you doing?" she gasped a few minutes later, as he aimed a flashlight at her face. "Dad, stop! Dad, this is insane!"

She pulled on the chains that were holding her tight, but he already knew that there was no way she could force her way out.

"Okay," she continued, "I'll do anything. Do you hear that? I'll do anything and I'll say anything, you just have to let me go. I'm sorry, okay? I'm so sorry, from the very bottom of my heart, and I'll never do anything like that again. I was wrong, I see that now, and I swear for the rest of my life I'll be a good person. Chrissie's death wasn't your fault and I don't know why I said it was, except I was hurting and I don't really understand why my brain was working the way that it was."

She waited, hoping against hope that she'd managed to get through to him, but with each passing second she was starting to worry that he'd really snapped. Squinting, she tried to look past the flashlight, and she could just about make out his eyes staring back at her.

"Where's Mum?" she sobbed. "I want to talk to Mum."

"I failed you," he replied.

"Dad, I -"

"It's my fault that you're like this," he continued, "so I'm the one who has to set you straight. Your mother and I tried so hard to raise you right, Jane, and I thought we'd done a pretty good job. I'd never have put us forward for an award or anything like that, but I still thought we'd raised you to be a decent human being. Obviously there are still a few rough edges that need sorting out, though. A few dark spots in your soul that need to be scrubbed away. And I can do that, I'm sure of it, I just need a little time to make you see the error of your ways."

"I see it all now," she told him. "Please, Dad, I know what an awful person I've been and I'm so sorry. Please, you have to let me go."

"I don't *have* to do anything," he pointed out. "You, on the other hand, are obligated to try to become the best version of yourself that you possibly can, and I think we both agree that you've failed in that regard of late. You've been let down, by both your mother and myself, and now it's up to me to set you straight. The process shouldn't even take that long, I just -"

"Please, Dad," she cried, as tears streamed down her face and her body began to shake violently. "Just tell me what to do!"

"It's easy," he replied. "You have to convince me that you really mean it when you say you'll change."

"I really mean it..."

"That doesn't sound very convincing."

"I mean it!" she shouted.

"I'm sorry, but it still seems like you're just telling me what you think I want to hear. I can see it in your eyes, Jane, you're just -"

"I mean it, you son of a bitch!" she screamed, suddenly reaching out and trying to kick him, only to miss by a few inches. "I mean it," she cried, barely able to get the words out as she broke into a series of shudders that shook her entire body. "What else do you want from me? I mean it. No-one's ever meant anything more, not ever. You have to believe me, Dad."

"Believe me, I want to," he told her, before lowering the flashlight and stepping closer to her. "I know you have it in you, Jane. I know that deep down you're a good person, you just need a little extra help to get it out. That's what this process is going to be about, and it *is* going to be a process. A long one, perhaps. Certainly a necessary one. And when you come out the other side..."

He paused, before reaching over and touching the side of her face, wiping away her tears.

"And when you come out the other side," he continued, "you're going to thank me so very much."

Looking up at him, she opened her mouth, but for a moment she couldn't get any words out.

"Please," she whimpered finally, "I'm sorry... Dad..."

"We'll start tomorrow," he told her, "but first there's just one more thing I need you to do, Jane. Don't call me Dad, not while we're down here." He leaned closer, until their faces were almost touching. "Call me Ted. Ted Armitage. After all, isn't that how all of this started?"

## CHAPTER TWENTY-NINE

*Fifteen years later...*

"No!" Charlotte said as soon as she saw the open hatch set into the forest floor. "I'm not going down there!"

She stopped and turned to run, but Doyle shoved her forward before holding the knife up so that the blade caught the moonlight.

"What do you want from me?" she asked, trying to play for time as she figured out which way to run. She knew she probably only had one more chance to get away, and she needed to make sure that there'd be nothing to slow her down.

"It's not about what *I* want," Doyle told her. "I've got my instructions, and I simply have to deliver you to Mr. Noad. Once I've done that, my role in this is over." He paused for a moment. "Are we going to do this the easy way or the hard way? Because, frankly, I'm not too bothered, but it'd be nice to know in advance. I thought you might be smart, Ms. Walker, but you're kind of starting to look a little unsure of yourself."

She took a deep breath, but she knew that the moment had come. She looked to her left, then to her right, and then at Doyle again.

"You're about to do something stupid, aren't you?" he said, before letting out a heavy sigh. "Charlotte, for once just -"

Turning, she began to race toward the treeline, only for Doyle to catch her almost immediately. He grabbed her and hauled her back, and then – as she kicked and screamed and tried to get away – he carried her over to the hatch and threw her down into the hole, sending her clattering down the steps until she landed in a heap at the bottom.

"You're a pain in the ass, do you know that?" he muttered, adjusting his tie for a moment before starting to climb down after her. "I've more than earned my money tonight."

\*\*\*

"Move!"

Sent stumbling forward, Charlotte bumped against the wall of the narrow passageway, and then she stopped as she realized that she was at the entrance to some sort of chamber. A flashlight's beam immediately hit her in the eyes, causing her to step back, but at that moment Doyle reached her and shoved her forward.

"Ms. Walker," Noad said, lowering his flashlight so that she could see him a little better, "I was wondering when you'd arrive. You're just in time. We appear to have found Mr. Armitage's hidden lair."

Staring up at him with an expression of absolute horror, she began to crawl back until she bumped against the wall.

"Did he bring you down here last time?" Noad asked, stepping toward her. "I know it must be difficult for you to think back to those awful few days, but I don't recall you mentioning this in any of the transcripts I read. And I did read them, by the way. I read everything. I'm sorry I didn't get in touch with you at the time, but... Well, other matters delayed me."

"Just get it over with," she replied through gritted teeth.

"Get what over with?" he asked, lowering the flashlight a little further as Doyle stepped into the chamber.

"You want to -"

Suddenly she stopped as she saw two bloodied, emaciated figures hanging from chains on the chamber's other side. For a moment she tried to tell herself that they weren't real, that they had to be models, but somehow deep down she knew the truth; the two women seemed different to the ones in the barn somehow, certainly much older but also still very much in possession of their heads.

"Ted Armitage's wife and daughter, I believe," Noad explained somewhat nonchalantly. "This is probably how the whole thing started. It's going to take quite some time to get to the bottom of the man's depravity, but that's something I hope you can help with."

"What are you..."

Her voice trailed off for a moment.

"*You're* Ted Armitage," she stammered finally.

"I'm sorry?" he replied, tilting his head.

Staring at him, she tried to figure out exactly what he meant, but she was starting to realize that he seemed different somehow. He was still definitely the same man who'd kidnapped her five years earlier, and who she'd encountered just a few hours earlier in the forest, but this time he was standing up straighter and there was something different about his voice, as if he was actually trying to be a different man. Of, if he wasn't *trying*, then the change seemed to be happening naturally, almost as if...

"You don't know," she whispered.

"What was that?" he asked.

"You don't know who you are, do you?" she continued, struggling to believe what she was seeing. "You have no idea."

"Can I go now?" Doyle asked. "I need to get back to the farm and find out what the armed response unit's up to. For all we know, they might have accidentally started to wander in this direction. Plus, I need to clean up the mess after the crash."

"What are you talking about?" Noad asked, turning to him.

"I don't have time to fuck about, okay?" Doyle continued, stepping toward him and holding out his right hand. "Just pay me and I'm out of here."

"Pay you?" John replied, furrowing his brow. "What would I pay you for?"

"You want to try to be smart with me?" Doyle asked, raising a skeptical eyebrow. "Okay, listen, you might want to pretend that you don't remember for everyone else's benefit, but we have a deal. Come on, quick, switch into your Ted Armitage mode and give me my money."

"I have absolutely no idea what you mean," Noad replied, clearly confused. "Ted Armitage is the man we're hunting, he's the -"

"Don't try to bullshit me!" Doyle snapped, shoving him hard against the wall. "You wanted me to deliver this bitch to you, and I delivered her. And believe me, it wasn't the easiest job in the world. She wouldn't stop yapping in the car, I had to bite my lip to stop myself punching her. You promised me a grand, cash in hand, and you should just be grateful that I'm not asking for double that."

"No," John said, shaking his head, "I've never offered you money for anything."

"I..."

Doyle hesitated, staring at him with a faint smile, before turning to Charlotte.

"Do you see this?" he asked, before letting out a loud sigh. "The old fool's completely cuckoo. He's either playing us all for fools, or he's genuinely out of his mind." He turned back to Noad. "You owe me a grand, old man," he continued, "and I need that money, and I'm not leaving here without it. I don't care if you want me to call you John Noad or Ted Armitage, it's all the same time me. Just hand it over!"

"Stop saying these things," Noad replied, as tears filled his eyes. "None of it's true!"

"Would you mind filling him in?" Doyle asked, turning to Charlotte again. "He might take it better coming from you. After all, you've had a ringside seat for the whole mess, so tell him. Tell him that he's Ted Armitage."

"I -"

Suddenly Noad lunged at Doyle from behind, slamming a knife into the back of his head and sending him crashing against the opposite wall. As he began to slide down to the floor, Doyle let out a series of faint gasps, before Noad reached down and pulled the knife away, only to grab the man's head and start slamming it against the rocky ground. Doyle tried to cry out, but his words were quickly stifled as his teeth broke and his jaw shattered.

"You don't know what you're talking about!" Noad screamed, overtaken by the anger that had been bubbling up through his chest for hours. "You're a liar! You're trying to trick me, but I won't let you! You're nothing but a filthy liar and I refuse to play your games! I'm not Ted Armitage! I never have been! I'm John Noad!"

He continued to smash Doyle's head against the rocks, until the front of the man's face had been entirely bashed away and pieces of his brain began to leak out onto the ground. Even this didn't deter Noad, and he hit Doyle's skull again and again until the back cracked open. Blood had splattered across the floor, but Noad paid no attention to that as he stepped back breathlessly and finally bumped against the other wall.

"You can't break me," Noad murmured. "I won't let you. You can't get into my head and... I refuse to... I..."

His voice trailed off.

Charlotte turned to run, but Noad grabbed her and pulled her back, sending her crashing down at his feet.

"Not so fast," he said firmly. "I've missed you, Charlotte."

Looking up at him, she saw a familiar grin, as if he'd changed in an instant.

"What's wrong?" he continued. "Don't you have anything nice to say to your old buddy Ted Armitage?"

## CHAPTER THIRTY

"You're insane," Charlotte stammered, staring up at Ted as he towered over her. "You know that, right? I mean, I knew you were crazy five years ago, but this..."

She hesitated for a moment, as she tried to figure out how she was going to get away.

"This is something else," she added finally. "You're actually two people, aren't you?"

"Poor Mr. Noad never seems to remember too well," Ted replied, as he aimed the flashlight at her face again, forcing her to turn away. "Sometimes I wonder what he does when he's tucked away in here. He must be aware on some level, but for the most part he seems to be completely oblivious. I guess that's how he likes things to be. Nice and simple. He leaves me to do all the dirty work."

"When did it happen?" Charlotte asked, trying to keep the conversation going so that she could think a little more. "When did your mind split like this?"

"I'm not really one for thinking about the past," Ted told her, before turning and looking toward the far end of the chamber. "Let's just say that my wife and my older daughter disappointed me a long time ago."

Following his gaze, Charlotte flinched as she saw the two figures hanging from chains. Both still had their heads, and both were so badly hurt that it seemed impossible for their bones to be holding together.

"Janice and Jane," Ted continued. "It was Jane who really made me angry. She's the reason poor John Noad snapped. Before that, Ted Armitage was just a name he used when he was posting crap online. He used me whenever he wanted to vent. At some point, though, everything flipped around and I became the dominant personality. He stepped back and let me do my thing to Jane. That girl really should have listened when I tried to teach her, but I never believed she was sincere."

He looked over at the second woman, whose body was even more badly damaged than the first.

"Then Janice just couldn't bring herself to understand why I'd had to do all this. She screamed so much, I genuinely wasn't sure what to do about her. Eventually, killing her was the only option. I wanted some peace and quiet, and John wanted to be left in peace to search for little Chrissie. Not that he ever had a chance of finding her, of course, but he was never quite able to accept that. Even now, at this exact moment, I can feel the sliver of hope that sits in his heart and tortures him. Chrissie'd be well into her twenties by now, it's not like she's going to magically reappear, but the old fool refuses to accept the truth. It's kind of pathetic, if you think about it."

"Why the rest of them?" Charlotte asked. "Why did you keep killing?"

"I suppose I just got a taste for it," he replied. "That, and I wanted to figure out what I'd done wrong with Jane. I should have been able to fix her. I wanted to prove that it had been her failure, and not mine, so I kept on trying with new girls until..."

He hesitated.

"Vicky," he added.

"Vicky?"

"A nice girl who actually listened," he continued. "I knew I could do it, but it's still nice to get the validation."

"What about the heads?" she replied. "Why did you take some of the heads and put them on that spike?"

"That was a monument to my work," Ted explained. "I was always worried that one day John would seal me away and stop letting me out to play. I figured that I needed to leave something out that he couldn't ignore, and it worked. Whenever he saw those heads, he was reminded that I was still lurking inside. He played his part, by making sure that this place stayed off the map, and I played my part by continuing the research. Besides, he had a bit of a thing about cutting off heads. I think deep down it excited him. It might even have been the one thing he and I had in common."

"And he let you?"

"Why wouldn't he?"

"You killed his wife and daughter!"

"Did I?"

He stared at her for a moment, before tilting his head slightly.

"Are you sure about that?"

She opened her mouth to reply, but at that moment she heard a faint rasping groan. Almost too scared to react, she hesitated for a moment before forcing herself to turn and look, and to her horror she saw that one of the two bloodied women had begun to shiver slightly.

"It's amazing what the human body can endure," Ted said with a smile as he looked at Jane. "I did a lot of research. Janice has been dead for years, but I kept Jane alive. And now that I succeeded with Vicky, I think I finally know how to force this selfish girl to see the light."

"Kill me," Jane groaned. "Please..."

"You can't be serious," Charlotte whispered, horrified that somehow one of the women had survived what looked like an immense bout of torture. "How long have they been here like this?"

"Fifteen years," Ted told her. "And do you want to know something? They'll be here for as long as it takes. In fact, if Jane never convinces me that she understands what she did wrong and how she needs to change, I daresay they're going to be here forever. Because there's one thing I can promise everyone in this room... I won't ever bow down. I'll do whatever it takes to make Jane see the light, and then..."

He paused, before stepping over to Jane and putting a hand on the side of her face. She flinched, but he simply moved his hand slowly down to her chin.

"Then John Noad'll get his daughter back, and she'll walk out of here with him," he purred. "She'll be so grateful. She'll be on her knees, sobbing and thanking me so much."

"So that's what the rest of us were?" Charlotte asked. "Practice?"

"Not practice exactly," he replied, "more -"

Suddenly Charlotte turned and tried again to run. This time she managed to get out into the passageway, only for Ted to grab her and haul her back into the chamber. She fought frantically, but he shoved her against the wall and pressed her against the rocks.

"You were supposed to be just a loose end, Charlotte," he snarled, leaning close to her ear. "I'm glad you're here so that we can finish what you started, but I haven't been entirely honest with you. You see, despite everything that you've done, despite your lack of gratitude and your rudeness, you still have a chance to show me that you can learn. Don't you want to do that? Don't you want to prove to me that even after five whole years, you might actually have what it takes?"

Reaching into his pocket, he took out a knife and pressed it against her throat.

"Or do you just want to give up?" he asked, leaning even closer. "Think carefully. Whatever you choose, it'll be a lesson for Jane. The question is, what type of lesson do you want to be?"

Charlotte struggled to speak for a moment, before finally realizing that she couldn't bring herself to lie to him.

"Go to hell!" she sneered.

"Oh dear," he replied, as he pressed the knife more firmly against her throat, "that's what I thought you might say, but I still had to give you the opportunity."

With that, he began to slice her throat open, only for something heavy to slam against him from behind. Letting out a pained gasp, Ted crunched against Charlotte, just as Pacey grabbed him by the shoulders and pulled him away.

"Charlotte, run!" Pacey shouted, dragging Ted further toward the far side of the room. Bloodied and beaten, and barely alive, he tried desperately to put his arms around Ted and keep him secure. "Get out of here! You have to -"

Before he could finish, Ted slammed an elbow into his face and then turned, slicing the knife straight into his chest. As Pacey began to fall down, Ted pulled the knife out and then stabbed him again and again, unleashing a furious attack that ended with him driving the knife repeatedly into the man's neck.

"Run!" Pacey groaned. "Charlotte -"

Ted thrust the knife up into his lower jaw, pushing hard until the tip of the blade burst out through his left eye socket.

Turning, Charlotte scrambled out of the chamber, trying to get back to the steps. Barely able to see anything in the darkness, she slammed straight into the bottom step and fell forward, before starting to clamber up on her hands and knees until finally she emerged in the forest.

"You should know better than this!" Ted shouted from the darkness below. "You won't get away from me again, Charlotte! I'm coming for you!"

## CHAPTER THIRTY-ONE

Racing between the trees, barely able to see where she was going as the canopy above blocked almost all the moonlight, Charlotte desperately tried to get as far as possible from the underground chamber.

She was running downhill, which she knew meant that she'd soon reach the river. She was trying to think back to the route that she'd taken five years earlier, and she remembered that after a while she'd followed the river to a waterfall, and then she'd climbed down the waterfall; she wasn't entirely sure of the route that she'd taken after that, however, and she told herself that there had to be a better way. First, though, she had to -

Suddenly she lost her footing and fell. Letting out a startled cry, she tumbled down onto the steep ground and began to roll, slamming into exposed tree roots as she careered through the darkness. She reached out in an attempt to grab hold of something and slow herself down, but instead she simply continued to fall until finally she hurtled off the edge of a raised ridge and flew through the air. She tried to find some way to prepare herself for an impact, but for a few seconds she wasn't entirely sure which way was up until finally she slammed into the ground with such force that her right leg immediately broke just below the knee.

Screaming, she came to a stop and rolled onto her back, and then she slammed a hand over her mouth in a desperate attempt to not make any more noise. She reached down to touch her leg, and she immediately felt a sharp piece of bone poking out through a hole in her jeans. She pulled her hand away, but the pain was getting worse by the second and she knew that this time there was no way she could possibly hobble through the forest.

Sobbing breathlessly, she tried to sit up, but the pain was too intense and she could barely even think straight. At least she could see a little better, as moonlight bathed the riverbank and she saw the water running past just a few meters away. She glanced over her shoulder and realized that most likely she could follow the river and find the same waterfall from five years earlier, although she knew that there was no way she could ever climb down again, not with her right leg broken.

Nevertheless, she began to try to get up, only for the pain to stop her.

"Come on," she whispered, trying to find some strength from somewhere, "you can do this. You're not going to let him win. You got away from him once and -"

Before she was able to finish, she realized she could hear a faint humming sound in the distance. She froze, telling herself that there was no way Ted could be after her so quickly, but deep down she knew that she recognized the sound. She took a deep breath, and then she turned and looked back up into the forest.

Sure enough, a small, bright light was moving between the trees, although it was far too high up for it to be a man with a flashlight. As the humming sound became a little louder, Charlotte realized with a growing sense of dread that there could only be one possible explanation.

"You've got to be kidding me," she stammered. "Another drone..."

For a moment, she simply watched as the light continued its slow progress, but she knew that soon it'd reach the river. After that, Ted would have to decide which way to send it next, and she had no doubt that it was most likely fitted with some kind of night vision. Looking around, she realized she was a sitting duck, and when she turned back toward the drone's light she saw that it was already heading her way.

"Not this time," she muttered, as she began to drag herself toward the water's edge. "I'd rather die."

Reaching the side of the river, she looked down at the water. She knew that her leg would hurt even more if she went beneath the surface, but she also knew that Ted's drone would reach her in a matter of minutes. She took a deep breath as she tried to think of some other option, and then she looked over her shoulder and saw that the drone was steadily getting closer. She thought of Ted watching through some app on his phone, and in that moment she understood that she had no choice.

After taking one more deep breath, she rolled over the edge of the riverbank and crashed down into the water, and she immediately felt a burst of agony in her right leg. She instinctively began to scream, but underwater all that emerged from her mouth was a rush of bubbles as she reached out and grabbed some rocks before hauling herself back up.

By the time she pulled her face above the surface, she'd managed to hold the scream back, but she was shivering in the darkness and she could barely see a thing other the faint glow of the approaching drone. She looked up and realized that the damn thing was almost with her, and she listened as it slowly made its way past. Although she didn't quite dare to believe that she'd actually managed to hide, she could hear that the drone was now getting further and further away, and she told herself that soon she'd be able to drag herself out of the water and...

And what?

Soaking wet and freezing cold, and with a broken leg, she couldn't even begin to figure out how she was going to get away. She told herself that the alternative was to simply die in the river, to at least deny Ted the satisfaction of being the one to kill her, and she began to realize that she didn't really have any other options. There was simply no way she was willing to let Ted hunt her down again; even if she died in the water and he was the one who found her body, he'd always know that she'd managed to escape.

"I'm sorry, Mum," she whispered, thinking of her dead mother. "I don't know if I... I don't..."

As her voice trailed off, she realized that she was starting to shiver. Her teeth were chattering and she felt that – even if she came up with a plan – she'd never find the strength now to climb out of the water. Her mind was strangely calm, and she was starting to worry that somehow she was shutting down, that her body was accepting the inevitable. She didn't want to die, but at the same time she could no longer find the strength to save herself, and after a few more seconds she began to slowly slip down until her face was about to dip beneath the water's surface.

And then she saw her.

Forcing herself to stay up, Charlotte looked across at the river's other bank and saw that a young girl – no more than seven or eight years old – was standing in the moonlight, staring straight back at her. Although she blinked, convinced that the pale little face couldn't possibly be real, Charlotte felt almost as if the girl's gaze was burning into her mind. She immediately had a million questions, but finally she realized that the girl might actually be her ticket to freedom.

"Hey!" she gasped, convinced that the girl had to have wandered away from some campsite. "Can you get your parents? Can you fetch them for me?"

When the girl failed to respond, Charlotte raised her right hand and waved.

"Hey!" she continued. "It's not safe out here! Are your parents nearby? It's the middle of the night, you can't be out in the forest all alone! There's a madman on the loose!"

She waited, but now she was starting to realize that the girl's expression seemed unusually intense in its sadness, and she couldn't help but feel that something about her seemed unusual.

"Can you even hear me?" she called out, waving again. "I'm down here! Little girl, please, don't be scared. Just go and get your parents, or whoever you're here with. Ask them to call the police. Tell them -"

She blinked, and in an instant the girl was gone.

Charlotte stared at the spot where she'd been standing. She knew there was no way the girl could have simply disappeared like that, that she'd not had a chance to run away into the forest, but somehow she'd vanished. Still shivering in the water, Charlotte tried to make sense of what she'd just seen, but she knew that the girl had simply been...

Impossible.

She began to lean forward.

Suddenly a hand clamped tight over her mouth from above, and an arm reached down and hooked her around the throat.

"Nice try!" Ted Armitage sneered as he leaned down to start pulling her out of the river. "Got you again!"

## CHAPTER THIRTY-TWO

"No!" Charlotte screamed, lunging forward in a desperate attempt to get away, only to find that he was holding her too tight. "Leave me alone!"

"That's not a bad hiding place," he replied, as he adjusted his grip and tried once again to pull her out. "I very nearly walked right past you!"

"John Noad!" she shouted, hoping to get through to his other personality. "You're a good man, you don't want to do this!"

"He's buried deep right now," Ted sneered. "In fact, I don't think I'm going to let him out ever again. Not unless I need something from him, at least."

"No!" she screamed again, and this time she twisted around and dragged him down.

Losing his balance, Ted crashed into the water, and this was enough to make him let go. Turning, Charlotte began to swim out across the moonlit river, pushing past the pain and desperately trying to get to the other side. She could already hear Ted calling after her, but she didn't even dare to stop and look back; instead, she aimed for the spot on the opposite bank where the strange little girl had been standing, and soon she was almost all the way across. She reached out, grabbing some tree roots, and finally she began to haul herself the rest of the way.

"You're just dragging this out," Ted spluttered as he set off after her, just about managing to stay on his feet as he waded neck-deep through the water. "I'm going to give you one more chance!"

Trying to ignore him, Charlotte pulled herself across the roots, although she quickly found that she was getting caught instead. She briefly dipped beneath the water, before pushing back up and gasping for air. Reaching out toward the riverbank, she tried to start hauling herself up, only for the mud to fall away in her hands. Realizing that she still wasn't close enough, she grabbed the roots and pulled again, and then she froze as she saw something pale poking out from the packed dirt that ran along the river's edge.

Somehow, deep down, she knew immediately what she'd found.

"It's taken five years," Ted said, as he continued to make his way up behind her, "but I'm finally going to get to put you to the test."

With her trembling right hand, Charlotte scraped away some of the mud, and she felt a shiver run through her spine as she saw a small skull staring back at her. She tried to pull the skull free, but for a moment the mud refused to let it go, until finally an entire corpse began to lean out from the soil, held back by trailing roots.

Scraps of a yellow and red sweater were still wrapped around the ribs, and strands of pale hair hung down from the skull's sides.

"Sometimes you seem so smart," Ted said breathlessly as he finally caught up to Charlotte and grabbed her shoulders, "and sometimes you seem so -"

Stopping suddenly as he saw the human remains, Ted stared in shock, as if he couldn't quite believe what Charlotte was holding in her hands.

Slowly, carefully, Charlotte moved the skull closer, and in the process she inadvertently pulled it free from the rest of the corpse. She could already tell that the skull wasn't that of an adult, and as she held it out in the moonlight she realized that somehow she'd been drawn to the exact place where the body had been hidden. She stared into the skull's empty eye sockets for a moment, before looking up at spot where the strange little girl had been standing.

"Did you *want* me to find this?" she whispered.

"Give me that!" Ted snarled angrily, grabbing the skull so that he could take a closer look. "This can't be real! What are you trying to pull here?"

Turning to him, Charlotte saw genuine shock in his eyes, and she realized that she had one more chance to get away. While Ted seemed mesmerized by the skull, Charlotte tried to pull herself up from the river, grabbing the roots tight but finding that she was too weak; she tried again and again, until one of the larger roots broke away in her hands and she fell back down into the water.

As soon as she was able to get back above the surface, she reached for the roots again, only to realize that Ted was still staring in shock at the skull in his hands.

"Chrissie," he whispered, as he gently stroked the few remaining strands of hair. "You were here all along. Why didn't anyone find you until now? Why..."

His voice trailed off for a moment.

"It's me," he added finally, as a faint smile crossed his lips. "It's Daddy. You recognize me, don't you? I'm so sorry I looked away all those years ago. You forgive me, darling, don't you? I searched for you, I swear. I looked everywhere, I don't understand how I didn't find you, but I've got you now and I won't ever let you go. Mummy's going to be so happy when I..."

Again, he hesitated.

"I have to take you to her," he said, as his voice began to tremble with emotion, and as tears filled his eyes. "I'll make her understand. It might take a while, but eventually she has to see that I only did all of this because I wanted our family to be happy again. Jane'll understand that as well. We're going to be together again, Chrissie. All of us. The Noad family."

He took a deep breath, and then – hearing a splashing sound – he looked over at Charlotte.

"This is my -"

Suddenly Charlotte screamed and lunged at him, slicing a broken branch straight into his chest. The jagged tip sliced through his ribs and heart, before bursting out the back as Charlotte shoved him against the riverbank. Still screaming, she twisted the branch and pushed it in harder, until he was fully impaled and pinned to the side of the river.

Ted let out a faint gasp, but blood was already running from his mouth and after a moment he let the skull fall from his hands as his head tilted back and the last breath left John Noad's body.

\*\*\*

"It's not my fault there was a roadblock," Ian said as he drove the car back along the twisting road. "We'll just have to take the long way round, that's all. Don't worry, we'll get to the cottage tonight. We'll just be a couple of hours late."

"I still don't get why the police couldn't just let us through," Mary muttered as she checked the map on her phone. "What are they even doing up here, anyway?"

"Didn't you hear about that serial killer they're chasing?"

"Don't talk about that now!" Mary hissed.

"Mummy?" Cavan called out from the back seat. "What's a serial killer?"

"Nothing, sweetheart," Mary replied, turning to look at him for a moment. "Just carry on reading your book."

She turned to her husband.

"Let's not talk about things like serial killers while the kids are listening, okay?" she continued. "Seriously, that's not a conversation I want to be having right now."

"Have you found us a route yet?" he asked.

"I'm working on it," she muttered, "but the automatic tracker hasn't picked up on the roadblock yet. It keeps telling us to go straight through Twist Valley, and it won't let me override that. Sometimes I hate these things so much."

"Let me take a look."

"I'm fine."

"You're doing it wrong," he told her. "You *can* override the suggested route, you just have to know how. Give me the phone and I'll sort it out."

"I'm fine," she said again.

He reached over and tried to take the phone, but Mary moved it out of his grasp.

"I'm serious," he continued, glancing at the road for a moment before trying again to grab the phone. "We're just going to waste a lot of time if we try to figure it out ourselves. Mary, don't get funny about this, I -"

"Ian, look out!" she screamed suddenly.

Looking ahead, Ian saw a figure slumped in the middle of the road. He instinctively turned the wheel, and the car missed the figure by inches before screeching to a halt just a short way further along.

"What the hell was that?" he gasped, momentarily too shocked to know how to react.

"It's a person!" Mary replied, scrambling to climb out of the car. "Did you hit her?"

"No," Ian stammered, before opening the door on his side and stepping out. "Stay in the car, Cavan," he added, before making his way around to the rear of the vehicle and watching as his wife knelt next to the unconscious woman. "Is she..."

He watched as she checked for a pulse.

"Barely," Mary said, before looking down at the woman's legs and seeing a broken bone poking out through a hole in her jeans. "It looks like she dragged herself here, out of the forest," she continued, before turning to Ian. "Call the police! Hurry!"

# EPILOGUE

*One year later...*

"And on this day," Commissioner Adrian Prentiss said, as he stood in front of a large picture of John Noad, "it's only appropriate that we take a moment to remember a man who typified the very best in all of us."

A smattering of applause broke out across the crowd, and Prentiss stepped aside so that everyone could get a better view of the photo.

"Chief Inspector John Noad gave his life in the line of duty," Prentiss continued. "I want everyone gathered here today to remember that the hunt for Ted Armitage remains our number one priority. We still don't know exactly what happened when John Noad died, but we're operating on the assumption that he was killed by Armitage. That means that one of our own was murdered by a man who's still at large. I'm sure I don't need to explain to anyone in this room why it's so important that we track this bastard down."

He paused for a moment, to let that last comment sink in, and then he nodded at the men.

"Dismissed. Get out there. Find him."

As the officers filed out of the room, Prentiss turned and looked once again at the photo of John Noad. Although he and Noad had occasionally had their disagreements, he knew full well that the man had been a dedicated soldier in the fight for justice, and he felt personally responsible for the fact that the man's killer had never been captured. Every day, he told himself that they'd find Armitage, and every day he was disappointed.

"Hard to believe it's been a year, huh?" Chief Inspector Andrew Lassiter said as he wandered over to join Prentiss. "We lost a lot of good men out there in Twist Valley. Noad, and Sergeant Doyle, and Warren Pacey. And somehow this Armitage guy is still out there. At least he hasn't killed again."

"That we know of," Prentiss murmured.

"Do you really think he's out there... doing stuff to more women?"

"Every time I hear about someone going missing," Prentiss replied, "anywhere in the country, I wonder whether it's him. Sometimes I can't sleep at night because I keep thinking about all the awful things he could be doing out there. Ted Armitage haunts this department, and he'll *keep* haunting us until we know we've got him. It's almost as if he's toying with us. As if he's enjoying himself. As if he gets some kind of sick, cruel satisfaction out of the way he plays us for fools."

"At least Noad's at peace now," Lassiter continued. "I'm glad that he could be buried with his wife and daughters. I know we tried to keep Jane alive after we found her in that awful place, but deep down I'm glad that she died at the hospital. She was in such an awful state, I don't think she could have lived a proper life. And at least Noad found them, right before..."

His voice trailed off.

"Well," he added, "it must have given him at least some comfort. For so many years, he didn't know what had happened to them. Finally, at the very end, he did."

"Something doesn't ring true about this case," Prentiss told him. "We're missing something, something simple that could turn this whole investigation on its head."

"We just need to be patient."

"We've been patient for the past year," Prentiss replied, turning to him. "At what point does patience start to become a problem rather than a virtue? Armitage is out there somewhere laughing at us, and we're no closer to catching him. I've been hunting scum for long enough to know when a case just doesn't smell right, and this case..."

He turned back to look once more at the picture of John Noad.

"This case stinks," he added.

"There's always the woman," Lassiter suggested. "Charlotte Walker. If she wakes up -"

"She's never going to wake up," Prentiss muttered darkly. "It's a million to one chance. Even if she *does* wake up, she might not remember." He let out a heavy sigh, before turning and leading Lassiter to the door. "The truth, I'm afraid, is that we can't rely on anyone to come riding to our rescue. We're going to have to track this Armitage guy down the hard way."

"I'm sure you're right."

"We'll find him," Prentiss added, as he let the door swing shut. "Wherever he is. And whoever he is. We'll find Ted Armitage eventually."

Back in the room, the picture of John Noad remained proudly on display. He'd been given various posthumous awards, a wing of the new academy had been named after him, and a bursary had been set up in his honor. There was even talk about having a statue of the man erected outside one of the divisional headquarters. Everyone in the force knew that John Noad was a hero. Even his photo betrayed a hint of a smile.

*\*\*\**

"Have you checked on the patient in room nineteen?" Nurse Kate Asher asked as she glanced up from the desk and looked along the corridor. "How are her numbers today?"

She could just about see the patient in that room, Charlotte Walker, through the open door at the corridor's end.

"I'll go and see now," Nurse Annie Wilcox replied, stepping away from the desk and heading toward the room. "I should've ducked in there earlier."

"Annie?"

Stopping, Annie turned to see her colleague Heather leaning out from one of the other rooms.

"Can you help me get an I.V. line in?" Heather asked. "Please?"

"Sure," Annie replied, before turning to see that Tom Boone was making his way past. "Tom, do me a favor, will you? Check on Charlotte Walker in nineteen and make sure she's comfortable."

"I was just about to go to -"

"Just help me out, yeah?"

Without even waiting for him to reply, she disappeared into the room, leaving Tom standing along in the corridor.

"Sure," he muttered, as he turned and began to make his way toward room nineteen, "I guess my lunch isn't important. I mean, I've been on my feet since six this morning, but it's not like I need to sit down or eat or anything like that. I'm basically a robot."

"Tom!"

He turned to see that Sally Briggs was waving at him from the door to room seven.

"Can you come and help me deal with Mr. Oliver?" she asked. "He needs to sit up, and you know he likes you best."

"Fine," Tom replied, before nudging Swan Chaudhury as he wandered past. "Swan, check the woman in nineteen. See that she's got everything she needs."

"Isn't she the one in a coma?"

"Just do it, man," Tom said as he headed into room seven. "I'll owe you one."

"For a change," Swan said with a sigh, before turning and heading toward room nineteen. He told himself that it'd only take thirty seconds or so to check on the patient.

"Swan," Kate Lucas said, suddenly stepping out in front of him, "can you help me with Howard Warner?"

"I'm supposed to -"

"It'll only take a minute."

"Okay," Swan said, before spotting Ally Maker walking right past room nineteen. "Ally!" he called out, waving at her in the hope that he might get her attention. "Can you check on the patient in nineteen?"

Stopping, Ally looked momentarily confused.

"Sure," she said finally. "Sorry, I was in a world of my own there. I'll take a look right now."

She turned and stepped into room nineteen, making her way toward the bed where Charlotte Walker had spent an entire year in a coma.

"Okay, Charlotte," she said with a smile as she approached the various machines, "let's just take a -"

Suddenly she heard an alarm sounding, and she looked over her shoulder just as several nurses ran past the room.

"I have to go and check on that," she said, hurrying back out of the room. "Sorry."

Voices shouted in the distance and more footsteps rang out, as Charlotte Walker remained on her back in the bed. A monitor nearby was beeping steadily, showing Charlotte's vitals on the display, as various tubes ran into her body. Her stillness was a marked contrast to the mayhem somewhere in the distance, and the only sign of movement was a faint flicker beneath Charlotte's closed eyelids. In the year since she'd been admitted to the hospital, she'd undergone a battery of tests and she'd shown absolutely no sign that she might wake up any time soon. In fact, some of the nurses had even developed a few nicknames for her.

In the distance, the alarm fell silent.

Suddenly Charlotte's eyes opened and she began to sit up with a horrified gasp.

*Also by Amy Cross*

## The Haunting of Nelson Street
## (The Ghosts of Crowford book 1)

Crowford, a sleepy coastal town in the south of England, might seem like an oasis of calm and tranquility. Beneath the surface, however, dark secrets are waiting to claim fresh victims, and ghostly figures plot revenge.

Having finally decided to leave the hustle of London, Daisy and Richard Johnson buy two houses on Nelson Street, a picturesque street in the center of Crowford. One house is perfect and ready to move into, while the other is a fire-ravaged wreck that needs a lot of work. They figure they have plenty of time to work on the damaged house while Daisy recovers from a traumatic event.

Soon, they discover that the two houses share a common link to the past. Something awful once happened on Nelson Street, something that shook the town to its core.

*Also by Amy Cross*

**The Devil, the Witch and the Whore
(The Deal book 1)**

*"Leave the forest alone. Whatever's out there, just let it be. Don't make it angry."*

When a horrific discovery is made at the edge of town, Sheriff James Kopperud realizes the answers he seeks might be waiting beyond in the vast forest. But everybody in the town of Deal knows that there's something out there in the forest, something that should never be disturbed. A deal was made long ago, a deal that was supposed to keep the town safe. And if he insists on investigating the murder of a local girl, James is going to have to break that deal and head out into the wilderness.

Meanwhile, James has no idea that his estranged daughter Ramsey has returned to town. Ramsey is running from something, and she thinks she can find safety in the vast tunnel system that runs beneath the forest. Before long, however, Ramsey finds herself coming face to face with creatures that hide in the shadows. One of these creatures is known as the devil, and another is known as the witch. They're both waiting for the whore to arrive, but for very different reasons. And soon Ramsey is offered a terrible deal, one that could save or destroy the entire town, and maybe even the world.

## BOOKS BY AMY CROSS

1. Dark Season: The Complete First Series (2011)
2. Werewolves of Soho (Lupine Howl book 1) (2012)
3. Werewolves of the Other London (Lupine Howl book 2) (2012)
4. Ghosts: The Complete Series (2012)
5. Dark Season: The Complete Second Series (2012)
6. The Children of Black Annis (Lupine Howl book 3) (2012)
7. Destiny of the Last Wolf (Lupine Howl book 4) (2012)
8. Asylum (The Asylum Trilogy book 1) (2012)
9. Dark Season: The Complete Third Series (2013)
10. Devil's Briar (2013)
11. Broken Blue (The Broken Trilogy book 1) (2013)
12. The Night Girl (2013)
13. Days 1 to 4 (Mass Extinction Event book 1) (2013)
14. Days 5 to 8 (Mass Extinction Event book 2) (2013)
15. The Library (The Library Chronicles book 1) (2013)
16. American Coven (2013)
17. Werewolves of Sangreth (Lupine Howl book 5) (2013)
18. Broken White (The Broken Trilogy book 2) (2013)
19. Grave Girl (Grave Girl book 1) (2013)
20. Other People's Bodies (2013)
21. The Shades (2013)
22. The Vampire's Grave and Other Stories (2013)
23. Darper Danver: The Complete First Series (2013)
24. The Hollow Church (2013)
25. The Dead and the Dying (2013)
26. Days 9 to 16 (Mass Extinction Event book 3) (2013)
27. The Girl Who Never Came Back (2013)
28. Ward Z (The Ward Z Series book 1) (2013)
29. Journey to the Library (The Library Chronicles book 2) (2014)
30. The Vampires of Tor Cliff Asylum (2014)
31. The Family Man (2014)
32. The Devil's Blade (2014)
33. The Immortal Wolf (Lupine Howl book 6) (2014)
34. The Dying Streets (Detective Laura Foster book 1) (2014)
35. The Stars My Home (2014)
36. The Ghost in the Rain and Other Stories (2014)
37. Ghosts of the River Thames (The Robinson Chronicles book 1) (2014)
38. The Wolves of Cur'eath (2014)
39. Days 46 to 53 (Mass Extinction Event book 4) (2014)
40. The Man Who Saw the Face of the World (2014)
41. The Art of Dying (Detective Laura Foster book 2) (2014)
42. Raven Revivals (Grave Girl book 2) (2014)
43. Arrival on Thaxos (Dead Souls book 1) (2014)
44. Birthright (Dead Souls book 2) (2014)
45. A Man of Ghosts (Dead Souls book 3) (2014)
46. The Haunting of Hardstone Jail (2014)
47. A Very Respectable Woman (2015)
48. Better the Devil (2015)
49. The Haunting of Marshall Heights (2015)
50. Terror at Camp Everbee (The Ward Z Series book 2) (2015)
51. Guided by Evil (Dead Souls book 4) (2015)
52. Child of a Bloodied Hand (Dead Souls book 5) (2015)
53. Promises of the Dead (Dead Souls book 6) (2015)
54. Days 54 to 61 (Mass Extinction Event book 5) (2015)
55. Angels in the Machine (The Robinson Chronicles book 2) (2015)

56. The Curse of Ah-Qal's Tomb (2015)
57. Broken Red (The Broken Trilogy book 3) (2015)
58. The Farm (2015)
59. Fallen Heroes (Detective Laura Foster book 3) (2015)
60. The Haunting of Emily Stone (2015)
61. Cursed Across Time (Dead Souls book 7) (2015)
62. Destiny of the Dead (Dead Souls book 8) (2015)
63. The Death of Jennifer Kazakos (Dead Souls book 9) (2015)
64. Alice Isn't Well (Death Herself book 1) (2015)
65. Annie's Room (2015)
66. The House on Everley Street (Death Herself book 2) (2015)
67. Meds (The Asylum Trilogy book 2) (2015)
68. Take Me to Church (2015)
69. Ascension (Demon's Grail book 1) (2015)
70. The Priest Hole (Nykolas Freeman book 1) (2015)
71. Eli's Town (2015)
72. The Horror of Raven's Briar Orphanage (Dead Souls book 10) (2015)
73. The Witch of Thaxos (Dead Souls book 11) (2015)
74. The Rise of Ashalla (Dead Souls book 12) (2015)
75. Evolution (Demon's Grail book 2) (2015)
76. The Island (The Island book 1) (2015)
77. The Lighthouse (2015)
78. The Cabin (The Cabin Trilogy book 1) (2015)
79. At the Edge of the Forest (2015)
80. The Devil's Hand (2015)
81. The 13th Demon (Demon's Grail book 3) (2016)
82. After the Cabin (The Cabin Trilogy book 2) (2016)
83. The Border: The Complete Series (2016)
84. The Dead Ones (Death Herself book 3) (2016)
85. A House in London (2016)
86. Persona (The Island book 2) (2016)
87. Battlefield (Nykolas Freeman book 2) (2016)
88. Perfect Little Monsters and Other Stories (2016)
89. The Ghost of Shapley Hall (2016)
90. The Blood House (2016)
91. The Death of Addie Gray (2016)
92. The Girl With Crooked Fangs (2016)
93. Last Wrong Turn (2016)
94. The Body at Auercliff (2016)
95. The Printer From Hell (2016)
96. The Dog (2016)
97. The Nurse (2016)
98. The Haunting of Blackwych Grange (2016)
99. Twisted Little Things and Other Stories (2016)
100. The Horror of Devil's Root Lake (2016)
101. The Disappearance of Katie Wren (2016)
102. B&B (2016)
103. The Bride of Ashbyrn House (2016)
104. The Devil, the Witch and the Whore (The Deal Trilogy book 1) (2016)
105. The Ghosts of Lakeforth Hotel (2016)
106. The Ghost of Longthorn Manor and Other Stories (2016)
107. Laura (2017)
108. The Murder at Skellin Cottage (Jo Mason book 1) (2017)
109. The Curse of Wetherley House (2017)
110. The Ghosts of Hexley Airport (2017)
111. The Return of Rachel Stone (Jo Mason book 2) (2017)
112. Haunted (2017)

113. The Vampire of Downing Street and Other Stories (2017)
114. The Ash House (2017)
115. The Ghost of Molly Holt (2017)
116. The Camera Man (2017)
117. The Soul Auction (2017)
118. The Abyss (The Island book 3) (2017)
119. Broken Window (The House of Jack the Ripper book 1) (2017)
120. In Darkness Dwell (The House of Jack the Ripper book 2) (2017)
121. Cradle to Grave (The House of Jack the Ripper book 3) (2017)
122. The Lady Screams (The House of Jack the Ripper book 4) (2017)
123. A Beast Well Tamed (The House of Jack the Ripper book 5) (2017)
124. Doctor Charles Grazier (The House of Jack the Ripper book 6) (2017)
125. The Raven Watcher (The House of Jack the Ripper book 7) (2017)
126. The Final Act (The House of Jack the Ripper book 8) (2017)
127. Stephen (2017)
128. The Spider (2017)
129. The Mermaid's Revenge (2017)
130. The Girl Who Threw Rocks at the Devil (2018)
131. Friend From the Internet (2018)
132. Beautiful Familiar (2018)
133. One Night at a Soul Auction (2018)
134. 16 Frames of the Devil's Face (2018)
135. The Haunting of Caldgrave House (2018)
136. Like Stones on a Crow's Back (The Deal Trilogy book 2) (2018)
137. Room 9 and Other Stories (2018)
138. The Gravest Girl of All (Grave Girl book 3) (2018)
139. Return to Thaxos (Dead Souls book 13) (2018)
140. The Madness of Annie Radford (The Asylum Trilogy book 3) (2018)
141. The Haunting of Briarwych Church (Briarwych book 1) (2018)
142. I Just Want You To Be Happy (2018)
143. Day 100 (Mass Extinction Event book 6) (2018)
144. The Horror of Briarwych Church (Briarwych book 2) (2018)
145. The Ghost of Briarwych Church (Briarwych book 3) (2018)
146. Lights Out (2019)
147. Apocalypse (The Ward Z Series book 3) (2019)
148. Days 101 to 108 (Mass Extinction Event book 7) (2019)
149. The Haunting of Daniel Bayliss (2019)
150. The Purchase (2019)
151. Harper's Hotel Ghost Girl (Death Herself book 4) (2019)
152. The Haunting of Aldburn House (2019)
153. Days 109 to 116 (Mass Extinction Event book 8) (2019)
154. Bad News (2019)
155. The Wedding of Rachel Blaine (2019)
156. Dark Little Wonders and Other Stories (2019)
157. The Music Man (2019)
158. The Vampire Falls (Three Nights of the Vampire book 1) (2019)
159. The Other Ann (2019)
160. The Butcher's Husband and Other Stories (2019)
161. The Haunting of Lannister Hall (2019)
162. The Vampire Burns (Three Nights of the Vampire book 2) (2019)
163. Days 195 to 202 (Mass Extinction Event book 9) (2019)
164. Escape From Hotel Necro (2019)
165. The Vampire Rises (Three Nights of the Vampire book 3) (2019)
166. Ten Chimes to Midnight: A Collection of Ghost Stories (2019)
167. The Strangler's Daughter (2019)
168. The Beast on the Tracks (2019)
169. The Haunting of the King's Head (2019)

170. I Married a Serial Killer (2019)
171. Your Inhuman Heart (2020)
172. Days 203 to 210 (Mass Extinction Event book 10) (2020)
173. The Ghosts of David Brook (2020)
174. Days 349 to 356 (Mass Extinction Event book 11) (2020)
175. The Horror at Criven Farm (2020)
176. Mary (2020)
177. The Middlewych Experiment (Chaos Gear Annie book 1) (2020)
178. Days 357 to 364 (Mass Extinction Event book 12) (2020)
179. Day 365: The Final Day (Mass Extinction Event book 13) (2020)
180. The Haunting of Hathaway House (2020)
181. Don't Let the Devil Know Your Name (2020)
182. The Legend of Rinth (2020)
183. The Ghost of Old Coal House (2020)
184. The Root (2020)
185. I'm Not a Zombie (2020)
186. The Ghost of Annie Close (2020)
187. The Disappearance of Lonnie James (2020)
188. The Curse of the Langfords (2020)
189. The Haunting of Nelson Street (The Ghosts of Crowford 1) (2020)
190. Strange Little Horrors and Other Stories (2020)
191. The House Where She Died (2020)
192. The Revenge of the Mercy Belle (The Ghosts of Crowford 2) (2020)
193. The Ghost of Crowford School (The Ghosts of Crowford book 3) (2020)
194. The Haunting of Hardlocke House (2020)
195. The Cemetery Ghost (2020)
196. You Should Have Seen Her (2020)
197. The Portrait of Sister Elsa (The Ghosts of Crowford book 4) (2021)
198. The House on Fisher Street (2021)
199. The Haunting of the Crowford Hoy (The Ghosts of Crowford 5) (2021)
200. Trill (2021)
201. The Horror of the Crowford Empire (The Ghosts of Crowford 6) (2021)
202. Out There (The Ted Armitage Trilogy book 1) (2021)
203. The Nightmare of Crowford Hospital (The Ghosts of Crowford 7) (2021)
204. Twist Valley (The Ted Armitage Trilogy book 2) (2021)
205. The Great Beyond (The Ted Armitage Trilogy book 3) (2021)
206. The Haunting of Edward House (2021)
207. The Curse of the Crowford Grand (The Ghosts of Crowford 8) (2021)
208. How to Make a Ghost (2021)

For more information, visit:

www.blackwychbooks.com

Printed in Great Britain
by Amazon